LOVE MAY FAIL

ALSO BY MATTHEW QUICK

FOR ADULTS

The Silver Linings Playbook

The Good Luck of Right Now

FOR YOUNG ADULTS

Forgive Me, Leonard Peacock

Boy21

Sorta Like a Rock Star

Matthew Quick

PICADOR

First published 2015 by HarperCollins Publishers, New York

First published in the UK in 2015 by Picador
an imprint of Pan Macmillan
20 New Wharf Road, London N1 9RR
Associated companies throughout the world
www.panmacmillan.com

ISBN 978-1-4472-4751-7

1 3 5 7 9 8 6 4 2

A CIP catalogue record for this book is available from the British Library.

Printed and bound by CPI Group (UK) Ltd, Croydon, CR0 4YY

Visit **www.picador.com** to read more about all our books
and to buy them. You will also find features, author interviews and
news of any author events, and you can sign up for e-newsletters
so that you're always first to hear about our new releases.

FOR MY TEACHERS AND MY STUDENTS

"[Kids] don't remember what you try to teach them. They remember what you are."

—JIM HENSON, *It's Not Easy Being Green*

"We are what we pretend to be, so we must be careful about what we pretend to be."

—KURT VONNEGUT JR., *Mother Night*

Portia Kane, Official Member of the Human Race! This card entitles you to ugliness and beauty, heartache and joy—the great highs and lows of existence—and everything in between. It also guarantees you the right to strive, to reach, to dream, and to become the person you know (deep down) you are meant to be. So make daring choices, work hard, enjoy the ride, and remember—you become exactly whomever you choose to be.

PART ONE

Portia Kane

CHAPTER 1

I'm kneeling in one of my own bedroom closets—peering E.T.-like through the white door slats—when the following epiphany hits me harder than a lawn dart to the eye: I am a disgraceful woman.

Gloria Steinem would call me whatever's the feminist equivalent of an Uncle Tom.

An Aunt Jemima?

Why does that sound like such an awfully racist statement? It's a mixed metaphor of some sort, certainly. But is it racist?

I'm so depressed and angry that I can't even figure out why it might be racist, let alone think up a politically correct metaphor for being an atrocious feminist.

I once read that Gloria Steinem had worked as a Playboy Bunny in an effort to expose the sexism of the job. Regardless of her motivation she was indeed a Playboy Bunny, letting men view her as a sexual object.

Gloria probably even got off on it, if only secretly.

I mean, politics aside, we all want to be desired—even lusted after—deep down, if we're being honest.

And maybe if Gloria Steinem let men ogle her and pinch her ass before she rose up to be the spokesperson for an entire gender, well then, maybe, just maybe, that means I too can transcend hiding in my own closet—literally—and once again become a respectable woman who young, intelligent girls will look up to and maybe even choose to emulate.

What was that old saying?

The truth will set you free.
But first it will piss you off.

Gloria Steinem said that, I'm pretty sure.

I remember reading all about Ms. Steinem in my Gender and Prejudice college course, back when I was a good—albeit untested—feminist.

Being a feminist is so easy when you're a college freshman with enough scholarship money and financial aid to cover tuition, room, and board. A woman with a clean slate. Compromises come with age.

Someone's going to quote me someday, when I'm once again saying intelligent empowering things, like I used to a long, long time ago in a size-four body.

"That's right, Portia Kane," I say to myself in the closet, with a Louis Vuitton stiletto heel stabbing the meat of my left ass cheek. I lean my weight—135 pounds, which isn't all that bad for a relatively tall forty-year-old woman—into the four-inch spike like a medieval priest punishing his lust-driven flesh. "Get pissed off! Because you're about to see the truth. *Ouch!*"

I ease up on the Louis Vuitton heel.

I'm really not all that tough.

But I can change.

I can be the woman I always wanted to be.

Somehow.

Right now, I don't even think the sluttiest teens in today's most godforsaken high schools, girls giving it up for nothing more than, say, a meal at Burger King—onion rings and a Whopper, maybe a chocolate milkshake if they're good negotiators—not even those

Burger King hoochies would sympathize with my current position, let alone look up to yours truly.

I should probably declare that I've been drinking.

A lot.

Hennessy Paradis Imperial.

A $2,000-plus bottle.

Ken was saving it for a special occasion—like maybe when he finally hits a hole in one.

His "lifelong dream." To put a ball in a hole with one swing of a club. What ambition! Ken is a caveman. The way he polishes his clubs with a fist full of terrycloth for hours—not one stroke short of masturbatory.

Tonight is *my* special occasion.

It's a real bitch of a hole-in-one, what's about to happen, let me tell you.

Earlier in the evening, I poured myself a pint of what Ken calls his Hen over ice, and then I poured the rest into Ken's suitcase-size "heirloom" humidor full of illegal Cuban cigars—a well-aged collection acquired over a decade through dubious olive-skinned business contacts and worth untold thousands. Then I left the humidor lid open, which is "worse than raping the pope," according to my husband, who is ironically a practicing and self-proclaimed devout Catholic. How can a pornographer be a devout Catholic? you might be asking yourself now. But let's get real. Every religious person you know does *something* on a regular basis that goes against his or her professed religion. That's just a fact.

Okay, I spit on the cigars several times too, but refrained from urinating on them, which was the original plan.

I also added a jar of Ragu spaghetti sauce with mushroom chunks, just to make sure the heirloom humidor was completely unsalvageable.

Oh, how I hate listening to Ken talk about the beautiful little white spots that appear when he has aged his "sticks" for the proper time and at the prescribed temperature and humidity.

"Look how they flare up when the cherry reaches them, baby," Ken says, holding the filthy lit cancer log in front of his nose and squinting at it, mesmerized, like his stick is the Hope Diamond. "Tiny little comets," he says, smiling with boyish wonder, and for nine years I've smiled back, pretty as a lipstick idiot, an aging Barbie doll.

Ah, trophy-wife me.

It always looks like he has a cock in his mouth when he smokes.

Yeah, I know what you're thinking. Women shouldn't use words like *cock*, right? Well, bullshit on that, because I'm an adult, this isn't a church here, and Ken really does suck salaciously on his cigars.

"No homo," he likes to say whenever he hugs or compliments another man or expresses anything resembling affection or kindness, because Ken is an unabashed homophobe.

How the hell did I end up in this place and time?

How did I end up married to a cartoon?

How did I end up so seduced by money, living in a tropical palace of marble floors, twenty-foot ceilings, cathedral archways, palm trees, crystal chandeliers, lap pool, hand-carved furniture, and high-end stainless steel appliances—all of which make my childhood dwelling look like a mud hut that barnyard animals would refuse to enter?

And yet . . .

"*E.T. phone home*," I say to myself in the closet—and then I take another slurp of Hen, which Ken calls "the preferred drink of the brothers," meaning black people.

Definitely racist.

If only I had some Reese's Pieces.

Here in the closet, I even do the freakishly long E.T. index-finger thing, pretending my nail is glowing as orange as my Hennessy when I hold it up to the bedroom light striping the inside of the closet door.

"*L . . . eeee . . . it*," I say, just like the alien whenever it talks to the little boy Elliott in the film.

I hear the front door open and the alarm beep.

Every muscle in my body stiffens.

I hear her laughing as he punches in the code—our birth dates mixed up.

My month, his year.

Her voice is childlike and makes me think of Smurfette, or maybe it's because she calls Ken "Papa."

Seriously, she calls him that. *Papa*. Like he's Ernest Hemingway.

"Disarmed," says the robot security system.

"Angry hysterical wife in the closet," I whisper. "Beware."

What I haven't told you yet is that I have Ken's beloved Colt .45 in my hand.

He claims you can stop a speeding truck with this gun just by firing a shot into the engine, so I'm pretty sure I can cut short the impending sexcapade.

I've convinced myself that I'm going to shoot them both dead.

Imagine that.

Their heads exploding like wet piñatas.

He must be feeling her up, because she's giggling now as they climb the steps toward me.

"Is that your wife, Papa?" I hear her say, and I imagine her point-ing to our portrait at the top of the stairs. Ken in a gray pinstriped Armani suit. Me in my best black Carolina Herrera cocktail dress. Both of us looking like some Tony Montana–inspired version of

7

American Gothic. She doesn't sound all that concerned that Papa may be married.

"She's dead," Ken says. "Woman's cancer."

He's a pragmatic man, after all—not very creative, but effective.

And for a second I actually believe him and allow myself to *feel* dead.

Nonexistent.

Already gone.

Nothing.

"Sad," muses the girl, who apparently prefers one-syllable words, except for the Papa business. "Did you love her?"

"Let's not talk about uncomfortable things," Ken says, and then she's screaming and laughing again.

"You're so strong!" she says, and I vomit a little into my mouth as I imagine him carrying her toward me.

Thresholds.

Ken often boasts that he's never cheated on me with any of the "actresses" in his movies, as if that—if it is indeed true—is an amazing accomplishment. He's always telling his employees, "Don't get high on your own supply," meaning, Don't fuck the girls we film and sell—but it's apparently okay to fuck the rest of the female world. That's the type of ethics Ken subscribes to. My Catholic husband.

I wonder if she's a hooker playing a role, because she sounds too dumb to be real.

It's funny how the possibility of her being a prostitute somehow gives me pause and definitely makes it harder to shoot her in the face, maybe because a whore would only be doing what Ken paid her to do, i.e., her job. But if I kill him, I'm going to have to kill her, as I don't want any witnesses, and the only way I'd get a lenient sentence is if the judge is a woman who believes the murders were a crime of passion. No woman controlled by passion and with a huge gun in her hand could resist taking a pop at the girl screwing her husband.

I put two hands on the Colt .45, readying myself, preparing to burst into the room, firing away like a Quentin Tarantino character.

I try to channel my inner Gloria Steinem and Angela Davis—my inner Lynda Carter even.

Be pissed!

Take control!

Be a true feminist!

Through the slats in the closet, I see that Ken's latest is, of course, tiny, blond, and maybe all of twenty years of age.

If she weighs one hundred pounds, I will happily eat my hand.

A size zero.

A college student who probably cannot even drink legally.

A child.

Ken is forty-six years old, but looks younger.

He's a bit like Tom Selleck circa 1983, with his throwback moustache and his chest hair, which has suddenly made an appearance.

His tie and jacket are on the floor.

She's got his shirt unbuttoned.

Off goes her dress—over her head.

Her pink bra and cotton panties make her look even younger.

They're sort of dancing now, looking into each other's eyes, swaying their hips almost like the slow part of "Stairway to Heaven" is playing and they can't wait for the fast part.

(Ah, junior high dances, your memory haunts me even at a time like this.)

She's sucking on her bottom lip like it's made out of hard candy.

I tell myself to wait until he does the deed, so I have undeniable proof. I will pop out of the closet like a neglected-wife-in-the-box wielding Ken's very own hand cannon as soon as he sticks his stubby little wang into her.

It doesn't take long for them to slip into bed, and even though they are under the covers—my Calvin Klein Acacia duvet—I can tell he has officially committed adultery because he's doing that little annoying there-is-a-bug-in-my-throat cough thing he does just before he is about to ejaculate.

It's only taken about ninety seconds.

And yet I don't spring out of the closet but just watch the blue comforter rise and fall with the final dying thrusts of Ken's infidelity—his covered ass like an air-starved whale resurfacing spastically every other second—and all I can think about is how his girl du jour looks like the actress who plays Khaleesi on *Game of Thrones*.

Well, I'll never be able to watch *that* show again.

Ken climaxes and then coughs some more. I don't think Khaleesi got off, and since Ken is now on his back, panting, I don't think she will.

Somewhere, Gloria Steinem is shaking her head—appalled. Angela Davis has revoked my woman card. Lynda Carter wants to confiscate all of my cuff bracelets and star-adorned blue panties before hanging me with her Wonder Woman lasso.

Thirty minutes ago, I was thoroughly prepared for life in jail.

It seemed heroic, even.

But if you were really going to kill Ken, why ruin the humidor and cigars?

Ah, smart reader, you know me better than I know myself.

And now it all seems like a practical joke.

My collected experiences thus far have no weight and are of no consequence whatsoever.

I start laughing and I cannot stop.

I'm powerless against the comedy of my life.

My mind flashes to the first time I met Ken, across the state in Miami. I was wearing a red sundress, a Coppertone tan, and my old knock-off Ray-Ban Wayfarer sunglasses, sitting on a veranda at a Cuban restaurant with a waitressing friend, basking in the unearned royalty of our already fading but still technically passable youth. We were eating the best black bean dip and still-warm-from-the-fryer plantains—amazing the details I recall under duress—and Ken walked right up to us and offered Carissa $500 for her seat.

"Will you trade places with me?" is how he put it.

Carissa and I both laughed until he fanned the money out on the table—crisp, never-been-folded hundreds that he pulled from the inside pocket of his jacket, like some Colombian drug lord.

He was dressed in a white suit and was carrying a ridiculous cane with an ivory handle, which should have been my first clue.

I mean—*a cane*, in 2002?

But he was knee-weakeningly handsome.

That's how he does it.

Earnest eyes.

Confidence.

Money.

A fuck-all fashion sense, gaudy and entitled enough for a plantation owner of old.

When I gave Carissa a kick under the table, she scooped up the five hundred-dollar bills, tapped them even, and said she'd meet me at the terrible tiny, smoky cockroach-infested hotel room we had booked for a week. Then Ken sat down and said, "I'm going to marry you."

"Are you now?" I said, oblivious to my doom.

Flattered even.

Ten years later I'm drunk in my own closet watching him fuck a teenager and I'm laughing my head off, because what is the alternative?

They call this life.

Beware, young women who may be reading.

It happens in a flash.

One day you're a young cub roaming the forest free, without a care in the world—and then bam! Your hind leg's bleeding in a bear trap, and before you know it, your claws and teeth have been removed, they've got you addicted to drugs, and you're performing tricks in a Russian circus, being whipped by your trainer—who is always a man—as cotton-candy-sticky children point and jeer.

Again, I've been drinking.

"What the hell?" Ken says as he rips opens the closet. "Whoa." He takes a step back with his palms in the air, his eyes on the mouth of his beloved Colt, which is unsteadily aimed at the sticky, mauve, spade-shaped head of his now-deflated penis.

Before an accident can occur, I toss the impossibly heavy gun into the corner of the closet.

Jail time for this joke of a man?

I think not.

"I'd never be able to hit such a small target anyway, Ken," I say and then giggle my drunk ass off.

"This isn't what it looks like," says Khaleesi, covering her perfect vanilla-ice-cream-cone breasts with one of my Calvin Klein decorative throw pillows.

I can't stop laughing.

"What are you doing in the closet?" Ken asks. "I thought you were going to visit your—Listen." He's holding his palms in the air, and his fingers are spread wide. "I can explain. Really, I can. We can work our way through this, Portia. Trust me. Everything is going to be okay."

Hilarious!

"Why are you laughing like that?" Ken says. "Are you okay?"

Khaleesi says, "I better go."

"No, no, no, sweetie. Stay. Please. *I insist.* My husband hasn't even made you come yet," I say. "I'm leaving anyway. So make yourself at home. You can fuck Ken as many times as you like. If he can get it up again, that is. But spoiler alert! It doesn't get any better than what you've already experienced."

I laugh so hard tears spill from my eyes as I stand and exit the closet.

I start stuffing underwear and bras into my Michael Kors weekend bag.

Naked Ken watches me with his mouth hanging open, like I have just invented fire.

I shake my head.

Fucking caveman.

How did this happen to me?

"Portia," he says. "Portia, come on. Where are you going?"

"*E.T. phone home*," I say, using the E.T. voice, and then laugh until I cough and gag.

"Portia," Ken says. "You're scaring me. Are you okay?"

I stop packing and look him dead in the eyes. "I've never been better in my entire life, Ken. Thank you. Seriously. Thank you so much for being this awful. I might have stayed if you were even a tiny bit more human. But you've spared me from all that. My hero. Thank you. Thank you one million times."

I decide to pull a suitcase from the walk-in and pack enough for a few weeks.

"Do you need any help?" Khaleesi asks, the sweetheart. And I realize that she is even dumber than she looks. I actually start to like her. Maybe I pity her, to be more precise. I imagine saving her from Ken and becoming her mentor. We could join some sort of group for women addicted to horrible men.

ABMAA.

Asshole Boy-Men Addicts Anonymous.

Forgive her, universe, for the little bimbo knows not whom she screws.

"No, just stay where you are," I tell Khaleesi. "I'll be gone soon. You can listen to Ken snore and then wake up for his postsex shit. No courtesy flush. He won't even bother to shut the door. He's a national treasure, let me tell you."

"Portia," Ken says. "Can't we just talk about this for a minute? That's the whole problem. We never even talk anymore!"

I laugh again, but this time it's only a snicker.

"It's been fun, Ken," I say, and then stick out my hand like we just finished a grueling ten-year tennis match.

"Portia, admit it," Ken says, completely naked, gesturing with his open palms extended. His little Khaleesi-coated wang has shrunk like a turtlehead into a graying shell of pubic hair. You'd think he'd manscape before dating teenagers. He says, "Things haven't been right for a long time now, and I have needs. You haven't, well, I'm only—"

"That's true," I say, cutting him off before he can say it's my fault. That I should have fucked him more. That I'm inferior. Not what he bargained for all those years ago. That I dared to age and no longer have the body and sex drive of an eighteen-year-old girl, that I want something more substantial and meaningful than his playboy lifestyle, and should be ashamed even though I haven't been eighteen for more than two decades and was long past my teen years when we met. I pull my hand back. "Correct."

"I'll take care of you, moneywise. Don't worry. You know I'm not a bad guy like that."

"I'm not a whore, Ken. Thank you very much."

"So you're not mad at me? We're still pals."

Pals.

Unbelievable.

After watching him fuck a teenager, I'm supposed to tend to *his* fragile emotions.

I look at Khaleesi, who has the covers pulled up to her nose, hiding. She's watching us with wide-eyed Kewpie-doll interest, like we're some live soap opera.

The Middle-Aged and the Pathetic.

The Betrayal of our Guys.

Portia Kane Is An Aging Fucking Idiot.

"I'm actually happy, Ken. For the first time in years. I'm happy. Fuck you for cheating on me. *Again.* But thank you too." I wave to Khaleesi and say, "Thanks and fuck you, as well."

She nods, but looks confused.

"*E.T. phone home*," I say once more, using the voice, pointing my index finger at Ken's nose.

He squints at me, cocks his head to the side. "You weren't really going to shoot me, were you, baby? Not after all we've been through. We've had some good times together. You and me. We'll always love each other deep down. Admit it. Right?"

I actually believe he cares about the answer—that it's important for him to think I still love him in some sort of dependent, subservient-daughter way, and always will.

Forever.

He wants to be my emotional pimp—the owner of my heart.

I decide to kill his memory, no matter how long it takes.

Obliterate Ken Humes.

Delete him.

Recover from a decade of dependency.

I deserve better.

And better shouldn't be all that hard to get when you've started at the absolute bottom of all men.

"Good-bye, Ken." I slap his little dank pecker and testicles hard with the bone of my open palm. "Low-five."

He doubles over and calls me a fucking bitch before dropping to his knees.

I think I hear Khaleesi squeal with fake delight, like she's suddenly riding on the back of a jet ski, her naked arms around the sculpted abs of an NFL player—an image I've actually seen on a TV commercial for a best-selling brand of underarm deodorant.

This is the world we live in.

Khaleesi's playing her role again.

Girls like this really exist, I think. They really do. Men like Ken can't get enough of the facade. And I've played this game for too long.

"Fuck this life," I say. "Fuck it. Fuck you, Ken Humes. Fuck everything!"

And then I'm gone.

CHAPTER 2

"I shouldn't have dropped out of college," I say to my regular driver, Alfonzo. I'm in the backseat of the town car. I'm sipping directly from a little one-serving bottle of Riesling. He's in his standard black suit and skinny tie, gripping the wheel with his smooth and steady almond-colored hands, acting statue-stoic as always. "Do you know how hard it is for a woman without a college degree to support herself?"

"I don't know anything about college. And I know even less about women, Ms. Kane," Alfonzo says, keeping his eyes on the road. "I stick to driving."

I guzzle the rest of my tiny bottle. "I couldn't keep my grade point average high enough to maintain my scholarship. I had a four-point-oh in my literature and writing classes, but the stupid other required classes outside my major—I mean, why did I need to take chemistry again in college? Memorize the periodic table? I'd rather carve out my right eyeball with a box cutter. I wanted to be a writer, not a scientist. And they were going to kick me out. *Me!* I was hovering around a three-point-three average while working twenty hours a week at the food court too—mopping floors, frying food, creepy twice-my-age janitor Old Man Victor constantly hitting on me, saying perverted things like 'I have a leather couch that feels good on the skin.' I was overcoming so many obstacles, and yet *I* was the one on academic probation! Why are some people drivers and some people passengers in the town car of life, Alfonzo? Have you solved that riddle?"

"No," Alfonzo says. "I have not."

"My freshman roommate was a passenger. She had something like a two-point-five GPA, but it didn't matter because her daddy was a lawyer who could pay for her ride. Oh, how I hated Casey Raymond! Designer clothes. Expensive makeup. You've driven her type a million times. It took her ninety minutes to get ready in the morning. Our dorm room became a beauty salon every time the sun rose. She even had a car. At eighteen! A brand-new Volvo! Can you imagine, Alfonzo?"

Alfonzo doesn't respond, but the alcohol coursing through my veins keeps me talking.

"College was just one big sorority party for her. She exploded with *fun, fun, fun* every time a guy hit on her. All while I was forgoing sleep to study and then nervous puking before every midterm and final. Smoking Camels like a fiend. Mainlining coffee. Anxiety like a giant fist shoved down my throat while I bit hard on its elbow to fight the pain. I had no support system. None. And I know you know what I'm talking about. The inequity. I see it in your eyes, Alfonzo. You and me are cut from the same cloth."

Alfonzo and I lock gazes in the rearview mirror for a second.

I can't tell if he's wearing too much aftershave or if I'm sweating alcohol.

"So I left before they could kick me out. Because fuck them, right? Just walked off campus with my suitcase and took a bus home. Didn't even tell them I was leaving. I don't know, maybe I had a breakdown. Maybe I'm having a breakdown now too. But it was a mistake. I see that now. I *needed* college, whereas Casey Raymond was going to be okay no matter what she did or didn't do, because her daddy was her Ken Humes. She was a born passenger.

Or 'a client,' as you like to say into your little phone. *The client is aboard.*"

"I don't think I should be hearing all this, Ms. Kane," Alfonzo says. "I'm just your driver."

I backhand the air between us. "Everyone knows that Ken has a sex addiction problem. He'd screw the hole out of a doughnut. He just can't help himself. And I was such a good little pretender. For an entire decade. I just wanted a nice life for myself. I wanted nice things. Who doesn't want nice things? And nice things made life okay for a time. Especially after years of waitressing long shifts at the Olive Garden until my spinal cord and all the bones in my feet exploded. Endless salad bowls. Oh, endless salad bowls! If I ever see another garlic breadstick, I'll stab myself in the heart with a screwdriver."

"Ms. Kane, are you okay?"

We're passing a line of palm trees now, and their symmetry is frightening, juxtaposed to my mental state. Finally I say, "You can wash away a lot of life's pain with money. You can hide from the past with money too. You can quit the Olive Garden. And it cures backaches. You should see the Jacuzzi in our en-suite. It makes your voice echo when it's empty. That tub alone was worth it at first."

"Maybe I should turn the car around and take you home."

"Even our marriage counselor liked Ken better than me. She always took Ken's side. Even about the possibility of an open marriage. AN OPEN FUCKING MARRIAGE! Do you know why?"

"Ms. Kane, you're yelling, and—"

"HE PAID FOR THE THERAPY! Everyone likes the man who's paying. That's just the way it goes."

"Ms. Kane, this isn't—"

"Ms. *Kane.* That's right. I didn't take Ken's last name. Because I'm the sexist pornographer's feminist wife! Isn't that just hilarious?" I laugh until I begin coughing. "I mean, there is porn made *for* women and sometimes *by* women—feminist porn where we aren't objectified and are actually in *control*—but my husband doesn't make that kind because he believes there's no money in it, or at least not enough. Don't you think I tried to get him to make feminist pornography? I even talked to his actresses once, telling them they should unionize maybe, which pissed Ken off mightily and accomplished absolutely nothing. They laughed at me. It's like some women actually *want* to be oppressed, right?" I'm starting to sense that Alfonzo is uncomfortable. He's rolling the back of his head against the headrest, so I say, "All right. The speech and the pity party are over. I'll just shut up back here."

Alfonzo doesn't say anything else.

Here's the truth, dear reader: it wasn't really Ken's affair with his latest teenage lover that destroyed me, but a simple offhand comment he made a little more than a year ago.

I don't remember why I started, but I'd been writing some fiction again, like I used to in high school. At first it was just a hobby. Something to pass the time while Ken was off doing whatever. But then I started to really feel something. I produced a few raw personal pieces about my mother that seemed to have promise. So I began wondering if I might have a shot at publishing someday. Of course, I didn't share any of this with Ken at first, but over dinner one night at our favorite restaurant, while I was feeling champagne hopeful, I casually mentioned that I had been writing and that maybe publishing a novel was a life goal of mine—something I had secretly wanted since I was in my favorite high school English teacher's class. As I spoke, I could hear the excitement reverberating in my words and I felt myself becoming vulnerable—as if I was letting Ken see the real naked me for the first time.

When I finished, Ken smirked, stared down at his meal, and said, "Go for it, baby."

"Why did you just smirk?" I said.

"I didn't smirk," he said.

"You did so. *Why?*"

"You should do it. Write your little book."

"*Little?* What the fuck is that, Ken?"

"I don't know, Portia." He smirked again, looking at me now. "Sometimes you just have to know who you are."

"And who am I exactly?"

"You're my wife," he said, pinning me down with each syllable.

"So your wife can't publish a novel someday?"

"You didn't exactly grow up among novel-writing people, did you? And you're not exactly among those types now."

"What does that have to do with anything?"

"You didn't even graduate from college, Portia," Ken said as he knifed his way through his chicken cordon bleu. "You and me aren't exactly the book-writing types, am I wrong? I don't want to see you get your hopes up for something that's never going to happen. That's all. I know how emotional you get. Anyway, you're much too pretty to be a novelist."

I hate you, I thought, but I didn't say it.

It was our wedding anniversary, after all.

I even let him fuck me later that night the way he likes and I hate—from behind.

Hooray for feminism!

He'd belittled me so many times before, but for some reason on this night, as he got off inside me, something shifted.

The best part of me knew I had to escape Ken right then and there—that it wouldn't get better, that he was slowly killing everything good inside of me—but it took a while to find the courage to give up financial security and make a break for it. Especially since Ken had me sign an airtight prenuptial agreement before we were married, so leaving him meant an immediate and most likely permanent decline in social status.

Why did I make a break tonight?

Why does a rotten tree branch come crashing down to earth one day?

Everything has its breaking point—even women.

And I'm courageously drunk too.

"I don't think Maya Angelou ever earned a college degree," I say as Alfonzo pulls up to the US Airways terminal. "But I read somewhere that she has more than fifty honorary doctorate degrees. *Fifty.*"

Alfonzo shifts into park and turns around to face me. "Are you okay, Ms. Kane?"

"What?" I say, blinking repetitively for some reason.

"I couldn't help noticing that you've been crying pretty hard the whole ride. You're still crying right now. I know it's not my business, but this just doesn't seem right to me, Ms. Kane."

I look out the window at the cars and taxis pulling away from the curb. "Well, nothing worth doing is painless."

He reaches back to hand me a few tissues, and when I take them, he says, "Are you sure you want me to leave you like this?"

I dab my eyes and say, "Do you know what happens when you do nothing? Nothing. My high school English teacher said that to me a long time ago. And he was right."

CHAPTER 3

Next thing I know, I'm on a plane.

I stumble my way to the last row.

A tiny wrinkly woman is already seated in the window seat. She's dressed in a nun's habit. She even has her head covered, which makes her look absolutely adorable.

Present-day Sally Field reprising her *Flying Nun* role—only this time she's old and wrinkly (and cute!) as a shar-pei.

Her spine is curved so that the middle of her back is touching the cushion, but there is a good five inches between the headrest and her shoulders.

She resembles the letter C.

When I sit down, the old woman says, "Hello, I'm Maeve. How are you doing tonight?"

It's almost like she's the hostess of our row.

I sit.

I buckle myself in, which proves a bit hard after the two blue martinis—which looked like Windex but tasted like Kool-Aid—I had at the airport bar.

I turn, look into her old eyes, and say, "Sister, I'm glad you asked, because I'm not doing all that well, honestly. And I could talk. Yes, I can. Talk all the way to Philadelphia. Because I'm in trouble. Trouble with a capital T that rhymes with P and that stands for Portia. My name. My curse-id stupid name."

I offer my hand, and she shakes it with her eyebrows lifted.

Her hand feels like a branch ripped from a small tree, left to dry for many years, and then stuck inside a surgical glove.

If I squeeze hard, everything will snap.

Even though I'm drunk, I handle with care.

And then I start to cry again, because I have enough alcohol in me to fuel a small dump truck.

"Oh, dear," she says, pulling endless tissues from her bag like she's David Copperfield. "What's the matter?"

"Seriously?" I take a wad of tissues and dab my eyes.

"Of course."

"You really wanna know? Be sure before you answer, because I could just pass out here and let you be. I'm appropriately medicated. You don't have to hear my depressing pathetic story." The businessman seated across the aisle from us is staring at me, so I point my finger at his nose and say, "You, sir, can mind your own business!"

His eyes snap down to the magazine in his hands, and I feel like a powerful woman capable of making men in suits do whatever I say.

When I spin my face back toward the old nun, she says, "I'm happy to listen. What else is there to do on a flight? Half the fun of flying is learning the stories of fellow passengers. I collect them!"

I notice the wooden rosary beads wrapped around her hand and catch a glimpse of Jesus's naked and well-toned body, which is meticulously carved.

All of the good men are either gay or the sons of gods with martyr complexes. I swear, we heterosexual women are a doomed lot.

"You collect the stories of strangers?" I say.

"Why, certainly. Everyone's story is precious."

I can tell this woman is a little nuts, but she seems kind, and kindness goes a long way at a time like this. "Okay, then. But remember. You asked for it."

As we taxi, I tell her everything, slurring away.

I say the word *wang* several times and describe Ken's tiny penis at great length before I think better of using such vivid sexual imagery while conversing with a nun, but she seems fascinated—riveted.

She squints and smiles when I say the word, maybe in spite of herself and her religious convictions.

Wang.

Hilarious!

Like I'm tickling the old woman with dirty words.

"Do you remember that song 'Everybody Have Fun Tonight'? No, of course not," I say. "*Everybody Wang Chung tonight,*" I sing. "You really don't know it?"

"Oh, my," she keeps saying, and then she suddenly pushes the button above us.

I have a paranoid thought: What if this nun is going to report my drunkenness and try to have me removed from the plane?

My fists clench.

The flight attendant appears in the aisle.

Maeve holds up two pink wrinkly fingers and says, "My friend here has had an awful day. Simply awful. We need vodka and some rocks immediately. If you have any of the citrus flavors, we'll take those. Any citrus flavor will do."

"Beverage service hasn't begun yet, Sister," the flight attendant says.

"Oh, I'm very sorry to ask, but this is a bit of an emergency," Maeve says. "I can hold you up in my prayers if you oblige us. The whole sister house will pray for you"—she squints at the flight attendant's name tag—"Stephanie."

"Okay, Sister," the flight attendant says, smiling now. "I'll take that deal."

"People will do anything for nun prayers. Even atheists!" Sister Maeve whispers to me as Stephanie walks away. "Between us girls only. One of the perks of sisterhood."

"Are you the type of nun who goes around saying you're married to Jesus?" I ask.

"I don't know if I 'go around saying' that. But, yes. I am married to Jesus."

"If all nuns are married to Jesus, that would mean he currently has thousands of wives and has had maybe millions over the past two thousand years, right?"

"Well, I guess so."

"You're okay with Jesus having multiple wives? Jesus the polygamist."

"You can't think of it that way—it's not sexual, or anything like that. He's not your Ken, after all."

Ha! Funny old nun. Still sharp as a razor blade in a Halloween apple.

"You would totally have sex with Jesus. Admit it," I say. "He has an amazing body."

Maeve shakes her head, laughs, and looks up. "Oh, Lord, what have you sent me this time?"

"You talk to Jesus?"

"Every waking hour of every day."

"Right now. You can talk to him here?"

"Certainly."

"What does Jesus say about me? Ask him."

"He says you need more vodka," Maeve says.

The flight attendant returns on cue with glasses of ice, which she hands us before bending down and pulling the mini bottles out of her pocket and slipping them to my nun friend with a wink.

"Enjoy your flight, Sister," she says and then proudly strides away down the aisle like she's just done a good deed.

As if Sister Maeve makes such sneaky deals every day, she simply pours two glasses. "To new beginnings." She hands me mine. We tap plastic and begin sipping citrus-flavored alcohol.

"So you've never had sex?" I wonder if that would have been a good decision for me—complete and utter abstinence.

"Do you always handle pain like this?" she says. "By trying to make others uncomfortable?"

"Pfft." I wave her words away with my hand.

We sit in silence for a time.

"I just want to be a good feminist," I say out of the blue as the plane takes off and we begin to fly. "I really do. But you wouldn't know anything about that, would you? Nuns are the opposite of good feminists, wouldn't you say? Submitting to men is sort of your thing, right?"

Sister Maeve smiles and nods, and then she even chuckles.

"Have you read Gloria Steinem?" I ask.

"No, I have not."

" 'A woman needs a man like a fish needs a bicycle,' she said— Gloria Steinem. I wonder if she'd include Jesus as a man."

"Wouldn't know." Sister Maeve's voice seems tired and distant now.

I've already worn her down with my flippant and obnoxious comments—I'm very good at wearing people down whenever I'm upset, although I'm not proud of this.

I wish I had been nicer to Sister Maeve, but what can I do about that now? I can't go back in time and start over. And I'm having a bad day. When you catch your husband screwing a girl half your age, you are permitted to be bitchy, even when talking to adorable nuns on airplanes—nuns who buy you vodka, even.

Right?

No.

I'm a terrible person.

I'm sorry, I think I say, but I'm not sure if I've actually moved my mouth and tongue, which is when I realize I'm fantastically drunk.

Maybe I should have used Ken's Colt .45 on myself.

Suddenly nothing seems funny anymore.

I stare at the seatback in front of me for a minute or so before I pass out.

When I wake up, I'm disoriented and my head's throbbing.

My shoulder is wet from my own drool.

"Where am I?" I say.

The nun to my left says, "Welcome to Philadelphia. I drank your vodka for you, Ms. Lightweight. Time to exit."

I look up. The plane is empty.

"We've been shaking you. I think they might have gone to find a doctor," the nun says.

"I'm okay," I say, but when I try to stand, I feel sick.

I make it to the bathroom just in time to empty my stomach.

Someone is knocking now, aggressively.

"Ma'am? Are you okay?"

I wash out my mouth in the sink. "Coming."

I look in the mirror and see a monster.

An old-looking mythical creature.

Red eyes.

Makeup running.

I might as well have snakes for hair.

"*Great*." I open the door, trying to avoid eye contact. "I'm okay. Nothing to see here."

I push past the flight attendants.

"Ma'am, your friend left this for you."

I turn around, and the flight attendant extends a folded piece of paper.

I snatch it from her, say, "Thanks," and then head for baggage claim, each step echoing in my skull like land mines exploding on impact, trying my best not to throw up again.

My nun friend is nowhere to be seen, so I read the note while I wait for the machine to cough up my suitcase.

Dear Portia,

It was very nice meeting you on the plane. Sorry we didn't get to talk more. I will pray for you. Very hard! Daily! And I will ask "my husband" to intervene in a special way for you. He says he's not mad at you for making sexual jokes, so if you are worried about that now that you're sober—don't be.

Galatians 3:28—There is neither Jew nor Greek, there is neither slave nor free man, THERE IS NEITHER MALE NOR FEMALE; for you are all one in Jesus Christ.

Good luck with your quest.

Love,
Sister Maeve
PS—Here's my address, should you ever want to write me. I love letters!

Sisters of St. Therese
Sister Maeve Smith
(Wife of Jesus Christ Number 2,917,299)

16 Waverly Park
Rocksford, PA 19428

Weird, I think, and then stuff the note into my pocket.

Am I on a quest?

Maybe the quest to become a novelist?

But why would she write that? Did I mention something I don't remember now? I don't think I ever used the word *quest*.

I'm too hung over to care all that much, so I drop it.

I try to remember if I really said "wang" to a nun, repetitively.

Did I actually describe Ken's horrible inadequate stubby penis in excessive detail to Sister Maeve?

It's impossible to know for sure, and so when my bag finally slides down the conveyor belt, I grab it and catch a cab.

"Take me home," I tell the dark-skinned man in the driver's seat.

"Where is your home, please?" he says as he turns on the meter. His accent is sort of sexy. Seal without the scars on his face, I think, but then I quickly remind myself not to say that aloud, because it seems racist, even though I compare white strangers to famous Caucasians all the time, and without guilt.

"Across the Walt Whitman Bridge," I say. "Westmont. You?"

"Me what?" he says.

"Where's your home?"

He pulls away from the curb and says, "Philadelphia."

"Yeah, but you weren't born here, I can tell by your accent. So where are you really from?"

Silence.

There are mounds of exhaust-smoke-gray snow on the ground outside. I'm no longer in Florida, that's for sure.

"Are you afraid to tell me where you were born?" I say.

Our eyes meet in the rearview mirror. "Nigeria."

"Is it nice in Nigeria?"

"No," he says. "There is too much violence. Please. Never go."

"Westmont is pretty fucked too."

"It is better than Nigeria."

"Maybe," I say. "But it ain't like I have a choice tonight."

"You always have a choice. Look at me. Here in America. *A choice.*"

"Do you like it here in America?"

"Yes," he says. "Very much. I will bring my family here one day. Soon, I hope."

"You have a wife?"

"In Nigeria. And five children. Three strong sons."

I ignore his sexist favoritism. "You love her—your wife?"

"Yes."

"She's lucky." I hate myself for envying this woman in Nigeria whose husband drives a cab halfway around the world, saving money to rescue her from whatever hell Nigeria currently offers. It sounds like a fairy tale. She might as well be in an ivory tower. So romantic—beautiful even. Their struggle.

Portia, you are a terrible person, I think. Terrible.

"I am lucky. Very lucky. My wife is a strong woman. Very beautiful. Good mother. She will make me more sons here in America. I am the lucky one."

I look at my ruined reflection hovering in the window as we pass the Philadelphia professional sports complexes on the left.

What is this guy smoking? Because I want some.

He takes me across the Walt Whitman Bridge.

"I do not know this area. Will you please advise me?" he says.

I advise him.

We navigate away from Camden and toward safer suburbia, with me yelling out rights and lefts. Finally I say, "Over there. The one with the highly embarrassing metal awning."

He pulls up to the row home in which I grew up, across the street from the Acme grocery store.

His index finger taps the glowing red numbers hovering over his dash, and he quotes the price.

Instead of paying, I say, "Have you ever cheated on your wife here in America?"

"What?"

"Have you had sex with a woman since you left Nigeria?"

"No!" he yells in a way that lets me know he is highly offended.

"Do you consider your wife to be your equal? Do you encourage her to have ambitions and dreams?"

"Why are you asking me these questions?"

"Tell me you love your wife."

"I do not understand."

"Just tell me you love your wife."

"I do love my wife! I miss her very very much. Now you must pay."

"I believe you. You're not lying. I really believe you," I say. "Wow. You're the needle in the haystack. The real deal. I can tell."

"I do not understand you. Please pay. I have to drive new people to make money."

"You'll do it. Bring your wife to America yet." I stick five hundred-dollar bills through the plastic hole, feeling a bit like Ken in that Cuban restaurant, back in Miami, except I'm a more altruistic feminine version of Ken. Maybe I'm the Gloria Steinem to Ken's Hugh Hefner.

"This is too much," the Nigerian taxi driver says. "Far too much."

"Bring your wife to America. And don't cheat on her in the interim. Be a good man."

"I *am* a good man!"

I exit the taxi as Mr. Nigeria keeps saying, "Too much, please, take some back, please. *Please!*"

I don't have the strength to confront my mother, so I walk around the block to the alley behind our row of homes.

I open the ripped screen door, which still creaks, step into the grave-size back porch, pull a few blankets from the old army chest, wrap myself up, and lie down on the shitty plastic-cushioned rusted-springs gliding couch, which is even older than me.

It's musty and damp from the snowy weather, but I don't really care.

Just like high school, I think. After a night of drinking in the woods. Running from the cops. Eating fried grease at the Crystal Lake Diner. And then sleeping off hangovers out here.

I lost my virginity on this couch.

Jason Malta.

He was terrified.

He was nice, though.

Really sweet.

It didn't hurt because he was so timid and gentle—and a bit on the small side, which I didn't mind one bit.

Despite what I have been saying about Ken's tiny penis, it's not the shape or size of a man's dick that counts, it's the character of the man himself, if you ask me. Most women over thirty-five would agree, I'm betting. Somehow I knew this when I was seventeen, and then I forgot.

When I took Jason Malta inside me, I kept thinking it was like I was sucking away the worst of his life, cleansing him, making him pure, which I realize is strange and unusual thinking for a seventeen-year-old virgin.

But I swear he knew what I was doing for him—he knew I was taking his pain away from him, or at least lessening it, and that it was more like a favor than true love.

We both knew.

And we were okay with it.

I didn't come.

Not even close.

But I enjoyed it.

Giving him pleasure.

Relieving his anguish, if only for a few minutes.

Jason was a good person.

And he had been in so much pain.

After he ejaculated, he kept whispering "Thank you" over and over again, and then he started to cry and shake, but he couldn't explain why when I asked him, or maybe he just couldn't verbalize it, because we both just knew.

We knew that the moment we shared was about much more than getting off.

His mom had died the year before.

I don't even remember what she had, but I remember he missed a lot of school, and then when he started attending every day again, everyone knew it was over, and he seemed like a ghost.

I just wanted to bring him back from the dead.

Resuscitate him.

I remember he used to be funny in junior high. We had been in a play together, a comedy that he had written called *Charles Barkley Goes to the Dentist.*

The funniest part was that Charles Barkley never even makes an appearance in the play, maybe because we had no black classmates to play the role. But I remember it was set in a dentist's office. Jason played the dentist. I played the woman who worked the office, answering phones and greeting patients, and Jason had me wear these huge red Sally Jessy Raphael glasses. And a few other classmates played the people in the waiting room, reading magazines and newspapers, looking up curiously every time the phone rang. Reporters kept calling and asking when "The Round Mound of Rebound" was coming in to get his teeth cleaned—Jason had our science teacher, Mr. Roorbach, play the reporters, speaking into a microphone off-stage, almost making the calls sound like the voice of some absurd Samuel Beckett version of God, even though none of us knew who the hell Samuel Beckett was back then. I had to keep saying I couldn't "give out Mr. Barkley's information," and when the people in the waiting room overheard, they kept saying, "Charles Barkley? The Round Mound of Rebound is a patient here?" and, being a bad secret keeper or an unethical dental assistant, my character kept winking and whispering, "Well, everyone has to take care of their teeth—even professional athletes!"

It seemed funnier when we were in eighth grade, but our parents laughed—well, Jason's and other people's parents laughed. My mom didn't attend the performance, of course.

Jason tried to send Charles Barkley—who was a rookie playing for the 76ers at the time—free tickets to our play, but the organization never returned his call.

Jason Malta's mom got sick shortly after that, and he stopped writing comedies. He became transparent as a window. You could see right through him for years. And when he made love to me for the first time, I swear to God, he became flesh and bone once again, if only for a few seconds, which was when I first realized that sex and womanhood were powerful.

He used to buy me roses from the Acme, a dozen at a time. Cheap flowers that wilted and turned brown within hours. I thought I loved him, and maybe I did. He wasn't very good-looking—red hair, pale skin, and a concave chest. But he was kind. Even when he stopped being funny, he was still kind.

The smell of trash from the alley behind my childhood home

makes me feel nauseous again, but I manage to avoid the dry heaves.

She's inside, my mother; I know it. I can feel her heavy presence. But I'll need strength to face her, more than I have right now.

The finality of what has happened—it sinks in.

It cuts.

It mutilates.

I try to shiver myself to sleep.

In the cushions, I think I smell the Drakkar Noir cologne I once gave Jason Malta for Christmas, and which he wore dutifully for the rest of our high school tenure. I hope Jason Malta's happily married with kids and is wildly successful. Maybe he's even writing comedies again. Maybe.

It's a nice thought.

"Portia Kane," I say to myself, thinking about the vibrations of those syllables floating away into the night. "Portia Kane. Portia Kane. What has become of you, Portia Kane?"

I close my eyes and try to erase the world.

In my mind, I keep seeing a fish riding a bicycle.

The fish is singing a song about how she loves to pedal her bike, and I can't figure out how she can move both pedals with a single tail, which is when I realize I'm still drunk.

I'm spinning.

Bile runs halfway up my throat like some horrible acidic tongue and burns as it licks its way back down.

"Fuck you, Gloria Steinem," I say, although I am not exactly sure why.

CHAPTER 4

"Portia?" I hear. "Portia? What are you doing out here on the back porch?"

I open one eye and see my large mother in a pink bathrobe. Her breath is visible; her short gray hair—which she cuts herself—juts out in untamed triangular bursts that make her head look like a weird diseased flower.

"I took out the trash this morning, and what did I find? *You*. Happy! Happy! May I give you a kiss? May I hug you, my darling? Are you real? Am I dreaming now?"

She doesn't wait for an answer.

Every inch of my face is kissed.

It's like an octopus has attached itself, her mouth sucking like so many tentacles, somehow all at once.

Or maybe it's like being licked by a hippopotamus.

She throws her ample weight on me. I feel the rough burn of her aging terrycloth robe and make a note to buy her an update, even though I know she won't use it and probably has a dozen brand-new unworn backups stuffed somewhere in a closet.

"I can't breathe, Mom."

"Have you been drinking, Portia? You smell like alcohol. Stinky, stinky."

"I could kill a Bloody Mary right now," I say, and think about why I haven't been home for years.

My mother's lack of a filter.

Her penchant for being honest as a mirror.

Her often creepy childlike demeanor.

Her proclivity to annoy and embarrass and depress, like a genetic oracle that screams out my doom whenever I am within earshot.

It all strikes blunt as a hammer to the thumb.

"Where's Ken?" she says.

I listen to cars driving up and down Cuthbert Boulevard for a second before I say, "Ken died. Was shot with his own handgun. Colt .45. They made it out to be a random intruder. A burglary gone wrong. But Ken had many known enemies. Made the five o'clock news in Tampa even. But they didn't get the story right. Not even close. The detectives said they could make Rorschach tests out of the blood-splattered wallpaper and then laughed like hyenas, which I thought was insensitive, even if their observation was completely accurate. Regardless of all that—so long, Ken. Nice knowing you and all that. Sucks to be you."

Mom pulls in a dramatic gulp of air. "That's simply terrible, Portia! Horrible! What is a roar-shock test? I feel so sad for you. Ken is really dead? Or are you kidding? I can never tell. Why didn't you tell me earlier? I'm so confused."

"Didn't want to worry you, Mom. It's probably for the best, Ken's murder," I say, thinking I really shouldn't be talking like this anymore now that the booze has worn off. But I can't seem to stop myself. "I was getting tired of him. He couldn't even get hard anymore. I'd been wanting to recycle him for more than a year. Our sex life had passed away long before that."

"Portia!"

"Why did you name me Portia anyway? You'd never even heard of *The Merchant of Venice*, let alone read it."

"Was Ken really shot? Is he okay? You *are* kidding, right?"

"Ha ha! No. He wasn't shot. He's not really dead. But he's definitely not okay either. He is the antithesis of okay. And—"

"You're making my head hurt! One minute you tell me Ken was murdered, the next you're asking about your name—and I haven't even seen you in *many years*. You just show up and—"

"Focus, Mom. One thing at a time. Forget all the rest. Concentrate. Why'd you name me Portia?"

She closes her eyes and shakes her head hard enough to make her cheeks ripple like two red Jell-O molds experiencing a small earthquake. Then she looks up at the porch ceiling. "I guess your father liked the name."

Liar!

"Why?" I say.

Her eyes grow huge. "How would I know that?"

"Didn't you talk about what my name should be when you were pregnant?"

"I'm sure we did. We must have."

"Well, then?"

"Too long ago. Too, too long. I can hardly remember what I did yesterday, and you want me to talk about all of the old things. Your father was a good—"

"And kind man," I say. "Yeah, I know. I would have loved him."

"The accident—"

"The accident," I echo, cutting her off, because it's all just bullshit and we both know it. A nameless coworker took advantage of her simplemindedness and knocked her up. She made up the story of a nice and kind man without ever bothering to report the rapist, let alone hold him responsible for child support. I'm okay with her lying about all that in the past, because I let go a long time ago, but the never-ending ongoing lies are inconvenient when you want answers—real answers. You can get lost in Mom's madness. It's like a maze of tall bushes, all thorns and no roses. And she insists I navigate while blindfolded. "So you really have no idea why you named me Portia?"

"It suits you, doesn't it? It's a pretty name. I love the name Portia. It was the best I could think of. The best *we* could think of. *The best.*"

My name sounds like the type of sports car middle-aged men buy while fantasizing about fucking girls half their age, the type of car Ken will buy now that he is free and clear of me. I see him and Khaleesi riding around with the top down, her golden mane trailing like a comet over the hand-sewn leather interior and a candy-apple-red paint job.

"Did you like Ken?" I ask. "You can tell the truth now. He's gone. Finished. Not coming back."

"He's very handsome, but I only met him one time! And for only ten minutes!"

Mom's smile is childlike, and I feel a wave of guilt overtake me.

Has it really been three years since I've seen her? And did she really only meet Ken that one time?

Are those things possible?

Absolutely.

Portia, you are cruel in addition to being stupid.

"What's the state of the house?" I ask.

"You're not throwing anything away!"

"Easy, Mom. Do you have any orange juice? Coffee? Basics?"

"Sure. Sure. Come on in. We'll both catch our deaths out here."

"One can dream."

"What?"

"Nothing. Let's go inside."

"Welcome home, Portia," she says, and then kisses both of my cheeks once more. "I've missed you. Thank you for visiting me."

"Is the house *that* bad?"

"I just—it's that . . . well, I . . . I have Diet Coke for you! With lime inside!"

"I bet you do."

I mentally prepare myself as Mom and I stand.

She looks like she may have become even more rotund—Grimace, kids used to call her when I was in elementary school, referring to the fat purple McDonald's monster, and I never stood up for her, even though she would have happily flayed off her flesh with a blunt butter knife if I had asked her to.

She's looking at me, blocking the door. She outweighs me by at least a hundred pounds, and she's shaking.

"It's really good to see you, Portia. So good," she says, squeezing my arm until it hurts.

"Good to see you too, Mom."

"I didn't know you were coming."

"It wouldn't have mattered. We both know that."

"I would have straightened up for you at least."

"You would have worried and obsessed, but you wouldn't have gotten rid of a thing."

"I have Diet Coke for you. With lime inside!"

"I know, Mom."

"Portia, this is *my* home."

"I promise I won't throw anything away. You have my word."

She lights up like a plastic lawn Santa on Christmas Eve. "*Promise?*"

I draw an X across my heart with my forefinger and say, "Swear to God."

"I love you," she says. "I love having you home!"

She opens the back door, and when I step inside I see the cans of Diet Coke with Lime stacked three feet high, twelve or so deep, on the counter, and I want to cry. Boxes of cereal and rice and bags of flour and crackers are all piled around the cabinets so you couldn't reach them if you tried, let alone open any. Not one square inch of counter space is uncovered.

"Would you like a Diet Coke with Lime?" she says.

"Okay, Mom. But it's, what"—I look at the timepiece hanging above the sink, a black cat turned gray by dust with the face of a clock in its belly; its tail acts as a pendulum; its eyes insanely darting in the opposite direction of the tail . . . right, left, right, left, right—"almost eight a.m. Yep, just about time for a Diet Coke with Lime."

She opens the refrigerator. The bottom three shelves are stocked wall to wall with silver soda cans.

Mom doesn't drink Diet Coke with Lime—ever.

These are all for me, on the off chance I might come home thirsty enough to drink seven hundred or so cans in a single visit. I'm sure most are at least five years old.

"Mom," I say, and wipe tears from my eyes, because I have almost allowed myself to forget how my mother's life is even more fucked up than mine.

"I know you love Diet Coke with Lime, right? Right?"

"Yeah, I do. You know me," I say, taking the cold can from the clutch of her plump fingers and thumb.

When I bend the tab, the drink hisses, and a million bubbles come to life.

I sip.

"Good?" Mom says, nodding and looking up at me from under her thick gray eyebrows.

The truth is that this is a bribe. My mind flashes back to the last time I tried to clean out the house and get her help. I had my old Olive Garden waitressing friend drive Mom and the insanely long shopping list I gave her to Kmart. Armed with more than one hundred extra-strength trash bags, I started stuffing like a madwoman. I had the living room completely done when Carissa and Mom returned, much too early. Kmart had run out of pink sweat suits on the sale rack, which had triggered one of Mom's panic attacks. When she found me cleaning, Mom started screaming, "No! No! No! No! No!" for minutes, then began punching herself in the side of her head hard enough to leave a bruise. Carissa and I restrained her on the cleared-from-shit-for-the-first-time-in-years couch. Since Carissa and I were planning a move to Florida at the end of the summer, we acquiesced and calmed Mom by helping her rearrange her piles of trash. She kept mumbling over and over, "Your room is yours, Portia. The rest is mine. Your room is yours, Portia. The rest is mine," which muted Carissa and drained all the color from her skin.

Back in the present moment, Mom says, "Like you remember from the last time you were here? Diet Coke with Lime? Good?"

"Very good. But they have Diet Coke with Lime in Florida too, Mom. You can get these pretty much anywhere in the world, so you don't have to keep so much of it—"

"Your room is just as you left it. I haven't touched a thing!"

"A little Portia Kane museum. Just like the dining room, I bet."

I walk into the next room, which doesn't have a dining room table in it like you might think, but instead boasts a five-foot-square tower of my grandfather's lifetime magazine collection, *National Geographic*s stacked with yellow spines out, the rest with spines facing in—who knows why, maybe they're old girlie magazines— and the whole thing towering so high the cheap dusty gold chandelier rests atop, its chain piled limp next to it. These were moved up from the basement when we started getting water leaks. The dining room table is now down there, each leg up on a cinderblock, mostly because that makes no sense whatsoever and this is a mad,

mad home. You could kill someone by pushing the magazine tower onto them. The walls of this room are wallpapered floor to ceiling with taped-up pictures of me. There is a two-foot-wide walkway separating the four sides of the magazine tower from the million or so versions of my always-aging face.

If I could bear to look, I could trace the history of my entire life.

Baby pictures. First day of kindergarten and every other year, all the way through college. Every Halloween costume. Every Easter and Christmas outfit. My fat phases. My acne. Every date in an ill-fitting suit or out-of-fashion tuxedo who ever slid cheap flower arrangements around my wrist while pretending not to look at my hoarder mother's many piles of dusty junk before taking me to a dance—me wearing poofy Disney-princess sleeves and shiny cheap fabric that made me into the shape of an uppercase A.

My mother's life work is on these four walls.

I am her single contribution to the world, the poor woman.

It's amazing that she's never had an existential crisis.

Of course, the fourth wall is mostly pictures of Ken's and my wedding, all removed from the very expensive leather-bound album I sent her and in which she doesn't appear, because—even though Ken purchased her first-class airline tickets and an ocean-view suite at the hotel—she refused to travel to Barbados to attend the ceremony, claiming it was "too dangerous for an unmarried white woman."

And then beyond the wedding photos on the fourth wall are all of the shots I've sent her over the years from trips Ken and I've taken around the world—scenes I do not wish to revisit. And yet I know them all by heart already and can't help imagining me smiling stupidly in front of the Eiffel Tower holding a flaky baguette like a sword in two fists, the Great Pyramid of

Giza resting like a tray of food in the palm of my hand, me in a black bikini sipping rum and sugary milk from a coconut with a ring of flowers around my neck in Hawaii, me pretending to talk on the phone in one of those red booths they have in London, me standing next to a koala bear in a tree at an animal refuge in Australia, the underwater shots of me and Ken in flippers and the silly snorkel gear floating over the Great Barrier Reef, me with my arms spread Christlike with the great white iconic statue looming over my shoulder in Rio de Janeiro—so many stupid pictures we took all over the world ended up here in this hellish place, with my mother circling endlessly around her *National Geographic*s tower to fuel the merry-go-round narrative of my life, wearing out the dusty carpet even, an endless zero of obsession and insanity keeping her from having any adventures herself, from ever experiencing anything but the piles of trash with which she surrounds herself.

For some reason, I envision ancient ape people finger-painting on cave walls, the glow of a torch illuminating their Neanderthal faces as they squat and make stick figures and hide in sunless godforsaken dankness from the saber-toothed tigers that roam freely with huge top-of-the-food-chain teeth and ferocious appetites.

What is my mother's real-life saber-toothed tiger? I'll probably never know.

Now we have reality TV shows, memoirs, and all sorts of information and resources about hoarders, but when I was a child I didn't even know the word for what my mother was. There was never a diagnosis, so how could there have been a solution? No one found my mother grotesquely fascinating enough back then to put her on television and make her disease part of popular culture. I can't decide if that was a blessing or a curse. And regardless, I've come to believe that there is no cure for Mom now.

Her mind's been rotting for far too long. Some people you just can't resurrect, no matter how much you love them.

The living room is almost inaccessible, as Mom has made a mini city of out-of-date phone books and expired coupon clippings tied up with string. There are pyramids of cheap teddy bears and plastic-faced baby dolls, more cases of Diet Coke with Lime stacked and waiting to quench my mythical thirst, Johnny Cash and Dolly Parton records purchased by mail order and still in the original plastic because Mom owns no record player, shoe boxes crammed with receipts older than me, endless cans of spaghetti sauce, never-been-cracked cookbooks, my grandfather's childhood baseball card and tool collections in boxes labeled DADDY'S STUFF, and so many other useless items, stacked and teetering in a way that reminds me of Dr. Seuss cartoons.

"Don't move anything," Mom says. "Just don't. I know where everything is!"

"Where can I sit?" I ask facetiously, because sitting anywhere but in Mom's crumb-infested pink recliner is an impossibility.

"Your room," she says. "That's your space. I haven't touched it."

"Have you been saving the money I've been transferring into your account?"

"Of course! We have lots of money! I have bank statements. Every single one!"

"I bet you do."

"I would never ever—"

"Mom, I've left Ken. We're done."

"You'll work out your differences. Couples fight. That's the way it—"

"No, Mom. He cheated on me. With a very young woman— among others. He's not been nice to me. He's been subhuman. Awful. Really shitty, Mom. I've completely fucked up my life."

"Don't curse like that, Portia! Not in my father's house!"

"Mom, can I stay here awhile? I don't really don't want to live in a hotel right now. And I don't have the energy to rekindle any of the old friendships that I failed to maintain because I'm a bitch who chose money over true connections."

"You can stay in your room! Right here! Sure, sure, sure! I can get more Diet Coke with Lime at the Acme right across the street. Please stay. Please! I would *love* for you to stay."

"Thanks, Mom. But we have enough soft drinks, I think. And I'm getting more and more worried we might kill each other. You did hear the part about Ken cheating on me, right? That was a pretty significant part of the story, which probably requires acknowledgment from you. I'm really leaving him."

"Don't rush to conclusions, Portia! Family is family."

"We got by before Ken. We'll get by now. Somehow. I'm starting over. I'm kind of in pain. My heart is broken. As high school as that sounds. I should warn you that I've been drinking a lot, and I don't plan on stopping anytime soon."

"I haven't touched your room. That's *your* space. The Diet Cokes too. With lime. Drink those! Those are for you. Just don't touch anything else in the house. Okay? Everything will be fine. Everything has a place. Everything. Even you. On the walls of the dining room and in your bedroom upstairs. That will always be your space. It's so good to have you home!"

"I can't live like this again," I say to the ceiling.

"Would you like another Diet Coke with Lime?"

"Why not?"

Mom waddles around her mountain of *National Geographic*s and returns with a fresh Diet Coke with Lime. I hand her my old one, which is still full.

"This new one is much colder," she says.

I nod.

I sip.

It *is* colder.

I look around the house at all of the various collected shit piled high and the many dust bunnies. Then I look deep into the sick kind doughy eyes of my mother, the only person to ever love me unconditionally, maybe because she's absolutely bonkers.

But she does love me.

That's my one absolute.

She would bring me a new Diet Coke with Lime every ten minutes for the next six months if I asked—hell, the next six years, without sleeping more than nine minutes at a time—and she'd do it with boundless joy in her heart, completely satisfied to offer what she thinks I desire.

I wrap my arms around my mom and bury my face in her plump shoulder, feeling her bra's thick shoulder strap cut into my chin.

"Portia—why are you hugging me so hard?" she says.

"Just because."

"I love hugs!"

"I know, Mom. I love you. I really do. But I fucked up my life."

"Please don't use profanity in my father's home, Portia. I raised you better. Your grandfather didn't allow cursing in this house, and neither do I."

"You *did* raise me better." I start to sob. "It's true."

Mom rubs my back and offers me another Diet Coke with Lime, but I just cry into her shoulder and think about how I can't quite get my arms all the way around her and wonder how many inches separate my two middle fingers that are resting on her shockingly thick bra strap.

I guess five inches, and then—in my mind—tell myself to stop crying.

"Can I take you to breakfast?" I ask.

"Why are you crying, Portia?"

"Let's have breakfast at the diner."

"Now?"

"Yeah. Right now."

"Can I go like this? Where are we going? Which diner? Who will be there? How can we even know? Is it a safe time to go? Maybe we should wait until there are less people there. I don't know, Portia. I just don't know."

She's in the pink sweat suit she wears every day, brown stains floating like continents in a pastel sea of cheap, worn cotton. She has at least fifty different pink sweat suits stacked in her bedroom, which she purchases whenever she gets up enough courage to take the bus to Walmart and finds a pink sweat suit on sale for less than $9.99, which is the maximum she will pay. All of her extra pink sweat suits still have the tags attached, because she wears the same damn one over and over again, and wants to have the option of taking the extra ones back should she ever run low on money. She has receipts for pink sweat suits from the Clinton administration. And yes, she and the entire house reek.

Mother goes to the Acme across the street once a week at 9:43 on Tuesday night, because that's when the fewest cars are in the parking lot. She counts the cars from the living room window obsessively and keeps a chart. Tuesdays at 9:43 has been the best time to go shopping for some time now, unless it's changed since the last time we spoke on the phone. She always diligently reports the number of cars in the Acme parking lot, whether I ask or not, and I never do. She has a record going back several decades. It's a shame there isn't a market for this sort of data. She'd be the Bill Gates of food-store parking statistics.

"If you really love me," I say, making a preemptive strike to her Achilles heel, "you'll go to breakfast with me right down the street at the Crystal Lake Diner. We'll have waffles maybe. You could use a walk. We need to get you outside more. You look sort of pasty."

"A walk! In the daylight! They'll see me! They have small planes now with cameras. Drones, they're called! I saw this on TV. The drones can shoot you dead too! Anywhere in the world!"

"The government is not watching you, Mom. They could care less about you, believe me. The US government only cares about rich people! Last time I checked you've never lived in Faddonfield."

"I don't know. I don't know." Mom taps the soft flesh of her right palm against her forehead. "I don't know. I don't know. *I didn't vote for Obama.* And *not* because he's black either. But they have records! And now that we have a black president—it's hard to trust anything these days."

"You haven't voted for anyone in three decades, white or black."

"They'll shoot me for being unpatriotic then!"

"Listen, Mom." I lift her chin with my index finger until our eyes meet. "I promise it'll be okay if you eat breakfast with me at the diner. I promise."

"We could eat here!"

"We can leave the house and be okay. I swear. Do this for me, and I won't throw anything away for at least a week. You can rest easy for seven entire days. And a week is long. I might lose interest in cleaning the house by the end of it. I won't touch a thing. You'll have my word."

"This is *my* house! *My* father gave it to *me*!"

"Mom. Focus. Breakfast. At. The. Diner," I say, karate-chopping the periods into the air between us, thinking about how Ken and I have paid her taxes and debt for the last seven years just so she won't lose this wonderful little shithole. We've actually prepaid everything for the next few years too—taxes, cable, water, electricity, everything. Less than Ken spends on his monthly cigar and scotch supply.

"I don't know," she says, but she's nodding in a way that lets me know we have a deal.

After she's wrapped everything but her eyes up in a pink scarf, covering enough of her face to appease the strictest and most sexist Taliban members, we walk down the street holding hands, just like we did when I was a little girl, only now it's my mother who waits at corners looking in my eyes for permission to cross and flinching whenever cars roar past and begging me not to let go of her.

She's shaking the whole time.

Leaf-in-a-hurricane shaking.

"Can I just wait outside?" she asks when we arrive at the Crystal Lake Diner. "I can stay right here until you are finished eating, yes? I'll be good."

"No," I say, and drag her inside by the arm.

It looks like every diner in South Jersey—booths, a bar with permanently fixed-to-the-floor stools, old people nursing cups of coffee, overweight people enjoying heaping portions of greasy heart-attack-inducing delights, kids in high chairs at the ends of tabletops, solo men reading old-fashioned newspapers.

In other words, this is home.

We don't have to wait, but we're seated in the back room.

"I don't like this. I don't like this. I don't like this one bit," Mom says several dozen times. Her scarf is still covering her forehead and chin, making her look like a cross between a fat ninja and a wounded earless Easter bunny, but she's uncovered her nose and mouth. To be more precise, she looks like a homeless person, like someone to pick up off the streets and lock up for her own protection. "This isn't enjoyable for me," she says. "Not in the least!"

"You're doing this because you love me, and mothers and daughters who love each other go out to breakfast from time to time. In South Jersey, they go to the diner. That's normal. Obama actually passed a law stating that mothers have to eat breakfast out at a restaurant with their daughters two times a month or else they will be fined a lot of money and people will come and straighten their houses for them. Congress is thinking about using the drones to enforce the law and—"

"Stop teasing! I hate this! How much is the fine? I'll pay it. Just no drones!"

"Mom, I swear to God, if you complain one more time, I'll clean out the house today."

"No! No! No! No! No! No!" she shrieks loud enough to make people turn and look.

I've pushed her too far already.

Yes, I remember you, old friend, Mr. Guilt.

"Shhhh, Mom. Relax. *I'm sorry.*"

"I don't—"

"Coffee?" a woman says.

"Please. For both of us," I say, because my mother is looking at her lap and pretending to be invisible, which she does often in situations like this. I study our waitress's face and red dye job and then say, "Hey, aren't you Danielle Bass?"

"Yeah," Danielle says as she finishes filling Mom's cup with coffee. "That's what it says on my name tag. . . . Wait." She looks at my face and then says, "Oh, my god! Portia Kane? Is that really you?"

"Just add a few dozen wrinkles to your memory," I say.

"I haven't seen you for— What are you doing here? I heard you escaped to Florida. Married some . . . is he a movie maker?"

She's being polite here. Ken owns a company that makes extremely popular porno flicks specializing in spring-break college-girl fantasies. I guess word got around.

I should add that meeting people you know but haven't seen for decades is quite common in South Jersey diners—they are like time machines that way—but you have to have attended kindergarten through high school in the diner's school district for the magic to work.

South Jersey diners also have secret homing calls that they send out around the globe, summoning you back to eat unhealthy food.

"Came home to visit my mom," I say, lying for no apparent reason. "And for a trip to the old Crystal Lake hangover cure."

"Hi, Mrs. Kane," Danielle says, but gets no response.

"My mom's not very talkative," I say and give Danielle a wink, hoping she'll just move on.

She nods. "Yeah, well, I'm waitressing here. Straight out of 'Livin' on a Prayer.' I bring home my pay for love. Only my name's not Gina. And I ain't got a man. Just a boy. He's five. Guess what his name is? *Tommy*. Swear to God. That's his name. He doesn't work on the docks. Obviously, because he's only in kindergarten over at Oaklyn. And I didn't name him after the guy in the song. I wasn't working the diner by day when Tommy was born either. Just a stupid coincidence. You must think I'm a moron. But we sing the song together anyway, often during bathtime. Tommy and me. He likes it. My little man. And Bon Jovi—never gets old, right? Classic. Especially for us Jersey girls."

"Congrats." I raise my coffee mug to her. "On Tommy and all the rest."

"Yeah, big winner me."

Danielle looks so ashamed of her situation that I blurt out mine before I can think better of it. "I just caught my husband screwing a teenager, so maybe you're doing better than I am. I've left him."

"Oh, my god. Gross. Men are such pigs."

"No argument here."

"I'm sorry."

"Yeah, well."

"At least he married you. Tommy's dad just took off when I told him he was going to be a father. Poof. Gone. Simply vanished. Instantly became a sperm donor."

"I'm sorry," I say, thinking about my own unnamed rapist father.

"Good riddance, actually. You know what you want to eat? Or do you need some time?"

"Hell yeah, I know what I want."

"Shoot."

"Waffles for both of us."

"Whipped cream?"

"Mom?"

"I'm invisible," Mom whispers. "No one can see me."

Danielle Bass raises her pencil-thin dyed red eyebrows.

"One with whipped, and one without."

"You got it, Portia," Danielle says as she slides her notepad into her waist apron. "And you look friggin' great. Like you beat time. No wrinkles either."

"You're a beautiful goddamn liar." I break eye contact and shake my head.

"Your ex-husband's a moron."

"You look good too, Danielle. Better hair than Jon Bon Jovi circa 1986," I say, because she still poofs up her bangs, which seems rather anachronistic here in 2012, even in South Jersey.

"You know, I saw the Slippery When Wet concert at the Spectrum. Jon Bon Jovi flying around on wires high above. My mom got my brother and me seats. She was dating—um, cough, cough, screwing—a radio DJ at WMMR."

"Lucky you."

"I would have gladly been the teenage mom of Jon's baby." She laughs. "Still have my fringe leather jacket. It even fits. Why did male rock stars look like women in the 1980s? Why were we so turned on by androgynous men back then? Poison. Def Leppard. Mötley Crüe. All fronted by men who looked like women. Remember Cinderella?" She squints, raises an imaginary microphone to her mouth, and sings, "*Shake me. All-ALL-all night!*"

"Remember how sexist everything was back then? In every video there was a girl dressed in ripped spandex crawling around on the floor like a cat."

"Ah, bullshit. Eighties hair metal was fun. It's *still* fun. God, I miss guitar solos. Where did those go? They were like the orgasm of the song. Why would you ever cut those out? What do teens even do in mirrors now if they can't play air guitar?"

"Hey, do you remember Mr. Vernon?" I ask, although I'm not sure why. "God, I loved his class. He was a good guy. If ever there was one. You were in that class, right? Mr. Vernon's? Senior English. Remember those little cards that he—"

Danielle's face goes slack. "You haven't heard about Mr. Vernon, have you?"

"What?"

"How could you not have—"

"Danielle, I don't pay you to talk the customers' ears off!" a man yells from the other room. He looks exactly like that fat hairy terrorist they kept showing on TV a few years ago, the one in the white T-shirt with the extra-wide neck hole and the carpet of black hair ringing his jowls.

"My boss, Tiny," Danielle says. "Asshole supreme. I'll be back."

Danielle hustles off, and I look at my mother, who is staring at her reflection in the window.

"Do you know what happened to Mr. Vernon?" I say.

"I'm invisible," she whispers. "No one can see me."

"Do you even remember him? My senior high school English teacher? I used to talk about Mr. Vernon all the time. The teacher who encouraged me to write. Remember?"

Mom doesn't answer.

"How much I loved his class? Why I tried to major in English? All those books I read?"

Mom says nothing.

"Do you know who Gloria Steinem is, Mom?" I say, although I'm not sure why. Maybe because I know Mom doesn't, and I wish she did. Maybe because I wish Gloria Steinem was my mother and I secretly believe that if she were, I would be living a much better life right now. Maybe because my mom is a whale riding a bicycle all alone, with no one paying her any attention but me.

"*I'm invisible*," Mom whispers more forcefully.

"I know, Mom. I know."

I remember the first day of my senior year in high school. I had heard rumors about Mr. Vernon. Some kids said he was some kind of poet-philosopher, like a bad-looking unmusical Jim Morrison or something, and all of the musicians and art room kids were ready to abscond with him to some Central American country and force him to be their leader. Some of the jockstraps called him "Fag Vernon," and there were serious rumors about him being gay, because he wasn't married and never talked about a girlfriend, which was a crime back in the late 1980s, around here anyway.

Rock-and-roll front men were allowed to wear makeup and tease out their long hair—androgyny was being sold on MTV every day—but homosexuality was still taboo.

The lead singer of Skid Row, Sebastian Bach, definitely teased his hair out to look like a woman, and he also used to wear a shirt that read AIDS KILLS FAGS DEAD.

It didn't even seem wrong to wear that T-shirt when I was in high school, which is insane now, looking back.

When I walked into Mr. Vernon's classroom on the first day of school, he announced we were having a pop test worth twenty-five percent of our marking period grade.

I instantly hated him.

Everyone in the entire class groaned.

More than one of the boys whispered, "This is bullshit."

And I agreed.

My heart was pounding.

Worse yet was the fact that this thirtysomething man in canary-yellow shirtsleeves, with a lumpy tire of flesh around his midsection and a hairline that was racing toward the back of his neck—he used to gel long wispy strands to his pink scalp so it was sort of striped—was so sure of himself. It was offensive.

He's a high school teacher, for Christ's sake, I remember thinking.

Follow the rules, pal.

"Clear your desks of everything except a writing utensil," he said. "Let's go. This will take the entire period. You'll need every minute."

My palms began to sweat, and I felt nauseous.

I had pretty crippling test-taking anxiety even when I studied for days in advance and was prepared, so this was my absolute worst anxiety nightmare turned real.

We had not been assigned summer reading.

What the hell could he be testing us on?

As backpacks were dropped to the floor and kicked under desks, Mr. Vernon passed out lined paper. He instructed everyone to take two sheets and then wait for directions. Once he had all of the paper passed out, he said, "Do not even think about looking at one another's answers, because I will be watching you like our school mascot—a hawk. If I even so much as suspect you are cheating, I will fail you on the spot. Today's test will be worth one-fourth of your first marking period grade. And this test is pass/fail. Zero or one hundred. If you fail today, the best grade you can receive for the first quarter is a seventy-five, and that's if you score hundreds on everything else for the entire marking period and never miss a homework assignment."

"That's not fair!" someone yelled.

I agreed.

"Starting now, if you speak—even one word—for the rest of the period, you automatically score a zero. So do not speak. I'm serious. You don't want to test me."

Oh, how I hated Mr. Vernon at this moment. I fantasized about marching right out of the room and straight to guidance so that I could demand to be transferred to another teacher.

"Write your full name on the first line of your first piece of paper."

We all did that as Mr. Vernon paced our rows.

"Skip a line and write the number one, followed by a period. After that, I want you to write a paragraph about how you feel right now. Do you think this test is fair? Are you looking forward to being in my class? Tell the truth. If you lie, I will know. And I will fail you. I will not be offended by the truth. I promise. I want you to be honest here. It's important. So how do you feel? That's question one. Go."

Everyone stared at Mr. Vernon. We were dumbfounded. Was this some sort of joke?

"You have three minutes. So I suggest you start writing. Remember, this counts for twenty-five percent of your first marking period grade."

Someone began writing, I don't remember who it was, but then the rest of us followed suit like so many dumb blinking sheep.

I remember thinking that if Mr. Vernon wanted the truth, I would give it to him. And so I wrote about how I had always had test anxiety, and his surprising us with this stupid and completely unfair test was unprofessional and unkind. I said I was not looking forward to his class based on what I had experienced thus far and was strongly considering transferring out as soon as possible. I finished by writing something about absolutely loving my previous English classes, just to make him feel bad and also to let him know I wasn't a math and science person predisposed to disliking any and all literature classes. I wanted him to know this was about him specifically, and I did so with unbridled seventeen-year-old righteousness and fury.

I was still scribbling angrily when he said, "Pencils down. Skip a line and write the number two. Then answer this question: What do you think should happen on the first day of senior English class? What would you have the students do if the roles were reversed—if you were me? Remember to be honest. You are being graded on your honesty."

I remember being incensed.

I would definitely NOT ask my students to do impossible things, I remember writing. I would maybe make them feel welcome. Talk about what books we were going to read. I don't know, maybe it might be a good idea to hand out a syllabus? Pass out the first assigned novel? Act like a normal regular teacher and not some freak on a power trip? Be gentle and kind and . . .

I erased many of those lines, but Mr. Vernon saw me, walked over to my desk, and said, "That's the wrong side of the pencil, Ms. . . . Ms. . . . What is your name? I don't know you."

I pointed to my lips to remind him that he had forbidden us to speak.

"You may answer this question," he said.

"Kane. It's Portia Kane."

"Ms. Portia Kane." He smiled kindly at me. "Be honest. I can take it. Rewrite exactly what you wrote the first time. Don't doubt yourself." He winked at me once, and then addressed the class. "All of you need to stop doubting yourselves!"

I blew away the tiny pink eraser worms and quickly retraced my cursive into the dented grooves of the paper.

"Okay," Mr. Vernon said. "Take the second piece of paper and make a paper airplane. And if you are thinking you don't know how to make a paper airplane, shame on you! There are no rules. Make a paper airplane any way you want. And then decorate it with drawings or doodles or your name or anything you wish. But you must make a paper airplane and decorate it. Make it uniquely yours!"

This was getting very weird.

"Why are you looking to your peers for answers?" Mr. Vernon said, holding his palms up in the air and shrugging in disappointment. "There is no right or wrong way to make a paper airplane at this very moment in time. Just do it and then decorate it the best you can. Make it yours!"

One of the boys in the front row began folding, and then the rest of us did too.

I had no idea how to make a paper airplane, so I began to glance around the room.

"Ms. Kane," Mr. Vernon said.

I met his eyes.

"No cheating."

I returned my gaze to the paper on my desk, felt my cheeks burn, and cursed Mr. Vernon in my mind.

Why was he picking on me?

I'm sure other girls were looking at the boys to see how it was done. What a sexist thing to ask us to do. Would Mr. Vernon be asking us to build racetracks for Matchbox cars next? I was so angry.

But I began to fold and fold and fold some more until I had something that resembled a paper airplane, if only in an abstract way, and then I was writing my name on the body of it.

Portia Kane Airways.

I smiled in spite of myself.

I drew little windows and then little faces in the windows.

My airline would have women pilots, I thought, and then drew a picture of myself looking out from the chair in the cockpit. Why not?

"On your first piece of paper, skip a line and write the number three followed by a period. In a brief paragraph describe and evaluate your paper airplane. Remember, you are being graded on your honesty. So be truthful. Is your airplane any good? Do you like how it came out?"

I studied my paper airplane, and even though I had enjoyed creating it just seconds ago, the folds didn't look even and the faces in the windows looked childish—like what a four-year-old would draw—and then I thought that you wouldn't even be able to see faces looking out of an airplane because of the glare maybe, but I wasn't sure. I had never been on an airplane in my life, and that made me feel ashamed too, because everyone else I knew had flown at least once. Of course, Mom hadn't had enough money to send me on the British Literature trip to London the year before. I remember writing something about my airplane being the worst one in the class, but insisting that it wasn't my fault. If I had known what this test was on, I would have surely spent the summer reading books on how to make a superior paper airplane. I would have practiced my folds every day. I would have consulted origami how-to books even, and then I felt proud of myself for using the word *origami*.

I wasn't finished writing when Mr. Vernon said, "Skip a line and write the number four followed by a period. Now I want you to close your eyes."

We all began to look at each other again.

Mr. Vernon was insane if he thought we were going to close our eyes.

"What are you afraid of? Just close your eyes. You do it every night before you fall asleep, so I know you know how. Remember, this test is worth twenty-five percent of your first marking period grade. If you don't close your eyes in the next five seconds—and keep them closed until I say—you will receive a zero. No peeking!"

My eyes snapped shut, and I guessed everyone else's did too, because Mr. Vernon continued.

"I want you to imagine standing with your paper airplane in your hand, walking over to the windows. Admiring the world outside. The beautiful day that seems to be everywhere but in this school, at least judging by the looks on many of your faces. Imagine your arm reaching out into this warm September day. The sun on your skin. The palpable feeling of escape accelerating your heartbeat. Now see your hand coming back toward the classroom. Your paper airplane is between your thumb and forefinger. You push it out toward the sky and let go. Watch its flight. Does it soar off into the heavens like a fierce majestic eagle? Does it take an immediate nosedive for the ground before crashing and burning? Or does it do something else entirely?" He paused for a second. "Open your eyes and describe the flight of your plane exactly as you imagined it in your mind."

Everyone began writing.

I saw my plane fall from my hand like a dead rat—I couldn't wait to let go of its tail so I could wash my hands of it—straight down to the grass below. I remember being very proud of my rat simile, as trite and inaccurate as it sounds now. I also remember writing FAILURE in big capital letters too, almost as if I were proud of my own perceived incompetence.

"Skip a line and write the number five followed by a period," Mr. Vernon said. "When I say go, I want you to stand—remembering that if you talk, you fail—and take your paper airplane over to the window, stick your arm out into the sunlight, give your plane a throw, and watch it fly. Keep watching until it hits the ground. Make a mental movie of it. Then I want you to go outside and retrieve your airplane quickly—without running—return to your desk, and describe your airplane's actual flight in great exact detail. Remember, you are not being graded on the flight, but on the degree of honesty you employ while describing the flight. If you are honest, you will receive an A. Go."

No one moved.

"What are you waiting for?"

I remember James Hallaran standing first. He always wore a black leather jacket, drove a late 1970s Camaro painted aqua, and kept a pack of Marlboro Reds rolled in his T-shirt sleeve. Outside of school he'd have a cigarette tucked behind his left ear like he was John Travolta in *Grease*, although he looked more like Billy Idol.

This cliché of a rebel walked to the window and threw his airplane.

I remember him grinning as he watched it sail through the air.

Then he laughed in this curt way, like he had just gotten away with smoking a joint in front of the principal, and made his way to the door.

"Very good, Mr. . . ."

James spun around, pushed his lips together, locked them with an imaginary key, shrugged comically, and then spun around on the heel of his left boot quickly enough to make the chain that connected his wallet to his belt loop rise.

"You and I are going to get along," Mr. Vernon called after him, smiling.

James lifted a thumb over his head as he walked out the door.

Then many of the other boys began giving their paper airplanes the gift of flight, and soon many of the popular girls did the same.

Being neither male nor popular, I was one of the last to stand.

It felt good to be moving in class, and the sun warmed my skin when I extended my arm out of the window, although my plane didn't fly, but spun and sadly seesawed its way to the ground.

I was embarrassed as I exited the classroom, walked down the hallway and the stairs, and found Portia Kane Airways' first female manned aircraft stuck in a bush.

Does a female pilot make it an un*man*ned plane? I thought, and smiled.

Back up in Mr. Vernon's classroom, I wrote exactly what I had seen, likening my plane's flight to that of an oak leaf plucked free from a tree by a gust of September wind, and feeling more than a little proud of the metaphor.

"Pencils down," Mr. Vernon said. "Now I want you to reread your answers. Put a plus sign next to the answers that seem optimistic and positive. Put a minus sign next to the answers that seem pessimistic and gloomy. Remember, you are being graded on your honesty."

As I reread my answers, I realized that I would be giving myself all minuses, because all of my answers were "pessimistic and gloomy." And this made me angry, because I wasn't a pessimistic and gloomy person.

Or was I?

Mr. Vernon had tricked me somehow. I wanted desperately to put little plus signs next to all of my paragraphs, because I had always thought of myself as a reasonably optimistic person, but it would be dishonest, and we were being graded on honesty.

"Pass your papers forward. You may keep your airplanes."

We did as he asked, and once he had all of the papers in his hand, he tapped the pile straight. "How did you feel when I announced that you were going to be tested today? What did you write? Be honest. You may speak when called upon."

A few kids raised their hands and said they felt betrayed, scared, worried, annoyed, anxious—mostly what I would have said. When Mr. Vernon asked, "How about you?" and pointed to me, I shrugged.

"You can tell the truth, Ms. . . ."

"Kane. I just told you that ten seconds ago."

"Forgive me. I have more than a hundred new names to learn, and it's only the first day of school. But how did you feel when I announced the test today, Ms. Kane?"

"Angry," I said, too quickly.

"Why?"

"Because it wasn't fair."

"Why wasn't it fair?"

"Because you didn't give us a chance to study. We didn't even know what the test was about. It wasn't fair."

"Would studying have helped you today?" he asked.

I could feel everyone's eyes on me. I didn't like it.

"I could have read up on how to make paper airplanes."

"Do you think that would have improved your grade, considering the fact that you're being graded on honesty today and not your ability to make paper airplanes?"

I felt my face turning red.

Mr. Vernon picked another victim—and in my memory it's Danielle Bass. I see her red hair teased out wildly and stiff with hair spray, like Axl Rose's in the "Welcome to the Jungle" video.

"It was just different," she answered.

"And different is bad?" Mr. Vernon asked her.

"Usually," Danielle said. In my memory, she's wearing black lip-stick.

"Why?"

"Don't know. Just is."

"Don't give average answers," Mr. Vernon said. "You're better than that. I can tell. Try to be articulate. You can do it. You're smarter than you think. All of you are. Trust me."

Danielle squinted at him.

"Is it safe to assume that everyone found the idea of a pop test on the first day of class unpleasant?"

We all began glancing around the room.

"Don't be such sheep!" he yelled. "Think for yourself. That's the problem. Consensus kills art and intellectual progress! I could see it in your eyes. You were all terrified by the word *test*. Just four little letters. Ridiculous. But let me ask you this question: Have you ever taken one of *my* tests before? No, you haven't. So how would you know what that experience entails, let alone if you would like it? Why did you all think it was going to be a bad experience?"

James Hallaran called out without raising his hand. "We assumed it would be a bad experience because all of the tests we've been taking since kindergarten have sucked—emphatically."

Mr. Vernon smiled and nodded. "I like your use of the word *emphatically*. Yes, I do. But if you are going to use sexual metaphors in my class, Mr. Hallaran, please be more original. Also, raise your hand when you want to speak, okay?"

James nodded back, and I noticed that he too was smiling. I could tell he liked Mr. Vernon, and it was then—right at that very moment—that I began to realize we all were going to like him. That he was in complete control, and he had tricked us. James Hallaran was the first to figure it out. Maybe I was the second.

Mr. Vernon slowly waved his index finger over the class. "You limit yourself with a bad attitude. Those of you who are lazy will blame the system. You've been conditioned to retch at the word *test*, no matter what the actual testing may involve. But it's a choice too. You don't really want to be Pavlov's dog, do you? And that's the point of today. When was the last time you got to make paper airplanes in class and then throw those airplanes out the window?"

He looked around at us, but no one raised a hand.

We were on unfamiliar ground, and while most of us were smiling at this point, we were still reluctant to speak before we knew what sort of game was being played here.

"How many of you wrote scathing reviews of your plane and its flight? Even worse—how many of you envisioned your planes crashing and burning before you even gave them a test flight?"

He seemed to be searching all of our eyes at once, scanning us for lies.

"You gotta believe once in a while, kids. That's what I'm trying to tell you here. The world will try to crush that belief out of you. It will try its damnedest. 'If people bring so much courage to this world the world has to kill them to break them, so of course it kills them. The world breaks every one and afterward many are strong at the broken places. But those that will not break it kills. It kills the very good and the very gentle and the very brave impartially. If you are none of these you can be sure it will kill you too but there will be no special hurry.' Does anyone know who wrote that?"

I raised my hand before I could stop myself. "Ernest Hemingway. It's from *A Farewell to Arms*. We read it sophomore year."

"Very good. And do you believe that the world wants to break you?"

"I don't understand."

"This is your senior year, Ms. Kane. Next year you will be squarely in the real world. It's important for you to understand these things. Imperative."

"What things?"

"The cost of being strong."

"I'm not sure I understand."

"You will," he said, looking directly into my eyes. "You will, Ms. Kane. I promise. You all will," he said to the class. "And I know before I even begin that many of you will be consensus people. Herd members who will cower at the word *test*. People who look around the room before speaking or doing anything. But you can free yourself. There's still time, kids. To be free. To tell Pavlov that you are not a dog. Do you want to be free? Do you?"

Mr. Vernon paused too long—it made all of us feel uncomfortable. You could hear the red second hand ticking on the standard school clock hanging next to the American flag.

"You all scored one hundred on your tests today. Every one of you starts the year with one hundred percent. And I'm a man of my word. That's twenty-five percent of your grade already perfect. No homework tonight either. And no boring average predictable syllabus outlining what we may or may not do. Instead I offer you adventure. Who knows what lies around the curve for us? I promise you one thing only—it won't be boring."

The bell rang, but no one made a move for the door.

"When your head hits the pillow tonight, when you close your eyes, just before you drift off into your dreams, I want you to ask yourself these two questions, and answer honestly: Doesn't Mr. Vernon give the best tests? And if day one was so interesting, what the hell will the rest of the school year be like? What was that word you used earlier, Mr. Hallaran? Assume? Makes an ass out of u and me, is the old cliché. Check your assumptions at the door tomorrow before you enter my domain. Ms. Kane, see me after class. The rest of you are dismissed!"

I swallowed hard and remained seated as the rest of my classmates filed out.

Mr. Vernon walked over toward me slowly, and then, with the fingertips of his right hand resting on my desk, he said, "Are you a fan of Greek drama?"

"What?" I said.

"Your T-shirt. The masks. Comedy and tragedy. Classic symbols, thousands of years old."

I looked down. "Um, this is a Mötley Crüe concert shirt. *Theatre of Pain*. 'Home Sweet Home'? Mötley Crüe is a band."

"Those masks represent tragedy and comedy. Been around a lot longer than your assorted crew. Look it up. You're smarter than you realize, Ms. Kane. You don't have to pretend. Do you like Hemingway?"

I shrugged, but inside I was pissed about the "smarter than you realize" comment. He didn't know me. And he sure as hell didn't have the right to talk to me like this—like he was my father or something. It was bullshit.

Mr. Vernon said, "Do you find him sexist? I mean, Papa was a bit of a pig when it came to women, but goddamn could he write. Do you agree?"

I just stared up at Mr. Vernon.

No teacher had ever talked to me like that.

"You don't know what to do with me, do you?" He laughed. "You don't like me yet either. *Yet*. But you will. I can look into all of your eyes on the first day and know which of you will get my class. You will get it, Ms. Kane. I can tell. You're free to go now."

I grabbed my backpack and left as quickly as I could.

When I was far enough down the hall, I whispered, "*Freak*."

But in my heart, I didn't mean it.

I went to the library during lunch and looked up Pavlov, learned about the conditioned reflex, and how you could make dogs salivate when they heard a bell ring even when there was no food in the room, if only you'd rung it enough times previously while the dog was eating.

I sort of got what Mr. Vernon was saying about us.

I didn't want to be anyone's dog.

Maybe I *had* been conditioned.

That night when my head hit the pillow I caught myself smiling and realized I was doing as Mr. Vernon had instructed—I was thinking about him and his class. I wondered what the rest of the school year would be like, and if any of the other kids in my class were also thinking about Mr. Vernon before they drifted off to sleep. I bet they were. And then I wondered if he was doing to us what Pavlov had done to his dog. Would I think about Mr. Vernon every time my head hit the pillow for the rest of my life?

Back in the Crystal Lake Diner, Danielle says, "One with whipped and one without," as she plops plates of waffles down in front of Mom and me.

"I'm invisible," Mom whispers.

I blink a few times, and Danielle says, "You okay, Portia?"

"What happened to Mr. Vernon?"

"Here," Danielle says, and then slips me a piece of paper. "Enjoy your meal."

I unfold the paper and read it.

Can't talk here. Boss is a Nazi. Off at 6 pm. Dinner? Call at 6:20?

Her phone number is underneath.

"Mom," I say.

"Invisible."

"You haven't heard anything bad about a teacher at Haddon Township High School, have you? Mr. Vernon? My senior-year English teacher? Anything at all? It could have been a few years ago?"

"Can we leave yet?" Mom says, covering her eyes with her right hand and then gritting her teeth convincingly enough to make me believe she is really truly suffering through this.

I look down at my plate—at the four-inch-high pile of waffles and the additional three-inch fluffy white pyramid of whipped cream on top—and I actually start to feel sick.

"You're not going to eat a bite, are you?" I ask Mom.

"I'm invisible. *Can we leave yet?*"

"Okay, Mom. You win."

I flag down Danielle, ask for take-home containers, explain that my mother is not feeling well, and let her know I'll call later. I leave a hundred percent tip on the table, thinking of little Tommy at home, who doesn't yet work on the docks but may someday, since his mother already works the diner by day, and also remembering my own waitressing days. I pay the cashier, and then walk Mom home hand-in-hand.

As soon as we're in the door, she asks if she can eat her waffles, and I say, "Sure."

She grabs a fork and eats lustily out of the white Styrofoam box. She's seated in her pink recliner among the towers of junk and lurking dust-bunny filth.

"Yum," she says. "Aren't you going to have any, Portia?"

"You got what you wanted, didn't you, Mom? This is what you want."

"Waffles with whipped cream!" she says, which is when I realize that she's eating *my* waffles.

"Enjoy," I say. "I'm going to my space now."

"Your room is yours. I haven't touched a thing!" she says, flashing a mouth full of half-chewed waffles, white whipped cream, and sticky brown syrup. "It's yours!"

I turn and approach the steps, which are only half as wide as they should be. Mom's stacked sundry boxes of crap two feet high along the left side, where there is no railing. She needs the railing on the right side to make it to the upstairs bathroom, which is the only thing she uses up there, since the halls, closets, and her entire bedroom are stocked floor to ceiling with what-have-you.

She's been sleeping on the pink recliner for decades.

I stand at the bottom of the steps, wondering if it's safe to climb, or if there is so much stuff up there that my added weight could bring the second floor crashing down. But then I remember that my mother outweighs me by an entire person, so I begin to climb, trying not to look at the six hundred or so rolls of toilet paper stacked eight feet tall and four feet wide, the bathroom door trapped behind them so that it's no longer possible to shut it while sitting on the toilet or taking a shower.

I enter my room and try to ignore its museumlike qualities. My mother has preserved the past with freakish dedication. Only one thing has been missing here: me. If my mother could have put me in a bottle of formaldehyde and kept me a little girl forever, she probably would have.

I ignore the red varsity letters that hang on the wall because I played the flute, wore a ridiculous uniform, and lettered in marching band.

A life-size poster of Vince Neil making an orgasm face and grabbing his crotch through ripped jeans hangs eternal and slightly faded on the back of my door.

My old flute is in its case on the bureau.

My collection of stuffed animal unicorns has grown because Mom still buys me one for my birthday and one for Christmas.

You know what you call a herd of unicorns?

A blessing.

True.

There are six less-dusty members of the blessing who I have not yet met, and the thought of Mom placing these on my bed because I'm no longer here and I've told her she's not allowed to mail me anything makes me so sad.

I'm a horrific daughter, yes.

But I'm also back in the exact place I ran from all those years ago.

I'm a homing pigeon.

What goes up must come down.

Then I remember why I came up here in the first place and rifle through my underwear drawer, tossing twenty-year-old panties—which would split in half if I tried to fit into them now; I'm not exactly fat, but I'm not eighteen anymore either—over my shoulder as I search. Finally I have it in my hand.

"Incredible," I say to myself.

I stare down at the Official Member of the Human Race card and examine the picture taken by Mr. Vernon the week before I graduated high school. He took everyone's picture—well, everyone who was in his senior English class. My face looks thinner, my skin smooth—absolutely no wrinkles—and I appear . . . innocent, completely oblivious to what's ahead.

Hopeful.

God, I was so beautiful. Stunning, even. Why did I feel so ugly back then? Was I blind? I'd kill little old adorable Sister Maeve and all of her nun friends—figuratively speaking, of course—to look like this again.

My bangs are teased up a little—okay, they're teased up so high they barely fit into the picture—and the rest of my brown hair hangs down straight, disappearing behind my shoulders.

Here in my bedroom, I look to my right and see my old curling iron on the nightstand, next to an aerosol can of Aqua Net hair spray that belongs in a real museum.

I smile.

On the card, even though it must have been June—maybe it was a cool June, but I don't remember—I'm wearing a white jean jacket and there are buttons pinned over the breast pockets. The buttons are hard to make out, but I can name them all anyway.

Over my right breast: Bon Jovi, Guns N' Roses, Metallica, Mötley Crüe, of course.

Over my left: A purple peace sign. A yellow smiley face. Kurt Vonnegut Jr. smoking a cigarette. Sylvia Plath looking smart and sad in misbehaving bangs. They're all still pinned on that white jacket—all I have to do to check my memory is open the closet door and take the relic off the hanger.

In the photo I'm holding now, I'm smiling in a way I haven't smiled for a long time. I look unburdened. Naive—in the best of ways. Like the rest of my life was going to be a late May afternoon on the Jersey shore, a walk on the beach in the most pleasant weather with the ocean tide tickling my toes.

I read the words that Mr. Vernon printed next to my photo. What happened?

Portia Kane, Official Member of the Human Race!
This card entitles you to ugliness and beauty . . .
. . . and remember—
you become exactly
whomever you
choose to be.

CHAPTER 5

I call Danielle Bass at 6:20 p.m.

I thought about googling Mr. Vernon on my phone to see what happened to him, but I didn't. I don't know why. Maybe because I want to hear whatever happened from someone who knew him? Maybe I'm worried that he did something deplorable like fuck one of his students—exactly like Ken and every other base man with whom I have ever come in contact would probably do? I don't know why it's suddenly so important for me to keep Mr. Vernon in the scarcely populated Good Man column, but it is. And if he isn't a good man, I want to hear it from a living breathing, person—preferably a woman—whether that makes sense or not.

"Portia!" Danielle says, after I tell her who it is. "You left me a nice tip. Thanks!"

"Well, good service should always be rewarded," I say, and hope it doesn't come off as condescending.

I'm relieved when she lets it go. "Glad you called," she says. "You wanna eat dinner with me and my kid at the Manor? I'm starving. And my treat. I insist."

"The Manor?"

"You know, that bar in Oaklyn. Near the school? I live in an apartment cattycorner to the Manor. I could hit it with a stone."

"The place with the deck, with the train tracks behind it? Next to the trestle?"

"That's it."

"I haven't been there for—"

"It's exactly how you remember it. The place never changes, which is the beauty of it, right? It's a constant. You wanna eat with us?"

"Um, sure. But I'm wondering if you could quickly tell me what happened to Mr.—"

"I just walked through the door, and I haven't seen my boy all day. Meet us at the Manor in, say, a half hour. I'll tell you whatever you want to know then."

"Okay, but—"

I hear her yell, "Tommy, Mommy's home!" just before the phone goes dead.

"Shit!" I say, remembering that I have no car.

I don't know why I open my closet and pull out my white Levi's jean jacket from high school, but I do. All of the pins are still affixed.

I try it on. It's snug, but chic. We used to wear them a little baggy, back in the day. It's definitely retro, but I like it—it takes me back and makes me feel like I'm home again—so I leave it on, almost like a costume.

Pre-Ken me.

I skip every other step down to the first floor, which is when I realize I'm sort of excited.

"Mom," I say.

"Did you say that Ken died earlier?"

"Yes, but he didn't really."

She's staring at the Buy from Home Network on her boxy old television set. A middle-aged woman is twisting her wrist under an intense light so that the faux-diamond-encrusted face of an imitation Rolex watch—which they are calling a "Roll-Flex" on the screen—sparkles and dazzles with fabulous faux brilliance.

Mom looks up at me from her recliner. "You must be careful, Portia. Sometimes when you wish for things, you get your wish! Maybe Ken really died today! It would be your fault then!"

"I could live with that, believe me," I say, and then quickly add, "but I'm going out with Danielle Bass."

"Who's Danielle Bass?"

"Our waitress today. Remember her?"

"I was invisible then."

"I know."

Mom turns and faces the television again. I can see the saleswoman now. A tanning booth has turned her face into a catcher's mitt, but she speaks and moves with the sensuality of a Victoria's Secret model half her age.

"With only five easy payments of fifteen ninety-nine, this beautiful classic cubic zirconia Roll-Flex can be yours! Perfect for any occasion, whether you are shopping at the mall or spending a night on the town! You'll be in style and the envy of your friends with this little equalizer on your wrist."

"*Equalizer?* Why do you watch this shit, Mom? You never buy anything unless it's on sale at Walmart."

"Father doesn't allow profanity in the house, Portia!" she says without taking her eyes off the screen. "You grandfather simply won't—"

"I might be out late, okay?"

She doesn't answer, so I make my way around the various junk piles to the front door.

I pause for a second before leaving just to see if Mom will break away from the Buy from Home Network long enough to say, "Have fun!" or even "Bye," but she doesn't, of course.

Never has.

Never will.

Outside I use my phone to google a local cab service, make the call, and wait on the sidewalk, hoping the nice Nigerian driver will show up again, but instead it's a tiny old man in one of those Irish caps that look like a duck bill sticking out of his forehead.

I tell him to take me to the Manor in Oaklyn, and he puts it in drive without saying a word.

Why don't I ask him where he's from and whether he loves a woman?

I'm not the same person I was last night, I guess. I'm sober, yes, but it's more than that. The rush of leaving Ken—taking action—is running out, and I wonder if I'll need another fix soon.

What's he doing tonight?

Is he with Khaleesi?

Are they screwing in my old bed?

Should I be talking to a lawyer pronto?

Why am I not more upset?

And Ken hasn't even called or e-mailed.

Is there something wrong with me?

Am I too old?

And what exactly happened to Mr. Vernon?

"Ten bucks," the old man says, and I realize we are outside the Manor. I remember the sign—a suspiciously young-looking man sitting on a barrel and downing a pitcher of beer.

There are red-and-white-striped metal awnings, and the building is made out of sandy-colored bricks. What looks like a double-wide red phone booth juts out from the front corner to protect the door from letting in gusts of cold air in the winter and hot air in the summer, maybe.

I give the cabbie what he asks for plus a few extra bucks and make my way to the side entrance.

The wooden tables and booths inside are old enough to make the flat-screen TVs seem like futuristic technology. Thick, dark wooden beams run along the ceiling and a brick archway divides the room, which is full of people who work and live hard in the various surrounding blue-collar towns—Oaklyn, Audubon, Collingswood—a patchwork of small homes with tiny yards. Many of these people are wearing orange-and-black Flyers jerseys, red Phillies caps, kelly-green Eagles coats.

"Portia!"

I spot Danielle in a booth at the other end of the room, waving me over with her hand in the air.

I make my way through the tables and notice a kid sitting next to her.

Tommy has shaggy blond hair that is maybe a little too long to be in style and makes him look a bit androgynous, but he's adorable. I immediately recognize Danielle's eyes and nose on his little face, although he has a strong chin, which is weird to say about a five-year-old, I realize. I imagine his father as a classically attractive Brad Pitt type.

When I sit down across from Danielle and Tommy, he says, "Hello, Ms. Kane, I'm going to perform soon!"

"Are you now?" I say.

Danielle doesn't say hi, but watches her son the way I've learned mothers do, as if their child were the most amazing thing in the world and therefore they remain mute out of sheer awe—like they don't want to interrupt what they think will be the best part of your day, talking with their kid.

I realize that will sound harsh to some readers, especially mothers.

I'm not looking down on Danielle so much as identifying what's going on.

Child-free women do this—observe with all the objectivity of an outsider—whether you want them to or not, and I am a child-free woman.

"Chuck and I are in a band," Tommy says.

"You're just in time for the show!" Danielle says to me and then musses Tommy's hair. "Tell her the name of your band."

"Shot with a Fart," Tommy says and then giggles so hard he can no longer open his eyes—he even tears up.

"And you're to blame!" Danielle says, poking Tommy's ribs with a forefinger to the rhythm of each syllable, and then tickles him.

I wonder if this is the performance.

But then a curly-haired blond man who looks to be about our age or maybe a few years older enters the room from the front bar. He's wearing a long-sleeved black T-shirt, faded blue jeans, and black high-top sneakers. Into a microphone he says, "Ladies and gentlemen, please put down your two-dollar Coors Lights, your deep-fried chicken wings, your cheese fries, and your tuna melts, for you are about to see the greatest show South Jersey has to offer before five-year-old bedtime."

I look around the room, and the patrons are clapping and smiling in anticipation.

"You know me as Chuck the bartender—the man who's continuously provided you with free Chex Mix and who will always be there to turn the channel for you sports junkies. The man with the remote control. Quick wrist on the tap. The guy who gives you a generous pour every time. The man who works extra hard for your tips. But I also lead a double life as the awesome uncle of Oaklyn's best-kept secret, the pint-size man who fronts South Jersey's most supreme Bon Jovi cover band, Shot with a Fart, the one and only Tommy Bass!"

The room explodes with applause.

Little Tommy jumps up out of the booth and runs behind the side bar.

The applause grows, and then everyone starts chanting, "Tom-MEEE! Tom-MEEE! Tom-MEEE!"

After thirty seconds or so another bartender—a beefy bald guy with the Phillies P tattooed in green on the side of his neck—lifts little Tommy up onto the bar, only Tommy is now wearing fake leather pants, a little leather fringe jacket, a long purple scarf, mirrored cop sunglasses, and a blond wig that makes him look like he has a lion's mane on his head.

Chuck hands Tommy the microphone and then picks up a broom.

Tommy says, "How you doing tonight, Oaklyn, New Jersey?"

Everyone cheers.

"This one's for my mom over there in the corner," Tommy says and then looks down at his feet on the bar, which is when I realize he is wearing little cowboy boots. He looks up again and says, "She really works at a diner. It's true."

Someone puts two fingers in his mouth and lets out one of those eardrum-piercing whistles, and the cheers get louder.

I look over at Danielle, and she's staring at her boy intensely—she's smiling, but she looks like she could break down crying too.

The beefy bartender puts some money in the jukebox, punches in a number, and then we hear the synthesizer chords and that jingling baby rattle. When the drums kick in, Tommy begins to gyrate in rhythm and the now straight-faced Chuck does his best Richie Sambora, strumming his broomstick, nodding his head, opening and closing his mouth to imitate that voice-box sound that Sambora does for "Livin' on a Prayer."

"Everybody up!" Tommy yells into the mic, just before he starts singing along. I'm surprised that everyone actually gets up and also that Tommy can sing pretty well for a kindergartner. The little guy has more confidence and swagger than seem possible.

And while he works the entire room with his shades and finger pointing, most of his glances and gestures go toward his mother in the corner, which is when I realize he's doing this for her, to pump her up and keep her going, and even though I know he's five and has no idea what he's doing at all, but is most likely naively running on instinct, I love the kid instantly.

I watch Chuck lean back and make comical faces during his guitar solo. He's terrible compared to Tommy, but sacrificing himself for his nephew and I'm guessing Danielle too, who must be his sister if Chuck is Tommy's uncle. I sort of remember him from high school. Maybe he was a grade or so ahead of us? And he's still pretty fit—actually *very* fit. And his face has remained kind after all these years.

Tommy cocks his head to the side, points at me when he sings, "*You live for the fight when that's all that you got!*" and then does a pelvis thrust that makes me more than a little uncomfortable, since he's five, but I seem to be the only one thinking about age-appropriate behavior, because the rest of the bar is pointing back at Tommy and singing along.

He's too young to be this captivating, and yet there are fifty or so Bud-bottle-drinking adults dancing and singing and clapping and enjoying the hell out of the performance.

I look over at Danielle and catch her wiping a tear from her cheek as she nods and dances and sings along, which is when I realize that this is the pinnacle of her week—this moment right here at the Oaklyn Manor bar with her brother and son performing a Bon Jovi song.

This is what she has.

And it makes me so sad and happy at the same time.

It makes me think about Mom watching me drink Diet Coke with Lime.

And before I know it I'm screaming too, "Whoa! We're halfway there!"

Which is crazy, because I'm not halfway to anywhere, but maybe that's the point of the song.

Shot with a Fart gets a thirty-second standing ovation before Tommy disappears behind the bar again and Chuck makes his way over to kiss his sister on the cheek and say "Did you like the show?" to me.

"Very much," I say, laughing. "I sure wish I had an uncle like you."

Chuck smiles proudly, but breaks eye contact before saying, "What are you drinking? On the house for Danielle's friends. Especially those who wear Mötley Crüe buttons." He makes the devil horns with his right hand and sings, "*Shout at the devil!*"

I raise my own devil horns and in a deep, put-on voice sing, "*Home sweet home.*"

"Best rock ballad ever. Fucking *ever*," he says. Then he quickly covers his mouth and says, "Sorry," to his sister.

"Ewwwww," Tommy says. "Bad words!"

"What do you think, Tommy? 'Home Sweet Home.' Best rock ballad ever?" Chuck says quickly, redirecting like a pro.

"We should perform that one next week," Tommy says.

"We'd have to change our cover band name if we started doing Crüe songs."

"But Shot with a Fart is *the best* name!"

"I completely agree, little man!"

"This is Portia, Chuck," Danielle finally says. "She went to good ol' HTHS. In my class."

Chuck smiles with nothing short of movie-star charm and shakes a finger at me like I've been very naughty. "I thought I recognized—"

"Chuck, we need you. Get up here!" the beefy bartender calls from the front.

"To be continued." Chuck gives two sets of devil horns to Tommy, sticks out his tongue like Gene Simmons, and then says, "Dude, you totally rocked."

"You rocked too, Uncle Chuck." Tommy returns the devil horns before Chuck jogs back to the front bar and yells something at a blonde, who smiles as Chuck points me out.

The blonde delivers two bottles of Budweiser to our table and says, "From Chuck. If you break his heart, I'll kill you."

"Easy, Lisa," Danielle says.

"I'm serious." Lisa holds my gaze for an uncomfortable beat and then walks away.

I look to Danielle for an explanation and she says, "Lisa and Chuck have worked together for years. She acts like his mother. What can I say? It's weird."

"Okay."

Several people come over to our booth to congratulate Tommy, and Danielle keeps telling them that it's not necessary to give Tommy tips, which seems strange to me because—from what I've gathered so far—she could certainly use the money.

Chicken wings and tuna melts arrive as Tommy colors with crayons in a blank notebook and Danielle tells me all about the Oaklyn public school system and how Tommy is "special" and "gifted" when it comes to performing, but those skills aren't appreciated in towns like Oaklyn and Collingswood and Westmont and Haddon Township.

I'm tempted to point out that her kid just got a standing ovation for performing right here at the Manor in Oaklyn. The people here at the bar seemed to appreciate the hell out of Tommy. But I know from experience that you should never disagree with a woman when she is speaking about her children. Women lose their objectivity when they give birth. There is no reasoning with a mother when it comes to her child, especially her firstborn.

"It's an okay school, but I mean, it's not Faddonfield," Danielle says, referring to Haddonfield, the wealthiest town in the area—the one that always seems to outperform the rest of us no matter how hard we try, proving that money and contacts help a whole bunch in America.

"Fuck Faddonfield," I say. "You want your kids to grow up snotty and entitled?"

"Portia!" Danielle says, and gestures to her son with her eyes and head. "Yo!"

"Sorry. I'm not used to being around kids."

Tommy is drawing what looks to be Guns N' Roses' *Appetite for Destruction* album cover—a cross with the skulls of the band members decorating it.

Her five-year-old knows that album, which features an illustration of a raped-and-left-for-dead-in-an-alley woman with her underwear around her ankles on the inside flap AND uses the word *fuck* multiple times on different tracks, and Danielle's worried about my using profanity in front of him?

"Do you want kids?" she asks.

"No."

"Oh," Danielle says in a surprised way, trying to mask her disappointment. Or maybe it's disapproval.

I don't elaborate on the many reasons I don't want children. I know it will win me no points tonight.

I always think of Philip Larkin's poem "This Be the Verse" whenever someone asks when I'll have children. My mom fucked me up, and I don't want to pass that on. Imagine if I had children with Ken the misogynistic porno king? Khaleesi and company would have hurt much more than my pride. But I also don't want to be like Danielle, who seems to live solely for—or through—her kid. I want *my* life to count. And I've seen how so many women have kids as a way of contributing when they no longer feel as though they are contributing. Their college dreams and hopes are crushed by the world, so they fall back into the traditional role of motherhood, where they will be praised for simply taking a man's seed into their bodies and then allowing it to grow. They become livestock, really. The simple fact that they've reproduced makes them palatable to society. A woman could be the worst mother in the world, but if she is holding a baby in public, everyone will smile at her with admiration usually reserved for saints and deities. She's not just some woman anymore, but a life giver, a Mother Mary. That's how they trick us into going through the pain of childbirth and all the rest. Just reproduce, and people throw you parties and buy you gifts and sympathize with you. You enjoy a sense of belonging and achievement simply because you had sex successfully. And who can resist that?

I guess I can.

My own mother had sex with a stranger and gave birth to me, and I'm sure people congratulated her for it along the way, but she was a criminally bad mother, who I must now take care of for the rest of my life or suffer extreme guilt. Motherhood is no bulletproof plan for happily ever after, that's certain. But will anyone say that openly? Not even I have the stomach for that.

"Portia?" Danielle says. "Where are you?"

I shake my head and blink a few times. "Must be the beer."

Danielle looks at my full bottle of Budweiser and raises her eyebrows. "Do you want to come over to my apartment? Once I tuck in Jon Bon Jovi here, we can talk about Mr. Vernon if you want. That's why you came, right? I didn't bring it up before because"—

she shields her mouth with her hand and whispers—"it's not a story for kids."

I nod, and it occurs to me once again that Tommy is a strange little boy. I mean, he gets up in front of strangers and performs but then says nothing during dinner. Come to think of it, he didn't even eat anything. He just colored in his blank notebook. "Sure," I answer.

I'm tired and can see that Danielle and I have little in common, but I want to know what happened to Mr. Vernon.

I reach into my purse, which sits next to me on the booth, and finger the little Official Member of the Human Race card, digging the sharp corners into the soft flesh under my fingernail for as long as I can take the pain.

I try to pay, but Danielle explains it's not necessary since Chuck works here. "One of the very few perks," she explains. "We eat and drink for free at the Manor."

Outside we cross the intersection diagonally, little Tommy holding his mother's hand and yawning now, appearing absolutely exhausted before nine, which is strange for a Saturday night, I think, but then again, he's a unique kid.

Their apartment is tiny.

A small TV is set up on what looks like a card table. I take in the dusty dorm-room-style metal frame futon, three wooden chairs that look like they are from three different 1950s-era dining room sets, probably all trash-picked, I think. Plastic crates of records— real old-school vinyl—are stacked next to an old record player with huge faux-wood box speakers that appear to predate the Jimmy Carter administration.

When she sees me looking at her collection, Danielle says, "Tommy gets one bedtime song. We rock out every Saturday night. What are you going to pick, Tommy?"

He doesn't answer, but runs into another room and returns wearing a disturbing mask that looks like it was made from papier-mâché and then spray-painted silver. There are two rectangular eyeholes slanted downward, a ridge for the nose, dozens of holes the size of pinheads where the mouth should be and straps that run around the back of the head.

When Tommy pulls Quiet Riot's *Metal Health* album from a crate, I realize that the mask is a damn good representation of the one on the cover we all loved in—was it fifth or sixth grade when that record came out?

Danielle helps him put the record on the turntable. "Do you still love Quiet Riot, Portia?"

"Hell yeah!" I say, forgetting that you aren't supposed to curse in front of elementary-school kids. "And I bet I know what song you're going to pick too!"

When I hear the snare and bass drum alternating, I know I'm right.

Tommy's doing a new show now, with the mask on, which strikes me as more than a little icky—not just this kid's need for attention, but the fact that he's wearing a Hannibal Lecter mask and singing about getting wild, wild, wild.

"*Girls rock your boys*," Danielle sings as she jumps around the room like we did when we were just a little older than Tommy, back when "Cum On Feel the Noize" was being blasted on MTV and every radio station in the country, back in hair metal's commercial heyday.

And before I know it, I'm jumping around the room too, getting wild, wild, wild, because how can you not jump and sing along with "Cum On Feel the Noize"? That song is genius, a litmus test for your love of life. If you aren't banging your head to the beat of that tune, you suck.

Suddenly we are all doing the guitar solo—Tommy on the futon,

Danielle with one foot on a chair, me kneeling on the floor, because I rock hard—and I think about the pre-Ken poor-metalhead-from–South Jersey days, that hopeful young Portia who hadn't yet been touched and tarnished by a misogynistic porn king. I existed free and clean of Ken Humes before, back when hair metal ruled, and so maybe I can again.

They call this nostalgia, Portia, I tell myself, banging my head to the beat, *and it feels great. Like being a kid again.*

Tommy probably gets his ass kicked every day at school for liking this old music, instead of Flo Rida or Ke$ha or Justin Bieber or whoever, but I see why Danielle shares it with him.

She gets her ass kicked every day at the diner too, no doubt—just because she's a woman and poor.

My tongue is out as I switch from air guitar to air drums, which is perfectly acceptable when you are rocking out with friends and their children to metal.

I think about Gloria Steinem and how metal objectifies women constantly as we all chant, "Girls rock your boys!"

But I also catch my reflection in the mirror—me in the old white jean jacket with my mane of hair rising and falling to my head banging, nose scrunched, eyes squinted in some sort of "cool face"—and I tell myself just to rock.

Even though he is wearing a mask, I can tell Tommy is smiling, and Danielle is too as she sings into her invisible microphone.

This is what these people have.

All they have.

And right now, it's what I have too.

The song ends, and we give ourselves a round of applause.

"Did you feel it?" Tommy says to me as he pulls off his Quiet Riot mask. "The noize?"

I nod and even tousle the kid's hair.

What the hell was that? I'm never affectionate with children.

"Time for bed. You can show Ms. Kane your bedroom, and then it's lights out, mister!"

"Uncle Chuck made this when he was little." Tommy hands me the mask.

I look at the inside and read these words:

Chuck Bass
Quiet Riot Rocks!
1983

"I turned twelve in 1983," I say absentmindedly.

"So did I, remember?" Danielle answers.

"The mask keeps the bad dreams away." Tommy snatches it out of my hands. "Uncle Chuck promised. And it's true!"

Danielle smiles at me, and we follow Tommy into his bedroom. He jumps up on his bed and hangs the mask on a nail over the headboard, just like in the old music video where the kid wakes up, his room is shaking, and the band finally breaks through the walls.

I think about Chuck being a boy himself, watching that video on MTV just like Danielle and I did, back in the day.

"Uncle Chuck made the mask. He sleeps over there." Tommy points to the single bed on the other side of the room. Over the headboard hangs a collection of everyday objects painted in bright colors on little four-by-four-inch canvases: a cell phone, a TV remote, a coffee filter. Weird.

"This is actually Chuck's place," Danielle says. "We're temporary guests."

"I like living with Uncle Chuck!" Tommy says as he slides into his bed.

"You better scrub those pearly whites!" Danielle says and begins to tickle Tommy. "I don't kiss boys with rotten teeth!"

When Tommy runs into the bathroom, I return to the futon and wait for Danielle.

I wonder why Tommy sleeps in Chuck's room and not Danielle's.

A few minutes later Tommy comes out in PJs to give me a kiss on the cheek, says, "Keep rocking, Ms. Kane," gives me the devil horns, which I return twofold, and runs back into his bedroom. I hear Danielle reading a book to him—something about a shark who wants to be a librarian and makes books out of shells and seaweed so that she can teach fish to read, because literate fish "taste better," which seems like a very creepy children's book. Danielle seems to be rushing the story a little, like she'd rather be out here with me.

As I wait, I start to think about Mr. Vernon again, and I wonder if he's dead. Could the news be that dramatic? I mean, it's been more than twenty years.

Danielle returns. "Jack on the rocks?"

"Hell, yes." I join her in the kitchen, which is just the left side of the living room really.

She puts ice into two small plastic cups and pours the Jack liberally.

My cup is from a fast food restaurant and advertises an Iron Man movie starring Robert Downey Jr. in a robot suit. I remember when Robert Downey Jr. was just doing regular roles about regular men.

I also think about the Baccarat crystal glasses Ken and I drank from nightly in Tampa and wonder how many hours working at the diner it would take Danielle to earn enough money for just one of those. An entire week's worth of pay and tips, maybe more.

"To good ol' Haddon Township High School," Danielle says.

"To rock and roll," I say.

We touch plastic and sip.

The burn is the same, but whiskey definitely tastes better out of fine crystal, no matter what your roots happen to be.

That's the problem with money—it changes your tastes. You can never go back to liking some things, like drinking alcohol from plastic cups, as much.

We return to the futon, and Danielle puts on Mötley Crüe's first album *Too Fast for Love* with the volume much lower than when we listened to Quiet Riot.

"You have this on vinyl?" I say.

"Original pressing," Danielle says proudly as Vince Neil sings "Live Wire." "It's Chuck's. He has quite a collection. Tells Tommy it's his when Chuck dies."

"Cool uncle."

"Did you fuck Mr. Vernon back in high school?"

"Excuse me?"

"That was the rumor. It was decades ago, Portia. No one would care anymore anyway. They're not going to send him to jail now."

"There were really rumors about that?"

"Sure. You were always spending time with him alone after class and before school. Some girls are into older men. Daddy issues. I heard you used to go to his apartment too. So of fucking course there were rumors. It was high school!"

"Unbelievable." I shake my head. "Mr. Vernon was the closest thing I had to a father figure in high school, so thanks for making my one good teen memory weird. Jesus Christ, Daddy issues? Yuck!"

"So you didn't fuck him?"

"No. I did not fuck Mr. Vernon. You didn't know him if you could even think that."

"Was he gay?"

"I have no idea."

"People used to say he was gay."

"Kids said everything and everyone was gay back then. It was the default adjective of our homophobic MTV generation."

"So what did you talk about all alone with Mr. Vernon?"

"Literature, writing, what I wanted to do with my life, becoming a novelist, if you can believe that," I say, leaving out the thing we talked about most—my mother—and the Christmas Eve I spent with Mr. Vernon senior year because Mom thought the government had bugged our house, so she was refusing to let me speak, and I was too embarrassed to tell anyone else but him. "What's happened to him? I'd really like to know."

Danielle studies me for a long moment, and it strikes me that she seems to be enjoying withholding the story. But then I tell myself that she doesn't want to be the bearer of bad news, that's all—she doesn't want to upset me. And yet I'm starting to wonder if the years haven't been downright cruel to Danielle Bass, and whether the bright, cheery side she's shown me so far isn't a bit of an act. The look in her eyes now seems almost sadistic, as dramatic as that sounds.

Finally she says, "One of Mr. Vernon's students beat him up during class with a baseball bat a few years ago. Fractured his legs and arms before the other kids broke it up. I remember a kid being interviewed on TV, saying that the attack seemed to come out of nowhere. In the middle of class one of the baseball players pulled a bat from an equipment bag—which he apparently had with him, who knows why—and just started swinging away. I remember the kid said he could hear the bones breaking and Mr. Vernon screaming in this very high-pitched squeal. 'Like a pig.' Some other students saved Mr. Vernon by tackling the baseball player, which I thought was heroic. The student they interviewed on TV hadn't helped take the baseball player down, and I remember thinking, Why the hell are they interviewing him? Get the heroes on camera! I heard Vernon sued the school for a lot of money and then retired. I got the sense—mostly from people gossiping in the diner—that there was some bad blood and some shit may have gotten covered up. A few people said Mr. Vernon was paid to retire quietly, whatever that means. And so he did."

Paid to retire quietly?

I'm shaking my head in disbelief. "Why?"

"Wouldn't you retire if a kid beat you almost to death with a baseball bat? I hear he has a permanent limp."

"Why would anyone attack such an amazing teacher as Mr. Vernon?"

"Maybe he did something fucked up to the baseball player? I mean you hear about teachers doing pervy things all the time, and then all of the community members being shocked as hell afterward. Some people seemed to think Mr. Vernon was having a gay affair with the boy who attacked him, or at least that's what a few were implying."

"No way. Not Mr. Vernon. He'd never do that to one of his students. Never."

"Well, then, maybe the kid just started swinging away for no good reason at all."

"Why would he do that?"

"Why would anyone blow up the World Trade Center? Why would anyone put a bomb in their shoe and try to take down a commercial airplane? Why do school shootings keep happening? People are sick, crazy, fucked up. It's a scary world we live in these days. No one can deny that."

I understand what she's saying, but she didn't know Mr. Vernon like I knew Mr. Vernon. He really cared about his students. He was a good man, the only teacher I ever heard of who would meet a student at the diner on a Saturday afternoon just to talk about fiction—reading her first fumbling attempts at short stories, even—

because her own mother's insanity made her home uninhabitable, and no other adults seemed to notice or care.

Nobody's one hundred percent good, I suddenly hear Ken saying in my head. It was one of his favorite mantras. *Everyone's a little bit evil.*

And he proved it time and time again by seducing young girls into making degrading pornography with his company. He'd send out good-looking, smooth-talking young men with alcohol and free lingerie and legally binding contracts with a lot of small print, and they'd never once come home without footage.

"Just put people in the right circumstances, and they'll do just about anything," my asshole husband would say as foul cigar smoke curled around his cocky, Tom Selleck–y head.

Every time Ken said something depressing like that, I'd think about Mr. Vernon and feel satisfied that Ken was wrong.

For all these years, Mr. Vernon has been my anti-Ken.

It was enough just to think of him teaching at HTHS—putting good into the world, one lecture at a time. At least *one* man on the planet was all good.

Why didn't I ever write to Mr. Vernon after I left high school?

Why didn't I ever thank him for all he did for me back then?

Do people actually do that—go back and thank their teachers years later, when they're no longer handicapped by youth and ignorance, when they figure out just how much their teachers actually did for them?

I mean, Mr. Vernon was probably the most influential person in my entire life. He believed in my potential. He gave me a handwritten card on my graduation night and wrote me a beautiful letter—the sort of thing you'd hope a father would write. I never even acknowledged it, never even said thank you, maybe because I didn't know how or what to write back. Maybe because I was leaving high school behind and Mr. Vernon was high school to me. Or maybe because I was a selfish white-trash bitch, too self-absorbed or too ignorant to show my favorite high school teacher common decency, let alone gratitude. And then when I dropped out of college I was too ashamed to face him again.

The young consume; the old are consumed.

"Are you even listening to me, Portia? *Hello?*"

I blink and say, "Where is he?"

"*Mr. Vernon?* How the hell would I know that?" Danielle starts talking about other teachers from Haddon Township High School.

"When did it happen?" I blurt out. "You know—the attack."

"Shit—I don't know. Maybe five years ago? Maybe more?"

"So he hasn't been teaching for more than five years?"

"I'm not sure, Portia. Are you okay? This really upsets you, doesn't it? I didn't realize that—"

"Do you still have that card he gave all of us on the last day of school?"

"That little driver's-license-looking thing with our picture on it? That was twenty years ago!"

"But didn't you keep it? The Official Member of the Human Race card?"

"You remember the name of it? Wow."

I wonder if I'm the only freak who actually kept the card. Then I start to wonder if it's because I'm my mother's daughter and will one day be a hoarder too, all alone in a shitty house, wearing pink sweat suits covered in stains and watching the Buy from Home Network among endless piles of carefully collected and stacked junk.

"It seemed important, that card—special. No one had ever given me anything like that before." Admittedly, my voice sounds too defensive, maybe even like Mom's when I start talking about getting rid of her junk.

"I might have it somewhere in a drawer or something, but— Jesus, Portia, you're sweating. Are you sick?"

"You know what, I'm actually not feeling great. I just left my husband last night. Caught him cheating and just took off."

Why am I bringing up Ken now?

"Last night? Like *yesterday?*"

"Yeah, I left him and Tampa all at once. It sort of just happened."

"What you told me in the diner about that teenage girl—that really happened *last night?*"

"Yeah. It's just sort of hitting me now. The finality of it. And someone really attacked Mr. Vernon in his classroom with a base-ball bat? *Really?* You're not fucking with me? That actually happened at our high school?"

"I'm sorry, but it's true. It was in all the papers. Like I said, on TV even. I'm really surprised you hadn't already heard. I assumed it was national news."

I've never really read the papers or watched the news, mostly because it's too depressing, as lame as that sounds.

I can't stop shaking my head no. "That's just so . . . so . . . *so fucking fucked.*"

"Yeah, it really is. But I'm worried about *you* now. You're pale as a ghost."

"Sorry. I better go home. I'll call a cab."

Danielle glances at her cell phone. "Chuck's off in ten minutes. He can drive you."

"I don't want to put him out," I say, remembering Lisa the wait-ress's threat.

"Don't be ridiculous."

Before I know it, I'm in a shitty old pickup truck with thick white stripes across the sides and a blanket covering the presum-ably ripped-up bench seat, being driven home by Chuck.

The engine is making a horrid whistling noise, like it's smoked two packs of unfiltered Camels a day for fifty years and decided to jog for the first time in decades.

"I'm sorry you're sick," Chuck says as we leave Oaklyn.

"I'll be okay. I dug your record collection. Very impressive," I add, just because he seems slightly freaked out by me, and I don't want to make this any weirder than it already is.

"How do you like the old man's Ford?" He pats the steering wheel.

I glance at the emblem on the dash. "Isn't this a Chevy?"

"Yeah, it is. Can't get anything past you. But I was just making a reference to eighties rock. And sort of hitting on you at the same time, but in a completely lame way. I suck at being cool. It's true. I'm really terrible at women. Fuck, I've said some pretty weird shit already, haven't I? Well, I'll just shut up now and drive."

His actually admitting to hitting on me is a surprise, and I'm not sure how I feel about that. He's obviously a great guy, based on his interactions with Tommy, and he's in shape—I glance over, confirm that his jeans and shirt bulge in all the right places and none of the wrong, notice his luscious biceps. He has an amazing body. And he even has kind eyes. Really kind. Turquoise, almost—they seem to shine every time oncoming headlights illuminate his face. So unlike Ken's oily shark eyes. Chuck's actually pretty cute in a nervous-innocent kind of way. I think about why the hell he might ask if I like "the old man's Ford" when we're in a Chevy. Where have I heard that phrase before, "the old man's Ford"? Then suddenly I understand the reference. "Poison. 'Talk Dirty to Me'? Were you really referencing *that* song? *'In the old man's Ford!'*" I sing.

"Yeah, pretty stupid, right? I don't actually expect you to talk dirty to me, but I wanted to impress you with my knowledge of hair metal lyrics from our shared youth, and I get nervous around exceptionally beautiful women. Really nervous, if you haven't already noticed."

"That's me, right over there. The one with the retro and supercool awning." I point to the row home where I grew up, pretending not to have heard the words *exceptionally beautiful* come out of his mouth.

Chuck makes a U-turn and pulls up right in front of Mom's home of shit.

"I'm sorry," he says. "I shouldn't have referenced Poison, right? Fuck Bret Michaels. Fuck that guy. So dumb to quote him. And that song, of all songs! But I've gone this far, so maybe would you like to have dinner with me sometime? Maybe? I promise I will not talk dirty to you."

Wow, I think.

A man who is concerned about how I feel—aware that I might actually have preferences. Kind of nice, for a change. And flattering too—I mean, I get asked out on the first day I'm officially on the market. And by a guy who publicly sings Bon Jovi with his adorable nephew.

"Just forget it." He waves his hand in the air, maybe trying to swat away what he just said. "It was really stupid of me to think—"

"Um, this has been a weird night for me, so I'm just going to be honest. I actually find you very attractive, and you seem like an amazing uncle, which is cool. I'd probably sleep with you just so I could steal your *Too Fast for Love* original vinyl and then feel guilty and ask you out for a meal or something afterward to make you feel better about losing such an amazing rock artifact. We might even make it a regular thing, who knows? But I just left my husband—like yesterday. I'm back in South Jersey for the first time in years, and I'm now forced to deal with my incredibly fucked-up mother.

I'm not in the best shape emotionally. I should probably tattoo the word TRAP on my forehead for the well-being of nice honest men like yourself. Then I find out about Mr. Vernon being beaten with a baseball bat, and—"

"I loved Mr. Vernon. That was a real shame, what happened to him."

"You were in his class?"

"One of the best experiences of my life. I'll never forget it. He gave us these cards on the last day of school. 'Official Member of the Human Race,' it says. Did he do that for your class too? I can actually quote the whole card by memory, because I've been carrying it in my wallet—I have it on me now, in fact— and I read it at least once a day just to remind myself that . . . well, anyway, I loved Mr. Vernon. Loved him like a father. Best teacher ever."

I fight an urge to wrap my arms around Chuck's neck.

I'm blinking back tears.

What the fuck is wrong with me?

"You think that's weird, right? Still carrying that old card Mr. Vernon gave everyone at the end of high school? Dorky, I know, but that class—and, well, that card got me through a really tough time in my life. Why am I telling you—I've never even told Danielle about—I'm such an asshole. Why would you even care about any of this?"

"I really have to go, Chuck," I say.

"Yeah, I'm a douche." He smacks himself in the head. "Who quotes 'Talk Dirty to Me' as a pickup line the first time he meets a woman? Ridiculous! Not even a shirtless Bret Michaels in his prime could get away with that!"

He's sweating.

It's like he's fifteen.

I think of Jason Malta, and suddenly I'm smelling Drakkar Noir in my mind.

I'm tempted to believe in good men again.

Just a tiny bit.

His still having that card Mr. Vernon gave us on the last day of school, our shared love of Mötley Crüe, those bright eyes . . . it all seems like some sort of undeniable sign—maybe even like the beginning of something—but it's all happened much too quickly, and I need time to think, process, and catch my breath.

"Good night, Chuck," I say, and then walk up the steps of my mother's home.

Inside I find Mom asleep in front of the Buy from Home Network.

An attractive middle-aged man sporting a sharkskin suit and a widow's peak is encouraging viewers to build a crystal menagerie piece by piece as lights shine and sparkle off various glass animals— panda bears and giraffes and wolves and pelicans and starfish and so many other alluring shapes that easily persuade people like my mother to spend what little savings they have, only to stick the knickknacks on shelves to collect dust until their owner dies and the menagerie gets sold at a fraction of the purchase price or thrown away by uninterested daughters like me.

My mother looks like a passed-out-drunk-on-its-back rhinoceros in a pink sweat suit—tree-trunk-thick neck, giant belly, stubby arms and legs.

There is junk stacked everywhere around us.

And I think about how that nun I met on the airplane used the word *quest* in the letter she wrote me.

Like I'm a modern female version of Don Quixote.

Quest.

I'm going to write that crazy nun, I think.

Why not?

I'm not afraid of windmills.

"You can have a crystal zoo in your cabinet," the slick man on TV says. "Gaze at your sparkly little friends daily and feel a little less alone."

"Bastard," I say.

I stare down at my mom, and then I have another lawn-dart-to-the-eye moment.

I will not become my mother.

I will leave this house and have adventures. Go on quests, even. Hear the universe's call.

And Mr. Vernon is out there somewhere—most likely alone. He's probably a mess after what happened. Who wouldn't be absolutely fucked in the head after being beaten almost to death with a baseball bat by one of his own students?

I need to make sure he continues to do what he was called to do—teach. Who will help the fucked-up kids if he quits?

Save Mr. Vernon.

My three-word quest.

Maybe this is why my marriage failed, why I haven't been able to accomplish anything in life so far, why I never even attempted to write the novel Mr. Vernon encouraged me to write "when I was ready." Maybe I was being groomed and conditioned and led to this very mission. By the universe. By God? Whatever you wanna believe in.

And to think I almost killed Khaleesi and Ken with the Colt .45 just last night—how close I was to failing.

Fate.

Greek fucking theater.

I'm living it now.

"Everything suddenly makes so much sense," I whisper in the glow of my mother's TV. "It has to."

PART TWO

Nate Vernon

CHAPTER 6

Albert Camus and I begin the day as we always do, by eating breakfast.

He has once again beaten me by cleaning his bowl in less than thirty seconds, inhaling the food as if he's afraid I might take it away, which I believe happened to him on a regular basis before we began living together.

As I swallow my last spoonful of Raisin Bran, I look Albert Camus in his one adoring eye, and then I quote him: " 'There is but one truly serious philosophical problem, and that is suicide.' I'm thinking about the first question again. It's true. To be or not to be."

Albert Camus cocks his head to one side as if to say, *"Pourquoi?"*

" 'All great deeds and all great thoughts have ridiculous beginnings.' Remember when you wrote that, Albert Camus? *The Myth of Sisyphus*. Remember? Before you were reincarnated as a dog? You also wrote this about the inevitable weariness we all face: 'It happens that the stage sets collapse. Rising, streetcar, four hours in the office or the factory, meal, streetcar, four hours of work, meal, sleep, and Monday Tuesday Wednesday Thursday Friday and Saturday according to the same rhythm—this path is easily followed most of the time. But one day the "why" arises and everything begins in that weariness tinged with amazement.' Do you remember? Did you think about the first question during your fatal car crash? When the wheels skidded across the ice? When the engine wrapped around the tree? Right before you died in your last incarnation? In that last moment of your life, did you regret never having finished writing *The First Man*? Did you regret anything? Could you still answer the first question as you left this world?"

Albert Camus cocks his head the other way, lets out a sigh, and then rests his chin on his outstretched paws.

He pretends to be resigned, but secretly he loves it when I quote his former self—I can tell.

In his present incarnation, Albert Camus is a toy poodle with a graying Afro and beard; the rest of his coat's as black as his eye and nose.

When I look at Albert Camus's face I sometimes think of the late PBS painter Bob Ross, who was always painting happy little things—happy little trees, happy little mountains, happy little clouds.

The Joy of Painting, his show was called, if I remember correctly.

Was there ever a nicer, more positive person?

Bob Ross—in this wonderfully inclusive way—made us all believe we could paint. I used to watch his show and think he was perhaps the best teacher I had ever seen practicing the art of passing on knowledge.

If I remember correctly, he died of lymphoma in his early fifties, which is five years or so younger than I am right now.

"Why were you reincarnated as a dog that looks like former PBS star Bob Ross, Albert Camus?" I say, and then reach down and sink my fingers into Albert Camus's Bob Ross Afro. I find his tiny skull within that globe of fur, give Albert Camus a good scratch behind the ears, and he blows air through his nose in appreciation. "Maybe you are here to keep me from reaching any conclusions regarding the first question, Albert Camus. Because I can't remember the answer anymore. I used to know why I should keep living, but now—well, I have you. We have each other. And maybe someday Mrs. Harper will stop wearing black. What do you think, Albert Camus? Is that our answer?"

He looks up at me lovingly with his one eye, but he offers no reply today.

I spark up a Parliament Light and take a drag, feeling the hollow little recessed filter between my lips.

I try to pretend Albert Camus and I are in a Parisian café in the mid-1950s, smoking and discussing the absurd.

In my fantasy, I am fluent in French.

I tell Albert Camus he will be reincarnated as a dog one day—*Vous serez réincarné en chien!*—and be rescued from a shelter days before he is to be euthanized just because no one wants to adopt a one-eyed dog.

"Maybe when you were in that tiny cage, you were hoping to be killed so that you could move on to your next incarnation," I say to the present-day Albert Camus. "But that was before you knew the joys of living with me, Nate Vernon, your master."

His right eye was cauterized shut by some monster of a man whom Albert Camus cannot name, because he is now a dog and no longer has the power of speech.

When I saw him in the shelter, I knew I had to rescue him. They opened the small crate, I knelt down, and he jumped up into my arms like a fool, still trusting after the horrors that he must have endured.

"I told you he was an absolute sweetheart," the young girl volunteering at the shelter said before she realized I was crying. "Are you okay?"

"I'll take him," I said. "Today. Right now. Whatever he costs, I'll pay. I'll sign anything."

At first I tried to get him to wear an eye patch, just so he might have some dignity, but he wasn't having it. He'd paw at the patch until it descended to his chin like a beard, and then he'd cock his head to one side, look up at me with his one good eye, and bark once, as if to say, "Really?"

The eye patch was a ridiculous idea.

His scarred eye socket is mostly covered by fur, when the groomer trims him properly, and he's not a vain dog.

He's accepted his fate in life, as we all should.

Albert Camus pretends he is no longer interested in cigarette smoke, now that he has been reincarnated as a dog, but I can tell my smoking makes him nostalgic for his days playing goalie for the University of Algiers, exploring anarchy and communism, having affairs with María Casares, getting involved with revolutions, winning the Nobel Prize even, only to end up a cripple's dog in the next life.

"The absurdity! It's like we're in one of your books, Albert Camus! Or maybe more like Kafka."

I ash my cigarette into the remaining cereal milk and then study the smoke leaving my mouth.

I don't even inhale all that much of it, but I enjoy seeing the smoke exit my body, maybe because it reminds me that I'm really still here. Sometimes I even smoke in front of the mirror. I prefer this activity to television.

Smell is a powerful trigger of memories, as you probably know, and Albert Camus was a smoker in his last incarnation as a French rebel novelist.

Another one of my heroes, Kurt Vonnegut, was also a smoker novelist who used to quip about suing the cigarette companies for false advertising, since the warning label promised that the damn things would kill him, but they didn't. He died of a traumatic brain injury. Kurt joked that he didn't want to set a bad example for his grandchildren, and that's why he didn't commit suicide. That's how he answered the first question, basically saying that we were put on this planet to bumble around. But the truth is that Vonnegut attempted suicide at least once. Pills and alcohol, if I remember correctly. That's the problem with being a high school English teacher. Too many of the writers you hold up to teenagers as heroes ultimately failed to answer the first question.

"Do dogs ever commit suicide, Albert Camus? What would it take for your kind to commit self-slaughter?" I ask, but his eye is closed now. The earth has moved enough through space so that a cube of sun has crept across the floor to land on my absurdist dog, and he is simply enjoying the warmth sent down from that huge sphere of burning gas our planet orbits from just the right distance. "Why is ours the only inhabitable planet in our solar system? How did we get so lucky, Albert Camus?" I say, trying to stay positive, and then take another drag, wondering if I will eventually get lung cancer and die. Vonnegut also used to say smoking was a classy way to commit suicide. Kurt was quite quotable. Many times I held up Vonnegut to teenagers and said, "Admire this man."

I read the warning label on the azure Parliament box. It says something about pregnant women and harming fetuses.

These are old cigarettes.

I bought several cartons a few years ago, even though I don't smoke all that often. I wanted to avoid the embarrassment of having to ask Mrs. Harper for something so out of fashion and dirty as cigarettes.

One cigarette a day, right after breakfast. How can you explain that habit to anyone? It's as absurd as the rest of my life.

I drop my half-smoked butt into the remaining milk of my cereal bowl. It hisses as it dies.

My mother hated cigarette smoking, and as I hate my mother, each smoke is also a middle finger held high for good old Mom.

I pick up Albert Camus, and he quickly settles into my lap. He licks my hand. I repetitively stroke the length of his spine and tail. We sit at our small kitchen table in silence for maybe an hour. Neither of us has anything else to do.

I think about Mrs. Harper and other impossible things.

The best and worst aspect of our day is that we have all the time in the world, Albert Camus and I. All the time in the world may sound nice in theory, but in practice it can become a swift kick to the balls.

CHAPTER 7

Harper's is the local convenience store around here, only it's nothing like the Wawas and 7-Elevens I frequented when I lived in the Philadelphia area. Perhaps its most defining characteristic is the wooden-shingle sign outside:

WHISKEY, GUNS, AMMO

Even though I only have a need for the first of those three things, Albert Camus and I go to Harper's just about every day to buy sundry more mundane items not advertised outside on wooden shingles.

In the parking lot today, just in front of the hole where, in the spring and summertime, bees come and go from a hive that is on full display behind glass, buzzing in warmer months with a frenetic and intimidating work ethic, I say, "Do you think she'll still be wearing black today, Albert Camus?"

He sighs, but does not rise. He's in his harness, which keeps him strapped to the seat belt, because we wouldn't want history repeating itself here in icy Vermont. He never protests when I belt him in for car rides, but he doesn't particularly enjoy being buckled in either, which makes me wonder if he can still answer the first question now that he is a canine.

(I give him a good life—top-of-the-line dog food, he's with me twenty-four hours a day, and I've never loved anyone more—but that's beside the point. There are times when I wonder if Albert Camus really wants to be here in this world, even though I realize the work he did in his last incarnation challenges us to find meaning—hope and beauty even—amid the absurd. But the fictional worlds he created were often bleak, and so is our current life together, truth be told.)

"You don't like Mrs. Harper, do you?" I ask as I reach over and scratch his head. "Don't worry, nothing comes between us, Albert Camus. Not even a woman. Never. You and me. It's what we'll always have."

He lifts his head and begins to whine a little, so I undo his belt buckle and transfer him to my lap.

He climbs my torso, rests his front paws on my chest, and licks my face, because he is a lover.

"Okay, Albert Camus, renowned ladies' man. French Nobel Laureate. And courageous explorer of the human condition. Let's go over the old game plan."

He continues to lick my face.

"If she's still in all black, we buy our daily supplies and leave as usual. But if she is wearing any color at all, we will try to make small talk, as they say, and see if it leads anywhere."

My dog's face is centimeters away from my own—I can feel his warm, pungent breath and his cold, wet nose on my cheek.

"Maybe she will have a lady dog for you," I say, but I can tell he isn't buying it—or maybe he's worried that having only one eye makes him unworthy of a mate. It's hard to tell. "Okay, I'll be right back."

When I exit the car, Albert Camus barks and claws at the window with his paws, because he has separation anxiety. I'd bring him inside, but he's growled at Mrs. Harper on several previous occasions, intentionally trying to sabotage my love life. He doesn't want to share me. Leaning my weight on my wooden cane, I place my left palm on the glass where Albert Camus is scratching and say, "It's okay, *mon petit frère*. I won't be long."

Mrs. Harper is at the register, checking out a customer, a man in a flannel jacket who is buying a shocking amount of canned baked beans.

She's wearing a navy blue shirt.

All the blood drains from my face, and I feel lightheaded.

This is the first time I have seen her wearing any color but black since her husband died of a heart attack more than a year ago.

And yet navy blue is very close in nature to black. In certain lights, navy can be confused with black, which creates a rather unfortunate dilemma for me.

As I make my way under the various deer, moose, and even bear heads mounted on the walls, I wonder if Mrs. Harper has worn navy by mistake. Could it have looked like black in the early-morning light? Or might she be slowly transitioning her way to brighter colors, and if so, what would that mean? Have I been given the proverbial green light or not?

I dare to glance back over my shoulder, seeing that her silver hair is down. It rises like a wave over her forehead before it dives along the left side of her beautiful face.

Mrs. Harper has what I can only describe as a gorgeous Jewish nose, and for some unknown reason, the noses of Jewish women always stir up the dormant lust within me.

Behind the bread aisle I quickly adjust myself, because I am embarrassingly aroused.

Ridiculous.

All of this.

I started imagining a life together with Mrs. Harper long before her husband died. It was never sexual so much as it was intellectually stimulating. She never really says much when she scans groceries, hardly ever smiles, and so it was easy to graft stories onto her and her beautiful angular nose. I imagined her trapped in a sexless cold marriage with a man who named a store after himself and loved it more than the wife he also named after himself. I imagined meeting Mrs. Harper accidentally on one of the walking trails Albert Camus and I often stroll in the summer, the three of us falling into stride—in my fantasy I am cane- and limp-free—perhaps even talking about the novels we are reading at the time. Before long she is sneaking away from her husband to have dinner at my home in the woods, confiding in me, telling me all of her secrets over the meat her husband cut and weighed himself earlier in the day. Turns out, Mr. Harper is a woefully inadequate lover who finishes much too early and is snoring less than thirty seconds after he rolls off his wife. "The shame," she says through tears. "He's never once given me an orgasm. Not once in thirty years." And I pat her hand sympathetically. "It's like I'm an object. Just a warm mitten for his dick," she says after one too many glasses of wine. "Are other men any different?" In my fantasy I tell her that I would make her buzz in the bedroom until her heart was content, and she places her hand on her chest and blushes. And then one snowy night I see two lights glowing like God's eyes through the blizzard, winding their way up my driveway, and I open the door and she comes bounding out of her truck without even putting it in park. I wrap my arms around her as her husband's vehicle continues slowly into the snowbank. "I've left him," she says, and I say, "Welcome home."

In real life, Mr. Harper was a curmudgeonly cheap hairy WASP of a little ape in a white butcher's apron, always pressing his thumb to the scale when he was weighing your meat.

He killed things for fun, forever hanging carcasses up outside his shop and selling his freshly murdered cuts inside. He had an arsenal behind glass and sold his guns freely to all of the local yokels and rich yuppie skiers who also seasonally purchased his overpriced bottles of wine, local microbrewed beers, cheeses made from the milk of Vermont goats and cows, and whatever else they didn't feel like driving forty-five minutes to get at the nearest chain grocery store. These sales made Mr. Harper a wealthy man. A beautiful wife and a cash machine of a store. One of the biggest houses around these parts, nestled at the center of an ocean of land, overlooking a private pond. You'd think the old bastard would have known happiness, but he was meaner than a bee in your mouth.

I've overheard patrons whispering that Mr. Harper died in the store while marking up the high-end whiskey and scotch, just before ski season.

Dead before his head hit the floor, they say, but somehow managing not to break a single bottle, because he was a frugal bastard to the very end.

And that's when Mrs. Harper started wearing all black.

"Two rib eye steaks—one big, one small," I tell the middle-aged butcher behind the counter, and he pulls two cuts from the window and begins to wrap them in wax paper.

"Your little dog eats better than most people," Brian says.

I know his name is Brian, because he wears a name tag. He started working here shortly after Mr. Harper died. I think he runs the place for Mrs. Harper, who has remained a silent and beautiful fixture behind the cash register.

I nod and smile.

"Why don't you bring the little guy in here anymore? I miss seeing him," he says as he weighs the steaks. He doesn't leave his thumb on the scale, I notice.

"He gets a little anxious lately," I say.

"What's his name again?"

"Albert."

"I heard you use a last name too when you were talking to him. What was it again?"

"Camus. Albert Camus."

Brian itches his goatee with his wrist and says, "How'd you ever come up with a crazy name like that? Albert *Cah-mooooo*?"

"I named him after the French writer."

"That explains it. I don't even read *American* writers."

"Maybe you should read Albert Camus."

"Why?" Brian says as he passes the meat over the counter. He's smiling at me, and there's a twinkle in his eye. He's just making small talk as he takes off his disposable gloves.

"Well, for starters, he's one of the best and most influential authors of the twentieth century."

"Hey, listen up, friend. I'm a butcher here in Hicksville, Vermont." He points at his face. "You see this guy here? Does he read French writers? No, he does not. He reads *Field & Stream* on the hopper sometimes when he's feeling really intellectual." Brian smiles proudly at his joke. "When I get to feeling like Johnny College, I sometimes read *TV Guide*."

"To each his own," I say, and start to turn away.

"Hey, don't take it that way. I'm just having a little fun today. You have me curious now. Why should I read some French writer? Why would you say that to me? Were you serious? Come on now. Tell me."

"Old habit, I guess. I'm a former high school English teacher. Maybe it's in my genes."

He laughs in a friendly way. "I got a library card because you can check out DVDs for free down there, but I bet my card would work for books too. Imagine that. Me reading a book. That would be something. I'm telling you. What's the name of this writer again? I wanna read this Frenchy who made you wanna name a dog after him. I mean—you love that dog. So what the hell, right? What the hell! You friggin' *love* that dog. I've seen you with him."

"I do love Albert Camus."

"I never really talk this much."

"I've noticed," I say, lifting my eyebrows. He seems like a kind man, albeit a little simple. I like Brian. I do. He's bagged and tagged my meat many dozens of times before, and yet this is the first time we've spoken this freely.

"I'm sorry," he says, "but I don't have any family around here—except valued shoppers like you. And today's sort of a big day for me. So I'm a regular Chatty Cathy this afternoon. This store—it's changed my entire life for the better."

"Oh, really? I love this store," I say, although I am not sure why. This is getting a little too friendly, and my instincts are screaming, *Get the hell out of here!*

"Hey, can I ask you a question?" Brian smiles, puffs out his chest a little, and lifts his chin ever so slightly. "Did you notice anything different when you walked in today? Did you? *Anything?*"

Instantly, I know he's referring to Mrs. Harper's navy shirt, and yet I say, "No, I didn't. What's different?"

"Mrs. Harper?" Brian raises his gray eyebrows, cocks his head, nods, and smiles.

"I'm not sure I—"

"She's wearing a blue shirt. For the first time since—*you know.*"

I glance over my shoulder at Mrs. Harper. "Is she? I thought it was black like always."

"Guess what? Take a wild guess."

"Um."

"Give up?"

"I have no—"

"Did you happen to see what's on her ring finger?" he says.

Please, no.

God, no.

"She and I are getting married. Married! How about that, Mr. High School English Teacher? Mr. Albert *Cah-moooo* dog owner. Popped the question last night after we locked up Harper's. Got down on one knee while we were restocking cereal, offered her a ring, and she said yes. Can you believe it? Me, Brian Foley, getting married after all these years of being a bachelor! And to the best woman in the entire universe."

The world stops spinning for a second, and I lose myself in the black space between Brian's grinning two front teeth.

"Did you hear what I said, friend? We're getting married! Hitched. Yoked. United! Making it legal and legit and beautiful! Go tell it on the mountain, Teach: Brian Foley is in love! Reborn even. Today's the best day of my entire life."

"Um . . ." I'm sweating now. I place the steaks on the counter and pat my pockets. "Oh, shoot! I think I forgot my wallet. Let me run to my truck. Just give me a second. I'll be right back."

"You're not even gonna say congratulations?"

I move as quickly as my limp and cane will allow toward the exit.

"Are you even serious?" Brian says. "You gotta root for love, man."

I can't resist sneaking a peek at Mrs. Harper's beautiful nose as I leave, knowing that I will never again set foot in Harper's, even if I desperately need GUNS, AMMO, WHISKEY.

Mrs. Harper is glowing.

She looks radiant.

Happy.

And her nose arouses me like never before.

Cruel temptress!

I don't bother to buckle in Albert Camus. The truck fishtails back so quickly he falls off the seat and onto the floor mat. When he jumps back up, Albert Camus makes a mad dash for my lap, and I feel him trembling against my jeans.

On a little-used dirt back road, I pull over, rest my head on the wheel, and sob.

Maybe you think it ridiculous, my weeping over the unavailability of a woman with whom I haven't even exchanged more than a hundred or so words. But I did love her, or the fantasy of being with her, which has pulled me through a very hard lonely period, the way the hope of seeing a single green bud pulls many Vermonters through the coldest and darkest Marches.

Albert Camus continues to comfort me the only way he knows how—by licking my chin, neck, and hands.

Maybe I am also mourning the way my emotional and mental decline mirrors the crippled state of my body. I'm getting worse, all alone in the woods. The shadows are overtaking my mind with useless thoughts that fester and ache like the metal pins in my legs and arms.

Brian the butcher may not have known the name of France's most famous existential writer, but he knew enough to make his move on Mrs. Harper in a timely fashion, and when you have spent many months talking to a dog—albeit the best dog in the world—facts like these take on a heightened meaning.

You can't make passionate love to a book, after all.

And dogs can't trade words with you, no matter how much you pretend.

In the truck, with the engine still running and the heat on full blast, I contemplate the first question and briefly consider driving my vehicle into a tree at 120 miles an hour, which is the highest number on my speedometer.

But Albert Camus is still dutifully licking the salty tears from my chin; he deserves better, or at least a different ending, in this incarnation.

I get the sense that he truly enjoys our life together, and that's not me projecting either. I love this dog; he gives me purpose and reason, but my longings for more are quite strong, I must admit.

Teaching used to fill the void that has opened up inside me.

This must be what "weariness tinged with amazement" feels like, I think, and then I utter the most dangerous question of all: "Why?"

Albert Camus stops licking me, and with our faces only inches apart, we look into each other. I still see humanity in his shiny black eye, even though he is a dog now.

"I don't know if I can keep going, Albert Camus," I say.

He cocks his head to one side as if to say, *Vous ne m'aimez plus?*

"I do love you, Albert Camus. It's true. I really do. With all my heart. But I'm afraid I can no longer answer the first question."

Albert Camus licks my face again.

"Have you escaped the absurd, now that you are a dog? Is that why you can lick me and love me after some monster burned out your eye, and yet I have no longer been able to interact with my own species successfully since some monster gave me this limp?"

He yawns, and his breath assaults me.

It smells like a bucket of sea snails rotting in the August sun.

I stroke Albert Camus's back, feeling the bumps of his spine, and his tail thumps hard on my thigh.

"If you weren't so goddamn happy now, I might ask if you wanted to enter into a suicide pact with me. But can I live my life for a one-eyed dog? Can I find meaning in this?"

As if he understands my words, he ducks his head under my hand, begging for a scratch behind the ears, making me feel useful.

While I know this is just some sort of animalistic herd instinct—I am the alpha male in his mind, the provider of food and water and shelter—I find meaning, beat the absurd, answer the first question, via my one-eyed dog, if only for the moment.

He is enough.

We drive forty-five minutes to the chain grocery store.

Inside I order two thick prime dry-aged rib eye steaks and a bone from some pimply teenager in an oversize white butcher's coat. He gags and makes retching noises while he weighs the meat, mumbles the words *disgusting, sick, barbaric*, throws in the bone at my request and extends the bag over the counter, holding it at arm's length like a sack of dog shit.

"Are you okay?" I ask, because he's starting to look green.

"I'm a vegan, and my asshole boss forced me to work in the meat department today. What do you think?"

"That's the absurd, right there."

"What are you even talking about?" he says as he turns his back on me, and I recognize his type. He's practically begging for me to hug him. I imagine the parents at home who alternately ignore and criticize him, offering no promise of better—providing no philosophy, no religion, no belief system whatsoever, which is why he's chosen veganism, most likely the antithesis of his parents' diet, as a means of protest.

"Here's your tip, young man," I say. "Read Camus. Start with *The Stranger*. Read him. He agrees with you. A vegan forced to work as a butcher—absurdism at its finest. There's a whole world out there beyond this small town. You're not alone."

"Whatever," he says, and I fight to quell my old teacher instincts.

As I peruse the pet aisle, throwing into my basket several months' worth of overpriced treats for Albert Camus and some dental chews for his awful breath, I think about how that kid in the meat department would have become my favorite student by the end of the year, back when I was teaching high school English. I always won over those types—the ones who were desperate for adult guidance, so terribly wounded and bruised. If you could stomach the apathy for a few weeks, give their minds something real to chew on, offer them the alternative they craved instinctively, what people like them have been finding in story for many thousands of years, they'd always come around. I look down at my cane. *Well, almost always.*

Before I leave, I swing by the meat section once more, wave to get the teen's attention. "You probably think I'm just some silly old fool, but I'd be remiss if I didn't tell you that you're in existential crisis. Look it up. You're not the first. I've been there often. And, metaphorically, vegans have been working the meat counter since the beginning of time."

He squints at me. "I gave you your order. I did my job. Now just leave me alone, okay?"

"Albert Camus. Read him. You'll see."

"Listen, old man," he mumbles, looking around to see if anyone is listening. When he's sure no one is within earshot, he says, "What the fuck—are you gay for me or something?"

"No. No, I am not. I am heterosexual and heartbroken, if you really must know. And I was just trying to—"

"Then fuck off, okay? How 'bout you try that?"

Maybe I've lost my touch.

And what the hell do I know? I'm just a cripple who lives with a one-eyed dog.

The kid's behavior is a classic cry for help, but I no longer help teenagers.

Remember, Nate Vernon? You failed as a teacher. The universe beat the hell out of you with an aluminum baseball bat.

"Sure thing," I tell the vegan butcher, and cane my way to the checkout line.

I let Albert Camus sit on my lap as I drive home, and he does so eagerly, licking my right hand the whole time, completely ignorant of the fact that our not wearing seat belts puts us in serious danger, forgetting how his last life ended, when he was a famous French writer.

Dogs do not understand the laws of physics, which is why they have never invented anything like the seat belt on their own.

I drink half a bottle of wine as I cook the steaks.

Albert Camus and I listen to our favorite CD—Yo-Yo Ma playing Bach's Cello Suites.

It massages our souls.

The smell of meat warming, cow blood boiling and evaporating in the frying pan, a virtuoso playing a genius's compositions—all of it fills the house, and Albert Camus salivates worse than Pavlov's dog until there is a puddle of drool on the black-and-white tile floor of the kitchen.

It takes me a long time to cut Albert Camus's steak into tiny pieces on which it is impossible to choke, because little Albert inhales his meat, and I think about how I could really use a food processor, make a mental note to buy one the next time I visit civilization. The whole time I'm cutting, he paws sheepishly at my feet, and his saliva glands get an excruciating workout.

I try not to think about Mrs. Harper's erotic nose, and am mostly successful.

My four-legged friend eats a good portion of the meat before his bowl even hits the ground. He's licked the bottom clean and is working on his butcher's bone before I swallow my second piece of steak, which is warm, bloody, and pairs divinely with the pinot noir.

As the spicy juices fill my mouth and give my taste buds an orgasmic high, I think about the vegan butcher.

"He's like Sisyphus," I say to Albert Camus, "rolling the metaphorical boulder up the hill, knowing it will roll down again no matter what he does. Over and over. He sees no future for himself. 'Where would his torture be, indeed, if at every step the hope of succeeding upheld him? The workman of today works every day in his life the same tasks, and his fate is no less absurd.' Remember when you wrote that, Albert Camus? The vegan butcher sees no Mrs. Harper in his future. He sees nothing. What do we see in our future now that we've lost our Mrs. Harper, Albert Camus?"

He pauses his gnawing for a second to ponder the question, and then resumes scraping the bone vigorously with his little teeth.

I finish the first bottle of wine and open another, which I quaff deeply as Albert Camus gnaws and gnaws and Yo-Yo Ma works his magic bow and snow flurries outside and Brian what's-his-face the ignorant butcher who doesn't even know who the hell Albert Camus was—that guy probably makes passionate love to Mrs. Harper, who moans through her wondrous nose under the weight of her bare-assed, affable butcher.

The CD ends, and I finish the second bottle of pinot noir to the now slightly less fervent sound of Albert's teeth chipping away at cow bone. I envy him; he looks much more content on marrow than I am on wine.

I see Mrs. Harper's nose in my mind's eye.

She knows who Albert Camus is—she must.

In all of my many fantasies she was well-read and sophisticated.

Mrs. Harper paired divinely with me.

I try to mentally undress her, but the gap-toothed butcher keeps popping up in my thoughts like a traffic cop of masturbatory fantasies, and he's yelling, "Whoa, friend! Time out here. This woman is going to be *my wife*. She's engaged now. But there are other doe in the woods, if you know what I mean. So point your arrow elsewhere." Brian the butcher winks and nods, and then he returns to making love to Mrs. Harper, whose gray wave of hair rises and falls over her titillating nose.

I briefly contemplate opening a third bottle of wine as my eyes get heavier—*What is this lit cigarette doing in my hand?*—and then my head is somehow down on the table.

And then . . .

And then . . .

And then . . .

And then . . .

I'm in bed with a desert-dry tongue that seems to have been smoked and cured into beef jerky without my knowing about it. A mind-numbing pulse is sounding an angry war-drum-like beat against my temples—BOOM-BOOM-BOOM-BOOM-BOOM—when through the darkness I hear a scratching at the window. This seems impossible, because we are high in the air on the second-floor loft, and the window in question is maybe a good thirty-five feet above the wooden deck below. I wonder if a bird might be pecking at the window. What sort of bird would do that at the end of winter, in the dead of night?

When I turn on the bedside light, I see Albert Camus jumping up and clawing at the window.

"What's wrong, buddy?" I say.

I look at the bedside clock's glowing red numbers: 4:44 a.m.

Is that good luck or bad? All the same number. I can't remember what my students used to say about that—whether I should make a wish or hold my breath or do something else. They were always so superstitious.

"Go to sleep, Albert. Get in your bed. I need to sleep off this wine headache."

But he keeps leaping up and scratching at the window.

When I stand, my cane is wobbly. He begins to bark and growl as he continues to jump and scratch. He's never behaved this way before. Was there something in his bone? Maybe that vegan teenager sprayed it with some sort of drug.

You can't trust anyone anymore, I think. And that kid had motive.

But what sort of drug would make Albert Camus act like this, so intently focused on the window?

"Do you need to use the bathroom?" I ask as I make my way toward the light switch, feeling a bit dizzy and still very drunk.

My right foot sinks into a warm pile of Albert Camus's shit, which squirts through my toes.

My left foot lands in a warm puddle of his piss.

He has never before had an accident in the house.

Never.

I honestly can't remember if I took him outside before I went to bed, and I mentally berate myself for being a bad pet owner, an inhumane lovesick drunken oaf.

Before cleaning my feet, I need to apologize. "I'm so sorry," I say. "The indignity. I'm the beast. This will not happen again."

I kneel down next to him and try to pick him up and give him a few kisses, but he growls menacingly enough to scare me into letting him go.

"What's wrong, boy? What are you trying to tell me?"

He keeps jumping up and scratching at the window.

Over and over.

Am I dreaming?

"There's nothing out there. Nothing. Time for bed, buddy. Stop that. Come on now. Stop it!"

He keeps jumping and scratching, like he's trying to run up the wall and onto the glass.

"Okay. Let's see what's outside."

I open the window and feel the cold night air rush in.

When I bend down to pick up Albert Camus, so that I might show him there is nothing outside, he uses my thigh as a springboard and is through my hands and out the window before I know what happened.

"No!"

In the time it takes for him to fall, I remember that just yesterday I had the handyman shovel the snow from the deck, fearing that the weight was becoming too great for the wood; I immediately understand that a thirty-five-foot fall is enough to kill a dog the size of Albert Camus; and I also remember what I said to him earlier in the truck about the first question and the possibility of a suicide pact between us. And then I remember every single kiss he ever gave me, the feel of his Afro in my hand, the way he wagged his tail whenever I said his name, and my great love for him swells my heart to a dangerous size.

Do dogs ever commit suicide?

The thud of his skull hitting the wood below sounds like heavy knuckles striking a door.

I listen for a yelp, mentally beg for the sound of his toenails clicking on the deck below, but there is nothing but a deathly silence.

I race down the stairs just as fast as my limp and cane and drunkenness allow, tracking my dog's excrement through the entire house, flick on the outside flood lights, and throw open the sliding glass door.

Albert Camus's head is bent at a horrifically unnatural angle, and his little legs are limp, which is when some part of me knows he was killed instantly, that the impact snapped his neck. But I scoop up his little body anyway, cradling his head, trying not to damage the spine, retching at the lifelessness of the bones and fur in my hands. "Please don't die. Please don't. Don't. I love you, buddy.

Please. I'm sorry I talked so much about the first question. I haven't been an easy roommate, I know, but I'll change. I promise."

There's blood trickling out of his mouth, and his one eye has rolled into the back of his head, but I grab my keys, lay him gently on the passenger-side seat of my truck, and—even though my veterinarian is an hour's drive away and most likely won't be in her office for another four hours or so—still barefoot, I shift into drive and hit the gas.

"Wake up, Albert Camus. You're going to be okay, little buddy," I say, looking over at him, patting his still-warm head, paying no attention to the fact that I am driving a truck.

Toward the end of my steep dirt driveway, my right front tire slips into the rut I've been meaning to have the plow guy fill in, the steering wheel jerks right, and I smash into an old oak tree.

The airbag inflates, punching me in the nose.

I blink.

My vision blurs.

I throw up two bottles of red wine and a pound of bloody meat onto the deflating airbag and my lap.

I cry.

I punch the dashboard.

I hyperventilate.

I try to spit out the awful taste in my mouth.

A rush of blood fills my head and then drains away too quickly, like an ocean wave crashing on the shore, grabbing everything on the beach and retreating back to whence it came.

A strange feeling comes over me, and I hope it is death.

I'm done.

I surrender to the first question.

Finally, I black out.

CHAPTER 8

The winter sun wakes me rudely.

Albert Camus is dead on the passenger-side floor; he's stiff as a stuffed fox.

I grab my cane and get out of the truck.

The hood is crumpled. The front bumper has become a part of the thick and noble oak tree—almost like an accessory maybe, a tree belt.

Part of me knows that this is it for me.

I live at the end of a dirt road. I picked this property because no one is ever around. No neighbors. No passing traffic—the connecting road is three miles from my driveway, and I have not walked more than a half mile or so in one stretch since the series of surgeries that put this Humpty Dumpty back together again.

I do not own a telephone—land or cell. No computer or Internet. This is my Walden, the closest I'll ever get to being Henry David Thoreau.

I have no friends. No one would ever visit. I have to drive to my handyman's home whenever I need him. The plow man is contracted to come whenever more than three inches of snow falls, but we only had a dusting last night, and according to the paper I read on Sunday, no storms are forecast for the coming week, so I know I can pretty much die alone out here without anyone trying to save me.

The smell of gas is pungent, and I see that the truck is indeed leaking—most likely a fuel hose has come loose. I think about lighting the whole thing on fire, sending Albert Camus to his next incarnation in a blaze of glory, like he's a Viking dog king and our truck is his boat, which it sort of was. But instead I start to strip off my puke-covered clothes and throw them onto the snow piles melting on the sides of my dirt driveway as I cane my way back to the house.

Without bothering to take off my underwear, I enter the shower and let the hot spikes rain down on me until the water heater's tank is exhausted, at which point I towel off, dress, and examine the window in my bedroom, which is still open.

"What did you hear or see, Albert?" I ask the cold air.

I stick my head outside and look around.

Nothing.

No animal prints in the snow.

Nothing at the edge of the woods.

Nothing.

I shut the window.

I think about whether my dog may have actually committed suicide, and decide it is possible—especially since I named him Albert Camus, and went on and on about the first question for years.

It was like I had been training him to find meaning or perish, then I continually told him that there was no meaning. And the suicide pact I offered him—how was he to know I wasn't invoking it with my heavy drinking last night? I mean, he was only a dog. His brain was smaller than a peach.

What dog could live up to such a weighty name when it came to solving his master's existential crisis?

Maybe I put too much pressure on him.

Perhaps his heart was like an emotional tick, absorbing all of my anxiety and regrets and inaction and sadness, swelling until it outgrew his little toy poodle chest, until he just could no longer take the anticipation of the inevitable pop.

I remember once reading an essay by or an interview with David Foster Wallace, in which he says that suicide is akin to jumping from the top floor of a burning skyscraper—it's not that you are unafraid of jumping, but the fall is the lesser of two terrors.

Was jumping out the window preferable to living with me?

Had I emotionally abused Albert Camus without knowing it?

He had never before shown any interest in the bedroom window—none whatsoever—so why last night?

These questions are beginning to hurt my head. I go to the kitchen and open up another bottle of red wine—a rioja—and spark a Parliament Light cigarette for breakfast.

I pour a glass and down it in one gulp without even tasting.

I pour another glass, and try to figure out what to do.

I light a second cigarette just as soon as I've finished the first.

"You killed your dog," I say to myself. "What type of a man drives his dog to suicide?"

As I chain-smoke and drink away the morning, I can't help but think about Edmond Atherton, the kid who smashed my bones with a baseball bat and ended my teaching career.

For six months he sat against the right wall of my classroom, just under a black-and-white photo of Toni Morrison, and he never made a sound as the rest of the class discussed Herman Hesse, Shakespeare, Franz Kafka, Margaret Atwood, Albert Camus, Ivan Turgenev, Paulo Coelho, and so many others.

And then one day Edmond Atherton raised his hand and asked if he could speak with me after class. It was a strange request to make in the middle of the lesson, and out of the blue, but I agreed, and redirected the class back to the discussion at hand.

I remember Edmond stayed seated when the bell rang, waited patiently for everyone else to leave the room as he sat almost life-lessly. His calm gave me goose bumps; it was so eerie and . . . force-ful. Something had shifted inside him, I'm certain of that now, but it was just a suspicion on that day.

Once we were alone, I said, "What's on your mind, Edmond?"

He put his hands together with a clap and held them in front of his face like he was about to pray. "I hope you won't take this the wrong way, but I think I found a major flaw in your teaching philosophy. I didn't want to embarrass you in front of the entire class, which is why I asked to speak privately. But there's a serious problem regarding your message."

"Okay." I forced a laugh. But something inside me knew that this was not going to go very well—that the reason for this talk was more than just regular teenage attention-seeking bullshit. Part of me knew that I was in trouble. Even still, I said, "Let me have it."

"Are you sure?" he said, tapping his nose with the ends of his forefingers in this almost giddy way. "Because I think you might not be able to teach the way you do once I point this out."

"Believe me, Edmond, I'm a grizzled veteran with decades of teaching experience under my belt. I can handle it."

"Okay, then." He slapped his hands down on the desk hard, which made me flinch, and then he smiled and looked at me for too long, creating a silence that hovered like mustard gas be-tween us. "I admire what you're trying to do for us, I really do. I mean, it's nice to be told that we're all special, capable of the 'extraordinary.' Like in that *Dead Poets Society* movie clip you showed us. It's nice to think we can all seize the day. That we can all make our mark on the world. But it's not true, is it? I mean, just consider the definition of the word *extraordinary*, right? It's an exclusionary word, after all. There have to be many ordinary people for the word *extraordinary* to mean something!"

He was smiling in this madman way.

"What do you really want to talk about, Edmond? What's eating you up?"

"Your class. I'm getting a little tired of the happy bullshit."

"Happy bullshit?"

"Yeah. I stomached it for as long as I could, but I just can't anymore. And I don't think what you're teaching is right. I mean, all of the teachers in this school are full of shit, but what you teach is dangerous."

"Dangerous? How so?"

"I watched the rest of *Dead Poets Society*. The main character kills himself. Is that what you're trying to do? Get us to kill ourselves too?"

I could see the madness in his eyes, and knew right then that any attempt at defending myself would be unsuccessful, because we were no longer having a rational conversation. But this wasn't the first irrational conversation I had had with a teenager. So I swallowed my pride and said, "I'm not sure I understand—"

"You tell us that we should all be different, but if we were all different, we'd be the same. Can't you see that? Not everyone can be different, or we'd lose the sense of the word—just like everyone can't be extraordinary. You can't tell average people to be extraordinary and get away with it forever. It's a mindfuck. And it's a lie. A pyramid scheme. At some point, someone is going to make you pay."

"*Pay?* What are you trying to tell me here, Edmond? Because that sounds like a threat to me. Should I feel threatened here?"

"I knew you wouldn't listen to me. No one listens to me."

"I'm here, Edmond. And I'm all ears."

He stood up and put on his backpack very slowly.

Then he looked at his sneakers and giggled like an elementary-school kid who had farted loudly in the middle of class. "I'm sorry, Mr. Vernon. I'm really sorry. I'm just messing with you. You're the best. High five."

He raised his hand in the air.

I did not raise mine.

"Are you okay, Edmond?"

"Aces, teach. No five? Okay. I'll just go then. Off to be extraordinary. I won't let you down."

I let him go mostly because I was feeling exhausted that day, and then I forgot about Edmond Atherton as I taught the rest of my classes, went to meetings in the afternoon, and then helped settle a fight between the leads in the school play, who had apparently "hooked up," which didn't work out all that well, making their onstage chemistry dodgy at best—and there were tears, which took a lot of energy.

I thought about Edmond as I drove home that night and decided I would ask to speak with him again at the end of class the next day. Maybe he was looking for some extra attention and was attacking as a way to alert me to the fact that he had needs that weren't being met. I had seen this approach before, and Edmond Atherton was not the first teen to challenge me.

When Edmond arrived in my classroom the next day, I asked if he would stay after class so we might talk, and he said, "Sure, sure, sure. Sure thing," and then started giggling again.

"Something funny?" I asked.

"Nah," he said and took his seat.

We were discussing Paulo Coelho's *The Alchemist*, debating whether there really was a universal language, and whether each of us had a personal legend, when Edmond raised his hand again.

"What if the universe tells you to do something the rest of the world would condemn?"

"Many people have asked this question before. Think about our founding fathers writing the Declaration of Independence. England sure condemned that," I said. "And that's only one example."

"And it's good to do things that others don't do, right?" he said. "That's what you're always going on and on about in here. The importance of being different?"

Before I could answer, he pulled an aluminum baseball bat from his backpack and charged me.

I remember hearing these awful noises like tree branches breaking and then high-pitched screaming.

He'd hit me half a dozen times before my mind even registered what was happening—elbows, kneecaps, shins, forearms—and all before I hit the floor and lost consciousness.

Later in court, a straight-faced and utterly remorseless Edmond Atherton said he never aimed for my head because he wanted me "to remember" that what he had done was the punishment for my being "wrong."

They locked Edmond away in an institution for disturbed boys, covered my medical bills—which were astronomical—and gave me a settlement large enough to let me retire and move far away to the woods of Vermont, a place I had never been before in my life. After all the media coverage—not to mention all of the time spent in the hospital recovering from multiple surgeries and then the painful rehab, during which I couldn't even walk, so I was an easy target for any reporter who was heartless enough to stick a microphone in my face as I wheeled, crutched, and then caned my way through parking lots—I just wanted to be alone, far, far away, where no one would know my name or face. Vermont sounded like such a place.

And that's how I ended up in this two-story cabin in the middle of the woods, where I've rubbed my aching joints, downed Advil at an alarming rate, and served out my time in this ruined body where no one can see me.

"I never thanked the students who stopped Edmond before he killed me," I say to my wineglass as I light up another cigarette. "Was it because I secretly wanted to die all along? Was it because Edmond was right? He may have been my most extraordinary student ever. That's the truth, isn't it? It's almost funny, when you think about the word *extraordinary* and how many times I used it—like I was Robin Williams playing Mr. Keating."

I open another bottle of wine.

I also open a second pack of cigarettes and cough up a tremendous amount of phlegm before I resume smoking, wondering how long it will take for a strict diet of cigarettes and wine to kill me.

When I am drunk enough, I retrieve Albert Camus's body from the ruined truck.

On my deck, sitting in the wooden Adirondack chair, I lay him across my lap and stroke his stiff back, hoping that I can pet him back to life.

"I'm sorry, buddy," I say. "I shouldn't have talked so much about suicide. But a pact is a pact, right? And maybe we will be reincarnated, find each other again—just as soon as I manage to hold up my end of the bargain."

I'm very drunk, but I still realize it's morbid to be petting and talking to a dead dog, and so—through snot and tears and cigarette smoke—I put some wood into the clay chimenea, lay Albert Camus on top, retrieve the gasoline can from the shed, soak my friend, and then toss in a match.

Flames shoot up through the little chimney, followed by a steady thick black plume that is slightly less nauseating than the hissing and bubbling and crackling noises Albert Camus's carcass is making.

"I'm sorry," I say over and over as the cold bites my face and hands, while tears burn my cheeks.

When the fire goes out, I know I am truly alone.

I contemplate methods of suicide.

Jumping from the roof seems risky. I may not die immediately, and I don't want to be eaten alive by coyotes as I rot on the deck in a human nest of broken limbs.

The chain saw in the shed seems too extreme.

Kurt Vonnegut style is an option—I have pills and alcohol and cigarettes.

But I settle on starvation, as it will be a horrific penance for having caused my dog's suicide.

This is the death sentence I give myself: You will consume nothing but wine until you die, and you will die alone, because you deserve it.

I forgo the artifice of the glass and drink directly from the bottle as the sun sets, puffing defiantly on my Parliament Lights, which have long ago ceased to offer any sense of comfort or pleasure. The smoke now assaults my esophagus and lungs, and yet I puff and puff like a magic dragon who has slipped into his cave after losing the one little boy who believed in his existence.

My vision is blurry, but I believe I count four bottles by my feet.

"Albert Camus!" I scream up at the sky. "Albert Camus! Where are you, little buddy? Is there a heaven for dogs? Are you already reincarnated? I miss you! I'm sorry! I am a shit for brains! I am selfish! I am foolish! I should not be alive! I never should have been born! I am truly and utterly sorry!"

I listen to the word *sorry* echo over the bare maples and oaks that cover the downward slope of land behind my deck and race toward the base of the small mountains in the distance.

"Beautiful view," the Realtor said when he showed me this place.

"Perfect view for ending it all," I say now, and laugh. "A good place to die. This will be a happy death, and I will now play Zagreus, the old cripple.

"Albert Camus!" I scream up at the sky. "Edmond Atherton was right! My class was all bullshit! Everyone can't be extraordinary! It defies the very definition of the word! It's absurd! And there is no meaning! No meaning at all! It's just a cruel joke! That's the answer to the first question! Just a joke! So why not kill yourself?"

I swig more wine, feel red rivers burst from the corners of my mouth and run down my neck before being absorbed into my sweater. I swallow down my need to vomit, and then I'm crying again.

I must be even drunker than I thought, because—before I know what I'm doing—I start to pray.

My estranged mother is a religious woman—she actually became a nun after she was done raising me. Had a "vision" shortly after I graduated from high school. Told me that both Mother Mary and Jesus visited her. They apparently told her she was meant to join a religious community. I thought she had gone insane. The Catholic Church took her in. She raised me Catholic, and I had already unequivocally renounced my faith. I've since renounced my mother, mostly because I hate her. But we fall back on what we know when we are weak—and especially when we are drunk.

"What the fuck, God?" I scream up at the sky. "Can it get any worse? I'm not a praying man, but I'm going to ask you just once for help. If you're up there, give me a sign. If you don't, I'm going to end it, once and for all. And who could blame me? Help me please, if you exist. Fuck you, if you don't!"

God doesn't speak to me as I finish my fourth (or fifth?) bottle of wine and the sun dips down below yonder mountain.

I don't remember when it happened, but I must have fallen out of the chair, because my left cheek is pressed firmly against the wood deck now, and I don't seem to be able to get up.

It gets colder.

When my right eye gazes up, it sees that the stars have come out and are shining particularly hard and bright.

"Need to do a little better than that, God," I mumble.

I shiver in the fetal position, too drunk, too apathetic, to roll inside where there are blankets and heat.

Maybe I will freeze to death, I hope, and then I somehow manage to light up another cigarette, which I let dangle hands-free in my mouth as I lie there on the deck.

I'm on my back now, but I have no idea where my lit cigarette went.

Vision is blurry at best.

I blink several times.

I think I see a shooting star rip through the sky at one point, but I'm too drunk to know what the hell I'm seeing anymore.

And then—once again—everything goes black.

CHAPTER 9

"Mr. Vernon?"

I blink, and a woman is slapping my face.

"Mr. Vernon? Wake up. Are you okay?"

I close my eyes and try to disappear again into sleep.

I'm spinning.

I'm being rolled over onto my side.

"You're going to choke to death on your own vomit," the woman's voice says, and I wonder if she is an angel.

I remember angels coming to save people in the biblical stories my mother told me when I was a child—and I also vaguely remember praying before I passed out.

I'm still drunk enough to believe in such things.

But then I'm vomiting onto my deck—all wine and bile tinged with cigarette tar.

"You have a little party?" she says. "What happened here?"

"Albert Camus," I whisper. "He's dead."

"Um, yeah. For half a century now."

"You don't understand," I say, feeling the damage I've done to my throat. It burns like someone sandpapered my entire respiratory system. "I killed him."

"What the hell have you been drinking?"

I blink and try to look at her face.

The floodlight is right behind her head now, so all I see is her silhouette outlined in white.

"Are you an angel?" I say. "Did God send you?"

She laughs. "Um, I'm not really religious, Mr. Vernon."

"So you're not an angel?"

"I believe you may be intoxicated."

"I'm Zagreus, the old cripple. You have to kill me. Like in the book *A Happy Death*. By Camus."

"I don't want to brag, but I may have just saved your life. Never pass out on your back, Mr. Vernon. They teach you this in health class. You can choke and suffocate on your own vomit when you're passed out, which was what you were doing when I found you here."

"I was supposed to die. I made a suicide pact with Albert Camus."

"Okay," she says. "Let's get you inside. Maybe put on some coffee. Get some water in you. Change your shirt."

"You won't kill me? What if I give you my money—all I have? Would you be my Patrice Mersault? Like in *A Happy Death*."

"Isn't Meursault the protagonist of *The Stranger*?"

"There are two *u*'s in Meursault from *The Stranger*," I whisper. "Only one *u* in Patrice Mersault. Just let me die out here. Because I killed Albert Camus. I'm sorry, but I have to pay with my life."

"Okay, drunk man. Let's sit up."

She's behind me now, forcing me to do a sit-up, pushing my shoulder blades with her palms.

"Here's your cane. Use it, because I don't think I can carry you. Let's just make it inside. Three feet, we have to travel. Just thirty-six tiny inches."

"I can't stand," I say. "Too drunk. Legs won't work."

"Then you'll crawl, because it's too cold out here."

"No," I say. "Let me freeze to death. I don't deserve to live."

"Get your ass inside that house now," she says and then kicks my thigh.

"Ouch!"

"Move!"

Mostly because I am now terrified of this woman angel, I fall forward and crawl toward the sliding door, which is open. My head is pounding, and it takes a long time, but I manage to drag my body inside. She slides the door shut behind us and locks it.

"What happened to you?" she says. "My god. You're a mess."

"I killed Albert Camus."

"Have you lost your fucking mind?" she says, and then she starts to cry, which alarms me.

Do angels cry?

She seems vaguely familiar. I wonder if I have run into her, shopping at Harper's. Maybe she frequents my favorite pizza shop, Wicked Good Pie, or perhaps the local gas station—but I can't place her in my drunken state, let alone figure out why she would come to my home. She's beautiful though, in her late thirties, I would guess. Long brown hair. Slim figure. Although she seems to be wearing outdated clothes—a white jean jacket with rock-star pins on it. I haven't seen people wearing rock-star pins on jean jackets for decades.

"Why are you crying?" I say.

"I didn't think you'd be *this* fucked up."

I feel guilty for disappointing her, even though I didn't even know she was coming, let alone who she might be. It all adds to the sense of responsibility I feel for Albert Camus's death, and I instantly remember why I have sequestered myself.

"Why are you here?" I ask.

"I came to save you."

"How did you know I needed saving?" I say, uncomfortably remembering my prayer.

She covers her eyes with her hand and sighs deeply.

"Are you really an angel?" I say.

"Would you stop fucking saying that please?"

"Angels don't use profanity, do they?"

"You need to hydrate," she says, and then she's opening cabinets and turning on the tap and thrusting the rim of a glass at my teeth.

I sip just to be nice.

I wonder if I might be hallucinating, or maybe I have died and gone to some sort of hell or purgatory where attractive women force you to crawl and drink excessive amounts of water.

"What's going on here?" I say, still sitting on the floor just inside the sliding glass door.

"Drink." She lifts the bottom of the glass up, so that water fills my mouth.

Suddenly, I realize that I am very thirsty—also my throat is screaming from so many cigarettes—and so I gulp the water down until the glass is empty.

"Good," she says. "Let's do one more."

I watch her fill the glass a second time, and when she approaches me, I say, "Who are you?"

She doesn't answer, but pours water down my throat again, and I do my best to consume it, but immediately feel as though I might vomit again. The woman must have read my face. "Try to keep it down," she says, and then she's in the kitchen again, rifling through my supplies.

"Heavily buttered toast," she says as she sticks two slices of rye bread into the toaster. "That's what you need now. Get some grease in you."

Before long she's sitting next to me on the floor, holding warm bread up to my lips.

Even though I just vowed to starve myself to death, I take small bites—hearing the crunch of my teeth breaking through crispy nooks and crannies—and feel the warm velvety melted butter on my tongue. My nausea dissipates with every swallow, which seems miraculous.

Once the toast has been consumed, she cleans my face and neck with towels soaked in warm water, and it feels so good that I close my eyes and try to forget that I have a strange woman in my home, making me do things against my will.

Maybe because I'm drunk, I pretend I am an infant again, and my mother is taking care of me.

You are a baby.

You have no control.

You also have no responsibilities.

Nothing can be your fault.

Then I'm on the couch, she's covering me with blankets, and I'm mumbling, "I didn't mean to kill Albert Camus. I really didn't. I'm so sorry. Won't you kill me in my sleep? Please. Just kill me. End this."

"Sleep it off," she says. "We start saving you tomorrow."

"You already saved me—whoever you are. Even though I didn't want to be saved."

"No," she says. "We've only just begun."

I hear anger in her voice, but—even though the warm butter is working its way through my system—I still feel drunk and tell myself that four bottles of wine is enough to make anyone hallucinate.

"I wish you were real," I say. "I'm sorry you're not real."

"Go to sleep, Mr. Vernon."

"Why do you call me by my last name?"

"Shhh," she says. "It's okay. Just sleep."

My eyelids are too heavy to open, even when I hear her crying.

Why is this woman crying?

Why is she here?

Who is she?

"You're an angel," I mumble. "A prayer answered. There's no other explanation. Simply none. Maybe a curse too. Maybe. Maybe. Maybe. May . . ."

And then I'm gone again, dreaming of Edmond Atherton.

In my dream he's chasing Albert Camus with the aluminum baseball bat, and I'm looking down at the scene from a high tower that doesn't seem to have stairs or an elevator or any way down at all, except jumping out the window.

Albert Camus is running in circles below, and every time Edmond Atherton swings his bat, he gets closer and closer to killing my dog—so, even though it makes no sense at all, I jump out the window, feel my stomach drop. But just when I'm about to hit the earth and splatter to death, the entire world disappears and Albert Camus and I are in my living room again, sitting on the couch.

Edmond Atherton has vanished, along with his bat.

"I'm sorry, Albert Camus," I say.

He jumps into my arms and licks my face.

"Why did you jump?" I ask.

You were the one who jumped in this dream! he says, although his lips do not move.

"Why did you jump in real life? From the bedroom window. Were you acting on the suicide pact?"

Remember in It's a Wonderful Life, *when Clarence the angel jumps off the bridge to trick George Bailey into saving him? He says something like, "I knew if I jumped in, you'd save me. And that's how I saved you." We watched that movie together the past two Christmases. You sobbed both times. Remember? That's where I got the idea—figured out how to save you.*

"You jumped to save me?"

Albert Camus licks me once right on the lips, as if to say yes.

"But I didn't save you back."

You didn't kill yourself either.

I hold Albert Camus close to my chest, smell the familiar slightly metallic scent of his fur, and feel the beating of his little heart against my ribs as his tail repetitively taps my stomach.

"Regardless of whether this is real or not, I love you, Albert Camus. You were the best dog in the world. You were a wildly gifted emotional support animal."

This is just a thought—but if you ever get another dog, please name him something a bit less intense, less absurd. Something happier—maybe something uplifting like Yo-Yo Ma. You name a dog Albert Camus, and you yoke him to a certain fate. That's just the way it is. No offense.

"There's only one dog for me," I say as I scratch Albert Camus behind the ears and kiss the hard spot between his eyes. "I could never get another to replace you."

Beautiful sentiment, Master Nate. I appreciate it. But you have to move on.

"Do you think the woman on my couch could really be an answer to prayer—could she be a wingless angel like Clarence? Sent by God?"

Dogs don't really believe in God, Master Nate. We believe in regular feeding times, car rides with the windows down, a good scratch behind the ears, a walk in the woods, and chasing small mammals, shaking them to death in our teeth. Our brains are no bigger than peaches, so we keep it simple. No God or anything heady like that. Give us a car ride with the windows down over a deity any day. Tell you what, let's just snuggle this one last time and simply enjoy the sun streaming through the window in all of its full frontal nudity.

We snuggle cheek-to-cheek and belly-to-belly.

"I love you, my furry little buddy."

Yeah, you too, Master Nate.

CHAPTER 10

"Albert Camus," I say when I wake up. "I had the strangest dream."

When I realize I'm on the couch, I search my memory. I'm pretty sure I was not in a high tower looking down on Edmond Atherton trying to kill Albert Camus with a baseball bat, but is my dog really dead? And was there actually a wingless angel woman here last night?

"Good morning, Mr. Vernon," a woman says from the kitchen, and I jump.

"Who are you?" I say as I turn around. "What do you want from me?"

She hands me a cup of black coffee. "Perhaps you'd like to see some ID?"

The woman hands me a small rectangle of plastic. It looks like a driver's license at first, but on second glance, when my bloodshot eyes focus, I realize it's one of those ridiculous Official Member of the Human Race cards I used to give to my students on the last day of school. What a colossal waste of energy it was to make those things—it took me days of my own personal at-home free time. Why the hell I ever made those, I couldn't tell you. I used to find half of them on the hallway floors, discarded thoughtlessly like candy wrappers.

"Do you remember me now?" she says.

I read the name on the card.

Study the photo.

Look up at Portia Kane—she's just standing there in my living room, like it's the most natural thing in the world.

She has long brown hair and is dressed casually, in the same jean jacket she's wearing in the photo, which seems downright bizarre. Her face has aged, but she's still remarkably pretty. She sits down next to me on the couch.

"You're the girl who used to talk to me about her mother? The hoarder, right?"

"So you *do* remember me. I hoped you might, but it's been twenty years and—"

"What the hell are you doing here in my home?" The coffee cup warms my hands.

"I told you last night—I've come to save you."

"How did you know I was going to kill myself?"

"Were you *really* going to kill yourself?" she says.

"Albert Camus, he jumped out the window and died. I had to burn him in the chimenea. We made a suicide pact, and—it sounds ridiculous now. I can't explain it to you, and I don't particularly feel like doing so anyway."

"Is that your truck outside, smashed into the tree? I hope you're not concussed, because you aren't making any sense, Mr. Vernon. And I don't think people are supposed to sleep when concussed. Shit, I hope that—"

"I'm making perfect sense!"

"Okay."

"What do you want from me?" I say.

"To save you and—"

"You students always want something. You never come without ulterior motives. Never once in my entire tenure of teaching did I encounter an altruistic student. Students by their very nature are designed to take and take before they disappear, never to be heard from again, unless they need something—like a letter of recommendation, or some sort of free advice, or a shoulder to cry on. So what do *you* need? Tell me, because I'm very busy trying to drink and smoke myself to death at the present moment, if you haven't noticed. So let's get this over with."

Portia looks at her hands. When I subtract a few wrinkles and poof up her bangs, I remember a sweet girl who hung on my every word and used up every free minute of every single one of my prep periods. She was so wounded—father issues, if I remember correctly. Used to drop by my apartment uninvited too, now that I think about it. Was there something about a pregnancy scare? Young foolish heart-on-his-sleeve I-will-make-a-difference me gave her free therapy, allowed her to squeeze me like a sponge, all the emotional energy I had to give for an entire year, before she graduated and vanished without so much as a good-bye, let alone a thank-you.

"What do you want?" I say with a little less cynicism, because she looks sad now, and I am tired—too exhausted to fight.

"You were the best teacher I ever had," she says.

"Okay," I say. "But I'm not a teacher anymore. Did you not hear about my last day in the classroom? It made the news—pretty much every market."

"I'm sorry that happened to you," she says.

"Yeah, well. I got this very fashionable cane out of the deal." I reach down to pick it up. "See? Top quality. Makes me look almost old money—and on a teacher's pension too."

She gives me a look like I just admitted to something heinous, like drop-kicking infants for fun. "My life didn't turn out the way I dreamed it would either. I've met some truly awful men in the last twenty years—was married to one, actually. But when I needed to believe there was better out there—at least one good man in the world—do you know who I thought about every single time?"

I have a strong feeling she is going to say me, which means she is delusional and maybe even psychotic, so I say, "How did you get my address?"

"I thought of you and your class," she says, quite passionately, completely ignoring my question.

"How did you find me?"

"Don't you even care about what I'm telling you? That your teaching had an impact that affected me for two decades, that forced me to seek you out twenty years after—"

"Sounds like you sought me out when it was convenient for you, because your marriage fell apart and you needed something to take your mind off your own problems. I have some experience with this—all veteran teachers do. Trust me. We exist as public servants who are expected to uphold the morals of an entire community and drop everything just as soon as anyone has a problem."

"I'm not doing this for me," she says. To her credit, she does a good job of appearing to be completely astonished.

"Okay then. You *really* want to help me? This is about *me* for a change? I get to be on the other side of the teacher-student relationship? Are you sure?" I stretch and yawn here, because I'm exhausted.

"Absolutely," she says, clearly choosing to ignore my indifference. "I owe you a gigantic debt of gratitude."

"Then help me kill myself. I entered into a suicide pact with my dog, Albert Camus. He kept his end of the bargain two days ago by jumping out of my bedroom window. In a dream last night he said you'd come to help me. I want to be Zagreus—the cripple from Camus's *A Happy Death*. You can be a female Patrice Mersault. Patricia Mersault, maybe. Kill me, and you can have my house and all of my money. We can draw up a will, even. You can sell this dumpy place, which has appreciated remarkably since the local skiing mountain has expanded, and you can buy a beautiful house on the beach and begin your search for happiness and meaning, completely free of responsibility for the rest of your life."

"You need to teach again."

"You can't be serious."

"You have a gift, Mr. Vernon."

"I most certainly do not, and more importantly, I no longer even care."

"There are kids who need you. Troubled kids who need to believe in good men and hope."

"Look at me—take a long hard look." I wait for her to take in my disheveled, puke-covered, and still legally intoxicated appearance. I haven't shaved in days. I must look and smell like a homeless person babbling nonsense on the side of a highway on-ramp. "I am not a good man, Ms. Portia Kane. My dog committed suicide, most likely because I blathered on and on at him night and day, spilling the poison of my brain indiscriminately. And I am done giving. I have nothing left."

"You are a *good* man," she says quietly.

"How would you know that, when we haven't even spoken in decades? Tell me. Please."

"I remember your classes and all of the time you gave me during my senior year when I was going through a really—"

"That was twenty years ago. Are you the same person now? Has time not changed you? You've romanticized your high school experience—and me. Whatever horrors you've faced in the last two decades are easily trumped by imagination and—Why am I even having this conversation with you?"

"Because you care."

"I absolutely do not, Portia Kane. Maybe I did once, when I made you this card." I glance down at the face of eighteen-year-old Portia Kane, and my heart softens for a second. I vaguely remember now a Christmas Eve when she showed up uninvited at my apartment and spent an hour or so sobbing in my arms, and we somehow ended up listening to Frank Sinatra holiday songs on AM radio as we sipped nonalcoholic eggnog and watched snow fall from the tenth-floor apartment window. Did she call me the father she never had? And do I remember thinking she was entirely unstable but in great need of kindness? I hand the card back to her. "When you are beaten almost to death for caring about young people, it takes a rather hefty toll."

"That's why I'm here," she says. "That's what this is about!"

"I'm afraid you may be a bit too late. I'm sorry. I don't know what sort of fantastical idea made you go digging through your memories to find me, but—"

"You would have choked to death on your own vomit if I hadn't—"

"I *wanted* to choke to death on my own vomit!"

Her mouth is open, her eyes well up, and then she is in my kitchen washing dishes.

This is the absurd, I say to Albert Camus in my mind as I sip my stronger-than-I-like coffee. *My suicide attempt results in being stuck in my own home with a former student who wants me to teach again. This is any retired teacher's hell. It's like that Stephen King novel. My own personal version of* Misery.

My dehydrated brain begins to throb, and so I just sit on my couch, staring through the windows at the distant mountains.

But then my own stench overpowers me, so I shower and change my clothes before resuming my sulking on the couch, now wrapped in a fleece blanket.

I sit in silent protest.

Portia Kane begins to clean the rest of my home once she is done with the kitchen. She's found my cleaning supplies, and she scrubs and wipes and vacuums and mops for hours as I sit and stare, completely dazed and apathetic and resigned as Gregor Samsa. Turn me into a cockroach, and I wouldn't even blink. At one point she even goes outside with pots of boiling water and washes my vomit off the deck.

"Cleaned up all the shit on the floor," Portia Kane yells down from the loft above.

"That was Albert Camus's excrement, not mine," I yell back.

"He jumped from this window in the bedroom?" she yells down. "Why was the window open?"

"He was jumping and scratching at it in the middle of the night, which was unusual. I wanted to see what was out there, so I opened the window."

There is a long pause.

She yells down, "Why didn't you stop him from jumping?"

"He was very fast about it. I tried. Don't you think I tried?"

"That must have been horrible. I'm so sorry."

"You have no idea."

When Portia Kane finishes cleaning my entire house, it's midafternoon, and I am still on the couch, staring at the distant mountains.

She brings me a sandwich—turkey and American cheese on marbled rye with pickles and lettuce.

"Enjoy," she says.

I take the plate. "You cleaned my house because you aren't allowed to clean your mother's, am I right? The hoarder. You clean when you want to feel in control. So don't say you did this for me."

"Eat your fucking sandwich," she says, and then leaves my house.

After a few minutes I cane my way to the window and confirm that her car is still in my driveway. She must have gone for a walk wearing only her jean jacket, which is entirely inadequate for this kind of cold.

When the sun begins to set, I open a bottle of wine and pour a glass, but after my two-day drinking binge, I just don't have the stomach to take a single sip.

Portia Kane returns shortly after dark looking a bit pink and sweaty, picks up the full wineglass, downs it, refills, carries the fresh pour into the kitchen, and begins making dinner.

"Did you walk down to the lake?" I ask. "Albert Camus loved the lake. Although we had a hard time doing that in winter. Cane and a dog leash are a tough marriage in snow."

She doesn't answer but prepares asparagus, snapping off the ends and then coating them with olive oil, salt, and pepper before popping them into the oven.

From the dining room table I watch her bring water to a boil, dump in wheat pasta, and heat a small pot of red sauce over a low gas flame.

"I can't remember the last time someone prepared me a home-cooked meal," I say as she sets the table.

She doesn't respond, but pours herself another glass of red.

When the meal is ready, we eat in silence.

I can tell that Portia Kane is very upset with me, but what can I do about that? How could I begin to fight twenty years' worth of mythmaking and romanticizing the past? Even if I wanted to—which I don't—I could never live up to her expectations for me now. I start to pity her. To think, this is all because of those stupid little cards I used to give my seniors at the end of the year.

Official Member of the Human Race.

Ha! A lot of good that ever did any of us. Why does she even still have hers? She must be a hoarder like her mother.

As Portia Kane clears the table, I find myself saying, "The kid who knocked me out of the teaching racket—Edmond Atherton was his name—they let him out of the nut house last year. I hear he attends college now in California. Received a letter from an old teaching buddy. Mr. Davidson, if you remember him. Maybe Edmond Atherton will go on to lead a fulfilling and productive life. Isn't that nice?"

No response.

Portia Kane cleans my dishes by hand, even though I have a dishwasher.

"You're not going to leave, are you?" I say.

"I made a promise to your mother."

"My *mother*?" I squint at her. I haven't spoken with my dreaded mother in years. This is getting seriously weird. "How do you know her?"

"We met on a plane just almost a month ago."

"What?"

"A bit of a coincidence, although she'd call it divine intervention. I prefer coincidence, because I'm not really sure whether I believe in God. Full disclosure—I was drunk at the time, so I don't remember much about our initial talk. But she gave me her address, and we began corresponding. I sent her my contact info in a letter, and then she called my cell phone out of the blue and I began to visit her. We talked. She confided in me. And I eventually ended up making her a promise that I intend to keep."

"What did you promise her?"

"That I would save you."

As I sit at the table, Portia Kane dries my dishes.

Could this day get any more ridiculous? She's clearly insane, I say to Albert Camus in my mind, and then I chuckle like hell.

"What are you laughing at?" Portia Kane says.

"Everything," I say. "And I can't wait to see how you 'save me.' Do you even have a plan? Did Mother send you up here with some sort of Catholic idol, rosary beads, and a bunch of prayer cards? Maybe a flask of holy water? A swath of some saint's jockstrap? Did she tell you about her 'visions'? What a crock of shit. All of her religious mumbo-jumbo hasn't made a bit of difference in my life, or anyone else's so far. But what the hell? How *is* my dear old mother anyway, the righteous, self-indulgent ancient bitch?"

"She's dead. I attended her funeral yesterday."

CHAPTER 11

"My mother. She's really dead? *Dead* dead? You're serious about this?"

She nods solemnly. "I'm sorry."

"Why didn't anyone contact me?"

Portia tosses down the dish towel and tries to soften her face, but this just makes her look even angrier. "When's the last time you checked your PO box? Because it's full of letters from nuns—a few from your mother. She'd been working on your salvation for years—and not just your soul, but you here right now in this world too. Her words, not mine. We quickly found that we had a common goal: we both wanted to *resurrect* you."

It's been months since I've been to the post office. I prepay my bills for electricity and water six months in advance, I pay my yearly property taxes in full down at the town hall every February, my retirement checks are direct deposit. I do all my banking in person, I own no credit cards, and everyone else who does odd jobs for me—like the plow guy and handyman—I pay in cash. I have to admit, I'm curious now as to what the old lady wrote. I have a sudden desire to go to my PO box, a feeling I haven't felt in many months. I have so many questions now, and pressure is building in my throat. It feels maybe a little like regret, even though I didn't do anything wrong and was perfectly entitled to cut her out of my life after she laid that easy religious mumbo-jumbo on me when I needed her most—her, not some ideas about the origins of mankind and some fairy-tale benevolent spaceman controlling our destinies. Her earthly leader wears flamboyantly large hats and extorts money from the poor and uneducated while living in a palace, probably eating off plates made from gold, even though his own god said it was harder for a rich man to enter into heaven than for a camel to pass through the eye of a needle. But I digress.

"How did she die?" I ask.

Portia tells me and then adds, "It happened fast. She was planning on making a trip up here, but her doctors forbade her, and she simply didn't have the strength, so she wrote because there was no other way to contact you. She even overnighted the letters in the hopes of reaching you in time. And she wasn't sure you were still here, or else maybe she *would* have come looking for you. She tried to contact you—very hard. Finally, she 'gave you to God,' her exact words. Check your PO box. It's all there."

"Okay," I say, although I'm not sure why, because it's not okay in any sense of the word.

A wave of guilt overcomes me.

I don't feel like crying so much as vomiting, which is confusing, because maybe it means I am just still hung over.

"You're having a hell of a week," Portia says. "I'm sorry."

"Maybe you will find this a bit strange, but I'm not sure I can handle any more information," I say. "I just don't want to hear any more right now, okay? I'm sorry. But I need time to digest all of this, and . . ." I don't finish my sentence. I have no idea what else to say.

"I'll tell you anything you want to know whenever you're ready, but of course it doesn't have to be right now, if you're feeling overwhelmed. My showing up here like this and dropping the news on you—it would be a great shock for anyone under any circumstances. And we can start saving you in a few days. I've set some time aside for this."

"I don't need—," I say, but no more words follow, because I absolutely need some sort of help if I am to keep breathing and thinking and occupying space here on earth.

To her credit and my great surprise, Portia respects my request and doesn't push it, which makes her very unlike my deceased mother—and actually helps me to trust her a little.

Sitting on my couch, we both look out the window at the mountains in the distance and act like mountains ourselves—breathing stoically, silently.

Unmovable—if only for a time.

A *long* time, actually.

And I begin to respect Ms. Portia Kane's ability to just sit and be.

At first I'm mentally challenging her to beat me at this stillness, this passiveness, this giving up—and I'm looking forward to her failure. But somewhere along the line, I start to draw support from her, much like I did from Albert Camus, and if I am being honest, some part deep down inside me begins to worry that she will leave before I am ready to be alone, just like my best four-legged friend did—that no living thing is able to be around me in my present condition.

But of course we eventually get up off my couch and begin moving about again.

Albert Camus once wrote, "Nobody realizes that some people expend tremendous energy merely to be normal." And that is exactly what Portia Kane and I do for a few days as we take walks together, share meals, wash and dry dishes, stare at sunsets, and avoid speaking about anything of consequence whatsoever. We rely on politeness, common courtesy, to get us through the hours. It's almost like we are playing estranged father and daughter who are suddenly forced to spend awkward time together in the Green Mountains of Vermont—although neither of us would put it that way.

I think I am mourning my mother, but I can't be sure.

I'm definitely mourning Albert Camus, who was much more in tune with my emotions and feelings than my mother ever was. My dog was there for me, and even though he might have committed suicide to escape my existential crisis, he loved the real true me in his own way.

I'm not quite sure what I am doing allowing this former student to sleep on my couch and live in my house.

In no way whatsoever does it seem smart.

I sometimes think maybe she's just as sick as Edmond Atherton, but masking it to heighten her inevitable betrayal; she will kill me in my sleep and end all of this thinking I am doing—take the first question off the table permanently.

But after a few days it becomes clear that this woman is pure of heart, and her intentions—albeit delusional and wildly misguided—are driven by a need to make things right, if only in some simple-minded way. It's obvious that she has been deeply wounded, broken by life, and is now attempting to live by a code. And there are moments I find myself thinking back to when she was in my class, remembering snippets of why I spent so much time with her when she was eighteen, maybe because she showed promise simply as a human being. She had the altruistic heart of a dreamer and un-checked ideal notions about the world—the perfect fool, smiling up at the sky with one foot already over the edge of the precipice. For some reason the dreaded word *extraordinary* keeps popping up in my mind, and I try to kill it every time, even though a former student showing up at my exact moment of need—just in time to save my life, actually—is indeed out of the ordinary.

Could she be Edmond Atherton's antithesis?

The universe evening things out?

Some sort of cosmic order?

Or maybe Portia and I are each silently daring the other to speak first, to open up, to be prematurely vulnerable so that the other can strike first, wound deeply, and win.

Regardless, I don't ask questions and she doesn't offer answers.

We just politely exist together for a time, in a heavy silence that sometimes feels like being buried alive under twenty feet of snow—a foot or so for every year since we last danced this number. It's as if we're in a hollowed-out snow cave heated by the flame of a single candle, and we're wondering if some emotional rescue team will ever arrive with the metaphorical equivalent of Saint Bernards wearing small barrels of brandy around their necks, and yet we have no way of knowing for certain if anyone even knows we are still alive. I come to appreciate this trapped, helpless, loss-of-control give-up-to-inevitability feeling more than I thought was ever possible.

It's almost liberating, to the point where I no longer even want to be rescued.

One morning, as we bundle up—I offer her an old down vest that's too big for her, but she wears it anyway over her jean jacket—and walk the quarter-mile dirt road together to the frozen pond, I wonder if she might be a quasi reincarnation of Albert Camus, or maybe his ghost taking on a womanly form, because she leads me there just like my little dog did, forcing me to cane my way a bit more quickly than usual—always pushing me to be more mobile and cheery than I thought possible.

But just when I'm about to buy into the fantasy, my sanity points out the fact that she has a rental car with New Jersey plates and I've touched her hand on several occasions when she's handed me dishes to dry, so she is not ethereal.

She also consumes food and much wine, so I know she is no ghost.

As we're sitting on my deck one night, bundled up in hats, gloves, and quilts, drinking said wine, I say, "Okay, tell me the story of how you came to know my mother."

She keeps her gaze on the many stars above, rocking back and forth on the old wooden Mission rocking chair I purchased at a flea market in town. "You're ready to talk about this? Are you sure?"

"I am."

"Okay, then."

My former student goes on to tell me the most unbelievable and frustrating story I have ever heard, one that makes me never want to read the letters my mother allegedly sent to my PO box. Wild coincidences. Mystical forces. The Virgin Mary supposedly appearing on an office-building window in Tampa Bay.

She even uses the word *miracles*!

It's absolutely laughable, even for my mother, until my former student gets to the end where the old woman dies, which unfortunately is the most realistic part, and I'm pretty sure Portia Kane doesn't believe half of what she's told me because she keeps saying, "I know it sounds crazy, *but* . . ." and "I don't even believe in God, and yet . . . ," chopping her thigh with her right mitten as her wine sloshes around in her glass.

"Why didn't my mother ask her almighty and powerful God to save her life when she found out she was sick?" I say. "Did she ever think of that?"

"She asked him to save you instead."

"I see." It feels chilly to be on the other side of Mom's religious delusions. She always used to say it was me who was to do the saving, with my teaching. What a laugh!

"She absolutely thought that her death was part of her god's plan," Portia says. "I'm not saying *I believe* it is all part of any god's plan, but you have to admit, it's a strange coincidence at the very least. Your mother believed that this was all meant to be. And I *did* save you from choking to death. That is a fact we can both agree on, right? That I arrived at precisely the right moment. Just a mere five minutes later, and we might not be having this discussion. What we do with that information is still up for debate in my mind. But here I am regardless. And here you are too. Together. Despite the odds."

Portia seems to be taking a rather objective view of my mother's madness, and I must say that I'm impressed by her ability to consider both Mom's religious nonsense and my current and preposterous lot in life—and also the link that we have now formed, Portia and me, whatever is going on here, right now. She seems to be absorbing all of it in stride, without getting emotional.

I think about Portia Kane showing up after twenty years simply to turn me over just before I choke to death on my own vomit. How it's undeniably true that I might very well be dead if she hadn't met my mother on a plane, been given my Vermont address, and been convinced to drive eight hours north to "save" her former high school English teacher, who she had mistakenly put up on a pedestal to represent the goodness of all men.

Absurd.

These are the uneducated thoughts of wacko mystics, the mind tricks of charlatans eager to control and separate the masses from their wallets, not the sort of stuff you should allow into your thought process about anything, let alone the first question.

Albert Camus would want me to answer the first question with reason and objectivity, not superstition and convenient religious mysticism.

"You know what my mother said to me when I was in the hospital, after one of my very own students beat me to within an inch of death with a baseball bat? When I looked up at her, frightened and desperate and wounded and with nothing left to give whatsoever, let alone anything left to defend myself with, not even dignity? Do you know what she said?" I ask Portia, who is now sitting comfortably with her legs up on the arm of my couch, back inside my house. "She said my attack must have taken place for a reason. Can you believe that? Isn't that sick? Isn't that just cruel? Can you imagine saying that to someone who has experienced such brutality? That the actions of a sick mind are actually part of some divine plan for the universe—that Edmond Atherton's mental illness was an intentional part of some god figure's plan. That god said, *Hey, wouldn't it be a good idea to scramble some teenager's thoughts to the point where he is willing and able to commit a chilling act of violence so that it will begin an otherwise impossible chain of events? Because it would be far too easy just to communicate directly with mortals. I am all-powerful, capable of doing whatever I want, so let's make this into a bit of a challenge. Just for fun, or maybe a laugh.* Is that not ridiculous at best and abusive at worst? It would make God either the laziest being in the universe or the most sadistic."

Portia offers no rebuttal, but stares at the snowy mountains in the distance.

"Can you imagine? Your very own mother says this to you at your absolute lowest point. That her god meant for you to be beaten with a baseball bat? That it was an intentional part of something larger? That's exactly when I cut Mother out of my life. Her Jesus talk crossed the line that day. Went from ridiculous to dangerous. I don't trust religious people. Period. Don't want them around me."

"Listen," she says. "I'm not a religious person. I'm really not."

"What's that crucifix hanging around your neck, then?" I point to a medieval-looking cross I haven't noticed before, maybe because I was drunk and then hung over.

"Your mother gave it to me. It was a parting gift. It looks sort of metal, and well, I grew very fond of your mother, truth be told."

"Metal?"

"Heavy metal. I'm a metalhead." She raises a fist, only the pinkie and index fingers are extended like bullhorns. "Heavy metal, religion—just two different shows really. You'd be surprised how much they overlap. High dramatics. Cultlike followings, cool pendants, mystical, esoteric, and often nonsensical prose, men with long flowing hair—"

"I want to be Zagreus again. Kill me, please."

"Okay, I've been here for almost a week now, and I need to say this: Would you stop being such a pussy?"

I'm stunned by her use of that word.

I didn't think women used that word—*ever*.

"As hard as this may be to believe, I vowed to save you before I even started writing your mother," she says, "before I knew she even *was* your mother—and since I too don't believe in God or mystical forces, this isn't exactly easy for me either. I can't explain how I ended up here to save your life, but I did, and here I am. We don't have to understand what led to this very moment, but I suggest we use it to do something positive. Don't you remember that paper airplane lesson you used to give on the first day of school? How you demonstrated the power of positive thinking and resisting Pavlovian impulses? Have your responses become conditioned for the worse? Are you going to piss on everything even before you know whether it's good or bad for you? Eternally raise the middle finger high in the air just because a few things haven't gone your way?"

I'm surprised she remembers that paper airplane lesson I used to give; I'd almost forgotten about it myself. I stopped giving it long before Edmond Atherton ended my career, mostly because it seemed sort of hokey after so many years of doing it, and also administration didn't like me encouraging kids to throw anything out of the windows. I had been sternly warned on several occasions. Other teachers complained that I was interrupting their classes—that their students were distracted by my class moving through the hallways, and also by all of the airplanes flying in plain sight past the first-floor classrooms' windows. I endured a lot of bitching about that little lesson over the years, and eventually it was just easier to hand out a syllabus on the first day of school and act like all of the other resigned and apathetic veterans—much easier, actually. Pragmatism won out in the end.

I'm a little touched that Portia remembers that paper airplane–throwing business, which I once considered one of my best lessons. And yet there is still enough piss and vinegar in me to say, "I was beaten with a baseball bat in front of my students. My dog has committed suicide. And now I'm being haunted by the misinformed and untested optimism of my youth in the form of a delusional former student who can't even take care of her own problems, let alone mine."

"*You* are my problem now!" Portia says, and I notice that her eyelids are quivering. "I'm not leaving until we solve *you*. Like in those old kung fu movies—I saved your life, and now I'm responsible for it."

"Kung fu movies? Why do you want to solve me all of a sudden, when you were happy to leave me undisturbed for two entire decades? Why *now*?"

"Remember when you asked for volunteers to go down to the soup kitchen in Philly and read books to the kids in the day care there? More than half the class signed up because they were inspired by *you*."

I sigh. "If your life was happy and fulfilling, you wouldn't be here right now, would you? Don't you see the irony of what you're saying? You were my student, you believed what I told you, and it led you where?"

"Here! Remarkably, I'm right here with you *right fucking now*—even though you're being impossible."

"You are here because you want me to be something I'm not."

"You've just forgotten who you are."

"Enough semantics," I say. "I've given you my proposition. We reenact Camus's *A Happy Death*, with me playing Zagreus the old cripple, done with life, and you playing Patricia Mersault, the hedonistic young person who kills the old for money and a chance to exist free and clear of the average working person's life. That's my solution. Now what's your counterproposition?"

A tear rolls down her flushed cheek, and that's when I know I am breaking her—that I am winning.

"I want to bring you back to life—make you flesh and blood again."

"That sounds a lot like Mom's religious hocus-pocus crap."

"You used to be so alive! And now you're a ghost. Living like you're already dead."

"I want to be dead!"

"No, you don't," she says, shaking her head.

"How would you even know? You assume that you know the innermost workings of my mind when—"

"If you wanted to be dead, you would be already. You want to sulk at the end of the world all by yourself. That's really what you want. It's pathetic!"

"I just lacked the motive that I've recently found. I will be dead soon, don't you worry! With your help or without it!"

"I want to motivate you back into the classroom."

"Never going to happen. Not in a million years. I'm done."

She's shaking her head defiantly and crying a little more forcefully, almost like she doesn't even care that she's crying anymore. "It *will* happen."

"How can you be so sure?" I say, smiling, because she has lost before she's even begun.

"Because I know you. And you've become unacquainted with yourself."

I stand and cane my way out onto the deck, allowing the crisp cold air to bite my skin. Portia follows and stands next to me. "I can assure you, Ms. Kane. You do *not* know me. Trust me on this. Students never really know their teachers. It's all a bit of a show, and you are familiar with the show I used to put on twenty-some years ago, for a paycheck, health insurance, and a meager pension. I no longer play that role. I am no longer a public servant. Haven't been one for some time now. Threw out the required mask many years ago."

"Your mother believed in you. She saw what I saw."

"My mother was batshit insane. More than me, she loved a fictional father figure who lived somewhere at the end of the universe, who sat on a golden throne in a cloud land. She heard voices. Had visions. Probably should have been living in a mental institution for the past forty years or so."

"Do you really want to be left all alone here in the woods so that you can drink yourself to death? Is that what you *really* want?" Her face is now the color of a ripe Jersey tomato. "If you can look me in the eyes and say you wish to be left alone so you can kill yourself, I'll leave right now. But you have to have the balls to admit it openly and without looking away. I want to hear you say it without breaking eye contact."

I look directly into her eyes, which are quite red now in addition to being watery. "I'm sorry to disappoint you, Ms. Kane, but yes, I would like to die. I can no longer answer the first question, let alone inspire people like you. I've given all I can possibly give, and it didn't leave me in very good shape. I'm done living, so I am without question done teaching. If you will not help kill me, I suggest you leave and go do something more productive with your time. Go throw paper airplanes out of windows if it makes you feel nostalgic for your youth, but it was all just so much bullshit. Truly. I'm sorry."

Portia's crying even harder now, scrunching up her nose like a rabbit, although she's keeping her chin up—stiff upper lip.

"Okay." She goes inside, packs up her luggage, and then marches out the front door.

I have to admit that I'm pretty shocked by her leaving without putting up more of a fight. I think she's bluffing until I hear her rental car's engine come to life.

I quickly cane my way to the edge of the deck to watch her pass my wrecked truck and exit my driveway.

She steps on the gas, descends, and her back tires fire snow and stones up in her wake as she disappears behind the tree line at the end of my property, leaving me free to kill myself at will.

And then I'm alone again with my thoughts and the oppressive, relentless quiet.

Albert Camus? my mind calls, but of course there is no answer.

CHAPTER 12

I resume my death-by-cigarettes-and-wine plan and consume an entire bottle of pinot noir and the better portion of a pack of Parliament Lights within an hour.

As much as I try to forget about Portia Kane, I can't help but wonder what she would have done in her attempt to get me back into the classroom.

Would she take me to the top of the Empire State Building like we were some sort of platonic teacher-student version of Cary Grant and Deborah Kerr in *An Affair to Remember*, and have me throw a paper airplane through the chain-link fence to somehow symbolically erase all of the many unfair trials and tribulations of our lives?

Do they even have a chain-link fence at the top of that building?

Why would I even think of that building when I am here in Vermont?

I wonder what Portia Kane planned, and if there actually is anything I would like to do before I die. I decide I'd really like to learn how to blow smoke rings, because I have never done that before, never even tried, and yet it always looks so cool when actors in old-time movies do it.

That's my dying wish—to blow smoke rings.

Why not?

It's just as logical as meeting some fifteen-minute pop star or going to Disney World, when you really analyze the arbitrary and—let's just say it—silly nature of dying wishes.

As if getting to do one last thing can really make you feel less regretful about your existence coming to an end. It may make your loved ones feel better, but not you. And I no longer have loved ones.

Regardless, I take a large drag from the Parliament Light in my hand, make my lips into an O, open and close my jaw the way I've seen black-and-white movie stars do, push with the back of my tongue, and several perfect rings of smoke shoot out of my mouth.

At first, I'm amazed to have done it so easily.

Then I'm a little disappointed because it took so little effort that it hardly seems like an accomplishment at all.

What was the point?

And what is the point of sitting around drinking wine and smoking cigarettes now that I've decided that I am finished with this life?

Why prolong this?

I go up into my guest bedroom and pull out the old photo albums I've kept for some reason I cannot name, and I take in my mother's face before she became a nun, when it was just her and me, before she made Jesus her "husband."

Some instinctual core of me regrets not having the chance to say good-bye to the old woman, but I don't feel like crying or anything like that.

The photos I have are pretty typical mother-and-son shots, mostly snapped during birthday celebrations, Christmas and Easter dinners, vacations and the like. I'm sure you have all the very same photos, just with you and your own maternal figure inserted where my mother and I are in mine, so I won't bore you with the specifics.

I wonder if it's wrong to miss my dog much more than I miss my mother, and then I contemplate retrieving the letters from the PO box before I remember I have no working vehicle—my truck is still wrapped around the tree at the bottom of my driveway—and a limp that requires the use of a cane, which limits me to half-mile walks at one stretch on Vermont's seldom-flat roads. The post office is a good twelve or thirteen miles away, which means I will die without reading Mom's farewell to me.

Just as well, I think, as it was probably a guilt-inducing rant about my soul and ending up in hell if I fail to buy into what she bought into. I smile because I have already been to hell and survived, with the help of a little toy poodle who looked like Bob Ross. Or maybe hell is living on after your dog commits suicide.

"Pussy," Portia had called me.

Portia Kane's hardly a feminist, using that word.

But maybe I *have* been unmanly in my efforts to solve my problems. I feel my cheeks start to burn with some testosterone-fueled sense of self-worth or respectability, because killing myself is at least an action.

In the medicine cabinet I find an almost full bottle of aspirin, a bottle of NyQuil, an expired bottle of Percocet left over from my physical therapy days, some laxatives, a few antidiarrhea pills, and some Maalox.

In the kitchen, I dump all of the pills into a wineglass, pour the mysterious-looking green NyQuil over the multicolored fist-size ball of meds, and then retrieve a picture of my mother and one of Albert Camus from my bedroom.

He's sitting erect with his one eye sparkling, looking out over the pond at sunset. The water is aflame with twilight.

Mom is making homemade crust for her delicious rhubarb pie, leaning down on a wooden rolling pin, flour smudged across her left cheek and her still golden hair up in a loose bun.

Back in the kitchen, I place each picture on either side of my hopefully lethal cocktail. "Albert Camus, a pact is a pact. Mother, this is to prove once and for all that your god is a fairy tale; you were wrong."

I lift the glass to my lips, intending to down the entire contents as quickly as possible, hoping that many of the pills have already dissolved, not quite sure what the hell I am doing, wondering if I will even be able to get this green semi-liquid concoction down into my stomach with one tilt of the wrist and then quell the gag reflex long enough to keep it there—but just before the rim touches my lips, the kitchen door flies open with a bang and I drop the glass.

It topples over.

Goopy liquid and wet meds spill out across the table like a tiny forest-green tsunami full of pill-shaped debris.

Portia takes in the scene, examines the contents of my lethal cocktail. "What are you doing?"

"What are *you* doing?" I retort.

"You were really going to kill yourself? *Really?*"

"Have I not been clear on this point?"

She strides toward me, lifts her hand back behind her head, and smacks me hard enough to twist my head ninety degrees.

"Fuck you!" she screams.

I touch my cheek with my palm. "Ouch!"

She slaps my other cheek even harder.

"Why are you doing that?" I yell. "It hurts! Please stop hitting me!"

"FUCK YOU!" she screeches even louder. "FUCK YOU! FUCK YOU! FUCK YOU! FUCK YOU! FUCK YOU! FUCK YOU! FUCK!!! . . . YOU!!!"

Then she starts smacking my face with both hands at the same time, screaming, "You liar! You told us to be positive! I believed you! I trusted you! FUCK YOU, you have a responsibility to your students! FUCK YOU, you have a responsibility to yourself!"

"Why?" I yell. "Why? If you can tell me, I'd be most grateful. I was just a high school English teacher. No one cared! *No one at all!* The world does not give a flying hoot about high school English teachers! Why do I have a responsibility to anyone? What responsibility do I have?"

"To be a good man! Because you changed the lives of many kids. Because we believed in you!"

"Bullshit," I say. "I introduced you and others to the classics and helped you get into college. Handed out a few pointers about life— platitudes mostly, which you could have easily discovered by opening up Hallmark cards. And then all of you went your merry little ways and forgot all—"

"We didn't forget! *I'm here!*"

"My mother guilted you into this, and—"

"You believed in what you taught us! That's what made you different. I know you did. *You believed!*" She punches my chest hard enough to make me cough. "You can't fake belief. Not in front of teenagers, you can't!"

"Stop hitting me!" I yell.

She punches me again. "Fraud!"

"What?"

"Drinking NyQuil and pills just because life got a little hard. You're nothing but a *coward*!"

"You're being abusive and downright insensitive."

"You're being a *pussy*!" she yells back, and then she hits me a dozen or so times until it feels like my face is going to bleed and my ears start to ring.

I start flashing back to the day of Edmond Atherton's attack— experiencing it all again, my body flooding with anxiety, the sound of the aluminum bat breaking my bones, shattering my elbows and kneecaps like dinner plates, the hate in Edmond's eyes—until I break down and start to weep and beg. "Please! Stop hitting me! Please! Just stop! I can't take this happening again!"

I reach out to grab her like a hockey player trying to end a losing fight, and the next thing I know we're both on the floor crying and our arms are around each other and she's saying, "You can't kill yourself because you'll kill the best part of me," which is a hell of a thing to say, and I'm saying, "Thank you," over and over just because she's stopped hitting me.

After we finish crying, we eventually stand and clean up the wine and pills together silently and then retire to my living room again, where we sit on the couch.

"I feel as though I should be calling someone," Portia says, "because you are clearly a threat to yourself."

"Maybe I should call the police and file assault charges, because you just broke into my home and beat the hell out of me."

"Did you stop making Official Member of the Human Race Cards before the attack?"

"What? Why do you want to know that?"

"Just tell me."

"I stopped in the late nineties, actually. It felt like a waste of time. I used to spend *days* making those cards, and half of them ended up on the floors just as soon as the bell rang. The last year I had enough energy for Official Member cards, I saw several students throw theirs directly into the wastebin on the way out of my classroom. They disposed of them right in front of my eyes! If they had spit in my face, I wouldn't have felt as crestfallen."

"Do you remember Chuck Bass?" she says, undaunted. "Class of 'eighty-eight?"

"How am I supposed to remember a name from two and a half decades ago when I taught *thousands* of—"

"He still carries his Official Member of the Human Race Card in his wallet. He graduated before I did, and he *still* reads the card daily. Every single day of the year he reads your words. Your efforts, your message—it's gotten him through a lot. He hopes to tell you about it himself someday."

I find that hard to believe—anyone reading that stupid card on a daily basis—but I must admit that it gives me a little thrill, arouses something deep within.

"Okay," I say. "Sure, I'm glad that those cards helped a few people, but it takes a lot of energy to maintain a belief in—Why am I even trying to explain this to you? I should be dead by now."

"And yet you're not."

"I am not dead. Correct."

"Will you give me a chance to revive your spirit? Get you believing again?"

Her eyes are wide and hopeful enough to make me feel sorry for her.

I do not want to tell this little girl that there is no Santa Claus. Who would?

"I promised your mother," she says. "And I intend to make good on that promise."

"Then why did you leave earlier?"

"Because you were being an absolute bastard."

"Why did you come back?"

"You've been good to me more times than you've been a bastard. You're still in the plus column."

Goddamn, she looks so hopeful, it's killing me. "What do you propose, Ms. Kane?"

"Leave this place with me for a few days—just a few days. Allow me to take you on an adventure."

"Will we be hunting for pirate treasure?"

"No, we'll be hunting for you. The *old* you."

"What do you have in mind?"

"It's a surprise. You were just about to kill yourself. You have nothing to lose whatsoever! So why don't we hit the road like Sal Paradise and Dean Moriarty? We can be fabulous Roman candles exploding like spiders across the sky!" she says, paraphrasing the naively enthusiastic Jack Kerouac poster I had hanging on my classroom wall back when she was a student, back when I myself was wildly naive. I resist the urge to tell her that Kerouac drank himself to death.

"Is your mother still alive?" I ask.

"Yes. Why?"

"I bet she's still hoarding, right? Why don't you go save her instead? Keep all of this happy namby-pamby business in the family?"

"Because she isn't able to do what you can in the classroom. And not everyone can be saved."

I laugh. "Ms. Kane, you sure know how to romanticize the past."

"If you give me three days—just seventy-two hours—and at the end of it, you still don't want to teach again, I'll leave you alone forever."

"If I give you but three little days, you'll leave me the hell alone afterward? I'll be able to kill myself in peace? No more interruptions? You promise?"

She nods.

"And you aren't going to drive me to some psych ward and lock me away, right? Tell them I'm a threat to myself and throw away the key? I don't want to end up in a straightjacket drugged out of my mind, foaming at the mouth like a rabid dog."

"Paranoid much?"

"Your showing up like this is enough to make anyone paranoid!"

"I swear I will not take you to a psych ward. I don't even know where the psych ward is! Swear," she says, drawing an X on her chest with her index finger.

It's strange that I'm actually considering going—but maybe I'm just embracing the absurd. Why the hell not, at this point?

"If I agree, will you promise not to hit me again and refrain from calling me 'a pussy'?" I say, making air quotes with my middle and index fingers.

"If that's what it takes."

"Where are you going to take me?"

"You'll see," she says, smiling now, as if all that has transpired so far is part of some elaborate plan, like she's been in complete control from the very beginning.

I fear I might be caught in her web, that Portia Kane is a hungry spider toying with my emotions.

But then somehow it's settled.

CHAPTER 13

As Portia loads my duffel bag into the back of her rented car, I get an up-close look at her suitcases for the first time and see that they're designer, just like the clothes that she wears—except the retro jean jacket—and I begin to understand that this woman has the funds and the means to take me anywhere, which is not exactly a pleasant feeling. I get into the passenger side and rest my cane between my legs.

She starts the car. "Put on your seat belt."

"You're joking, right, Mom?" I say, staring at my ruined truck, which is still embedded in the tree.

She sighs. "The car will make an annoying beeping noise, and I could get pulled over by a cop if you don't buckle up."

When the car starts to beep, she points to a little flashing yellow light on the dash that depicts a man properly strapped into a car seat, which is indeed annoying, so I return her sigh and buckle up. "I'm old enough to remember when no one wore seat belts."

"Okay, Grandpa," she says, and then smiles.

"Getting cocky, are you?" I say as we navigate the dirt roads through the long piles of snow pushed to the sides by plows. "Where are we headed?"

"You'll see," she says, smiling again.

And then she drives in silence for a long time on the highway, headed south, following the dashes, becoming part of the blur of vehicles doing sixty to eighty miles an hour, like so many drops of blood flowing through a countrywide system of arteries.

Are we any different than the molecules that make up our bodies, I think, or are we just the molecules that make up something larger that we can't even fathom?

"What are you thinking about, Mr. Vernon?" she asks.

"Can I smoke in here?"

"No."

"You're a prison warden!"

And then we drive on for hours.

At one point she asks if I want to listen to music and what kind. I tell her, "Classical, please," and she searches until she finds a station that's playing Tchaikovsky, Piano Concerto no. 1 in B-flat Minor, op. 23.

"Is this good?" she says.

"It's divine." I remember listening to this very composition many times with Albert Camus curled up on my lap. He'd beat out the dramatic and wonderful piano notes with his little tail.

I lose myself in the music, and as the road dashes dance with the notes, I wonder if I could be dead. Could I have already killed myself, and might this be some sort of existential purgatory?

Massachusetts zooms by uneventfully, and then we are in Hartford, Connecticut, turning off the highway and entering what appears to be a financially challenged neighborhood.

"Where are we going?" I ask.

Portia smiles coyly.

But I see a sign for the Mark Twain house, and suddenly I know exactly where we are headed.

From taking my class, she must remember that I am a huge fan of Mr. Clemens's work. While I've never visited his home in Hartford, it's going to take a lot more than this to help me answer the first question, and so I'm afraid Ms. Kane has underestimated her sizable task.

"You do know that Mark Twain was an extremely ornery man," I say, "especially at the end of his life. If you read *No. 44, the Mysterious Stranger*, you'll see that ultimately Twain was not very optimistic. Vonnegut loved Twain, and he tried to kill himself. Are you sure this is a good idea?"

Portia ignores my comments as she pulls into the parking lot and shifts into park. "In your classroom you used to have a poster of Mark Twain and his quote: 'Keep away from people who try to belittle your ambitions. Small people always do that, but the really great make you feel that you, too, can become great.' Do you remember?"

I do remember, but instead of acknowledging that, I say, "Well, then, maybe you should keep away from me."

"Come on," she says and gets out of the car.

I follow and cane my way to the Twain house, which is brick, quite large, beautiful, and mysterious-looking.

Inside, Ms. Kane buys us tour tickets and we join a small group led by an almost oppressively eager young man who—to be fair—really does know a lot about Mark Twain, although he has an unfortunate love for posing unanswerable questions like, "If you were Mark Twain, living here back in 1885, what would you hope to have seen when you looked out this window?"

Our peppy guide leads us through various rooms as he discusses the "happiest time" in Mark Twain's life, showing us his telephone even, one of the first in the world, the angels carved into his headboard, and his attic billiards room, where he shot pool and smoked cigars (always in moderation, Twain said, "one at a time") and looked out from his lofty perch.

It's a little hard for me to do the steep stairs with my cane, but the tour is nice enough, and I think about how I haven't done anything like this in years—how once upon a time I would have been thrilled to be in Mark Twain's home.

Mark Twain!

The father of American literature!

And I would have schemed ways to get my students here too.

In the gift shop, Portia buys us matching little white pins with cartoons of Mark Twain's face in profile. She pins hers on her white jean jacket, adding to her collection of rock groups, Sylvia Plath, and my favorite, Kurt Vonnegut Jr.

I allow her to pin Mark Twain to my own jacket, right over my heart. "You know, Hemingway said that 'All American literature comes from—' "

" '—one book by Mark Twain called *Huckleberry Finn*. American writing comes from that. There was nothing before. There has been nothing as good since.' "

"You know that quote?"

"Learned it in your class," she says. "And it's on the T-shirt behind you."

I turn around and see that she's quite correct.

She says, "Your pin looks cool."

I look down at Mark Twain displayed on my chest like a military medal, and I have to admit the former English teacher hiding deep within does think it's "cool," but I don't tell Portia that because I don't want to let on that it was a pleasurable experience—and I sure as hell don't want to get her hopes up.

"I still have no desire to teach, let alone live," I say. "Nothing's changed."

"This is just day one," she says, far too cockily. "You ready to go?"

"Well, while we're here, we might as well see Harriet Beecher Stowe's house too, don't you think? It's right next door, after all."

"Isn't *Uncle Tom's Cabin* considered racist now?" she asks. "It's super uncool to call a black person an Uncle Tom. That's worse than the N-word, right?"

"I have no idea," I say as I cane my way toward the museum. But for some reason it's closed today, which disappoints me greatly, and so we get back in the car and continue driving south.

"Aren't you glad you didn't kill yourself yesterday?" she says to me.

"Because I got to see Mark Twain's home?" I say, thinking how silly that seems. How can seeing the home of one of your favorite authors help you answer the first question?

"No," she says, and then laughs mischievously. "Because now we're wearing matching Mark Twain buttons. That's pretty killer, right?"

It takes me a second to realize that she is serious—that she thinks wearing the same button is actually a significant gesture that implies or maybe even proves in her mind that we have made some sort of meaningful connection. This is the logic of an eleven-year-old girl—the equivalent of buying one of those cheap heart necklaces that breaks in two so that each friend can wear a jagged-edged half and yet the pieces can be put back together to form this phrase:

Best Friends Forever!

"I'm afraid it's going to take more than a button—albeit a 'cool' and 'killer' one—to save me, Ms. Kane. I wish it were that easy, but it's not."

"Okay," she says, but when I look over, she's smiling from ear to ear.

"You like that we are wearing matching pins—why does this mean something to you?"

"I don't know—you'll probably be mad at me if I tell you, anyway."

"Now you have to tell me!"

She pulls back onto I-84 South, speeds up, and says, "When I was in your class, I used to pretend you were my father, because I never had one—and if I got to pick, I would have wanted a father exactly like you. I used to fantasize about you taking me places like the Mark Twain House and teaching me about great writers, the way other fathers might teach their sons about baseball players at the ballpark. And now we've been to the home of a famous writer together. It's kind of like a childhood dream come true for me."

"So that little pit stop was for you and not me, Ms. Kane?"

"It was for *us*. Both of us."

"Why aren't you married?" I ask—out of the blue, I admit. "You are a smart, attractive woman. So why are you driving around with your fat old crippled former English teacher instead of doing something productive with an age-appropriate life partner? Why aren't you with a family of your own?"

"I *am* married—legally, anyway. To an asshole named Ken Humes. He cheated on me with a teenager. I caught him just a month ago. And this was after he treated me like shit for years, cheating on me many times, belittling my ambitions too. But catching him in the act, actually seeing him fuck a teenager, led to my getting on a plane home, which is where I met your mother, remember? Ken's moral low point started this whole chain of events."

I can hear the pain in her voice.

"Well, he's a fool to let you go," I say, almost reflexively, knowing that it's a mistake to offer her kindness. She will amplify it to mythical proportions until I can no longer possibly live up to her expectations, even if I try, which I am not about to.

"Was that a positive remark from Mr. Suicide? Mr. Gloom-and-Doom?" she says, beginning already with the amplification.

I do my best to redirect her emotions back to a safe place by saying, "Your husband let you down."

"He did."

"I'm sorry, Ms. Kane, but I will let you down too. It's inevitable. Fair warning."

"You may surprise yourself," she says in a way that depresses me. She's like a poor kid the night before her birthday who believes she will wake up to a surprise party and endless presents and a pony just because she's tried to wish these things into existence, and I'm the father who owes money to every bill collector in town and has no way of providing what his daughter needs, let alone what she wants—except that I am not even Portia's father but a man who was once paid to teach her how to write a five-paragraph essay and make sure she didn't graduate without knowing the difference between *then* and *than*—and let me tell you that an alarming amount of twelfth-grade students didn't know that difference when they first entered my room.

"Technically, you kidnapped me," I say after almost an hour of silent driving and thinking. "I'm not even here of my free will."

"What?" she says, snapping out of a daydream, oblivious. It would be disconcerting—she is behind the wheel of a car, after all—if I didn't wish to end my life.

"Nothing," I say, and we drive on south.

CHAPTER 14

"We're not going to the Empire State Building to throw airplanes off the top, are we?" I say, when it becomes apparent that we are heading into New York City. "Because I think that's illegal and dangerous."

"Now there's an idea!" she says.

"Why New York City?"

"We're going to have a Holden Caulfield day. Look for the ducks in Central Park, drink scotch and sodas in jazz bars, watch kids ride merry-go-rounds and reach for the gold ring—maybe even visit the museum and erase all of the Fuck You graffiti we can find."

"Are you serious?" I say, wondering how that would be beneficial for either of us.

"I'm joking, of course," she says. "Just a little American literature humor to get you back into the right head space."

"J. D. Salinger is always good for a laugh, right? What a role model for hope and living with open arms. I envy his solitude at this moment. You would have never even made it onto my property if I had a wall and maybe a moat. Did Salinger have a moat?" I sigh. "I wonder—in all that time alone—if he ever found an answer to the first question. Publishing became his boulder—like in Camus's *Myth of Sisyphus*."

"You have to stop obsessing about Camus. Jesus Christ."

It takes her a long time to navigate the traffic into Manhattan, but somehow she gets us to a hotel, and then she's handing the keys to a valet in a red monkey suit and men in green monkey suits are retrieving our luggage from the trunk.

Standing on a red carpet under heat lamps, leaning on my cane, I say, "I'm not sure I'm dressed appropriately for this sort of thing." I'm wearing jeans, a sweater with snowflakes stitched into it, a puffy ski jacket from the 1980s, a five- or six-day beard, and a black knit hat that makes me look like a cat burglar from the neck up.

Portia ignores me, and I follow her like a child to the front desk, where she refers to me as her father and checks us into a room.

In the elevator with us now there's a man in a blue monkey suit, whose job it is to push the proper button and carry our bags. I don't say anything. I've never before stayed in a fancy hotel like this, so I don't know the etiquette.

When we enter our "room," I see it's more like an apartment—two bedrooms, two bathrooms, a TV room, and even a formal dining room with a crystal chandelier, all of it overlooking Central Park.

The man in the monkey suit shows us how to turn on the lights and work the TV and close the curtains and offers suggestions for restaurants until Portia hands him some money and he leaves.

"You've done this before, I see," I say.

She smiles. "Surprised?"

"Who the hell is your husband, and what does he do?"

"What, you don't think a woman metalhead from the good ol' HTHS can earn her way up to this sort of lifestyle?"

"I didn't mean to imply that—"

"My soon-to-be-ex-husband made his millions in the pornography business, if you really must know. His is the misogynistic kind of porn, too. Made for misogynistic men. There's nothing even remotely artistic or empowering about his movies, at least from the feminist point of view. He's a producer-slash-owner. And he's sub-human, capable of turning 'the endless well of human lust into mountains of capital'—his words, not mine. Likes to use first-time college girls on spring break because they don't know how much they should get paid. Many of them will sign a legal document and appear on film for free drinks and a T-shirt. He also has a sex addiction problem. Ken'll stick his dick into anything blond with an IQ under seventy."

I don't know what to say to that.

"Anyway, he's a complete asshole, but he knows how to travel. I charged the room to his account here, the prick. So drink and eat as much as you want from the mini bar. Take a bathrobe, if you like. Trash the place. Smash the jumbo TV set with that expensive-looking floor vase over there, if you feel so inclined. Live it up like a rock star."

I raise my eyebrows ever so slightly in disapproval, or maybe pity.

She smiles at me, but it's a sad smile. "Why aren't you saying anything?"

"Um," I say, and suddenly I feel sorry for this woman who can stay in posh hotels because she married a pornographer. While I have nothing against what consenting adults do with each other behind closed doors, Portia's face tells me that her Ken is not a very nice pornographer. Maybe I should have taught more female authors when I was a teacher? Maybe I should have emphasized the importance of having one's own room, like Virginia Woolf suggested?

"Well, do you like the place?" she says, letting me off the hook.

"It's lovely."

"Hungry?"

I nod, and shortly after that we are eating room service— ginormous lobster salads, chilled sweet Riesling wine, and carrot cake for dessert—in our private dining room overlooking Central Park.

Portia seems tired from driving. She's not saying much, pushing the food around with her fork but not really eating either.

"I'm really starting to worry about you," I say, "which is strange, because it's you who's supposed to be saving me."

She looks up. "Why are you worried about *me*?"

"Because this trip is not going to end the way you hope it will. It's a really nice idea. Romantic, even, in a wonderfully platonic way. The former student returning after all these years to save the grizzled teacher who has suffered calamity and given up hope—it's poetic, but it's simply not real life."

"And yet here we are," she says, far too confidently.

"Look, I'm not going to pretend for you, so you can take all of my remaining strength and go on living your life believing in fairy tales. I won't lie. I don't wear a mask for people anymore—not even kids. I just can't."

"I don't want you to lie. I don't want to see a mask. I just want to awaken that part of you deep down that wants to be a good man again."

"What if the part of me that wants to be 'a good man,' as you say, truly is already dead? Hacked out of me like an appendix just before it erupted? What if it's simply gone?"

"It cannot die. It cannot be removed—because it's who you are—your fate," she says, as only a fool or a child could, and I start to worry even more, because she's talking nonsense now. Utter rot.

"My fate? You're starting to sound a lot like my delusional mother. Please don't start spouting her religious nonsense—"

"It's whatever I saw in you when I was in your class—the real true you," she says. "I don't know what to call it now. Maybe a spark."

"A spark? Of what?"

"I don't know. Just a beautiful spark."

"But a spark flickers for only a moment, and then it goes dark forevermore," I say. "By definition it cannot endure."

"Not the kind of spark we're talking about, and you know it. Those kinds of sparks set blazes that can be seen for miles and miles and provide warmth and beckon strangers to gather round and sing songs even and feel alive and dream under stars and become sparks for other people who will use the light to do great—"

"I'm sorry, Ms. Kane. I cannot follow this line of logic. I just can't—"

"The spark was there plainly manifested through the smile on your face when I pinned the Mark Twain button to your jacket, the little twinkle in your eye when—"

"Don't do this to yourself, Ms. Kane. Please."

She frowns, shakes her head, and then says, "Why did you agree to come with me?"

"So you would finally leave me alone. So I could get on with my suicide. No other reason," I say, and then add a quote for emphasis. " 'And in that patient truth which proceeds from star to star is established a freedom that releases us from ourselves and from others, as in that other patient truth which proceeds from death to death.' Albert Camus, from *A Happy Death*."

She squints at me for a few moments, looking like she just bit into a ripe lemon. "Oh, bullshit! Stop hiding behind the words of other men. And you can fuck Albert Camus in the ass with a crusty old baguette for all I care about him!"

"Excuse me?"

"Be a man! Stop hiding! I'm so tired of your constant Albert Camus quotes and references. Fuck him."

"But he's a Nobel Laureate!"

"Who cares?" She refills her glass and takes her wine into the sitting room.

Who cares about Albert Camus? Everyone with a working mind!

And yet I'm compelled to join her for some reason, to comfort her.

Damn you, teacher instincts, for you are a sickness never cured!

A few minutes later I find her slouched on the couch facing the grand windows, lined with heavy golden curtains.

Wineglass in hand, I sit at the other end of the Victorian-looking ornately carved twelve-foot cherry wood couch adorned with red silk cushions, which is not as comfortable as it is beautiful, and stare at the lit park through the window.

"You used to quote literature for good," she all but whispers, in this tiny voice.

"Albert Camus put good into the world. Like Thoreau, he inspires us to live an examined life and—"

"You twist his words in a cowardly way now, and it scares me."

"It ends in death for me. It ends in death for all of us—so why be afraid? And why put off the inevitable when the spark is gone?"

"Because if the world crushes my hero and reduces him to a weak man, then maybe there's no hope for me."

"I don't want to be your hero, Ms. Kane."

"You could have fooled the eighteen-year-old me," she says, and when I look over, I'm worried that she's going to start crying again.

"I was young and foolish back then," I say. "Maybe even younger than you are now. I had no idea what the hell I was doing, and I'm now very sorry I used to teach that way."

"You are not forgiven."

"Okay, then."

"It's not okay," she says, and glares at the window with a look of determination that I used to see in the mirror a long time ago.

When the silence becomes unbearable, I say, "Where are we going tomorrow?"

"Does it matter?"

She's staring even more fiercely at herself in the glass, or maybe only I can see her reflection from this angle. I feel myself wanting to comfort her—almost against my will—and so I say, "The Mark Twain button was the best present I have ever received from a student." When she doesn't answer, the wine and I stand and retire to my bedroom.

After I get ready for bed, I decide to crack my windows so I can hear the city.

The noise—traffic, wind, the bustling of a few million strangers—seems endless, and yet also ephemeral as my own heartbeat.

When I was a teenager, I dreamed of living in New York City. I fancied myself banging out a novel in some tiny one-room apartment in whichever of the five boroughs was the hip place for fiction writers to live at the time. Finding my own modern-day version of Max Perkins to edit my work, with whom I'd have three-martini lunches, talking endlessly about literature in general and the upward trajectory of my career with great specificity.

That dream was once so real I could touch it, if I only stretched out my arms far enough.

But I never reached with any effort, never even got a single short story into some semblance of a final draft form that I could submit with confidence, I think, as I lie in a king-size bed surrounded by furniture that I could never afford.

"I've been kidnapped by a former student," I say. Then, in spite of myself, I smile.

I drift off into a deeper sleep than I have known for months.

*   *   *

"Mr. Vernon, wake up. You have visitors," I hear. When I open my eyes, Portia is pulling back the curtains, letting in the early-morning sunlight with all its blinding intensity. She's barefoot, in a white and extremely fluffy bathrobe that reveals a small V of her chest.

I jump when I see three men in red monkey suits staring at me from the end of the bed, each with a portable table in front of him.

"What's going on?" I say, pulling the covers up to my chin.

"I didn't know what type of breakfast you took when you were visiting New York City, so I ordered you three kinds," Portia says, a look of utter delight on her face, gesturing with her hand like Vanna White. "Would you like the healthy breakfast?"

The first monkey suit lifts a silver half globe. "Steel-cut oatmeal, assorted berries, brown sugar, pineapple juice infused with wheat grass, a bran muffin, and green tea."

"A moderately unhealthy breakfast . . . ," Portia says.

The middle monkey suit lifts his silver lid. "Egg-white omelet with asparagus, turkey sausage, rye toast, grapefruit juice, and decaf coffee."

"Or death by breakfast," Portia says.

The third monkey suit lifts his silver half globe. "Eggs sunny side up, Angus steak cooked medium rare, fried potatoes, freshly squeezed orange juice, coffee, cream, sugar."

"Death by breakfast," I say. "Definitely death by breakfast."

"Very predictable, Mr. Vernon," Portia says, and then nods at the men. The first and second wheel their tables out of the bedroom as the third monkey suit places a fancy silver tray across my lap. It has legs, so it doesn't touch my thighs, but it's heavy enough that I feel the mattress sink where the four feet have been placed.

Without making eye contact, the monkey suit sets my personal table with silverware, a china plate full of wonderful-smelling food, a first-rate steak knife I think about stealing, and even a crystal vase with freshly cut roses. He pours my cup of coffee and then says, "Is everything to your satisfaction?"

"This is a dream, right?"

"Sir, we are very much conscious and here," he says. "May I do anything else for you, or shall I take my leave?"

"Is he real?" I ask Portia.

"Thank you very much," Portia says to the man. "That's all for now."

"Very well, Ms. Kane." He bows and takes his exit.

I cut into my steak, watch the juices pool across the plate, and say, "I have to admit, I like this part, Ms. Kane," before I fork a cube of meat into my mouth.

I close my eyes and savor it. This is the best steak I have ever eaten in my entire life—it explodes with bold, juicy flavor.

Portia sits down next to me on the bed as if we were a married couple. "Including the breakfast I already ate without you, Mr. Sleepyhead, and adding in the generous tip for all three men, we just spent seven hundred dollars of Ken's money."

I slice into my steak again. "This steak alone is worth seven hundred dollars."

"I hope you enjoy it," she says. "You need to fuel up, because we'll be doing a lot of walking today."

I focus on my food. It feels like I haven't eaten in days. I've missed food.

The roses in the vase smell wonderful too, and the satisfied look on Portia Kane's face is also a thing of beauty, I must confess. I begin to worry about disappointing her again when she fails to do what she's set out to do.

These temporary satisfactions—travel, gourmet food, even the praise of a former student—are novelties, no match for the eternal tides of my mind, which can wear down rock given enough time.

Portia's tricks are like the sand castles of children whose parents are smart enough to leave the beach before their efforts are inevitably destroyed and erased.

"You look happy," Portia says.

"Just chemical reactions—my tongue and stomach sending thank-you messages to my mind. Just the hardwiring of any man who ever lived."

"Breakfast in bed is nice."

"It's something."

"I'm glad to be here with you, Mr. Vernon."

"Don't get too attached," I say, and then attack my potatoes.

We gaze out the window at a beautiful winter's day in Central Park as I finish eating and drink my coffee.

"I wish Albert Camus were here," I say.

"Oh, fuck Albert Camus," Portia answers.

"Not the writer you wish to sodomize with a stale baguette," I say. "My dog, Albert Camus."

"Why did you name your dog Albert Camus?" she says, rolling her eyes.

"Maybe because I am a former teacher of literature—a man who forever monitored the great conversation and yet never added a line himself."

"What the hell do you mean by that?" she says.

"Nothing," I say, thinking I really do miss Albert Camus, wondering about what my mother's letters might say if I ever bother to retrieve them from my PO box, and sipping the best coffee ever to pass through my lips.

"Goddamn it, money is a wonderful thing," I say.

"I thought so too, for a while," she answers. "But the sad part is that you adjust quickly to it. I can't believe I'm going to say this, but like what happens to the protagonist in *A Happy Death*."

"So you've read it? Ms. Sodomize Camus with a Baguette has actually read his books?"

"I read everything by Camus in my early twenties—not just his novels, but his essays and plays too."

"You were assigned Camus in college?"

"I actually dropped out of college before I read much of anything. The pressure of maintaining the grade-point average my academic scholarship required led to a breakdown. There it is. The truth. No higher-education diploma for me."

"I'm sorry," I say, because she's obviously embarrassed and I don't know what else I can offer here.

"Anyway, I read Camus while I was waitressing. Mostly because the French Nobel laureate was greatly revered by my high school English teacher, who I admired even more. He gave us these cards on the last day of school that—"

"Okay, okay, enough with the sycophantic banter. I'm not even dressed yet, for Christ's sake. Can I not digest my breakfast first?"

"I will make you whole again, Mr. Vernon," she says, staring into my eyes with a dangerous intensity. "I swear to you. I will not fail."

I blow a lungful of air up toward my forehead, turn my eyes toward the barren trees in the park, and resume sipping my coffee.

This is not going to end well for either of us.

CHAPTER 15

Allowing her smart phone to lead us around, Portia walks the soles off my shoes—although there are a few cab rides thrown in here and there—to several buildings, telling me to take a good look up each time we stop.

"Why?" I keep asking.

"I'll tell you once we've seen all six!" she keeps replying.

I don't know the layout of New York City, having only visited once or twice, and many years ago, and so I have no idea what connects the various buildings at which we gaze.

The city buzz induces a high level of anxiety—everyone is marching quickly with blank faces, cars and yellow cabs slice through streets like so many angry sharks eating up free inches of asphalt—and while Portia seems to benefit from the New York state of mind, being here makes me feel like one of many insignificant ants that will crawl through the city for a time before being replaced by other ants that will also be forgotten, on and on ad nauseam.

As we gaze up at the sixth building, Ms. Kane says, "So, did you figure it out yet?"

"Figure *what* out?"

"Why I showed you six buildings in New York City."

"Does this have something to do with architecture?"

"No."

"Some form of birds that are flourishing in nests built high above?" I guess, shading my eyes with my hand as I look up, trying to see the tops, and whether there are any nests. "I read something about falcons thriving in cities."

"Not even close. Do you give up?"

"Does it mean we can stop running all over the city if I do?"

"The six buildings we saw house the six major publishing houses in New York—Simon & Schuster, Hachette, HarperCollins, FSG, Penguin, and Random House."

"Okay," I say.

"Which one do you think it will be?"

"Which one will *what* be?"

Portia smiles mischievously. "Which one do you think will publish my novel?"

"You've written a novel?" I say.

"Well, not yet, but I'm going to."

"Perhaps you better concentrate on writing the actual words before you start predicting who will publish," I say. "Selling a novel to a major house is extremely difficult."

"Have you tried?" she asks.

"Well, no—but—"

"Then how do you know?"

"I guess I don't." I can tell this is important to her, and even though I am beginning to sense a pattern of delusional hope, I really don't want to be the one who urinates on Portia's parade. I'm beginning to feel sorry for her in a way that I didn't think was possible. I admire her moxie and determination, even as I watch her jump off an emotional cliff without a parachute.

"Then guess again, just for fun. Which one will it be?" she says.

"Which house will publish the book that you haven't yet written?" I ask, feeling once again as though Mr. Kafka is writing my life as I live it. "I don't know."

"Doesn't it give you a rush to think that one of your former students might be published by a real New York City house someday? That your teaching might have a great ripple effect? That you may have encouraged a future *New York Times* best seller just when she needed it most? Haven't you ever dreamed of that?" she says, looking up at me from under this very cute pink hat, and I suddenly realize that she is wearing matching lipstick, eyeliner, and some sort of blush. She's done herself up to walk around NYC with me. *Me.* To Portia Kane, this day is worth makeup.

"So that's your dream now—to be a fiction writer?"

"It's always been, since I was in your class. We used to talk about it, remember?"

"No," I say, even though I have a vague recollection.

"Haven't *you* ever dreamed of becoming a published novelist? I mean you practically worshipped—"

"Never wanted to be a writer," I say, too quickly, I admit.

"Well, I'm going to be published someday, and I'm going to dedicate the book to you. That's a promise. You'll want to stick around to see your name in print, right? Right at the beginning. 'To Mr. Vernon, the good man who first helped me believe.' "

I stare at her and try to decide if she can possibly believe what she's saying—promising to dedicate a book to me, a book she hasn't even written, and guaranteeing that it will be published by one of the major houses in New York City. Aside from the dedication she has presumptuously penned *before* her dreamed-up novel, she probably hasn't even written a paragraph since her brief college stint, almost twenty years ago. It's a delusional promise at best, and probably psychotic otherwise. And yet she's looking up at me with these wonderful, childlike believing eyes, bathing me in that rare gaze I used to receive from my most promising students, who were not necessarily the most intelligent or the best read or the ones who had previously studied under the cleverest teachers, but the ones whom Kerouac called the mad ones, the people who were crazy enough to do something outside of the norm, just because it was in them to do.

Before I can stop myself, I say, "Ms. Kane, I don't want to speak about things I know little about anymore, and this doesn't change a thing regarding my ability to answer the first question—but that just might be a spark in your eye I see now."

When she smiles, a happy tear leaks out, and I instantly regret giving her hope. She doesn't deserve it—she has done nothing but dream and look up at buildings with her suicidal former English teacher—and I know that hers will most likely be what Mr. Langston Hughes called a dream deferred.

"Maybe there's one hiding in your eye now too—a spark," Portia says.

I shake my head. "It's a good dream for you, Ms. Kane. I hope you accomplish your goal. But this is your course, your dharma, if you will, not mine."

"You started it. You turned me on to this—literature, writing," she says.

I'm tempted to ask how many books she has read in the past year, how many words she has written, but I hold my tongue. This will all be over soon.

She takes me to Central Park, and we buy warm cashews and hot dogs from a vendor and eat on a park bench, neither of us saying much, and then we stroll, people-watching and feeling a bit awkward about everything—both of us, I can tell, because Portia seems to be running out of steam herself.

We watch the sun set through the barren trees, the dying light illuminating the melting piles of snow, and then we walk through darkness back to the hotel, order room service, and eat a light dinner in our suite before we resume drinking heavily from the mini fridge.

Three or four airplane bottles in, Portia says, "You don't believe I'll publish a novel, do you?"

"Plenty of people publish books every year," I say, trying to skirt the question.

"But never the daughters of hoarders—fatherless girls who grow up across the street from the Acme. No, they marry abusive men who discard them when they grow to be middle-aged and wrinkled."

"Perhaps you've had too many little bottles, Ms. Kane?"

"Do you know people used to say we slept together when you were my teacher?"

I don't know what to say to that.

"That, apparently, was the rumor. I just found out. Why do you think people would say that?"

"Funny. I thought the rumor was that I was gay," I say.

"Are you?"

"Would it matter to you?"

"No. I just—I mean, I wish you had someone in your life, like a lover. It would make all of this easier."

"Saving my life?"

"Yes."

"I was in love with Mrs. Harper, but she's going to marry the butcher—and he doesn't even know who Albert Camus is," I say, and suddenly realize I am a bit drunk too. "I found out he popped the question right before you showed up. That and Albert Camus the dog's suicide sort of triggered my . . . well, whatever we are in now."

"What did you love about Mrs. Harper?"

"Her nose, mostly, I guess."

"What?" Portia laughs.

I smile in spite of myself. "Mrs. Harper had a—well, a *Jewish* nose. And I have always been turned on by Jewish women, especially their noses, with the little bump. I don't know why."

"I'm pretty sure that's a racist thing to say."

"That I love Jewish women?"

"To say you love the bump in their noses, as if they only have one kind. You'd never say 'I love the slanted eyes of Asian women.' Or 'the big asses of African women.' "

"Um," I say, not sure how to proceed, because those examples seem extreme.

"Did you tell Mrs. Harper that you loved her?"

"I never even spoke with her. She was the checkout lady at the local store. She rang me up hundreds of times, but I never said anything to her other than pleasantries."

"But you wanted to."

"Yes," I say. "I did. Very much."

"There are other Mrs. Harpers in the world. Some of them have even sexier Jewish noses, you know. *Bigger bumps.*"

I sip my wine.

"You're not dead yet," Portia says to me. "There's still time for love."

"And how did love work out for you?"

"Shitty in the past, I admit, but I'm going to give love another go."

"Okay. You do that."

"The man who carries your Official Member of the Human Race card and reads it daily. Chuck Bass. You had him in your class back in 'eighty-eight. He put himself through college in his thirties and early forties by tending bar and taking out student loans. He's looking for an elementary school teaching job. He has no money, lots of debt, and he takes care of his sister and her five-year-old son. Not exactly the best suitor on paper, but he has a spark in his eye, yes he does, and he loves you as much as I do."

I'm tempted to roll my eyes, but I manage to refrain. "I don't even remember him. Sorry."

"He's a lot like you," she says.

"Then run away from this Chuck," I answer. "Seriously. You do not want to be yoked to a man like me."

"You're too hard on yourself," she says. "Too serious."

"Tomorrow is our last day together, right?"

"Yep."

"I'm still planning on returning to Vermont so I can kill myself. I want you to know that. And it's not your fault. You should absolutely write your novel. Forget about me. Be with this Chuck Bass and make a good life for yourselves. Dedicate your novel to him, because—"

"I have a good surprise for you tomorrow," she says. "It's going to be a game changer."

I look out the window and endure a very uncomfortable silence before I excuse myself and retire to my bedroom.

I toss and turn all night. This trip was a mistake. I'm passing on my misery by allowing Portia to get her hopes up. My suicide will destroy her, and yet that's not a good answer to the first question—or maybe I should say it's not a good *enough* answer for me, when I am alone with my thoughts, finally unfettered from the ridiculous notions of former students.

I rub my knees, because they ache tonight, probably from all the walking. I think about all of the metal in my body that will outlast my flesh and muscles and bones should I be buried—or maybe the metal will be found in my pile of ashes when I am cremated.

So strange to think about that.

Stranger yet to be in a presidential suite in this exclusive New York City hotel.

"This woman is not going to take her defeat very well—that's now certain," I whisper to myself through the darkness.

CHAPTER 16

I choose death by breakfast again, the monkey suits come and go like androids, and Portia and I eat together in the dining room's opulence, under the crystal chandelier, wearing our fluffy white bathrobes.

The steak is even better than yesterday's, somehow juicier, and I decide to consume all of it before I bring up the uncomfortable discussion I've been planning since four in the morning, because that's when I woke up for the last time and tossed and turned until the sun rose. I'm worried about Portia, who seems to be glowing with dangerous confidence this morning, but I'm smart enough to savor this meat, because I am certain I will not have better in the few remaining days that I'll be caning my way around this planet.

Just as soon as I've swallowed the last bite I say, "I think it would be prudent if we parted ways now, and I caught a train back to Vermont before this gets any more complicated than it already is. Because there is nothing—"

"Not a chance," she says, and the light in her eyes fades a little. "I have you for three days. A deal is a deal."

"I don't want to prolong this, Ms. Kane. And I don't want you to get your hopes up. There is nothing I want, except to be left alone. *Nothing.*"

"You just need to remember," she says, and then sips her coffee. "Who you once were."

"It was a mistake to come with you," I say. "I see that clearly now. I don't know why I—"

"Because some part of you, deep down inside, knows I'm right about you," she says, looking out at Central Park glowing in the morning sun.

"No. That's not it," I say, and then take a deep breath. "I'm not proud of this, but I think I came on this little adventure because I wanted to hurt one of my former students, as sadistic as that sounds. Wound you deeply the way Edmond Atherton wounded me, sans the baseball bat, of course. And this was a subconscious wish that was controlling me, but somewhere along the way it became conscious, and now I feel guilty about it and want to be open with you, protect you from any further pain. The conscious part of me wishes you no harm, and so I must protect you from my subconscious. Do you understand?"

She's looking at me as though I have just flashed her my private parts—half shock, half repulsion.

"You can't fool me," she says. "This is just a trick."

"Listen, what you are trying to do is beautiful, but it makes you vulnerable. I know, because I used to live this way myself. The world broke me in a big way, and then I was harder—hard enough to want to do some breaking of others. And you're a sweet, kind woman, Ms. Kane. I couldn't sleep last night because I felt so guilty—and so I feel it's best if we simply part ways now. Thank you for all you have done, for letting me know my class meant something to you. I wish you much luck with—"

"I'm taking you to meet my mother today," she says. "Whatever reason you had for coming, it doesn't matter. It would mean a lot to me if you simply met my mother. Maybe that sounds bizarre to you, but I would be very grateful. After that I will drive you home to Vermont and leave you alone for good. You'll be free and clear of me. I promise."

"You want me to meet your mother—the hoarder?"

"She's my mother."

"But why do you want me to meet her?"

"Because—I can't explain it, okay?"

"I really don't want to return to Haddon Township—I haven't been there since, well . . . since this," I say and hold up my cane.

"I know I'm asking a lot, but we can make it there in time for dinner, and then after we eat with my mom, I'll drive you directly home, right away. I won't even sleep."

"I don't think it's a good idea, Ms. Kane. I'm sorry."

"Please." She puts her hands together in prayer position. "I know it's dumb, but I really just want the two of you to meet. She was in no condition to attend any school functions or back-to-school night, and I've told her so much about you. She's not well, and I think she believes I made you up. I just want to show her that you exist."

"This is really important to you?"

"It would mean a lot to me. If you're going to disappear from the world, maybe you could do this one last kindness before you go? It's a simple thing, really. Do it, and you will never hear from me again. I promise."

"Dinner with your mother and you—that's it? I do this, and the game ends? You take me directly back to Vermont."

"And I forgive you for wanting to punish me," she says, looking up from under her eyebrows like a wounded little girl.

"Okay," I say, against my better judgment.

How can I refuse her this simple thing after what I just admitted?

She takes so long packing her things and getting ready that I begin to wonder if she is intentionally stalling for some reason, but I enjoy my view of Central Park, watch the late-morning light climb the trees, and I don't say anything when she finally emerges from her bedroom with her hair and makeup done.

"Let's get some lunch sent up and check out late, just to screw Ken a little more in the pocketbook," she explains.

"Sure," I say, thinking this will all be over soon, if I can just be agreeable a little while longer.

It's half past one by the time we are back in the rental car, fighting Manhattan traffic. Portia hits buttons on the steering wheel until she finds the classical station. My old friend, the best cellist alive, is playing.

I must make some emotional noise, because she says, "Are you okay?"

I don't answer.

"Mr. Vernon? Do you not like this music? I thought you liked classical, and—"

"It's Yo-Yo Ma," I explain. "Suite for Solo Cello no. 4 in E-flat Major, BWV 1010, first movement, 'Prelude.' Bach, of course."

"Of course."

"My dog, Albert Camus," I say, missing him more than I have since Portia first found me choking to death on my own vomit, "this was one of his favorite pieces."

"Your dog loved Bach?"

"He loved Yo-Yo Ma," I explain, and then emotion floods my chest, and I can't stop myself from crying. I turn my head away from her and pretend to look at New York passing by, but I'm making sniffling noises now.

"I'm sorry," she says. "I'm sure Albert Camus was a great dog."

"He was the best friend I ever had," I say, realizing how stupid I'm acting, crying over a dog.

Yo-Yo Ma works his magic—transports me.

And suddenly I'm with Albert Camus again in my Vermont

kitchen, listening to our favorite cellist play Bach. I'm cooking us steaks as Albert Camus thumps out the beat against the wooden floor with his tail.

In my mind, I bend down and scratch him under his chin and behind his ears the way he likes, until he stands up on his hind legs, paws at my chest, and licks my cheek in thanks.

"Why did you jump out the window?" I ask him in my fantasy. "Why? We had such a good life together."

He looks up at me lovingly through his one eye. *I told you already. I jumped to save you, like Clarence in* It's A Wonderful Life *does to save George Bailey. And I think you should listen to this woman who is driving the car, in real life. She has a good heart. She loves you!*

"I'm done, Albert Camus. Got nothing left to give!"

Then why not take a little, eh? he says. *Learn from me. Did I ever refuse a treat or a scratch or a ride in the truck with the window rolled down? Never! And what did I have to give back in return?*

"Companionship!" I say. "You were the best friend I ever had."

We are still best friends—best friends forever, he says, and then licks me furiously all over my face as I close my eyes and laugh. *Now stop being such a pussy! Let the girl help you.*

"Did you just call me a 'pussy'?" I say, making the stupid air quotes with my fingers.

Yes, I did, and it is the absolute worst thing a dog can call another dog. A pussycat. And you are acting like one. Snide. Selfish. Self-absorbed. An untrustworthy, taciturn pussycat. Be a dog, Master Nate. A true and good dog is affable and loving and kind and ready for adventure. Ready to piss on the entire world, marking every inch with his many drops of urine, which he believes to be inexhaustible!

"This is getting a little weird, Albert Camus. Even for me. I must admit."

Use this new life. Mark it with the urine of your essence.

"What did you just say?" Portia says a bit loudly.

I open my eyes and look at her behind the wheel of the rental car, blinking several times as my mind wakes up and my eyes focus.

"Did you just say something about 'the urine of your essence'?" she says.

"What?"

"I think you may have been dreaming, but that's disgusting. I'm stopping for coffee. Maybe you'd like some too." She pulls into a rest stop off the highway, where we get some overpriced java and sip it quietly at a little plastic table as scores of faceless background people swarm about.

"You're almost done," she says. "Almost free of me."

I nod at her, suddenly exhausted.

This is the longest I've been around another human being in many years, I suddenly realize. No wonder I'm so depleted of energy.

There's an endless slow-moving snake of traffic on the New Jersey Turnpike, which makes me think of that old song by Simon and Garfunkel about counting cars on this very road, but as the hours creep by in interims of standstill and five-miles-per-hour, Portia's knee starts to move up and down, and her bottom lip gets chewed fiercely.

"Why are you so agitated?" I ask.

"We're meeting my mother at seven," she says. "I don't want to be late."

I look at the clock on the dash: 5:30.

We take Exit 4 around 6:40, and Portia seems even more agitated. I can feel her nervousness filling up the car like some sort of poisonous gas; it's stifling.

I take a deep breath and remind myself that I only have to eat dinner with a crazy old lady before I'll be returned to my home in Vermont, where I can finally be done with everything and enjoy eternal rest.

Portia navigates through and mostly around the South Jersey rush-hour traffic, taking less-traveled residential roads through Cherry Hill, Haddonfield, Westmont, and then we are on Cuthbert Boulevard and she is pointing out the row home in which she grew up across the street from the Acme, and then she's pulling over and pointing at the Haddon Township High School public announcement board and football field.

"Why did you stop *here*?" I say.

"Thought you might like to reminisce," Portia says, and it's like all of my bones are being broken again.

Edmond Atherton.   Edmond Atherton.

Edmond Atherton.   Edmond Atherton.

Edmond Atherton.   Edmond Atherton.   Edmond Atherton.

Edmond Atherton.   Edmond Atherton.

Edmond Atherton.   Edmond Atherton.

Edmond Atherton.

Edmond Atherton.   Edmond Atherton.

Edmond Atherton.   Edmond Atherton.

Edmond Atherton.   Edmond Atherton.   Edmond Atherton.

Edmond Atherton.   Edmond Atherton.

Edmond Atherton.   Edmond Atherton.

Edmond Atherton.   Edmond Atherton.   Edmond Atherton.

Edmond Atherton.   Edmond Atherton.

Edmond Atherton.   Edmond Atherton.

Edmond Atherton.   Edmond Atherton.   Edmond Atherton.

Edmond Atherton.   Edmond Atherton.

Edmond Atherton.   Edmond Atherton.

Edmond Atherton.   Edmond Atherton.   Edmond Atherton.

"Keep driving!" I yell, and now it's me who is feeling anxious. "This wasn't part of the deal."

"Don't you want to take a second to—"

"Drive!"

She pulls away and heads toward Oaklyn.

"I'm sorry stopping by the high school upset you so much," she says, after my breathing returns to normal.

I don't respond, mostly because it upset me more than even I thought it would, and now I'm sweating and my heart is banging.

"You're really shaken," she says. "I'm sorry."

"I'll be okay. Let's have dinner with your mother, and then I'll be happiest if you return me right where you found me."

"Okay," she says, but there is a hint of music in her voice, like she knows something I don't, and when I look over at her, I see it clearly in her eye—the spark.

We pull into a rather full parking lot across the street from a place called the Manor in the small town of Oaklyn, and alongside my former student I make my way to the entrance door, over which hangs a sign featuring a suspiciously young boy sitting on a barrel and drinking beer directly from a pitcher.

Before we go in, Portia stops and faces me. Then she kisses me on the cheek, which shocks me. "You were the best teacher I ever had. Thank you."

Her eyes are watery, and I'm not quite sure what's going on, so I say, "Let's not keep your mother waiting."

She nods and then opens the door for me.

I cane my way inside, looking down so I don't trip over the step, and when I look up, I hear a few dozen people yell, "SURPRISE!!!!!!"

It scares the hell out of me, and I almost fall backward, but Portia is nudging me forward toward the mass of people who I quickly understand are my former students, because they are all holding up those stupid Official Member of the Human Race cards I used to make and distribute to my seniors on the last day of school. It feels like a dream at first—like something that can't possibly be true—and as I scan the beaming, smiling faces in the room, I recognize several and can even name a few.

My entire body is instantly slicked with sweat.

Everyone is looking at me.

Edmond Atherton's face pops out in the crowd dozens of times, peeking up from behind shoulders and around heads in rapid succession, so I know I am hallucinating, seeing my attacker everywhere I look, and all of these former students are waiting for me to say something. It's so deadly quiet, I can hear them breathing.

They want me to send their emotions soaring with goodwill and belief in possibility. Even though I would actually like to provide them with what they need, with what would keep them believing and carrying around those recklessly hopeful cards, I have nothing left in my tank. I no longer own the Mr. Vernon Super Teacher Mask. So I turn around, push past Portia, and limp my way out of the building.

"Where are you going?" she says. "Yo!"

I ignore her and make my way down the steps, onto the street, and under the trestle so I can climb my way up the hill and out of here.

Portia follows, yelling, "All of these people showed up for you! You can't just leave!"

"We had a deal," I yell back over my shoulder. "And this was *not* part of it. You lied to me!"

"Some of those people in there took off work to be here—drove hours! Tonya Baker flew in from Ohio!"

"Not my problem," I say, and attempt to escape.

"Hey!" she yells, standing in front of me. "At least have the guts

213

to tell me our showing up for you doesn't rekindle the spark and—"

"It means absolutely nothing," I say, looking her dead in the pupils. "It doesn't change a goddamn thing."

Portia Kane searches my eyes for a long time, maybe looking for the spark that is no longer there and never will be again, before she says, "I believed in you! You fake! You coward!"

And then she's slapping me again, and I'm flashing on Edmond Atherton, feeling my bones break along with my pride and confidence and maybe everything that was ever good in my heart, and she's no longer hitting me so much as crying into my chest and pounding my back with her fists, and then there's a man with us and he's yelling at Portia, telling her to stop calling me names, and restraining her, and so I try to escape once more, caning myself out of there as fast as I can, silently cursing my limp, thinking I can find a pay phone and arrange for a cab to drive me to the train station so I can get the hell away from here forever—or maybe I can just find some quiet place in South Jersey to end it all, because I am done, finished.

This woman has drained me dry.

There is nothing left.

And soon there will only be ash, this godawful cane, and the metal pins that once held my bones together.

I'm ready to follow Albert Camus's good example.

PART THREE

Sister Maeve Smith

CHAPTER 17

February 15, 2012

To My Sweet and Good Son, Nathan,

It's been some time since I last wrote to you.

Please know that I have prayed and will continue to pray for you every single day, multiple times, and ask my sisters to hold you up to God as well. There is an army of nuns praying for you always, and there is great strength in our prayers. I think about you with every breath I take. That will never change.

Then why have I not written to you for months? you might ask.

It is hard to write many letters and never once receive a reply. It's like talking loudly to a brick wall, never knowing if the person on the other side hears a thing you say, or if the bricks merely bounce your words right back into your face like well-struck tennis balls.

And so maybe you will now feel I have a lack of faith and have failed you once again in some way that I cannot see? I fear this greatly, but I also didn't want to be an overbearing mother, sending you so many letters that you didn't want.

I didn't want to become your equivalent of "junk mail."

When a son doesn't write back, it is hard for a mother to know what to do!

Nor did I want to upset you, and I began to feel as though God were telling me to give you space, that He would take care of you in His own way. That I was being asked to show my faith by doing nothing—letting go.

Trust and obey.

And I know you will find these ideas silly, because you don't share my faith.

But I gave you to God regardless.

I hope you will understand that it was not an easy message for a mother to receive—that she had to let go of her only son—and it is even harder now that I believe I may have misinterpreted what God was trying to say to me, which is what this letter is about.

Two weeks or so ago, completely out of the blue, Mother Superior forced me to get a physical; she insisted that I see a doctor even though I hadn't been to one in years, and my refusing to see any medical professionals had never been a problem before. I told her that God was the only doctor I needed, but she is a stubborn crab of a woman—albeit a strong wife of Christ—and she made the arrangements for me, and then when I refused to go, she threatened to take away access to our wine collection. An extra glass of red every once in a while is a comfort, so help me Jesus.

Long story short, they found a surprisingly large lump in my breast, which immediately prompted more tests—mostly womanly things you will not wish to hear about in great detail, I would imagine—and they ultimately concluded that I have stage IV cancer, which means that it has basically spread everywhere. It's uncanny, because I had been feeling fine! I've heard others say, "If you want to be sick, go to the doctor," and now, whether they are right or wrong, I finally understand why people say this.

Two days ago my doctor, a Japanese woman much younger than you named Kristina, sat me down in a room to tell me the news, and she looked as though someone had already died, God bless her soul. She was trembling even. I wondered if this might be her first day as a real doctor, and if I were the first person she had booked on a one-way trip to heaven with her diagnosis.

She took my hand in hers, looked me in the eyes, and said, "Your breast cancer is terminal, Sister Maeve. We caught it too late, and it's already spread, and rather aggressively at that. I'm sorry. There is simply nothing we can do for you at this point but make you feel as comfortable as possible."

I said, "I do not fear death, child. I know where I'm going when I die, so you don't have to worry about me. You also don't have to make that miserable sad face. Have you been sucking on lemons for lunch?"

Dr. Kristina squeezed my hand and said, "I admire your faith. I really do. But it's my job to inform you of what's to come, and I'm afraid it's not happy news."

She went on to describe at length all of what I will inevitably endure, and then she spoke of medicines that she could offer to help with the pain.

"How about some medical marijuana, Doc? Can you get me any of that good wacky tobacky stuff?" I said, just to break the tension, thinking the idea of a nun who smokes "reefer" would make her laugh. I had recently heard something about the legalization of marijuana on the news.

But she took me seriously. "We can certainly look into that, Sister, if that's the route you wish to pursue."

"It was a joke, Doc," I said. "I'm a red wine girl. Always have been. Always will be. Although vodka's good too."

She looked at me for too long before she finally said, "Sister, it's my job to make sure you understand the gravity of the situation here. You are going to die. It's amazing that you haven't already felt the effects of the cancer more strongly. These effects will be severely debilitating. Do you understand what I am saying to you?"

"Are you a religious woman?" I asked her, knowing full well the answer before I posed the question.

"No," she said—at least telling the truth. "I'm sorry. There are people here who can talk to you about religious matters. I can get Father Watson if—"

"No need to be sorry. I'll pray for you," I said. "And no need for a priest just yet. Do you know who my husband is? He's quite famous."

"I didn't know nuns were permitted to have husbands," she said, appearing very confused in her fancy white doctor coat with the stethoscope around her neck and one of those things they use to look into your ears sticking out of her breast pocket along with a few tongue depressors. She was so young, her outfit almost looked like a Halloween costume.

(Sin though it may be, I envied her thick mane of hair that was like the tail of a beautiful black stallion.)

"We nuns all have the same husband—his name is Jesus Christ," I said. "And I'm going to trust in Him to sort this out for me. Just like always. He's had much more practice than you have had and can heal without the help of a medical degree, no offense. He's been doing it for thousands of years."

"Sister," the doctor said, a bit more sternly this time, "I would be remiss if I didn't make it abundantly clear that you may only have a few weeks left. How you are not already in remarkable

pain is a mystery to me, I admit, but you need to know that you don't have a lot of time."

"With all of your education and expensive medical equipment, it's still a mystery to you, eh?" I said to her and then had myself a bit of a chuckle. "Well, my husband just so happens to traffic in mystery quite a bit."

"I don't think it wise to believe that you will be miraculously cured," the doctor said. "Statistically speaking, you have already received a bit of a miracle, making it relatively pain-free this far without any interruptions to your life. Science cannot explain—"

"We all die," I said to young Kristina. "And I've actually been looking forward to heaven, where I can finally spend some quality face time with Jesus." I winked, but she didn't laugh at my joke, maybe because she was one of those serious big-brain types, so I got back to business. "Exactly how much time do I have?"

She took a deep breath and said, "There's no gentle way to break this to you."

"Just give me a number," I said.

"You will most likely go downhill very soon, and rather quickly. If there is anything you need to take care of, you should do it immediately. Maybe a few weeks at the most. That's the best-case scenario. Again, you should already be failing. You're living on borrowed time, so to speak."

I nodded and thanked young Kristina for all of her good work, told her I was going to pray for her, ask my husband to work a little harder on saving her soul, and she smiled politely and wished me luck, because she didn't know that I have no use for luck. I have the awesome power of God—who created her science and the entire universe—in my corner.

Mother Superior was waiting for me, reading her iPad in the waiting room. She claims to read the Old Testament in Hebrew and the New Testament in Greek on that gadget. "It's much lighter than carrying the actual paper Bibles," she says. Every year, on her birthday, her brother sends her the latest computer product, which she shows off ostentatiously every chance she gets. I often wonder if she actually reads the Bible on that thing, or just wastes her time watching secular movies and playing mind-numbing Internet games. She never lets me see the screen.

"So?" Mother Superior said.

"I'll be with Jesus Christ within weeks and maybe sooner, according to Little Miss Doctor Kristina in there."

"There's nothing to be done?"

"Medication for the pain."

"Are you in pain?" Mother Superior said.

"Not yet. It's apparently coming, and in a big way, she said."

"We will pray," Mother Superior said.

"We always do," I answered, and then we made our way to the convent's trusty old Dodge Neon.

As she drove me home, I asked, "Why did you make me go to the doctor? What brought that on? You never made me go before. Did you notice something about my health that I missed? What aren't you telling me, old woman?"

She scowled—she is ten years younger than me, and hates to be called "old woman." Then she said, "My husband told me to make you go."

"Why would my husband tell you such a thing?"

"Mysterious ways, perhaps."

"Oh, bullshit!" I said to Mother Superior, whose face had turned to stone as she drove with her precious iPad resting on the console between us.

"Jesus Christ came to me in a dream again, Sister Maeve," the Crab said, without taking her beady little black eyes off the road. "He said it was the first step of many necessary steps. Taking you to the doctor would set in motion a grander plan, He told me. But let's not tell the other sisters about that, shall we?"

Mother Superior may be a crustacean, but she also has the visions, like I do, so she is an ally and a confidante, albeit an extremely ornery one.

Not all nuns have the visions—in fact, most don't.

And it is best to use the visions without making the other nuns feel jealous or lesser because they have no eyes to see, nor ears to hear.

"The first step toward what?" I asked her.

"He didn't say. But He obviously wanted us to know that your allotted time to put in motion His divine plan was . . . as we now know . . . extremely limited."

Back at the convent, I prayed my afternoon prayers and then ate dinner with the sisters, who all kindly inquired about my trip to the doctor. I told them the findings were inconclusive, although I wasn't sure why I misrepresented the truth at the time. Mother Superior raised her eyebrows at me from the head of the table, but said nothing to contradict what I had told my sisters in Jesus Christ.

When I retired to my room that night, I prayed the rosary, read my scriptures (in good old American English!), and then I thought about what to do with my remaining time. What unfinished business did I have in this world?

Of course, your name was first in my thoughts—my beautiful sweet boy.

After you were attacked, in the hospital, you yelled at me and told me never to contact you again, and have since *refrained from answering my many letters now for years, making it painfully clear that you have cut me out of your life for good—just like your father did to both of us, I might add—but I had also stopped writing you, and I didn't want you to think that I could ever relinquish the possibility of having you in my life again.*

With my last breath I will wish for your forgiveness.

My life here at the convent has been bliss, except for the rift that my faith has created between us—that is my one regret, or maybe I should more accurately say it is my one source of suffering.

I thought about you for hours, wished I could have called you on the phone even, but I have no number for you, and because I had searched for one many times and found none—not even a trace of you in any phone book or Internet website Mother Superior could find—I came to believe that you might not even have a telephone, but have removed yourself from the world, as you threatened to do so many times before.

My greatest fear is that you are no longer even alive. I worry so much about you, and on this night my worry was intensified one hundred thousand times.

Late in the night, and after some wine, God found it in his heart to calm my mind, and I went to sleep, which was a minor miracle in itself.

Soon I was dreaming, and I was in a warm vacation-type place—somewhere south where the sun shines bright and you can smell salt water in the air—and across the street was an impressive modern corporate-looking building covered in large rectangular windows that reflected like mirrors. Standing out front was a crowd made up of many different people of all backgrounds, some fervently praying the rosary, and when I followed their gazes, I saw reflected in nine window panes the Blessed Virgin Mary, appearing like a gas rainbow in a puddle on the giant mirrored windowpanes. She looked beautiful and so full of love and grace, her bust glowing some thirty feet tall maybe, as if she had taken Noah's rainbow and bent it into her own form.

"Come," I heard Mother Mary whisper to me in my dream. "Come, Sister Maeve, to this place, and you will have your closure. Have faith. Come."

Then I sat up in bed, wide awake, knowing that God had sent me another vision, so in my slippers and nightgown I tip-toed through the halls of the convent to the old Crab's palace of a bedroom—with her own bathroom even!—knocked lightly, and entered.

Mother Superior was snoring like a drunken bear.

I turned on her bedside lamp, but the light did not wake her, so I pinched her nose shut and covered her mouth with my palm. She was wide awake in fifteen seconds or so, swatting at my hands, gasping for air, and even letting out a little swear disguised as a prayer.

"Jesus, Mary, and Joseph!" she said, pupils opening up quickly. When she saw me, her eyes narrowed. She shook her head. "You—"

"My husband sent me a message in a dream," I said in a whisper, so we wouldn't wake up the others.

"What did my husband show you?" she whispered back.

"He showed me a flock of God-loving Catholic people—many of them olive-skinned, maybe Mexican—gathered in front of a big building made of huge—"

"Windows that reflected like mirrors?" She lifted her eyebrows.

"Yes," I said, and then Mother Superior and I were wearing the smiles of conspirators.

"The Virgin Mary," the old Crab said, cocking her head to the side.

"Was reflected in nine panes of glass."

"Like a gasoline rainbow," the Crab said.

"Exactly."

"My husband was showing me the same dream when you rudely woke me up."

"Then it must mean something."

Perhaps you will mock this series of events as religious mumbo-jumbo, the phrase you love to use when dismissing my beliefs and passions and dreams, and maybe you will wonder why we were not more amazed. Well, this was not the first time the old Crab and I had been sent the same vision. In fact it had happened dozens of times before—linking us as unlikely twins in Christ. And from experience, we have learned to act quickly when such visions come.

I tell you all of my secrets now, because . . . why not? What use do I have for secrets at this point in time?

And the Crab has big enough claws to scare away any doubting Thomases you might inform of our special talents through Jesus Christ.

Soon we were at the Crab's desk, using her brand-new, fancy, and terribly expensive computer—Is there anything she will not ask her brother for? Has she no humility?—to search for images on the Internet, which, I admit, I know nothing about. Into a small box on the screen she typed a description of the vision we had seen, hit a button labeled SEARCH, and soon we were seeing pictures of our dream, exactly as it had appeared to us.

We found an article in the St. Petersburg Times called "For

Mary's Faithful, a Shattering Loss," and from this we learned
that what we had seen in our dream was once a real place, that
Holy Mother Mary had appeared in Clearwater on a giant
building, and that pilgrims from all over the world had gone to
pray there and light candles. But we also learned that in 2004
someone had deliberately fired buckshot at the panels where
Mary's head appeared, shattering three glass panes and effectively
"beheading" the Holy Blessed Virgin. Yet faithful people still
flock to where she once appeared, albeit in smaller numbers, and
pray the prayers of pilgrims.

The old Crab and I shook our heads. The unfaithful can be
driven by the cruelest demons, set upon bringing darkness to this
world once and for all, and so it is sometimes a great struggle to
tend and spread the light.

"What does it mean, this vision?" I asked Mother Superior.

"I'm not sure," she said, "but maybe you are meant to go on
a pilgrimage, Sister Maeve—to this very shrine. Maybe God
is setting in motion something that will tie up the loose ends in
your life before you go. It is perhaps a great gift waiting to be
opened."

"Loose ends?" I said. "Are you referring to my son? Because he
lives in Vermont, not Florida."

"We must simply trust and obey," the old Crab said, and I
wondered if she hoped to get rid of me once and for all, sending
me to Florida so that I might get sick and die there far from her
jurisdiction, and then she would once again be the only nun in
the convent with such a direct connection to Jesus Christ, the
only woman to be blessed with visions. Mother Superior has
always viewed me as a threat to her authority, even though I
have never once challenged her in front of the other sisters, and
believe you me, there have been plenty of opportunities, because

Mother Superior is a proud old scuttling Crab whose gigantic claws are much scarier than her pinch.

But regardless of all that, the old Crab has since booked my trip, finding the money to pay for plane tickets somehow, providing me with a cell phone and maps of Clearwater. I must say she has been surprisingly kind and efficient about this, and when I asked her why, she replied, "I simply do as my husband commands."

And so, God willing, tomorrow I take a leap of faith and go on a pilgrimage. I fly to Tampa Bay and will go to Clearwater to see the beheaded Virgin Mary and look for a sign.

I am hoping that I may see you there at this sacred place, maybe making a pilgrimage yourself, or maybe you have moved to Florida in search of warmer weather, or perhaps you have conquered the great demons who plague your mind and you are once again doing what you were called to do here on this earth: teaching, changing the lives of young people, inspiring them to do the good work God intended them to do, which is always the harder path and will require the guidance and encouragement of gifted teachers such as yourself.

You are gifted. God told me you were meant for great things when I carried you in my womb, and when I used to hold you in my arms and stare into your wondrous baby eyes, Jesus Christ would whisper into my ears the most beautiful reassurances, saying, "This one has a perfect heart. He will help many. He's a teacher of the people, just like I was when I walked this earth."

And then you grew up and became exactly what God told me you were meant to be, which was the greatest gift I have ever received—the most supreme present for which a mother can ever hope, her son fulfilling God's purpose for him.

Regardless of whether you are teaching again, I would like to see you before I die, and apparently, according to that child of a doctor, Kristina, I have very limited time to accomplish this last remaining wish—to mend whatever rift has kept us separate for too long, however selfish that may seem to you.

So I send you this letter hoping for the best, and with an ocean of love flowing through my old veins.

Perhaps I will see you in Florida?

If not, I hope you will read these words and decide to break your silence.

My earthly flesh can't help feeling as though this letter is like throwing a penny in a wishing well and expecting a real miracle to come flying out.

I am an old dying woman, Nathan, and I love you greatly— more than you can even imagine. You come from my flesh, and when I rocked you in my arms back when you were tiny, the two of us became forever yoked by love in its purest form.

Please answer this letter, if only to spare yourself the remorse of not having closure with me, your only mother. Write back, or even better yet, call, and let me know that you are okay before I die. I will not allow myself to hope for a visit—to hold your beautiful face in my hands one last time. But a letter or a phone call—to put my heart back together again—perhaps we could start there.

Let's end this horrid silence.

Please.

Love and blessings,
Your mother

CHAPTER 18

February 22, 2012

To My Sweet and Good Son, Nathan,

When I returned from Florida, the Crab informed me that you had not answered my letter. No phone call. No e-mail. Nothing. She assured me she had overnighted my words, but you can never trust the Crab, because she is rather tight with the convent's money when it is not being spent on things that will benefit Mother Superior. I've asked her to provide me with receipts in the future to prove that she has sent my letters in a timely fashion. So I initially held the Crab responsible for your silence. Her back is broad enough to bear it. But days passed, and by now you would have my letter even if the Crab sent it at the lower and slower rate, and she is not quite cruel enough to lie about not sending it at all. Mother Superior may be cheap, but she is not a sadist. So my heart has sunk a little, and will continue to sink with every minute that passes until you contact me.

When I landed in Tampa Bay, with the money Mother Superior had given me I hired a cab to take me directly to the holy shrine, the building on which the Blessed Mother Mary had appeared. In the cab, I rolled down the window and allowed the warm Florida air to wash over my old skin, and I felt healthier than I have in years! Pish posh on that young doctor Kristina, I thought, and allowed myself to fantasize about being reunited with you at this holy place I was about to visit. I wondered if God had let you know I was coming, or would you be taken by surprise? Either way, I saw the tears fill your eyes before you ran to me and then we embraced and agreed to forget about all that had kept us separate for so long. I was practically drunk on Floridian air, with my eyes closed, dreaming about you, when the driver said, "We're here, Sister," and then quoted me the fare.

I paid with the Crab's money, grabbed my small bag, and nervously exited the car, looking for you, but you were nowhere to be seen.

My heart sank, and then I saw the decapitated Mother Mary—they've replaced the broken windows with new panes of mirrored glass, so the top half of her bust is gone.

I wept for the Virgin Mary who had given us this great miracle, only to have it thrown back in her face.

There were a few people there praying, again mostly olive-skinned people, and one of them—a young man—walked up to me and said, "For you, Sister," before handing me wooden rosary beads. "God bless you," the young man said, nodded, and then turned back to a stand where religious items were being sold.

"Thank you!" I yelled, and he looked back over his shoulder and smiled a holy grin.

I studied the wood in my hands—Jesus carved out of cedar, maybe, on the cross, a two-inch-tall version of him. I felt the strength return to me.

It's amazing how much power can be manifested through a simple act of kindness.

I prayed to the Blessed Virgin Mary, but she did not appear to me, nor did she provide me with any answers.

When it was time to leave, I realized that I had no ride to my hotel. I was so excited to see the shrine that I had forgotten to arrange for a taxi to pick me up. I stood by the edge of the road and hoped a taxi would drive by, but there were none to be seen.

"Do you need a ride, Sister?" I heard, and when I turned around, it was the man who had given me the wooden rosary beads. Before you tell me that I should not get into cars with strangers—and I usually don't!—this man had a kindness in his eyes.

"I'm an old fool," I said, explaining why I had no ride.

"I am happy to drive you," he said. "My name is Manuel."

I told him the name of my hotel, and he said, "Not far from here."

And then I was in an old truck, looking at the many strands of rosary beads hung from the rearview mirror—there were so many carvings of my husband twisting and spinning and bouncing up and down.

"How do you carve such tiny crucifixes?" I said.

"With a knife, Sister. As penance."

"Penance?"

"I am living the good life now."

What he was doing penance for was none of my business, so I said, "Do you always give lost nuns rides?"

"No, Sister. You are the first. It is truly an honor."

"Do you have a family?" I asked.

"The Catholic Church is my family."

"Mine too," I said.

He nodded.

"I thought I might see my son at the shrine, back there. I had him in my former life, before I took my vows, of course. That's why I flew down here from Philadelphia. Hoping to see him."

"Your son was supposed to meet you, Sister?" he said.

"No, he wasn't."

"I do not understand."

"I was hoping for a miracle."

He nodded again once.

"Do you believe in miracles?" I asked.

"Of course, Sister."

I smiled and asked, "Is your mother still alive?"

"She died many years ago."

"Were you there when she died?"

"I wish I could say I was, but I was far away doing shameful things. This was before."

"I'm sorry you didn't get to say good-bye to your mother."

"I regret it every day of my life," Manuel said, and when I looked over, I saw that he was trying very hard not to cry.

"She would be proud of you today, giving an old nun a ride to her hotel," I said, and reached over to pat his arm.

"It is nothing," he said. "Any decent man would have done the same."

When we arrived at my hotel, he told me to wait a moment, and then he ran around to open the door for me, like he was a chauffeur. "I will pray that your son appears to you, Sister. That God reunites your family."

I stood, and with my bag in my hand I looked into Manuel's eyes.

As I reached up and touched Manuel's face, I noticed the tattoos just under his ears, which he had tried to hide by flipping up the collar of his button-down shirt and wearing a faded red bandanna around his neck.

"You were my son today, Manuel," I said, and kissed him on the cheek. "I will pray for you too. And nun prayers are very powerful!"

Tears collected in his eyes as he stood up straight and kept a stoic face.

"Thank you, Sister," he said and then left me.

Maybe God had sent Manuel to me as a sort of surrogate son?

Or maybe Manuel was an angel?

I thought of Hebrews 13:2: "Do not neglect to show hospitality to strangers, for by this some have entertained angels without knowing it."

Inside the hotel, I found that the Crab had booked me a room with a partial view of the Gulf of Mexico. I had a small balcony from which I could watch almost one-half of the sun set over the greenish blue water, which is exactly what I did as I sipped on a minibar vodka over rocks, thinking that if death was really coming, I might as well have some vodka, because I loved it so much before I became a nun, as you know.

I thought about Manuel and I thought about you, wondering if you might be helping someone else's mother. I wished that I could let Manuel's mother know about his act of kindness, rescuing an old dying nun from her own stupidity. I hope to meet her in heaven, which may be sooner rather than later.

The water on the horizon burned orange and yellow and pink until it swallowed the sun and the stars began to pierce the sky above. I was not hungry, but I did empty the minibar of vodka, as there were only a few little bottles. As I sat alone on my balcony, I began to feel strange pains and aches in my chest and stomach. I shook my head and again wondered if that young doctor had made me sick with her tests and science and seriousness. I knew it was a foolish thought, but I had felt fine before she had me stuck into those awful machines and took pictures of my insides, before she gave me her learned opinion.

I tried to enjoy the sound of water lapping up the beach and the smell of the Gulf breezes in my nose—to relish the moment for all it was worth, because it had been a long time since I'd been alone in a hotel room, and I did manage to find some comfort that night.

The high-thread-count sheets and king-size comforter were like the clouds of heaven—I could have rolled over ten times before I found the end of the bed—and I fell asleep just as soon as my head hit the pillow.

In my dreams the Blessed Virgin Mary appeared to me in a vision, right in my hotel room. She looked no older than Dr. Kristina.

"My daughter," Mother Mary said to me, smiling mysteriously. "You must go home immediately."

"But I'm booked in this hotel for three nights."

"As soon as possible," the Virgin Mary said. "Return to the convent."

Then she blinked out of existence.

When I woke up the next morning, I was somehow sitting on the balcony, with my head resting on the small table and mini-vodka bottles all around my feet!

Did I sleepwalk?

I telephoned the Crab right away and told her what I had seen in my dreams.

Mother Superior said, "The Blessed Virgin visited my dreams last night as well. 'Confirm Maeve's message,' was all She said to me. And then I woke up sleeping in your bed. I don't even remember walking through the hallways. I prayed thanks that none of our sisters found me there."

"So what should I do?" I said, looking at the morning sunlight dancing across the distant water like so many lit sparklers.

"Did you discover anything at the broken shrine?"

"Nothing."

"We cannot disobey the Blessed Virgin. I will call you back in fifteen minutes."

When the phone rang again, the Crab had booked me a flight home to Philadelphia.

I boarded that night and found that I was in the very last row. Right up until they sealed up the plane for takeoff, I thought that I was going to have the row to myself, but then a drunken woman stumbled back to me and sat down. Her head was wobbly, because she had consumed so much alcohol. I couldn't believe they let her on the plane.

I was concerned at first, but then I thought maybe this woman had information for me—maybe she was the reason Mother Mary sent me home early—so I said hello and tried to strike up conversation, but she soon passed out.

They could not wake her when we landed, and so I was trapped between this drunk woman and the window as all of the other passengers exited.

After all I had been through, I was very tired. I just wanted to meet the Crab and return to the convent—maybe take a shower.

Finally the drunk woman woke up, and I was free.

I found the Crab outside in our idling car, pretending to read the Word of God in Hebrew and Greek on her iPad, and I got in.

"Well," she said, shielding the screen from me as she turned the machine off. "Find any clues on the flight?"

"Clues?"

"As to why the Blessed Virgin demanded that you return home early."

I told the Crab about the drunk woman.

"Disappointing," the Crab said as she drove. She has such little faith sometimes.

"Maybe I've not heard the last of this drunken woman. There was something about her that I couldn't quite put my finger on. But something."

"Well, then, you should have exchanged information with her," the Crab said in a condescending manner, because she is a haughty woman, albeit a sister in Jesus Christ.

"Oh, I did," I said. "She knows where to find me."

"Well, then," the Crab said.

"And the pain has begun."

"Is it bad?"

"It is getting worse," I said. "If only you hadn't sent me to that foolish young doctor!"

"You think our actions—what we do or do not do—are any match for God's plans, Sister Maeve?"

"I think you'll be glad to be rid of me when I go," I said, staring out the window.

"I'll be jealous."

"Jealous? Why?"

"You'll be with my husband, and I'll be with so many sisters who see no visions. Who have no eyes to see, nor ears to hear—"

"Ah, you'll be in your own little heaven once I'm gone, and don't you pretend otherwise," I said. A few minutes later I sighed and added, "I'm never going to see my son again, am I?"

"I cannot answer for God, but I can see you through until you go to heaven," the Crab said, and for the first time I felt as though she was being truly sympathetic toward me. "I will help you through your transition, regardless of whether your son comes or not. I will be there for you."

I was caught so off guard that I didn't thank the Crab for her kindness, but I will before I die—I have vowed it to myself.

I had no visions last night, and I wonder if I will ever have another vision again. I feel the power draining from me rapidly, and can tell that the young doctor was right, that my work here in this world is done.

And yet I have the strangest feeling about that drunk woman I met on the plane.

She was rude, obnoxious, and quite pathetic, but she was also something else too—something familiar that I just cannot name right now. Maybe because the cancer is eating away my brain. Who knows?

Maybe it was in her eyes—something familiar?

I cannot say.

So now I will have the Crab overnight this letter just as soon as I stick it in the envelope. (And I will ask for a receipt as proof that she paid the higher price, because we are running out of time!)

Will I hear from you, my son?

I hope so.

I've lived a good life and can die happy, and I know where I will go when I leave this world, I have my husband's assurance—but hearing from you would finish things, and allow me to die completely content.

This is my dying wish—to communicate with you just once more.

Please, Nathan.

Write or call.

Love and blessings,
Your mother

CHAPTER 19

February 27, 2012

To My Sweet and Good Son, Nathan,

The young doctor's science and machines were not far off with their predictions, because I am now in bed mostly, groggy from their medicines, weight falling off me daily, and many other things that I do not wish to share with you—and yet the worst pain of all is that you remain a silent mystery.

With almost every waking breath I pray to my husband and ask why He is refusing to answer my prayers. I even ask the Crab, and she recites scripture and makes many logical and calming assurances, but behind her mask, I see that she too is frustrated with our shared husband, because her answers are hollow as my innards will be when this awful cancer eats me all up from the inside out.

That is all I will say about the bad I must endure, because it is a sin to dwell on our misfortunes. We must count our blessings always, and God has sent me one more that you may find particularly interesting.

Remember the drunken woman on the plane I described in my last letter?

Well, she wrote to me!

I received her letter just shy of a week after she and I had our chance meeting.

She started off with many apologies for her intoxicated state and also for describing her ex-husband's anatomy in great detail—apparently he was not very well endowed, ha!—all of which amused me and was a welcome alternative to thinking about my sickness and the lack of communication I have received from my only son. A wonderful surprise, receiving this unexpected correspondence.

But then her letter took an interesting turn, because my young friend started to ask questions about what she called "destiny," which, of course, is just an unbeliever's word for God.

"Do you believe in destiny, Sister Maeve?" she wrote. "That maybe we are each called to do something in our lives and will find no peace until we do?"

What she was describing of course is a calling, and asking a nun if she believes in a calling is like asking a hungry robin if it believes in pecking worms out of the grass.

I laughed and smiled at her childlike naiveté.

Matthew 18:3—"Truly I say to you, unless you are converted and become like children, you will not enter the kingdom of heaven."

But then she went on to tell me that she knew a man long ago who had made a huge impact on her life, a teacher by the name of Nathan Vernon. Perhaps I had heard of him, because he became infamous after one of his students attacked him with a baseball bat, shattering all of the bones in his arms and legs.

I had to put the letter down and pray the rosary seven times.

Then I prayed to my husband first and Mother Mary second, asking them to forgive my doubts, for they had led me right to this naive young woman who was talking about destiny and my very own son, with no idea whatsoever that she was writing to her hero's own mother.

My eyes filled with tears when this woman—her name is Portia Kane, do you remember her?—described in great detail all of the many beautiful things you did in the classroom and how much these lessons had shaped not only her life but the lives of many.

Hubris is a sin, but my heart swelled up two extra sizes.

The letter ended with her fumbling for the right way to convey the fact that she felt called to assist you in some way— to "resurrect" you and help you find your way back into the classroom where you could continue the good work God had sent you here to do. (Mostly my words, not hers—but her sentiment. She just lacked the vocabulary to express herself properly.) Portia said she admired my conviction—becoming a nun—and that even though her current plan to rescue her former high school teacher seemed delusional, she felt as though she must take this "leap of faith" (her exact words) and return the many kindnesses that you had given her so many years ago.

I rang the bell the sisters had given me to call whenever I need help, and when Sister Esther came, I asked her to bring the Crab.

"But she is praying," Sister Esther said.

"God is in this room at the moment, not in her palace! Bring her quickly!"

The Crab appeared some fifteen minutes later with a sour look on her face.

"What could be so pressing that you'd interrupt my prayer time?" she said.

I held Portia Kane's letter up. "Read this and be amazed."

The Crab squinted her beady little eyes at me, but eventually she took Portia Kane's letter into her claws, sat down, and began to read.

"This is from the drunk woman on the plane," Mother Superior said without looking up at me.

Then a smile bloomed on the Crab's face—a wondrous grin, like an upside-down rainbow. I had never seen her so happy. And when she finished the letter, she covered her mouth with her hand and giggled like a schoolgirl.

"There's a phone number here," Mother Superior said.

I nodded.

"Well, why aren't you calling it?"

"I wanted to share this with you, because even though you are an old annoying Crab, you are part of this. You sent me to the doctor and then to Florida. So you might as well be in for the rest of the ride!"

"Shall I dial?" the Crab said, holding up her expensive "smartphone" that's covered in some sort of fancy red plastic, which no doubt cost her brother a lot of money.

I held my tongue and nodded.

When Portia Kane answered the phone—she was clearly sober—I heard goodness in her voice right away, like a ray of light through a stained-glass window.

I identified myself, told her I had received and read her letter, invited her to visit the convent, and promised to tell her the most amazing story she had ever heard.

For some reason, she warned me that she was not a religious woman, as if I hadn't gathered that already.

Ha!

"And yet you talk of destiny?" I said. "Well, how's this for destiny—the woman you just so happened to sit down next to on the plane is the mother of the very man you wish to save now, your beloved high school English teacher, Nathan Vernon."

It took her a few seconds to process the information. Then

she said, "You're Mr. Vernon's mother? But how? You're a nun! And you have different last names."

"He has the last name of his father, a man I was smart enough not to marry. Come visit me, and I will tell you everything—answer all of your questions—but come quickly, because I am dying and will soon be forever gone."

She arrived at the convent a little less than three hours later, sat by my bedside—I drew strength from her!—and we talked until late in the night.

Her love for you rivals my own.

She simply glows when she recalls the details of your class and the time you spent with her during her adolescent crisis. She said you once let her stay a night in your apartment because she was hysterical and afraid she was pregnant with the child of a weak boy she was trying to save with sex. Portia said there were no other friends or relatives to help her. She slept on the couch in your living room, after you talked her off a ledge.

Based on what she told me, you may have very well saved her life.

Again, I have reason to be proud of you.

Portia will be tracking you down and visiting soon, but has agreed to sit with this old dying woman a few more times before searching for my lost son.

Selfishly, I have asked Portia to visit with me in these last days—to tell me more stories about my son the teacher and the good deeds he did in the classroom.

Jesus Christ has sent Portia Kane to me, and I am confident He will send her to you when I no longer need her.

I have no idea if you are still in Vermont or if she will be able to locate you in the future, but I have made peace with the fact that I will not communicate with you again in this life. I *see now that everything is as it should be, and I was wrong to doubt.*

Portia is a funny woman—always cursing in front of me and then apologizing right afterward. There is something in her eye that suggests that perhaps she really has been called to do this thing she says she feels she must.

And so I will allow her to regale me with stories of my son the teacher until I die, because it is a great comfort, especially now when it has become apparent that you will not be responding.

I am thankful for this strange gift my husband has provided.

Love and blessings,
Your mother

CHAPTER 20

March 6, 2012

To My Sweet and Good Son, Nathan,

I'm dictating my final words to you through the old Crab, Mother Superior, which is why this letter is written in her chicken scratch and not my refined hand, if she hasn't bothered to type up her scribbling for you, like I asked her to do. (The Crab is giving me dirty looks now.)

I am going to die tonight—I feel sure of this. The drugs they shoot into my veins no longer allow me much clarity, and it hurts even to speak these words, so I must be brief. My husband has granted me the strength for these few last sentences, praise be to Jesus Christ.

I love you. I am not mad at you for failing to answer these letters. Maybe you didn't even receive any of them? Maybe the PO box address I have is no longer current, no one is forwarding your mail, and this last letter will never even be read by your eyes, and yet I will send it anyway, because a mother's hope is unending.

God has told me that He will take care of you—that your work is not yet finished here on this earth.

And there is the hope of Mother Mary arranging for me to meet your former student, Ms. Portia Kane, who has promised to find you and then do her best to get you back on track. I've given her my crucifix necklace as proof that we have been in contact, so that she might show it to you and you will know that we have been exchanging stories about you, my sweet son.

She is a misguided naive young woman who has suffered much, but her unexpected companionship has been a great comfort in these last days of my life.

I am glad you are not here to see me in this dilapidated withered state, whispering my last words to an old crab of a woman whose handwriting is probably unreadable because it is hard to hold a pen in a claw. Ha ha!

The Crab is giving me another nasty look now, so I must cease joking, because—in all seriousness—she has been a true friend in my time of need, and I have grown to love her very much.

You are a better man than you believe you are.

I love you always and know I will see you again in heaven.

Good-bye for now.

Love and blessings,
Your mother

CHAPTER 21

March 8, 2012

To Mr. Nathan Vernon,

*The purpose of this letter is to inform you that your mother
has died and gone to heaven, God rest her soul.*

*She passed into the hands of our Lord and Savior, Jesus
Christ, in her bed on the evening of March 7, 2012, almost at
the midnight hour. She had the prescribed intravenous medicine, so she did not experience excessive pain.*

*At Sister Maeve's request, there will be a closed casket funeral
mass given here at the convent on Wednesday, March 14, at
10:00 a.m. I've overnighted this letter to you and have delayed
the funeral for as many days as I possibly could.*

*I've taken your needs into consideration out of respect for
Sister Maeve, and that is the only reason, because, quite frankly,
cutting your own mother out of your life simply because she tried
to comfort you in your time of need—even if she did use what
you consider to be skewed logic—was exceedingly cruel in my
humble opinion, and caused her much unnecessary suffering,
far worse than the cancer. Granted, I don't know your side of
things, but I do know that she loved you very much, warts and
all, and in her time of need you were not here.*

*Perhaps her many letters did not reach you, and this is all
some sort of grand Shakespearean misunderstanding, an Eliza-*

*bethan tragedy, if you will. (I used to teach a high school liter-
ature class, too, a long time ago at a school for Catholic girls.)
Maybe. But I am fairly certain that there has been no mistake,
and rather, you have simply been weak when your mother needed
you to be strong. Such is the way with men and women, and
I'd be a liar if I pretended I was never before weak when others
needed me to be a pillar on which many could lean. But your
mother was my friend and confidante, so I am not impartial.*

*There is the funeral, yes, and while it would be decent of you
to make an appearance, it might also help you move on from the
beating your former student gave you and whatever else has you
so stuck.*

*There is also the rest of your life, which, regardless of your religious
views (or lack thereof)—make no mistake about this—is a great gift.*

Life is the greatest gift there is.

With life, there is possibility.

*The woman who brought you into this world was many
things—jealous, proud, quarrelsome, obstinate, myopic, to
name but a few of her lesser qualities—but she had a certain
talent for spotting the potential in people, the goodness, if you
will, that divine spark within all of us, but that for whatever
reason is capable of shining a little brighter in the chosen few
string pullers God calls to make His mysterious ways possible.*

*She talked about you incessantly, had us all praying round
the clock, which we will continue to do, and insisted that God
called you—gave you a gift, one that you used for many years to
help others, but then stopped using.*

*A gift is a great responsibility, a fact that your mother knew
well, and such gifts often force us to make sacrifices, be better
than we think possible, rise up for the sake of others—and while
employing said gifts often makes our lives more complicated than*

the lives of others less burdened, we are never more miserable than when we stop using our talents.

Are you happy, Mr. Vernon?

If not, when was the last time you were?

Perhaps you should resume doing what last gave you a sense of purpose and joy?

Put my religious views aside, and you will see that I also am fighting on the side of rationality here.

My condolences on the loss of your mother.

She was a woman of God, and she was my dear friend, however difficult she might have been—and believe me when I say Sister Maeve could be tiresome.

The truth is this: I will miss her deeply.

We hope you will be able to attend the funeral mass. You would be our honored guest.

"He's real!" the sisters who have been praying so hard and long for you will proclaim when they see you, because your mother's big talk about her only son has bestowed upon you a mythical quality.

Regardless of all that has transpired, you are welcome here at St. Therese.

All of the necessary information, along with directions from the north, has been listed on the enclosed card for your convenience.

Also, she's left her Bible to you, along with her beloved photo album, mostly containing pictures of you when you were a little boy. If you will not be attending the funeral, please provide me with an address so I can send you these items.

Love and light,
Mother Catherine Ebling (aka the Crab)
Mother Superior, Sisters of St. Therese
PS. Docendo discimus. (Latin. By teaching, we learn.)

PART FOUR

Chuck Bass

CHAPTER 22

I'm no writer. I'm just a regular guy, so please forgive me if I mess this up. I'm doing my best here. Just going to tell the truth. With that being said, I guess my part begins when I leave Mr. Vernon's party at the Manor and pull Portia off him under the trestle—I've never seen a woman attack a man like that before and I hope I never see it again. She's pounding on him with both fists, calling him vulgar words. And she's sobbing and yelling things about Mr. Vernon being the father she never had and his mother dying alone because of his selfishness and his needing to help kids—not completing sentences, hardly even making sense, losing her mind—and so I grab her, because she's out of control, and when she struggles to get free I see that Mr. Vernon is shaking and crying himself.

"You fake!" Portia yells, in my arms now, and starts to bang the back of her head against my collarbone, trying to free herself.

"I'm sorry, Ms. Kane, that I wasn't the man you hoped I'd be," Mr. Vernon says in this sad awful voice. It's depressing, and so unlike the teacher I remember. He's a shadow. Even I can see it plainly. He's done. Tapped out. And as much as I love teaching kids now, I honestly don't know that I could recover from being attacked by one of my students.

I get it.

Teachers have to believe. You have to care, and that takes a lot of work and effort. Teachers need people to give back once in a while too, if only a little. If you've never taught, maybe you won't understand, but I've done my student teaching and am subbing regularly now, so I'm starting to maybe get it for the first time.

Mr. Vernon turns his back on us and starts to make his way up the street, on the other side of the trestle now.

"Where are you going?" Portia yells. "Are you going to limp your way back to Vermont?"

"Stop belittling him!" I yell at Portia, and shake her hard enough to scare myself. I spin her around, grip her biceps, and look into her eyes.

She looks back the way Tommy sometimes does when he's overwhelmed, after a meltdown.

"I need to do something," I say to Portia. "Stay here."

I let her go and start jogging after Mr. Vernon.

"Mr. Vernon!" I yell. "Mr. Vernon!"

When I stand in his way, he stops walking.

He's still sobbing.

"Mr. Vernon, I'm sorry to do this when you're so upset, but I'll hate myself forever if I don't take the time to tell you something. Chuck Bass? Class of 'eighty-eight?"

He's shaking as he leans on his cane and tries to wipe the snot from his nose with the back of his hand.

He doesn't want to hear what I have to say. He's only stopped because he's unable to physically best me; he's cowering like a beaten dog, tail between his legs, and it kills me.

I have no idea if he remembers me or not, but it doesn't matter.

"I'm sorry about what happened to you," I say. "It's unimaginable and wrong. And there's nothing Portia or me or anyone else can do to erase that tragedy. *But*."

I pull out my Official Member of the Human Race Card and hold it up.

He's looking through me, weeping quietly, waiting to leave.

"I've carried this with me for more than twenty years because it's the nicest present anyone has ever given me. I didn't even thank you for it in person because I was just a teenager who didn't know any better, but it meant a lot to me. Long story short, I became a junkie in my twenties. The addiction made me do unforgivable things I don't want to list now, because I'm deeply ashamed of that period of my life. But when I hit rock bottom, as they say, and ended up in rehab, I had this counselor who said we were all in rowboats trapped in a fierce storm out at sea, and we needed to focus on a single light in the distance—like a lighthouse—and work our way back to it, rowing slowly but steadily through the storm, focusing only on the source of the light whenever it swept across the water and never on all of the tossing and turning and scary huge waves that threatened to suck us under at any time down below, where the real monsters were.

"Some people at rehab used their kids as lighthouses, other people used their careers, or making their parents proud. I didn't have a career or kids or parents, but I remembered how good I felt being in your class senior year—good enough to carry around this card for so many years and read it over and over whenever I was feeling shitty about myself, like I wasn't even a person anymore. You made me believe I *was* a person.

"And so I read this card every day in rehab and made you my lighthouse. I wanted to be like you. I told myself that if I could get clean and become a teacher like Mr. Vernon, make a difference— well, then the pain and the work and the excruciating detox and . . .

"I'm saying too much, I'm saying it all wrong, because I'm not as smart as you, but I wanted you to know that you made a huge difference in my life. You saved me. And I wanted to say thank you. That's it. *Thank you.*"

Mr. Vernon is breathing heavily, and the fist gripping his cane is bone white.

He glares at me for a long time before he says, "Please. Just. Leave. Me. *Alone!*"

He pushes past me and canes his way up the street as fast as he can.

I stand there feeling like a huge asshole.

Talk about an anticlimax. I've fantasized about telling Mr. Vernon all that for years.

I used to mentally play out the scene over and over again, in and after rehab too.

When I turn away, blinking back tears myself, Portia's looking up at me.

"Get your truck," she says, "because we're going after him. Let's go."

I've been in love with Portia Kane since the late 1980s, when I was a shy awkward fatherless virgin gawking at her whenever she passed me in the hallways of Haddon Township High School, wearing that same white jean jacket with her hair all teased out and a strength in her eyes that both attracted and scared the shit out of me simultaneously, and so I don't need to be told twice.

We get into my truck and drive toward the White Horse Pike, and we spot Mr. Vernon in front of the police station.

"Let's talk about this," Portia yells out the window. "Can we simply talk?"

Mr. Vernon surprises us by going inside the police station.

Portia jumps out and follows him, so I park the truck. By the time I arrive inside, they have Mr. Vernon hidden away, and Portia is arguing with my cop friend, a guy I often serve at the Manor. Jon Rivers. I even helped him crack a drug case once by sharing some insider info I acquired back when I was a junkie. Jon and I are pretty tight. He owes me a few favors, so I'm more than a little glad that he's the cop we run into tonight.

"Do you know this woman, Chuck?" Jon says. When I nod, he says, "Calm her down," and then disappears through a door to the space behind the thick glass separating the waiting room from the rest of the police department.

"Why did Mr. Vernon go to the police?" Portia asks.

"I have no idea," I say.

Twenty minutes later Jon comes out. "Mr. Vernon doesn't want to speak with either of you. He's willing to press no charges if you both just go home now."

"Press charges?" Portia yells. "What charges?"

"Kidnapping. Harassment. And you did just hit him under the trestle, right? So that's assault," Jon says. "Listen. Just go home and leave this poor man alone. He's back there sobbing and hyperventilating, okay? He's having a breakdown of some kind. Sounds like you two were trying to do a very nice thing that ended up being not so nice for your guest of honor. Let's not make this any more complicated than it has to be. Okay?"

"No! This is bullshit," Portia says.

Jon gives me a look that says, *Trust me on this.*

"Thanks, Jon," I say. "We're going now. Come on, Portia."

He nods once and then leaves us.

"I don't understand." Portia's shaking her head as I lead her out of the police station. "This wasn't supposed to be like this. It was supposed to be beautiful. What the fuck?"

In my truck, I say, "Should we go back to the Manor? People are probably still waiting. They're most likely very confused."

"Can you just drive me the hell away from here?" Portia says.

Her face is blank.

Her posture is defeated.

She doesn't look good.

I don't know what else to do, so after I call Lisa at the Manor and explain that the party is over, I drive Portia away from all of the unanswerable questions and confused former classmates and Official Member of the Human Race cards. An hour or so later, we somehow end up on the Ocean City boardwalk, walking aimlessly, listening to the ocean crashing, both of us shivering the whole time.

Portia says, "This all has to be for a reason. Right? What do you think?"

"What do you mean?" I have no idea what she's talking about.

"Maybe tonight isn't the end of Mr. Vernon's story," she says, and I can see the light returning to her eyes. "And maybe it's the beginning of ours."

"Ours?"

"Our story."

"We have a story?" I say, maybe a tad too eagerly.

She turns and faces me.

I'm looking down into her eyes, and I can't believe how quickly her mood has changed.

"Can I try something?" she says.

"Sure."

"Okay, here we go."

Then her hand's on the back of my neck and she's pulling my face down toward hers and we're kissing.

Tongues and all—passionately—and I'm not sure this is appropriate or even a good idea, but Portia doesn't give me any time to consider, because now her hands are running up and down my back, and it's like she's trying to devour me, suck me inside her.

When she comes up for air, I say, "What's going on?"

"This is the beginning of us, Chuck Bass."

"The beginning of us?"

"Yes. Absolutely. It must be," she says, and then we're walking hand in hand, and I'm absolutely drunk on Portia Kane and the freezing cold salt air.

We end up in a cheap motel four or so blocks from the beach, the Sand Piper. Before I know what's happening, clothes fly to every corner of the room, and then Portia and I are making love for the first time.

There's part of me that knows we shouldn't be doing this, that it's probably rebound sex. She has been so wounded and rejected by her hero, Mr. Vernon—and come to think of it, I was too—this person who had represented goodness in our minds for more than twenty years, but turned out to be beaten by the world at best and a complete fraud at worst. It's like there's this big gaping hole in both of us now, and maybe we're just trying to fill each other up, but the sex stuff happens quickly and it's mind-blowing and beautiful and sad and scary too, because I know that it's not just sex stuff for me, but much more, and yet I don't know for sure what it is for Portia, who is still technically married, if I have my facts straight.

And when I come, emptying myself inside her, in that seriously high moment—ejaculation is the closest thing I now have to a heroin hit—I can't keep myself from saying, "I love you, Portia Kane. I have always loved you," and then immediately wish I hadn't and feel like an ass, even when she whispers back, "I'm hoping you're my good man, Chuck Bass."

She rests her head on my chest and we just sort of lie there—her breathing, me stroking her long brown hair—until we both surrender to sleep.

In the morning, we shower, dress, and walk the boardwalk, holding hands again, listening to the waves crashing, and talking about the fact that we both need change in our lives without really going into specifics, neither of us bringing up Mr. Vernon, even though I keep wondering where he ended up last night—and also if he might actually eventually kill himself like Portia said he wanted to when she called me from New York City. I hadn't told the classmates we rallied about Mr. Vernon being possibly suicidal, and I'm now trying not to think about what they'd say if they found out he had actually gone through with suicide after our failed party.

"You don't think Mr. Vernon might have tried to hurt himself last night after he left the police station, do you?" I ask Portia when I can't take it any longer.

"It's out of our hands," she says, and then adds, "at least for now. We left him with cops. I'd say that clears us from any responsibility. What else could we have done?"

I think about how we could still get him professional help—maybe contact a therapist or call a suicide hotline or something like that—but I understand what Portia means. She's just driven all the way to Vermont, shown him a big fancy time in New York City. She will go on to tell me how she's saved his life twice already. How many times are you expected to raise your former teacher from the dead, after all? And yet I still can't shake the feeling that we could do more.

"Hey," Portia says, looking up into my eyes, her forefinger lifting my chin as seagulls cry and swoop overhead. "We tried. And maybe we haven't heard the last word from Mr. Vernon."

I don't understand what she means about "the last word," but we did try.

After late-morning pizza slices at Manco & Manco, I drive Portia home to her mother's row home across the street from the Acme in Westmont, and just before she gets out of the truck, looking sun-kissed and wondrous, I say, "This isn't going to sound very cool, I'm aware, but please tell me that I'm going to see you again soon."

She smiles. "How's tonight sound? You around?"

"I have Tommy tonight, but he'd love to see you too."

"Cool," she says. "Maybe you'll let me sit in on a Shot with a Fart session?"

I smile.

She gives me a kiss on the lips, and then she's climbing her mother's front steps.

"Portia Kane," I whisper to the dashboard, tasting each delicious syllable, "Portia Kane. *Portia Kane.*"

I pull away from the curb, and as I pass the Crystal Lake Diner, I feel like something really good has begun. Like I'm basking in the warmth of the best sunrise I will ever experience. Maybe this really is the story of Portia and Chuck, and I'm just at the beginning. Could I be that lucky?

And then I think of Mr. Vernon hobbling away from me as quickly as possible, and how my little speech seemed to make no impact on him whatsoever.

What do you do when the person you admire most literally turns his back on you?

I'm not sure.

How the hell did we end up at the police station last night? I think when I pass it.

Where did Mr. Vernon go?

When I pull into the parking lot across from the Manor, I see Portia's rental car, and my heart leaps, because it gives me a chance to call her right away, to hear her voice without coming off as needy.

So I dial her cell phone.

"What took you so long to call me?" Portia says. "I've missed you, Mr. Bass."

It takes me a second to answer, I'm so giddy—I feel like a teenager again—but then I say, "Forget something at the Manor last night?"

"Shit. The rental car."

"Should I come get you?"

"Please."

"I'll be there in five." I hang up, and when I check myself out in the rearview mirror, I see a happy man—more elated than he's ever been in his entire life.

CHAPTER 23

Tommy gets attached to Portia really fast, which scares me a little, even though Portia is great with him. For months, almost all of our dates are sexless because the little man is along for the ride, usually right between us, actually, holding both our hands.

We take him to the movies, where we see all of the animated films; to the Franklin Institute, so he can climb around in that huge beating human heart they have there; to the Academy of Natural Sciences, so he can marvel at the reconstructed dinosaur bones looming above; even to Longwood Gardens to smell the spring flowers, which I never dreamed Tommy would be into, but he is in a big way. Especially the tulips, of all things, like just how many there are, endless amounts—he even tries to count them, but quits around one hundred or so. We go to a few Phillies games at Citizens Bank Park when my Manor customers float me tickets as tips, and even though none of us really like baseball we have a good time watching the Phillie Phanatic dance, goof on people, and throw his big green belly around; we run the steps of the Philadelphia Museum of Art and victoriously hold our hands up in the air like Rocky before we eat cheese steaks at Pat's in South Philly, where Tommy—with electric-yellow Cheez Whiz all over his face—innocently asks, "Who's Rocky?" so we immediately rent the movie that weekend, and Tommy says, "Yo, Adrian!" for weeks. We go to the beach a lot when the weather warms up, and Portia looks drop-dead gorgeous in a bikini; at the zoo we take a ride up in their hot air balloon, which freaks me out a bit, to the point where Tommy reaches up and holds my hand because he sees how nervous I am; and when the temperature breaks into the nineties, we go fountain hopping, even though it is technically illegal now. "How can you make a Philly tradition illegal?" Portia says as she strides into the first fountain like a seasoned lawbreaker. We do all the stuff that most normal families do every weekend in and around Philadelphia.

Portia plans these adventures with a regularity and reliability that none of us have ever known before, maybe because our parents were too poor or lazy or, in the case of Portia's mother, mentally unwell to give us these experiences back in the day. It's like Portia's trying to prove something to Tommy and me—maybe to herself as well.

I tell myself to just enjoy this—this amazing gift that seems to have magically appeared, right when Tommy and I needed it most—but I wonder a lot about my good luck and just when it will run out.

Tommy does too, I can tell. He always hugs Portia for too long when he says good-bye to her, and I often have to peel him off her limb by limb.

At first Danielle joins us on a few of these family trips, though she's distant and she bristles when Portia pays for everything, which I understand, believe me. I do realize it's the twenty-first century, and I'm really not a sexist asshole, but I don't like letting Portia pay either, even though she insists she's doing it to get back at her husband, who is apparently loaded. But after the first few excursions, Danielle just stops joining us on our adventures, saying her feet hurt from waitressing, or she wants some time alone. Portia and I each talk to Danielle privately, asking her to be a part of things. Then we both ask to spend time alone with my sister, but she refuses, making up excuse after lame excuse. It's like we've suddenly caught some deadly disease. Portia takes it hard.

"What did I do wrong?" she keeps asking.

"My sister's not used to kindness," I offer. "And she has difficulty trusting people—especially people who are good to her. She pushes them away before they can let her down. It's a pattern that has nothing to do with you."

But we both feel bad and maybe even guilty about the situation.

I can tell that Danielle quitting our new family bums Tommy out, makes him feel conflicted, even though he never says anything.

After Tommy and I return home from watching Fourth of July fireworks with Portia in the park across the street from Collingswood High School, when Tommy says he had an amazing time and begins to list all of the cool snacks Portia packed for our picnic that was in "a real wooden basket" and "on a blanket in the grass like families on TV would do," my sister just says, "It's late, Tommy. You should have been in bed hours ago. Now brush your teeth, buddy."

When he blinks at her, confused, Danielle says, "You can tell me all about your picnic in the morning."

Tommy looks like he's not sure what to do, so I say, "Time to brush those teeth. You heard your mother."

He nods once at me and does as he's told.

Danielle has no steady boyfriend, and I'm madly in love. It's been hard for her, being the only Bass sibling not high on life these days. So I let her hostility slide.

Danielle quit drugs cold turkey, without rehab, and she still drinks alcohol, which I've always admired in a slightly suspicious way, because I needed a lot of help to quit drugs. Alcohol is also a dangerous drug for me, which is why I don't drink. And I worry that Danielle's never having been to rehab makes her more susceptible to a backslide and prone to start using again. But she seems okay lately, working a full-time job even.

I pour myself a Diet Coke and sit down on the futon.

In the bathroom, Danielle's getting Tommy ready for bed, and I hear him trying to tell his mother all about what happened tonight—which fireworks he liked the best, and the little American flags on sticks that Portia brought, and everyone chanting "USA! USA! USA!" after the grand finale—but Danielle only gives him instructions, moving him closer to bed.

After a short bedtime story, Danielle returns. She pours herself a large Jack Daniel's and then sits down next to me.

"Do you wanna watch TV?" I ask.

"You're not his father, you know."

"Tommy's?" I say, which is dumb, I admit, because I know who she's talking about. It's a strange comment, because when Tommy's real father left, Danielle practically begged me to take them in, and when I did, she gave me a big speech about how I *needed* to be her son's father, because we never had one.

"I appreciate all that you and Portia do for him, but he's still my son," she says.

"I'm aware of that."

"Good."

"What do you think about Portia and me?" I ask. "Truthfully."

Danielle looks down at the drink in her hands. "She's still married, you know. She could move back to Florida with her rich husband."

"My worst fear."

"You asked."

"So you don't trust her?"

She shakes her head. "I don't trust anyone. Remember?"

"Do you trust me?"

"Maybe eighty percent."

"What?" I say and then laugh. "You don't trust me twenty percent of the time?"

"Eighty percent is the most I've ever trusted anyone. Be proud."

"How much do you trust Portia?"

"Five percent. Tops."

My stomach drops. "So you think she'll hurt me?"

"Everyone hurts you eventually, big brother." Danielle sips her whiskey. "Can I have your keys? I could really use a drive."

"Where are you going?"

"Just out to clear my head."

"Are you okay to drive?"

"Should I walk a line for you, Officer Bass, or say the alphabet backward?" She smiles at me in this wonderfully sarcastic little-sister way. "A short drive around town is healthier than Jack Daniel's. I won't be long."

"Okay," I say, offer her my keys, and then she's gone.

I pick her barely sipped Jack up off the floor and dump it out in the sink.

A minute or so later, I hear, "Uncle Chuck?"

I turn around, and Tommy's standing there in his PJs, wearing my old Quiet Riot mask, which means he's crying and doesn't want me to see.

"Did you have another bad dream?"

He nods. "Where did Mom go?"

"Just for a drive," I say.

The boy leaps up into my arms, and I can feel his little heart beating too hard, which reminds me of all the nights I spent alone in bed trembling when I was his age, hoping my mother or one of her many dickhead boyfriends wouldn't enter the room I shared with Danielle.

"Can we watch your Mötley Crüe *Carnival of Sins* DVD?" He loves watching that concert, and his mother sometimes says—depending on her mood—that he's too young to be taking in metal shows, especially since there are women dressed like strippers onstage with the band. Danielle and Tommy gave me the DVD for Christmas, and watching it has become what Tommy and I do when his mother isn't home.

"Sure," I say, because I'd do anything to help the kid forget a nightmare.

I get him situated on the futon and fast-forward through the opening where two strippers simulate sex, the whole time feeling as though I too may be a horrendous role model for the kid, exposing him to 1980s metal at such a young age, and then Mötley Crüe is playing "Shout at the Devil" as pillars of fire explode upward behind them to the beat.

Tommy raises up the devil's horns through the first chorus, but then he takes off his Quiet Riot mask and nuzzles his head against my chest.

He's sound asleep before they finish playing "On with the Show," my favorite Crüe song of all time.

I hit stop on the DVD player and carry him into his bedroom.

Once he's under his sheet, I hang the Quiet Riot mask on the nail over his headboard for protection from nightmares.

I watch him breathe for a while, and I think about how there's nothing I wouldn't do for this little guy—not a thing in the world.

And then I crawl into my own bed on the opposite side of the room, and I think about where Danielle might have gone.

I'm woken up by laughter, and when my brain kicks in again, I hear Danielle in the living room with a man.

They put the B side of *G N' R Lies* on the turntable, and while

I agree that it is one of the best late-night B sides to put on after a party, they're playing "Patience" loud enough to wake up the entire fucking neighborhood.

"What's happening?" Tommy says.

"It's okay," I say, looking at my cell phone: 4:44 a.m.

"Stay here," I say.

I turn on the light so Tommy won't be afraid and then close the door behind me.

In the living room, my sister is slow dancing with some guy wearing a skintight Sex Pistols "Anarchy in the UK" T-shirt. His hair is all spiked up. There's a dog collar around his neck, and covering his arms are dark sleeve tattoos, which I instinctively scan for track marks, the old junkie in me thinking, What is this guy hiding?

"Who are you?" he says when he sees me.

Danielle laughs. "That's just my brother, Chuck. What the Fuck Chuck, I call him." She has never once called me that before. She's slurring her words a little and holding onto Johnny Rotten for support because she's hammered. "Chuckie Fuckie!" she adds, and then laughs uncontrollably.

I appeal to Johnny Rotten. "Her son's in the back, trying to sleep."

"You mean him?" Johnny Rotten says, and points with his long goatee, through which a thin white scar runs.

I turn around and see Tommy staring wide-eyed.

"Back to bed, Tommy," I say. "Everything is okay."

"Who is that?" Tommy says.

"Com-ear, Tom-hee!" Danielle says and then opens her arms. "You can stay up all night if you just give me a hug and a kiss."

Johnny Rotten laughs, and Tommy looks up at me with scared eyes.

"She's just drunk," I whisper to him. "She'll be okay tomorrow."

"I'm just *happy*," Danielle says, "which ain't no crime," and then tries to walk over toward me, but she trips and face-plants on the floor.

Johnny Rotten rushes over to my sister.

"Uh-oh," Danielle says, and when she sits up, her hand and nose are red.

"Mommy!" Tommy says.

"It's okay," I say to Tommy as I try to help Danielle up.

Guns N' Roses is now playing "Used to Love Her" on the turntable, which is still cranked up high.

"That tickles!" Danielle says when I put my hand under her armpit.

Johnny Rotten says, "Maybe we should put her to bed."

"You think?" I say.

"You can go home, man," he says to me. "I can take it from here."

"This *is* my home."

"Oh." Johnny Rotten looks genuinely surprised. "So they're staying with you."

"Yeah, he's like a superhero, my brother," Danielle says. "Likes to save people like me and Tommy. Best guy you'll ever meet. Chuck Bass. Gotta love him."

"Okay, drunk girl," I say. "Let's get you into your room."

"I love you so much, big brother. I really do."

The little man looks at me, and I can tell seeing his mother smashed like this scares him. "Tommy, go to our room," I say. "I'll be right there, I promise."

He listens, even though Danielle says, "No! Let's stay up all night long!"

Johnny Rotten and I get Danielle onto her mattress, and then I say, "*I'll* take it from here. Thanks."

"You sure you're good?"

"Yeah," I say, and escort him out the front door.

When I return to her bedroom, Danielle's giggling on her back with a fistful of bloody napkins on her nose.

"Please tell me you didn't drive home," I say to her.

"Relax. We were drinking at the Manor. Lisa made him *walk* me home," she says and then starts laughing. "But I do like him. Very cute. Noticed a rather large bulge in his pants too."

"You need to sleep it off, Danielle." I bring her some water, and then I go back to Tommy, who looks whiter than the sheet covering his legs and torso.

"I didn't like that guy," Tommy says.

"Neither did I," I say, wondering what would have happened to drunk Danielle if I weren't here to put her to bed and send her escort home.

Of course Danielle sees our man again and makes him her regular boyfriend. Johnny Rotten's real name turns out to be Randall Street, which has to be the dumbest name ever.

Many times, Tommy tells Portia and me that he doesn't like Johnny Rotten, and we fumble around for what to say back to him, because Danielle seems happy, albeit distant. I ask her to double date with Portia and me, so I can get to know Johnny Rotten better and alleviate my fears, but Danielle just laughs and says, "We're dating people from different planets. Let's not start an intergalactic war, okay?"

"What do you mean?"

"You're happy. I'm happy. Let's not push our luck. Just be happy with Portia independent of us. I'm fine. You've already done enough for me, big brother."

The truth is that while I love my sister, and I really do, carrying her financially and emotionally has been draining. The break Johnny Rotten provides is somewhat of a relief.

And so when Portia gets her own place in Collingswood, a little two-bedroom apartment above a flower shop on Haddon Avenue, I gradually move most of my stuff over there. She sets up a small sofa bed in her office for Tommy, so that he can sleep over whenever Danielle asks us to babysit, which is often. Even though I am still paying the rent on the Oaklyn place, Tommy tells me that Johnny Rotten's been staying there more and more.

Tommy doesn't like jumping back and forth between the two apartments, but he'll get used to it, and to Danielle's new boyfriend, who seems okay, from what I've observed. If he makes my sister happy, well, then I'm all for that. And so I tell Tommy, "Look for the good in this guy. He may just surprise you."

Portia's writing a novel now. That's what she does all day long.

I've never met anyone before who was writing a novel, and now my girlfriend is a full-time fiction writer, which makes me proud, I have to admit. It seems so glamorous, even though no one is paying her to write this book, it's just something she does alone in a room. She says she can get an agent when she finishes and then that agent can sell the book to a publishing house in New York City—"a real one," she's always saying. She reads books about how to do it and chats with all of these other writers on the Internet, which makes her hopeful.

Portia works with her door closed and always covers the laptop screen with her hands whenever I knock and stick my head in. She says she can't talk about her book because the talking will rob her of the creative energy she needs to write, which sounds a little like bullshit to me, but what do I know. She even wears this lucky hat when she's working—it's a pink Phillies baseball hat that they gave her for free on ladies' night at the ballpark when one of my customers slipped us tickets as a tip. The writing makes her so joyous—

she seems determined and driven—that it probably doesn't really matter what she's wearing or doing in that room. It's all good, as far as I'm concerned.

Late at night, after she's had a few drinks, she'll talk about how she first decided she wanted to write a novel back in Mr. Vernon's class, and how the world knocked the belief that she could do it out of her.

"How does that happen?" she says. "You can't look back and pinpoint an exact moment when you give up on your dreams. It's like someone stealing all of the salt from your kitchen, one tiny crystal at a time. You don't realize it for months, and then when you see that you are low, you still think you have thousands of little crystals left—and then bam, no salt."

Sometimes when she talks like that I feel stupid, because I don't think about the world the way she does, and yet I love Portia, so I nod and agree. I feel completely lost when she asks, "What do you think about that?" and I can't think of anything to say.

But she never seems to mind. Portia says I listen to her and "don't piss on her dreams." She never really talks about her husband directly—it's sort of a taboo subject—but I've been able to infer that he made her feel stupid and small and weak.

Apparently, when they were in New York City, Portia told Mr. Vernon that she would publish a novel and dedicate it to him, and now she thinks that if she can keep her promise, Mr. Vernon might discover her book, read the dedication, and maybe it will save him after all.

That's her new great hope.

Portia Kane's latest master plan to save our old teacher.

We asked the Oaklyn Police Department for information on Mr. Vernon, but by law they weren't permitted to share any developments or details, or so they said.

Late one slow night, when it was just Jon and me at the bar, he finally admitted after four or five pints that he had driven Mr. Vernon to the Amtrak train station in Philadelphia, and that was the last they heard of him. Because our former teacher had committed no crime, they didn't even ask him for any of his information.

"It's damn hard to see a grown man crying the way he was that night, Chuck," Jon said, staring down into his golden pint of Budweiser. "Shit. Especially after all that had happened to him. So I gave him a ride across the bridge in the cruiser. It's what any decent person would have done. You would have done the same thing."

Portia and I have both googled our former teacher's name many times, hoping to see "Mr. Nathan Vernon" listed on some high school faculty roster somewhere, or at least find some evidence that he's still alive and didn't actually go through with the suicide pact that he apparently made with his dog, according to Portia, which seems bizarre. Portia claims Mr. Vernon's dog actually held up his end of the bargain by jumping out a second-story window, if you can believe that.

In the public records we find that he sold his house in Vermont, so we can't even go looking for him there.

But no other new mentions of Mr. Vernon's name ever appear on the Internet, just references to his teaching at HTHS and his being attacked by Edmond Atherton years ago.

It's a consolation that we never find any evidence of his death either. Portia says that there would be some sort of official record, an obituary or a listing.

She's always so optimistic when she says this, so I never bring up the fact that many people die every day in this country without the media printing their names—just ask any former junkie who has spent time on the streets, where last names don't matter and people vanish into thin air on an hourly basis. According to what Portia found out from his since-deceased nun mother, Mr. Vernon had no known family left to even pay for an obituary to run in a paper. He could also have killed himself in some remote desolate place where his body would never be found, or even in some back alley in a bad city neighborhood.

But as I hear Portia clicking away on her laptop, often until late at night, I know exactly what hope is fueling the writing of her novel, so I keep my darker thoughts to myself.

I want to preserve whatever harmony we have for as long as I can. My life has never been better.

CHAPTER 24

Besides bartending at the Manor and taking Tommy places with Portia, I spend the summer applying and interviewing for jobs as an elementary school teacher. What I have going for me is that I'm a man applying for positions that are almost always filled by women, so I'm a bit of a novelty. What I have working against me is that I'm forty-two and have relatively little teaching experience.

My CV is mostly a huge blank.

Here's what I have to show: strong recommendation letters from my college professors and the cooperating teachers and principal of the school where I did my student teaching, a portfolio of work from my students that includes happy child drawings of me looking like a super educator, and several samples of six-year-old writing that often proclaims me "the number one teacher in the world." That's a direct quote from Owen Hammond's penmanship sample that I proudly include because it took us two months of encouragement and hand-over-hand coaching to get the little guy to stop writing his S's backward—one of the finest accomplishments in my entire life, if I do say so myself.

All of this goes over well enough, but the interview will inevitably arrive at the uncomfortable part where they ask what I did in my twenties and early thirties. I have no suitable answer for that, because when choosing role models for small children, you don't often hire men who used to shoot heroin as a full-time profession. I can't exactly discuss the many nights I passed out behind Dumpsters with a needle sticking out of my arm or the times when the cravings were so intense that I robbed homes for cash and jewelry. There are dozens of nights I don't even remember. How I was never arrested, I can't tell you. So when we reach that part of the interview, I usually just say something vague like I was still trying to find myself or I got a late start with my calling, and then I shrug and laugh in a friendly way. The interviewers never laugh back, and I've failed to get the job six times already this summer.

I've been extending my potential commute to ninety-plus minutes each way to increase my chances as I scour the Internet for job postings, so no one can accuse me of a lack of effort. Portia keeps saying, "Something will turn up. I'm absolutely sure of it," which is both encouraging, because she's so understanding, and infuriating, because her husband's money affords her the ability to be so nonchalant about the fact that I have no real job, no health insurance, and no equity at all. Why he hasn't cut her off yet is the biggest mystery of my life these days.

From time to time I ask Portia if it's not weird that we are living together so happily—making love now on a regular, healthy, and exciting basis—when she is technically still married to another man.

She always laughs and says, "Don't worry about him, because he's a complete asshole."

And when I try to push it, asking when she might actually file for a divorce, she always says, "Are you not having fun?" which makes me feel like I'm rushing her and also that she is just playing at love with me, which is my worst fear. But I keep telling myself to let things develop organically, although I worry about Tommy should Portia ever leave us. I'm not sure he could handle it.

I also worry that the seemingly endless supply of money Portia has access to will dry up and leave us unable to pay the bills, but I know it's not my business to ask about her situation, especially when she's not charging me any rent, which allows me to keep paying for Danielle and Tommy's place.

If I get a real teaching job, that's when I'll have a serious talk with Portia about money and our future together. How can I bring up the subject of cash when I am contributing so little?

My Narcotics Anonymous sponsor lives in South Carolina now, but we still talk on the phone regularly. His name is Kirk Avery, and he's about twenty years older than me. When he first agreed to be my sponsor, I thought he would give me all sorts of advice, like a life coach. I think I was secretly hoping for a Mr. Miyagi who would share ancient secrets and teach me how to solve all of my problems, give me a cool antique car, kick the asses of all my enemies, and even get me hooked up with the hottest woman around. But Kirk turned out to be just a regular American guy who likes to go deep-sea fishing and paint little portraits of random things found in anyone's house—a toaster or a bottle of Windex or a shoehorn or a roll of toilet paper—which he posts on his website and actually sells. It's like he's Andy Warhol or something, except he's the most normal guy in the world otherwise. He was an accountant by trade, but he just retired recently. And he's never really given me any advice at all. He just picks up the phone when I call, like he promised he would back when we were first paired up.

"That's my job," he said. "Just to pick up whenever you dial my number. And it's the most important job a sponsor can take on."

I thought he was insane when he said it, because it sounded so ridiculous. How could simply picking up the phone matter? I learned quickly just how much it mattered when I started calling him at all hours of the night because I wanted a fix and my life was falling apart. He'd stay up with me, just listening to me babble on and on about all of the stupid shit I was angry and worried about. And the monologues I delivered were so long that sometimes I'd stop and say, "Are you even still there?" and he'd always reply, "Eternally," which I didn't really understand at first, but now, in retrospect, I've come to see that Kirk Avery is the rare sort of man who keeps his promises, and I needed that type in my life more than I realized.

Every Christmas he sends me a four-inch-square painting, and I have them hanging in Portia's and my apartment now, over my dresser. These are all random things too—a fly swatter, a corkscrew, an electrical socket, hardly the type of art most women would agree to hang in their homes. But when I explained that these were from my NA sponsor, and that simply looking at the little squares of art helped to keep me on the straight and narrow path, so to speak, Portia told me to hang them up right away, wherever I'd draw the most strength from seeing them. I chose the bedroom, because the nights can be bad sometimes. These little paintings are a bit like Tommy's Quiet Riot mask for me. It's not what's actually painted that matters, but that the little artworks have arrived and continue to arrive with a regularity that I didn't think possible for most of my life. I like to count them in the middle of the night, like the tree rings on a stump, knowing that I've been sober one year for every little picture, and that Kirk Avery has been a witness to each hard-fought drug-free trip around the sun.

There are eleven paintings on my wall.

I've been asked to be a sponsor myself, but I haven't taken on that responsibility yet. I didn't think I could handle it when I was recently clean, and then Tommy arrived, and I immediately wanted to give him all I had—the best of me.

Sometimes I wonder if I'm kind of like Tommy's sponsor, even though he's not an addict, and I hope he never will be.

*   *   *

One day in mid-August it's too hot to be outside, and Portia's in her office typing away as usual, so I decide to call Kirk Avery because I haven't spoken to him in months.

"Mr. Chuck Bass," he answers now without saying hello, because my name comes up on his cell phone, and I remember when I used to call him mostly from pay phones, my front right jeans pocket bulging with silver coins that each bought me a few minutes, back before either of us had a cell. "Tell me that you're still clean and sober."

"I am," I say. "One hundred percent."

"Congratulations, friend. It's a clearheaded life for us."

"How are you?"

"Well," he says, like always, and I have spent many a night awake and thinking about how Kirk Avery rarely leaks any details regarding his life. He'll tell me about some fish he "fought," spending hours reeling in, or how many paintings he has recently sold on the Internet, but nothing else. Maybe that's all part of the sponsor gig, making it about me and not him, but it's weird how much I care about Kirk, when I know so little about the man. "What's up?" he asks.

That's my cue to tell him what's on my mind—to get to the point of the call. It used to bother me, how direct he always is with me, but I've learned to appreciate the efficiency.

So I tell him all about Portia's lax attitude toward her husband and how I can't find a teaching gig, even though I technically graduated last December and now have six months of subbing experience under my belt, during which I kissed the ass of every administrator within eyesight, but the interviews always ask about the past. "I mean—they make you submit your goddamn life history on a piece of paper."

"Use it to your advantage," Kirk says.

"How?"

"You beat heroin. You can do anything if you can do that."

"So you want me to tell them I was an addict?"

"Have you not been going to NA meetings for more than a decade now?"

"Yeah, but it's different when you're being hired to work with kids. It'll scare them away."

"I'd rather my son or daughter be taught by an openly reformed and honest addict than a liar with a shady past he's afraid to talk about."

I see his point, but he doesn't know what it's like to sit in those boardrooms at the end of a long table, being grilled by suits.

"How's Tommy?" he says, uncharacteristically changing the subject before I'm through.

I tell him how Tommy doesn't like Danielle's new boyfriend, who I really don't know all that well. "He seems like an okay guy, but he has these sleeve tattoos that make it hard to tell if there are any needle marks. And yet Danielle seems normal enough lately, so I don't know. Tommy's fine."

"Remember," he says, "you need to keep yourself healthy first and foremost. You can't be your sister's keeper for her entire life."

"You know, sometimes I feel guilty," I say, "because this new life with Portia—it's like heaven."

"Don't overthink it. Just let it be heaven," he says, almost Mr. Miyagi–like.

And I wonder if it can be that easy—just enjoying Portia without worrying too much about Danielle and Tommy and Portia's marital status and how the rest of the world views my bank account.

"Hey," Kirk says, "you've *earned* your sobriety, fought hard for it, fair and square, and that's more than most people can say. Don't be embarrassed of your accomplishments. You think Tommy cares that you were once an addict?"

I wonder what the little man will think once he's old enough to understand what that means—how low I once sunk—and I worry about it sometimes too. But I've already taken up too much of Kirk's time, so I don't say anything.

"You ever hear from that teacher of yours again, the one who left the party?" he asks.

"No," I say, embarrassed yet again.

"Maybe you will yet."

"I don't know."

"Life's funny, Chuck. People surprise you sometimes. And don't let anyone convince you different."

"Thanks," I say, though his bringing up Mr. Vernon makes me feel even worse about everything. Then I add, "Hope you catch some big fish and sell tons of paintings this month."

He laughs. "Roger that. You good?"

"Yeah," I say, even though I'm not really all that great, and then we exchange good-byes and hang up.

Like always, I think of a million things I could have asked the mysterious Kirk Avery if only I had more courage, but maybe it's like I don't want to mess with a good thing. I don't want to back him into any bad corners that would make him think twice about picking up my next call.

He's been my one constant since I quit heroin, and a constant is a powerful thing.

I spend the rest of the day listening to the clicking of Portia's fingers on her laptop and the steady buzz of her headphones playing the classical music she likes. She's become obsessed with some cellist named Yo-Yo Ma.

I wonder if all her typing will really help Mr. Vernon in the future. I definitely hope that it will, but I also worry that Portia is actually going to be able to help Mr. Vernon in a way I never could, and while I realize it's petty and low to be competitive like that with the woman I love, it is also hard to imagine her successes while I continue to fail.

Her determination and belief in her abilities are a little daunting, to say the least.

CHAPTER 25

Just before August ends, when I have all but given up hope, resigning myself to another year of substitute teaching and bartending, I get a surprise call from a small Catholic school in Rocksford, Pennsylvania, a sixty- to ninety-minute drive from our apartment in Collingswood, depending on traffic.

A Mother Catherine Ebling asks if I can possibly interview immediately. When I agree, she says, "How about this afternoon?"

Portia's clicking away in her room with the door closed, so after a shave and shower, I leave her a note and hop in the old man's Ford wearing my one and only suit, which is tan and dated and a little too snug, but hopefully adequate.

I drive with my jacket off, the vents on high and the windows open, but I end up sweating anyway. It's ninety-five degrees out, the old man's Ford has no air-conditioning, and I'm nervous as hell.

"Remember what Kirk told you," I say over and over as I drive. "That getting clean is an accomplishment—something that sets you apart, something to be proud of and not to hide."

When I arrive at the small school, I drive past the huge imposing black iron crucifix outside and pull into the parking lot.

I mop off my face with my lucky red handkerchief, look at myself in the rearview mirror, and say, "You are a fucking rock star, Chuck Bass. A first-grade-teacher rock star. And your jacket will cover the disgusting sweat marks under your pits and on your back."

With my jacket on and my portfolio in the leather briefcase Portia purchased for me when I first started going on interviews—I refused to let her buy me a new suit, although she offered at least a hundred times—I enter the school and am greeted by a cool blast of wind.

Hello air conditioning, my old friend.

My luck continues when I spot a men's room.

So I freshen up, washing my face with cool water, and giving myself another pep talk in the mirror. *"Not working, old approach. Another, you must try, Young Bass. Rock star, you are,"* I say like Yoda for some unknown reason.

I enter the office fifteen minutes early and introduce myself.

"Welcome!" yells the tiny woman behind the desk. She looks to be maybe ninety years old and is squinting so badly I wonder if she might be legally blind in addition to being hard of hearing, or so I assume based on the way she yells. She's in plain clothes, wearing a heavy sweater to protect her from the air conditioning. "We've been praying hard for a miracle around here! I hope you're it! Take a seat!"

I laugh and then sit down by the teacher mail cubicles and read the last names printed above each. I wonder who will have to move all but Mrs. Abel's name over should Mr. Bass get hired and take cubicle number two, by right of alphabetical order.

The old woman disappears and a minute or so later returns with another slightly less elderly nun, who is maybe six feet tall and rather manly looking, even though she's in a nun's habit. A large silver crucifix rests on her enormous breasts, she's wearing tan stockings in August, and her hands are so large and red that I wonder if maybe she started out life as the opposite gender.

"Mr. Bass, I presume?" she says, extending her gigantic mitt toward me.

I stand. "Mother Ebling?" When we shake, her grip pinches me unexpectedly, almost as if her hand were a claw.

"You may call me Mother Catherine." She lets go, saying, "Follow me," and I obey.

The tiny old woman who first greeted me yell-whispers, "Good luck! And I'll say a prayer for you!"

Even though I'm not really religious, her offer makes me feel a little better. So far, people are nice here, at least.

I wonder if Mother Catherine just moved in. There are boxes all over the floor, and nothing hung on the walls. She sits down in a throne of leather behind a large wooden desk and motions for me to sit in the much more modest wooden chair facing her, so I do.

She examines my face for a moment or two, like she's sizing me up. "This is my first week as principal here, and you are my first official order of business. Do you want to know why you were called in for an interview after the position had already been filled a month ago?"

"I'm happy to interview, regardless of why the position has opened up. I'm ready to teach," I say. I had no idea there had been a previous hiring for the job. I've shotgunned my CV around to so many places that I can't really keep track of them all.

"I see you're a no-nonsense type of guy. I like your style, Mr. Bass," she says, and then gives me a smile. "If you get hired today, you'll no doubt learn the gossip soon enough—that is, if you haven't already read today's local paper. There were some unethical hiring practices going on. The former principal is being accused of abusing his authority, and the attractive young woman he hired earlier in the summer has filed a sexual harassment lawsuit against us. So here I am, filling in as emergency principal, and here you are."

I don't know what to say, so I say nothing.

"Those are my cards. Right there on the table," she says. "Let's see yours."

"I beg your pardon?"

"Why haven't you been hired yet?"

"I don't know. I'm ready to teach, though. I'm an excellent teacher."

"Are you a practicing Catholic?"

"No."

"Are you a nonpracticing Catholic?"

I swallow once and shake my head.

"Do you believe in God, at least?" she asks.

"Yes," I say, and it's true—I pretty much believe in God, or maybe I don't *not* believe in God.

"Well, that's certainly a good start. Now, should we hire you, would you be willing to uphold the beliefs and morals of the Catholic Church in your classroom, or are you one of those teachers who want to Trojan-horse us?"

"Trojan-horse you?"

"Sneak inside our walls using some sort of philosophical disguise and then attack from within. I've seen it happen a million times. People take jobs working for the Catholic Church and then they want to challenge the roles of nuns and priests and debate all sorts of things just to get everyone upset. We don't need that, especially at an elementary school. You don't have to agree with everything the Catholic Church does, but if you want to work here and take home a check every two weeks, you have to at least be respectful of the institution providing you with a job."

This nun is intense, I think. "I just want to teach kids how to read and do math. Help them learn how to write. I have no other agenda than to educate. Especially regarding six-year-olds. I mean, it's first grade, right?"

She looks into my eyes for what seems like an eternity. "I believe you. Good."

I nod, because I don't know what else to do, and when the sound of the air conditioning blowing full blast starts to get uncomfortable, I say, "Would you like to see my teaching portfolio?"

"In order to speed up the process—and especially in light of recent events here at our school—I've already spoken with your references, including the cooperating teacher with whom you did your student teaching, Mrs. Baxter. She was absolutely lovely on the phone, and she's already told me everything I need to know about what you are capable of doing in the classroom." Mother Catherine pauses, smiles knowingly, and says, "Before I ask this next question, I would like to preface it by saying I am a Catholic woman, and Catholic women believe in redemption and the power of forgiveness. But we do not suffer liars all that well. No, we surely do not. So with that in mind, why is there a rather large blank on your CV? Who were you before you decided to teach little children?"

I can feel my throat start to close, my palms becoming slick, my tongue drying up, and my forehead turning bright red.

Remember what Kirk said, I tell myself. *Be strong for Portia so you can start building a future. Be the man she can admire.*

Mother Catherine is tapping the tips of her index fingers against each other, waiting for me to answer, but instead of opening my mouth, I open my wallet, pull out my Official Member of the Human Race card, and hand it to her.

"What's this?" she says, a bit surprised for the first time during the interview, which feels like a good sign for some reason.

"My high school English teacher made it for me," I say. "Go ahead. Read it."

I watch Mother Catherine's eyes move back and forth as she

reads the lines, and a smile creeps its way up her face. "Please explain," she says when she finishes.

So I tell her all about Mr. Vernon, and what an influence he was on me, and how I never told him thank you and always regretted it. Before I can stop myself, I'm telling her about my heroin addiction and how I finally came to admit I had a problem and then went to rehab, where I used Mr. Vernon as a lighthouse as I got clean, making teaching my ultimate goal. It feels so freeing to say all of this out in the open, in an interview, no less—so much so that I wonder why I didn't do it earlier. I am killing this interview now. There is a confidence in my voice that I haven't heard for a long time, and I can see it registering on Mother Catherine's face, which gives me even more swagger, and so I tell her all about Mr. Vernon being attacked in the classroom and how Portia and I tried to save him.

She interrupts me and says, "Who is this Portia?"

I know that living with a woman out of wedlock is probably still a sin according to the Catholic Church and will probably win me no points with a nun, so I skip that part and say, "She's my girlfriend. The great love of my life. And I'm going to ask for her hand in marriage just as soon as I'm on my feet financially."

A look of shock flashes across Mother Catherine's face, which terrifies me.

"You may find this a rather odd and intrusive question, Mr. Bass," she says, "but are you willing to tell me Portia's last name?"

"Why?"

"Just indulge me. Please."

"It's Kane. Portia Kane."

A beat of silence hangs heavy between us before Mother Catherine says, "Does she know you're here today interviewing for this job? Did you happen to mention my name to her?"

"I left her a note saying I was going on an interview, but I don't think I mentioned you specifically by name. May I ask why?"

"You may not," Mother Catherine says. "But you may tell me the end of your story."

"Excuse me?"

"Whatever became of this Mr. Vernon, the man who changed your life for the better?"

"We don't know," I say and then explain how he ditched his own party before it even began, demanded to be left alone, and had the Oaklyn police order us to stay away from him. I tell her about our efforts to find him since, but it's like he's vanished. "We tried our best to help Mr. Vernon. We really did," I add, thinking maybe this wasn't the best story to tell in an interview for a first-grade position, even if it distracts her from the fact that I am a recovered heroin addict.

She looks down at her desk for a long time. Finally she says, "All humans have access to Jesus Christ—but some of us are a little more connected than others, so to speak. And I'm not shy about my relationship with Jesus."

I stare back at her. I have no idea what she's talking about.

"If you are going to work in a Catholic school," she says, and I wonder if it means I already have the job, "you must get used to people like me talking about God and His mysterious ways. Are you okay with that? Again, we don't want to invite in any Trojan horses."

"I am definitely *not* a Trojan horse," I say. "I am more than okay with religious talk."

"Again, I do not suffer liars easily," she says in a way that makes me believe she'd take the wooden ruler to my knuckles if she had to, and judging by her size, I bet she could break more than a few with a single whack. "You are willing to lead your class in morning prayers, take them to school mass, and participate yourself too?"

"Absolutely," I say, without hesitation.

"Okay, then," she says. "You'll have my decision by eight o'clock tonight."

"That's it? The interview is over?" We didn't talk about my teaching philosophy, all of the ed psych I learned in college, nor did I even pull my portfolio from my leather briefcase.

"You are free to go."

"Thanks for your time." I stand, and then add, "I really do love kids. You hire me, and you will not regret it. You'll have a fully committed teacher."

"I know." She nods. "No need for histrionics, Mr. Bass."

I nod back, wondering what the hell histrionics means, and make my way to the door. But then I turn around, and before I can stop myself, say, "Why were you so interested in my girlfriend's last name?"

She smiles. "Is it possible for her to be there when I call you with my answer tonight? Tell her Mother Catherine Ebling of St. Therese's requests the pleasure of speaking with her on the phone."

"Sure," I say. "But how do you know Portia?"

"Oh, I do believe that she and I are linked."

"What do you mean?"

"Ask her."

"Does this mean I have the job?"

"You'll have my answer tonight, Mr. Bass."

When I arrive home, I tell Portia everything, and she laughs and laughs and explains Mother Catherine's relationship to Mr. Vernon's mother, how they both were nuns in the same convent and also best friends, "although they talked badly about each other all the time like an old married couple, which was hilarious. They bickered even when Sister Maeve was on her deathbed! Mr. Vernon's mom referred to Mother Catherine as the Crab."

"Wow. Mother Catherine does have these enormous hands," I say. "And you're not going to believe this. When she shook my hand—*I felt a pinch.*"

"Shut up!"

"I swear."

We both laugh.

Then I add, "But don't you think it's a little uncanny that I end up interviewing with a friend of Mr. Vernon's mom, after all that's happened?"

Portia touches the crucifix hanging around her neck. "No weirder than my meeting Sister Maeve by accident on a plane and then finding out she's the mother of my favorite English teacher."

At eight o'clock Portia and I are staring at my cell phone on the kitchen counter, and when it rings we lock eyes for a second before I pick it up and say, "Hello?"

"Let me talk to Portia," Mother Catherine says, without even identifying herself.

"She wants to talk *to you*," I say to Portia.

Portia's eyebrows arch as I hand her the cell phone, and then she's chatting away with Mother Catherine like they're long-lost friends.

For a half hour I sit there as Portia tells Mother Catherine all about her time with Mr. Vernon in Vermont and New York City, going on and on, when I just want to know whether I got the job or not.

They talk about Mr. Vernon's deceased mother next, and what a pistol she was. "So feisty," Portia says more than once. And then Portia is nodding and saying, "Um-hmm," over and over again, writing things down on the magnetized scratch pad we keep on the refrigerator.

I'm shocked when Portia hangs up without allowing me to speak with Mother Catherine, but then she says, "You want the good news or the bad news first?"

"Why didn't you let me talk to her?"

"She didn't want to talk to you. I'm sorry. You don't tell the Crab what to do."

"Bad news first," I say, because my heart is pounding.

"The nonnegotiable starting pay is only twenty-five grand a year plus benefits, and those are sort of shitty, from what I gathered."

"I got the job?"

"That's the good news. They want you to start tomorrow. Orientation begins at eight thirty sharp, and Mother Catherine recommends you give yourself plenty of time because of Philly commuter traffic. She says she doesn't tolerate tardiness."

"How does she know I'll be taking the job?"

"She said Jesus told her you would accept."

"What?" I laugh. "Is this weird or what?"

"Your getting hired to do what you've always wanted to do?"

"Just the way it happened, right? Bizarro!"

"Let's celebrate! Congratulations!" Portia says, and then she's in my arms.

We head over to Danielle's and Tommy's. Johnny Rotten's drinking a beer on the futon, looking very much at home.

I ignore the fact that he's living in my apartment for free and excitedly tell my sister the good news.

"Nice," she says, and then carries a bowl of Cinnamon Life and a Budweiser to the futon.

"This is what I've worked so hard for," I say, feeling a little kicked in the balls by Danielle's nonchalance.

"Congrats," Johnny Rotten says and lifts his beer in the air.

Danielle halfheartedly lifts her beer too. "Super congrats, bro. Happy for you."

They aren't exactly rude, but they clearly aren't excited for me either.

"Mind if we take Tommy out to celebrate?" Portia says, breaking the awkward tension.

"I bet he'd like that," Danielle says, and I notice that she's wearing long sleeves, which makes some part of my brain wonder if she's hiding track marks. The air conditioning is cranked up, and it's freezing in here, so I tell myself I'm being paranoid as I make my way to Tommy's bedroom.

He's got his headphones on like usual, so I sneak up behind him and tap his shoulder. I move left when he looks over his right shoulder, and when he turns the other way to face me, I remove his headphones. "Guess what? I got a teaching job!"

"Awesome!" he yells, and then he's in my arms and I'm lifting him up over my head so he can fly Superman style.

We take him to Friendly's and gorge on celebration sundaes.

When the bill comes, I insist on paying, and then we're driving home in the old man's Ford when Tommy says, "Can I stay with you guys tonight?"

"School night for me, buddy. I'm a legit working man now," I say. "Sorry."

"I don't want to live with my mom anymore," Tommy says.

"Why?" Portia asks.

"I don't know," he says.

"Did something happen?" I ask.

"No."

"You can tell us anything," Portia says.

"I know."

"Did Johnny Rotten do something to you?"

"No," Tommy says. "He's okay to me."

"Did your mom do something to you?" I ask.

"She doesn't do *anything* anymore."

Portia and I share a worried glance over his head.

In the Oaklyn apartment, Portia and I tuck Tommy in and read him a quick book as my sister and Johnny Rotten stare at the television and sip beer.

When we say bye to them, Johnny Rotten says, "Congrats again."

"Yeah, proud of you, bro," Danielle says, but her words are flat and empty.

In the truck, I say, "Was it me, or did Danielle seem underwhelmed by my good news?"

"You're changing your life for the better, and she's the same as always. Your drinking buddies aren't going to cheer when you get sober, right?" Portia says, and we drive back to our own apartment of bliss, where Portia toasts my new job with champagne, and we talk more about the strange coincidence of my connecting with Sister Maeve's best friend and then end up making celebratory love on the living room floor.

CHAPTER 26

The day after Thanksgiving, I have a precious day off.

Teaching has been going very well. I love my kids, the other teachers have been incredibly supportive—sharing lesson plans, lending me supplies, taking me out for after-work drinks and not grilling me when I don't order alcohol—and Mother Catherine seems pleased with my performance so far, but teaching full-time is much more demanding than I had originally thought. It's even harder than student teaching, which was difficult. And unfortunately, it's cut into the time I get to spend with my nephew.

So I use my rare free day to take Tommy out to buy a cell phone. He's been complaining about our not talking as much as we used to. My commute is long, so I figure we can catch up then.

Tommy and I pick out a cheap little flip phone at the Verizon store and I add him to my plan for next to nothing, especially since the only person he will ever call is me, and the sales guy sets it up so that calls from Tommy won't cost me anything extra.

"So I can call as many times as I want?" Tommy asks as we drive home. He's got the phone in his hand now and is examining it like it's some magical device from outer space.

"All you have to do *is* . . ."

"Hit the number one," he says, because we've programmed my number into his favorites.

"*And* . . ."

"Keep the phone charged."

"That's right! And I can call you from the truck now too during my commute!" I reach over to tousle his longish hair.

He pushes the one button on his phone, and mine starts ringing.

"I wonder who that could be?" I say in an overly dramatic voice that Tommy loves. It's so easy to entertain the little guy.

"Hello," I say into my phone.

"Uncle Chuck?" Tommy says into his.

"Speaking. Who is this?"

"Tommy!"

"Tommy who?"

"Tommy your nephew."

"That's an incredibly weird last name, Mr. Your-Nephew. Is it Greek?"

Tommy laughs and laughs and then says, "It's Tommy Bass."

"Oh, Tommy Bass, *my nephew*. I get it now. Why didn't you just say so?"

"I did!"

"Well?"

"Well what?"

"What is the purpose of your call?"

"To talk."

"Okay, then talk away."

"I know a secret you're not supposed to know," Tommy says, and suddenly the laughter has left his voice.

"What's that, Tommy, my nephew?"

"Mom's not working at the Crystal Lake Diner anymore."

"Really? Why?"

"I don't know. She told me not to tell you."

I swallow once. "Okay, Tommy. We'll find her another job."

Tommy hangs up his flip phone.

When we get to the Oaklyn apartment, I tell Danielle I purchased Tommy a cell phone so we can talk more. He shows it to her, and she says to me, "Um, do you think that maybe, just maybe you should have talked to me about this first?"

Sensing the tension, the little man retreats to his room.

It hits me that I definitely should have talked to Danielle about Tommy having a cell phone, but instead of admitting that, I say, "Went to the diner for lunch. Heard you lost your job." I glance down at her long sleeves. "What happened?"

"Jesus, *Dad*," she says, shaking her head. "I had the flu and called out a few days. My boss fired me. Does he really want me serving food when I have a virus, coughing on people's eggs and making everyone sick?"

"Tommy seems worried about you."

"I'm fine."

"You using again?" I say, before I can stop myself.

"*What?*"

"I haven't seen your arms in months."

She squints at me and says, "Are you even serious?"

"If you're using again, I'd be happy to take you to a meeting or—"

"I'm not using."

"Danielle, listen. I just want to—"

I'm shocked when she pulls her shirt over her head and then, in her black bra, holds both of her arms out for me to inspect.

My eyes speed up and down the soft white undersides of her wrists and biceps, but I see no fresh track marks, nor anything at all to suggest that she has been shooting heroin, other than the fact that her ribs are sticking out and she's lost quite a bit of weight. I wonder about other drugs, but am rather relieved to see that she at least isn't shooting junk. She never shot up anywhere else, back in the day—just in her arms. And my sister is a creature of habit, if nothing else.

"Are we good now?" she says. "You're being ridiculous."

"I'm sorry," I say, even though I'm only looking out for my little sister.

Danielle puts her shirt back on. "Just because my boyfriend has tattoos and no college diploma—"

"I'm concerned. That's all. I love you."

"Well, maybe I'm *concerned* that Tommy's too young to have a cell phone. Now if I take it away, I'll be cast as the bitch mom. So thanks for that."

"I told him we could talk during my commute."

"You have no Bluetooth in your truck, and you're not supposed to use cell phones when you drive. You could get into an accident. That would traumatize Tommy—scar him for life."

Her concern feels reassuring—like the old days—and so I say, "You're right. I'm sorry. Do you want me to take Tommy's cell phone back to the store?"

"What's done is done," she says, just like our mother used to, imitating Mom pretty well—lifting her palms above her head and shrugging her shoulders—and we both smile. "Is the interrogation over now?"

I nod. "Sorry you lost your job."

"Something will turn up. Randall's helping out with the bills too."

"What is it that he does?" I say, finally getting up the courage to ask what I've been wondering for months.

"He collects for bookies."

"Oh. Like—is he . . . *an enforcer*?" I ask, surprised, because he doesn't look all that tough or intimidating.

"No. Nothing that dramatic."

"Is it safe to have him around Tommy?"

"Please. The bookies he works for are regular guys with nine-to-five jobs and families. Randall just makes cash deliveries and pickups. He's like a UPS guy, only without the brown uniform."

"So. You're all right?"

"Yep. I'm dandy, big brother."

"Well, okay then."

I relay all of the above to Portia over dinner, and she says, "Danielle's a big girl, Chuck. And being a waitress sucks. Believe me. I know. Maybe it's the best thing that could have happened."

"I should have talked to her about getting Tommy a cell phone before I took him to the Verizon store. Right?"

"Yep."

"Shit."

"I would have been furious."

"Thanks," I say, but then my phone rings. "It's Tommy."

"Well, pick up," Portia says, and then starts to clear the table.

"Hey, buddy, what's up?" I say.

"Just wanted to make sure this phone works."

"You keeping it charged?"

"Got it plugged in next to my bed."

"Good man."

"Are we going to hang out this weekend?"

"Sure," I say.

"Mom cried after you left."

I watch Portia load the dishwasher for a second. "I'm sorry about that."

Tommy lowers his voice to a whisper. "Then she came in my room and promised to get a new job and make lots of money and take me to Disney World. Do you think she's telling the truth? I'd like to go. My friend Shawn at school has already gone *twice*."

"I bet she's going to do her best," I say.

"She also said I can call you as much as I want, even though she doesn't want to hang out with you for a while. Do you want to know why she doesn't want to be around you now?"

"Why?"

"She said she has to make you proud first."

I swallow hard, and then Tommy and I discuss maybe going to the Camden Aquarium this weekend and touring the battleship *New Jersey* before we hang up and I relay to Portia what Tommy said.

"I'll say it again," Portia says. "It's really fucking hard to be a single mother with only a high school diploma in this country." I make a note to remember that.

CHAPTER 27

Portia goes to see her mom a few times a week, but she never takes me, and I start to feel really strange about it, especially when we don't get together with her at all for Christmas or New Year's. Once in a while I casually suggest maybe introducing us, but Portia continues to visit her mother solo.

One night after dinner, I get up the courage to be more direct. "So what's up with you hiding me from your mother?"

"I'm not hiding you from anyone," Portia says.

"Then why have I never met her?"

"Because it's not necessary. I've never met *your* mother."

"She's *dead*," I say.

"But I'll never meet her, and it doesn't affect our relationship."

"Do you think your mom won't like me?"

"She's insane, Chuck. And I really don't want to get my worlds mixed up right now."

"Your worlds mixed up?"

"Things are going really well with us, right?"

"Yeah," I say, "except you won't introduce me to your mom. Does she even know about me?"

"We actually talk about you all the time," she says. "But she's sick. New things. Change is really hard for her."

"I want to meet her, because she's a part of your life, and I want the full Portia Kane experience."

Portia laughs. "You really want to meet my mother?"

"Yeah, I do. Are we there yet?"

"We've been there for a long time, and that's why I've been protecting you from Mom. I don't want us to *not* be there after you meet her. You might run away screaming."

"She can't be *that* bad."

"You sure?" The look in her eyes seems like a challenge.

"Let's take this relationship to the next level. Bring on your mom!"

It takes a few weeks for Portia to talk her mother into letting me visit, and I'm a little hurt at first, even though Portia explains that no one has visited her mother for decades, and so we are asking a lot of her. "And whatever you do," Portia says on the ride over there, "don't touch anything. We won't be able to sit down because there is so much shit everywhere, and it's important that my mother doesn't feel like you might want to alter the state of her home, which I must warn you will be absolutely frightening."

When we enter the row home, even though Portia said it would be bad, I'm shocked by the number of boxes and things that Portia's mother has fit into the small building. Endless piles of crap fill the rooms, leaving maybe only a two-foot-wide walking path to navigate. Every other inch of space is stacked almost floor-to-ceiling with boxes and junk.

Mrs. Kane is sitting in a recliner watching some home shopping program on TV. Her body odor is hard to ignore. She's wearing a very old pink terrycloth sweat suit covered in stains, and she doesn't even look over at us when Portia says, "Hi, Mom, this is the man I've told you so much about. Chuck Bass."

Portia gives me an I-told-you-so glance. "Mom, don't pretend to be invisible again, because I want you to meet my boyfriend. He's become a very big part of my life. I love him, and he wants to be part of your life too."

Her mother doesn't look away from the television, which is eerie, and I start to wonder if she isn't a little slow in addition to being eccentric.

"Hello, Mrs. Kane. Nice to meet you." I wave, but get no response.

"We're going to get some Diet Coke," Portia says.

"With lime!" Mrs. Kane says without taking her eyes off the man in the television who is trying to sell burn-proof potholders made with "NASA technology."

I follow Portia into the next room, where we are forced to navigate our way around an enormous pile of magazines, and I notice the photos of Portia taped to the wall. I scan the pics of her when she was an adorable little girl and then the awkward school photos and prom dates—"Hey, isn't that Jason Malta?" I say, and Portia nods. Then I make my way to the other side of the room, where I see a rather handsome man wearing a throwback mustache.

"Is this Ken?"

"Yep," Portia says.

The infamous Ken Humes.

He looks confident and rich and accomplished and used to getting what he wants out of life—and I burn with hatred and jealousy.

"Why does she still have these pictures of him up?" I ask.

Portia gives me a hurt or maybe perturbed look. "Seriously?" Then she whispers, "Did you not see the state my mother is in?"

When Portia opens the refrigerator, I see that at least half of it is stacked full with soda cans.

"Your mom must really love Diet Coke with Lime," I say.

"She doesn't drink it. These are all for me."

It takes almost ten more visits before Portia's mother acknowledges my existence, but she eventually does, and then she shows me the pictures that cover the walls of her dining room, narrating each and every one, even the shots of Portia with her husband, who Mrs. Kane says will be returning someday, and after spending so much time with Mrs. Kane it doesn't even really bother me anymore, because I can tell that my being acknowledged in this house by name means something.

I tell Portia's mother about the students I teach, and sometimes I show her the pictures my kids paint and samples of their handwriting and other various projects that I assign, and Mrs. Kane begins to pull out Portia's old elementary school projects. She has them all—nothing was ever thrown away. And while I can tell Portia is embarrassed by her mother, my girlfriend likes the fact that I have made this small connection, and I do too.

It takes some time, but eventually I start to stop by Mrs. Kane's home without Portia, just to check up on her or say hello or help her count the cars in the Acme parking lot, which she does obsessively almost every waking hour. And during one of these visits, when we finish our count and log it into her notebook, I say, "Mrs. Kane, I'd like to ask your permission to marry Portia. I realize it's traditional to ask the father, but since he's out of the picture—"

"Portia's father was a very kind and gentle man," she says, and I don't ask any questions about where he might be now, because Portia has told me the backstory.

"I bet he was. Do you think he would have given me his blessing? Would he have allowed me to marry his daughter?"

"Portia is married to Ken," Mrs. Kane says, turns on the Buy from Home Network, and plops down in her chair.

"They've been separated for a year now," I say. "And Portia is going to file for a divorce soon. My nephew helped me pick out a ring. Would you like to see it?"

I pull the small box out of my pocket and show it to her.

"Shiny!" she says.

"Don't tell Portia, because I want to surprise her. I have a trip planned."

"Do you want a Diet Coke with Lime?"

"I have one already," I say and lift the can in my hand for emphasis.

"Do you want a colder one from the refrigerator?"

"No, thanks."

"I'll go get you a lime Diet Coke." She stands and makes her way to the kitchen. A minute later she hands me a very cold can. "Here."

"Thanks," I say, two-fisting Diet Coke with Lime now. "I love your daughter, Mrs. Kane, and it would mean a lot to have your blessing."

"Yes," she says as she sits down in her recliner, but I don't know whether she is acknowledging the fact that I would really like to have her blessing or if she is actually giving it to me.

"I'll treat her right," I say. "I'm going to love her until the day I die."

"Is your Diet Coke good?"

I ignore her question. "Thank you for bringing Portia into the world. She's the best thing that ever happened to me. You did something amazing, making her."

"Portia is a *good* girl," she says, still staring at the TV. "A *very* good girl. Portia's father was a kind and good man."

The old woman isn't going to say anything appropriate—or even relevant—about my wanting to marry Portia. I begin to see how hard my future wife's childhood must have been. It takes patience to maintain dialogue with a woman who offers you Diet Coke with Lime in response to anything and everything you say. In theory, it hadn't seemed all that unbearable, but in practice, her mother's inability to engage is crushing.

I don't say anything else for a while, but just stand there watching a young woman in the TV trying to convince us to buy tennis sneakers in five different colors. "This will be the spring of the rainbow wardrobe," she says.

"I'm going to be good to your daughter," I say to Mrs. Kane.

As I look around the ruined house, completely full of one woman's memories, which are so trivial and unimportant to the rest of the world but everything to her, I think that Portia and I owe it to ourselves to be something more than what we came from.

In my truck, I pull my Official Member of the Human Race card out of my wallet and read it:

. . . the right to strive, to reach, to dream,
and to become the person you know
(deep down) you are meant to be. . . .

When I arrive home, Portia says, "Just talked to Mom, and she says you stopped by and told her a secret. Is that true?"

"I stopped by," I say, "but I'm not sure about the secret part. She gave me two Diet Cokes with Lime and we watched the Buy from Home Network like always."

Portia chuckles at me and then drains a pot of ziti through a colander in the sink. "I finished my novel today."

"Really?"

She looks back over her shoulder. "Yeah. It's done. But I need to revise, still, and that can take some time."

"Congratulations!" I say.

"Do you want to read it?"

"Hell yes!"

"When?"

"Right now, if you'll let me."

Matthew Quick

"Seriously? Because I'm feeling really paranoid about it, like it's only going to make sense in my head and no one else's, and it would be really helpful to know that at least one other person gets what the hell I'm writing about—and if you don't get it, maybe you could help me work through the kinks?"

"I seriously can't wait!"

"Really?"

"Really."

She goes into her office and returns with a stack of paper three inches thick.

"Impressive girth. Can you finally tell me the title?"

She smiles and says, "*Love May Fail*. Do you like it?"

"It's a reference to that quote at the beginning of that Vonnegut book Mr. Vernon used to talk about in his class, right? I think he had it hanging on the wall."

"I am *so* glad you got that," she says and kisses me on the mouth. "Can you read it right now, start to finish?"

"The whole book?"

"Yes."

It's a Saturday, so I don't have to get up and teach in the morning. I'm able to read through the night, which is exactly what I end up doing, reclined on the couch with my feet propped up on the armrest, stacking each page on the coffee table after I read it.

I haven't read too many novels since high school, so maybe I'm not the best judge, but I really do love Portia's book, mostly because I see her on every single page.

As I read, she keeps sticking her head in the room and saying, "What do you think so far?" And when I say, "It's good," she says things like, "Good or great?" So I say, "Fantastic!" and she says, "Fantastic how?" And I say, fake annoyed, "Would you let me read the damn thing first before we talk? How am I supposed to enjoy it

308

when you keep interrupting?" And she'll disappear until she hears me laugh at something and then she comes running in the room, saying, "What made you laugh? Which line?"

It's fiction, but I recognize so much of our lives in the story. There's a teacher who reminds me of Mr. Vernon and there is a little girl who could be Tommy's twin sister and there is an asshole man who seems an awful lot like Portia's husband and then there is the main character. Her name is Krissy Porter, and it doesn't take a genius to figure out that those are Portia's initials reversed. Krissy is funny and witty and damaged and broken, but she's also kindhearted, and all she really wants is to believe in people—that there is a goodness inside everyone. Her favorite high school teacher's wife dies, which sends him into a debilitating depression that leads to a failed suicide attempt that lands him in the psychiatric ward where Krissy just so happens to work as a therapist, specializing in matching patients up with emotional support dogs. There are a lot of specific details in the book that make me wonder how Portia knows all this stuff about psychology or whether she just made it up. And I must admit that I get a little concerned when Krissy ends up falling for her former teacher's handsome son, and they have this steamy love affair in a beach house in Maryland, especially since the sex scenes are remarkably similar to what goes on in the privacy of our bedroom. And I'm surprised to find myself wiping away tears as I read the ending.

When I place the last page on the coffee table and look up, Portia is biting her knuckle and staring at me. She's wearing her old Mötley Crüe *Theatre of Pain* T-shirt, a pair of silk panties, and nothing else.

"So?" she says.

"Best novel I've ever read."

"Seriously?"

I point to the tears running down my face and say, "Look at me. I'm a fucking mess."

"And the sun's up. You read the whole thing straight through."

I stand and take Portia in my arms.

Directly into her ear I whisper, "This book is so you. And I love you. Therefore, well, you can do the math."

"Do you think he'll like it?"

"Who?" I say, smelling her hair, my tired eyes closed.

"Mr. Vernon. The book's dedicated to him. Didn't you see?"

"I did. And how could he not?" I say, wondering if our old English teacher's even still alive.

"Do you think it's publishable?"

I know absolutely nothing about the publishing industry, but I say, "Yes," again anyway. Then I add, "I'm proud of you. It's a huge accomplishment, finishing a novel. And I really did love it. *I love you.*"

I reach down and put my hands on the silk stretched across her wonderful ass, thinking I am definitely getting lucky after reading her novel straight through, but then she says, "I'm going to start revising right away. I'll have a lot of questions for you, so can you be on call today for me?"

"Sure," I say, because it's what she needs, and then I lose Portia again to her office.

CHAPTER 28

A few weeks later, when I arrive at Danielle and Tommy's, I'm relieved Johnny Rotten's not there. Danielle's on the couch looking tired, watching TV. I notice that she's got her arms covered again, but I've already gone there once, and she came up clean. Portia's right. Danielle's a big girl. And tonight's about Portia and me.

"Hi there, little sis," I say.

"Hey," she says. "Tonight's the big night, right?"

"Yep."

"Think she'll say yes?"

"Hope so."

"She will."

"How can you be so sure?"

"She'd be a dumbass not to," Danielle says, smiles, and then looks back at the TV.

There's something going on during this moment, but I'm not quite sure what it is. Danielle seems happy for me, but she also seems resigned somehow. No hug. No kiss. Just a simple vote of confidence. I can't quite figure out what's off, but something deep down inside knows all isn't right. It's a moment that will haunt me for years, and somehow I know it right then and there. But I shake it off. "Tommy here?"

"Yeah. He's so excited for you—and Portia. He's in his room."

Danielle's wearing an oversize Hello Kitty sweatshirt, hugging her thighs to her chest underneath the fabric. Her chin is resting on

311

her knees. She looks like a kid, sitting like this. I remember when she actually was a little girl and I was her big brother, back when we used to watch MTV videos, alone in the apartment we rented from an old woman who had cable, wondering when our drunk mother might make her next appearance in our lives.

"Do you have on any pants under that?" I ask, going for humor again.

"I gave up the pants. Going through a Winnie the Pooh phase," she says and then flashes a mischievous smile.

I make another attempt at peace. "Danielle. I only asked those questions about your arms—this is stupid. Can't we—"

"It's okay, Chuck. Seriously. I'm not mad," she says, looking directly into my eyes.

I want so much to believe her, and so I do, even though she's chewing her bottom lip and tapping her toes.

"Okay," I say.

I knock, but Tommy doesn't answer. I hear his headphones buzzing, so I push open the door.

Tommy's little back is toward me. His headphones look gigantic on his kid-size skull. He's sitting at his desk, banging his head to the beat of his music and writing something. I watch him headbanging away and scribbling. He looks so content that I hate to interrupt, so I just enjoy watching him for a minute or so.

When I finally tap his shoulder, he turns around and then his arms are around my neck and I have him in the air. The old yellow Walkman I gave him long ago falls to the floor and the music stops playing.

"What are you listening to, little man?" I ask.

"*Too Fast for Love*. Mötley Crüe," he says, and gives me the devil horns.

"You have that on cassette tape now?"

"I taped it off the vinyl. Recorded over one of your old metal mixes. Put Scotch tape over the holes on the top of the cassette. Mom showed me how."

"You taped over one of my masterpieces?" I say, but I'm only joking. I'm impressed by the little man's ingenuity.

"*Too Fast for Love* is the masterpiece."

"You are correct, little man," I say. Tommy's still in my arms. Our faces are only a few inches way from each other. The kid's skin is so smooth, young, and unblemished. I wish I could stop time and keep Tommy just the way he is, because for a kid who loves bubblegum metal, he has the most innocent, pure heart. "But why would you want to listen to a secondhand bootleg recording of the best Mötley Crüe album ever, when you have it on vinyl?"

"Put me down and I'll show you," Tommy says, so I put him down. He runs over to his dresser, pulls out a large square he's covered in paper and tape, and hands it to me. He's written on it in red crayon:

> *Welcome to the family, Portia.*
> *You will be a great aunt.*
> *Love, Tommy*

And then he's drawn a picture of what I believe is Tommy and Portia holding hands and raising the devil horns with their free ones.

I say, "Is this your *Too Fast for Love* original pressing album in here?"

"Aunt Portia loves that record."

"Dude," I say.

"Is the picture cool?" he says, and looks up at me like he's really worried.

"You are a total rock star, little man," I say, and then I'm down on one knee, looking him in the eye. "This is seriously cool and generous of you. And you know you can come over and listen to this record with us whenever you want. It's still yours too—it'll be all of ours. A family record. And you'll inherit it back some-day."

"I wish I could live with you and Aunt Portia."

He's already begun calling her aunt.

"What? Why?" I say.

"Mom watches TV all the time. She doesn't do anything else."

"She's just going through a hard spot now, and—"

"I don't like Johnny Rotten. When he's here, Mom makes me stay in my room so they can kiss."

"You shouldn't call him Rotten. He's an adult, and your mom's—"

"*You* call him Johnny Rotten. I've heard you!"

"Okay. He's not my favorite," I whisper, looking over my shoul-der to make sure my sister isn't in the hallway. "But you have your cell phone, right?"

He points to his belt, where his flip phone is attached to his hip.

"You keeping that thing charged like I taught you?"

"Yep!"

"Give me a call right now, just so we know we're connected."

He opens his phone and holds the number 1 key.

My cell starts ringing, so I pull it out and say, "Hello?"

He holds his phone to his head. "Uncle Chuck?"

"Is this my favorite nephew, Tommy Bass? Front man for Shot with a Fart?"

"Yes, it is."

"You know you can call me anytime, right? Day or night. Even at four a.m. Wake me up. Why the hell not?"

"Bad word, Uncle Chuck."

"Rock and roll, kid. *Rock and roll.*"

"I wish I were going to see Mötley Crüe with you tonight."

"I'm going to buy you a concert shirt, little man. Promise. But tonight is about getting you the best aunt in the world—making it official. Have to do some romance—and that requires going solo. So why don't you give me that ring. Ring me. You still have it, right? You didn't let me down—shrug your best man duties. Not Tommy Bass. Hell no."

"No way!" he says, we both hang up our phones, and then he dives under the bed, reaches up into the hole in the box springs, pulls out the little red box, and hands it to me.

I open it up, and the diamond looks tiny. "Do you think it's too small?"

"I thought you measured her other rings when she was sleeping to make sure it would fit."

I tousle his hair. "I did. Do you think she'll say yes?"

"Give her my present first. That will help."

"Think so?" I say.

He nods earnestly.

"Why would she want to marry your loser uncle anyway?"

"Because you are taking her to see Mötley Crüe. She loves Mötley Crüe. It's her favorite band."

I look down, and the kid's hopeful believing face slaps the sarcasm right out of me. "It is her favorite band."

"And ours too. Lucky for all of us," he says.

I look at my nephew. Can he really love 1980s hair metal as much as his uncle, or would he love anything I told him to love just because he needs a father figure that much?

"I love you, Tommy, more than I love Mötley Crüe."

He smiles.

"It's true," I say.

"Do you love me more than you love Portia?"

"Yes, but never tell her that."

He laughs. "Go get me an aunt. I've never had one before. Go get her."

I give him the devil horns, and he gives them right back.

"Remember, you can call me anytime, right?" I say.

"Go! Have fun! Rock out!"

"All right. Love you, little man," I say, and then exit with Tommy's gift and the engagement ring.

Danielle's still staring at the television—some show about pregnant teenagers, which I've seen her watching before.

"Here I go. I'm actually asking Portia to marry me tonight."

Danielle stands, walks over to me, and gives me a long hug. She squeezes too hard, and it makes me worry a little, but it also feels nice.

When was the last time we hugged like this?

"Wish me luck?" I say when she lets go.

"You don't need it," she says.

"How about you let me take Tommy tomorrow night, and you can have some time to yourself maybe," I say. "Would you like that, if I—"

"I'm going to get a job. Don't worry."

"I'm not worried."

"I'm going to get my shit together, Chuck. I promise. This is just temporary."

"Good," I say, and then for some reason I add, "I love you."

"You too, big brother."

We share a smile, and then I'm gone.

As I hide Tommy's present behind the seat in my truck, I think about how hard my good luck must be for Danielle. I mean, when you compare Portia Kane to Johnny Rotten, my sister's definitely holding the 45 to my LP. But what can I do about that?

I have a ring in my pocket, and Mötley Crüe tickets are waiting for us in Connecticut because I didn't want to wait an extra few weeks for them to play a closer venue. "It's okay to be happy," I say to myself, and then I'm on my way to our apartment.

Portia's in her office, so I knock.

"Yes," she says as I open the door, but she doesn't stop typing.

"Do you trust me?" I say.

"Um . . ." She finishes recording her thought and then spins around in her swivel chair. "Did you just ask if I trust you?"

"I did."

"Would I be living with you, if I didn't?"

"So you trust me."

"What is this?"

"Just yes or no."

"Yes."

"Okay, save your work. Put on your retro jean jacket, pack an outfit you would have loved to wear in 1983, an overnight bag, and let's get the hell out of here."

"Nineteen eighty-three? What are you talking about?" she says, but she's smiling. "Are you serious? Where are we going?"

"It's a surprise. Trust me. You'll like it."

She laughs, wraps her arms around my neck, gives me a long kiss on the lips, and says, "The edits are coming out all shit today anyway. I'll be ready in fifteen minutes."

One of the best things about Portia is that she never makes me wait—she's always on time and doesn't spend hours primping in mirrors and asking me over and over again if she looks fat or what outfit she should wear, like Danielle always did when I was living with her and Tommy. She's not vain, but she isn't needy either.

In my truck, as we jump onto the New Jersey Turnpike, she says, "So where are we going?"

"It's a surprise!" I say. "Can't say."

She reaches over and grabs my hand. "Chuck Bass. My hero. I needed a surprise today. How did you know?"

Just riding in the truck, holding Portia's hand, driving north on a Saturday—I'm not even thinking about the concert—makes me feel like my life is okay, that I've finally dug my way out of the mistakes of my past.

After an hour or so, Portia says, "How far north are we going? Are you taking me for a night in New York City?"

I just smile.

When we pass New York City and continue on up into New England, she says, "Are you sure this truck of yours will make it wherever we're headed and back again?"

"The old man's Ford will do us proud," I say. I put more than a few hundred into it a few weeks ago when I had to replace the water pump, and the mechanic talked me into doing other stuff while he was in there. He also listed a few other potential down-the-road problems that I couldn't afford to fix without asking Portia for money, because I needed to purchase Mötley Crüe tickets and a diamond ring. I feel ashamed to be driving Portia around in this old piece-of-shit truck, especially knowing that her first husband was richer than Donald Trump, but it's definitely been reliable so far. And I love my job, even though the math regarding my hourly wage—if you were ever sadistic enough to do it—has me making something akin to minimum wage.

Portia playfully squeezes the inside of my thigh.

I raise my eyebrows. "You keep doing that, and I can't guarantee your safety. Driving while under the influence of Portia Kane is illegal in the state of Connecticut. I could lose my license."

"Well, then, no en route blow job for you."

"We definitely can pull over," I say, and then we both laugh in that good easy way.

When we stop for gas and sandwiches, she says, "I don't know where we're going, but I like today."

"We haven't even done anything yet."

"Yes, we have. We've taken an unexpected drive north."

"I was expecting it."

"You planned it for me, which makes it all the more special. How did I find you? How did I get so lucky?" Portia looks up at the sky. "Thank you, Khaleesi."

"Khaleesi?"

"Inside joke. From a former life."

"Okay."

"A life that sucked much worse than this current life."

"So this life sucks too?"

"Today is already the best day I've had in years."

I watch her take a bite out of her tuna on rye and think even the way she chews is sexy.

Then I start to worry that maybe I am rushing things by popping the question today.

"Are you okay?" Portia says to me. "You look a little worried."

"Just want to make sure we get there in time. I'm going to blow your mind, baby. Just wait and see."

"I love when you get all nervous and cute," she says, and then finishes her sandwich.

When we're maybe fifteen minutes away, I open my window and turn on the vent, because I'm sweating again.

"You okay?" Portia asks.

"Yep," I say. "Still okay."

When we pull into the Mohegan Sun casino and enter the parking garage, Portia says, "Are we going gambling? I didn't know you liked to play."

"I don't. I never gamble."

"Oh, good, because we are entering a casino. What's going on? There are casinos in our home state. A little place called Atlantic City. Have you heard of it?" she says.

"Indian chief in a headdress walks into a restaurant and says, 'I have a reservation,' " I say.

"Okay, now I know you are nervous about something, because you are making bad—and slightly racist—jokes."

"Saw it on a T-shirt once."

"What the hell is going on, Chuck?" she says, half laughing.

"You didn't like driving with me?" I say as I troll the parking garage for an open spot. "An hour ago you said this was the best day you'd had in years."

"But you didn't even talk dirty to me once in the old man's Ford," she says in this pouting voice that really turns me on.

I smile, pull into a parking spot, and kill the engine. "We made it. Now lean forward."

"What?"

When Portia leans forward, I tilt the seat and pull Tommy's present out from behind us.

"The boy wanted you to have this," I say and hand it to her.

"Is that supposed to be Tommy and me?" Portia says. " 'Welcome to the family, Portia. You will be a great *aunt*? Love, Tommy.' What does that mean?"

"Open the present."

"I don't understand," she says, and the concerned look on her face makes me even more nervous.

"Open it."

She peels off the paper carefully, trying hard not to ruin Tommy's artwork, and then—

"Is he giving me his *Too Fast for Love* original-pressing vinyl? Is he an idiot? Wait. Why did you drive all the way to Connecticut to give me a Mötley Crüe record?"

"Because Mötley Crüe is playing this casino tonight, and we have tickets."

"Don't even fuck with me, Chuck Bass."

"I'm not."

"Original lineup? Vince Neil. Mick Mars. Nikki Sixx. And Tommy Lee? They're all here?"

"Yep," I say, smiling proudly.

And then Portia's kissing me.

When we come up for air, she says, "I've wanted to see Mötley Crüe in concert since I was twelve!"

"I know. That's why I paid a small fortune for a hotel package that got us good seats."

"But what was Tommy talking about? Welcoming me to the family?"

I pull the little red box out from my pocket, open it, and extend it to her.

Her face drops, and I can't tell if her surprise is good or bad.

"I love you, Portia," I say, my stupid voice shaking. "I've worked really hard to be clean and sober and get my life in order. And you're the best thing that's ever happened to me. I want to spend the rest of my life with you. So will you marry me?"

She's staring at the ring, but she hasn't said anything yet.

"Did you want me to get down on one knee?" I say. "Was that important to you?"

"No," she says. "It's not that."

"Is the diamond too small?"

"No! It's beautiful. Perfect."

"Once I get on my feet, in a few years, I can get you a bigger—"

"This ring is the one I want. This one right here. I never want another ring. You hear me? Never. This one is the one."

"Put it on then."

Portia looks at me for too long; she takes off her silver chain and puts the ring on it, next to the small goth-looking crucifix she's been wearing ever since that nun friend of hers who died turned out to be Mr. Vernon's mother.

"Why'd you put it there?" I say, worried now.

She kisses me on the lips, rests her head on my chest, and starts to cry.

"This wasn't the reaction I was expecting," I say.

"Can you just hold me?"

I hold her, stroke her hair, massage her back, as she cries quietly with her cheek against my chest. After fifteen minutes or so, she sits up. Her makeup has run down her face, which is bright red now.

"I'm sorry," I say. "I obviously fucked up. Maybe I rushed things a little, but—"

"I'm going to say yes, Chuck. I am. I just need some time."

"Time? Like *away* from me?" An anger is rising inside of me, and I feel itchy, like I need a fix for the first time in a while.

"No, time *with* you."

"That's why I asked you to marry me!"

"And that's why I put the ring on my chain."

"Why won't you put it on your finger? I don't understand."

"I'm not even technically divorced yet, Chuck."

"Why are you crying?"

"Because you're perfect for me, and I wish we had met earlier before I fucked up my life. And I'm damaged—and I'm not sure if I will ever be undamaged. And—"

"I'm damaged too," I say. "Crazy damaged!"

"And yet you are so brave—and romantic, putting all of this together," she says. "So much stronger than me."

"So I completely fucked this up. That's what you're saying?"

"No. This is all perfect. Today. You. Perfect for me. And we are going to enjoy this. Mötley Crüe. Shit. It's like you're some heavy-metal Prince Charming, making all my dreams come true. I'm the one who's fucked up. But I'm working on it, and you're helping more than I deserve. So I'll wear the ring close to my heart for now, we're going to get a room here, I'm going to make love to you like never before, we're going to see the best metal band ever, and then we will continue on together. And at some point, I'm going to put this ring on my finger and marry you. I promise. I fucking promise you, Chuck. You're just going to have to trust me on this. Can you?"

"So you're saying that we go on as a couple, you wear the ring around your neck, and at some point in the future—once you sort a few things out—you put the ring on your finger and we get married? That's your answer."

"Yes, that's my official answer. And you are so getting laid before and after the Crüe concert."

"You are a beautiful and mysterious woman, Portia Kane."

"You make me believe in good men, Chuck Bass," she says, but her voice quivers and she starts crying again. "I'm sorry."

"It's okay," I say, even though I'm more confused than I thought possible.

The inside of Mohegan Sun looks like a gigantic futuristic tepee in outer space—like Native Americans built the starship *Enterprise* and docked it on Connecticut's Thames River.

Strolling around the slot machines and blackjack tables are many Jersey Shore–type guys with steroid-inflated muscles and

Ed Hardy shirts, but there are also Crüe fans in Harley-Davidson shirts and old concert T-shirts—the band on motorcycles for the *Girls, Girls, Girls* album is what I see most, but I also spot some *Theatre of Pain* tragedy and comedy masks and good old upside-down pentagrams on shirts too, with the band's teased-out hair making them look like they were the inspiration for the costumes in the musical *Cats*. The original look, the Mötley Crüe I loved best.

"Look at the moons on the carpet," Portia says, pointing down at our feet as we pass a poker pit. "This one is the Moon of Straw-berries."

I look down at a ten-foot-wide circle with three strawberries in it.

"There are thirteen moons in the Indian year," she says.

"How do you know that?"

"I read it on the wall back there," she says. "Look, there's a ro-botic coyote up on that fake mountain. Its ears are twitching!"

"Weird!"

"Kind of awesome," she says, and loops her arm through mine, pulling herself real close to me. "Let's go fuck, Chuck."

"If you insist," I say, playing the role, because she's smiling and seems to be enjoying herself again.

The whole time we check in, I keep wondering if her putting the ring on her chain is weird. But I keep telling myself not to go down rabbit holes.

She's with you.

Smart women like Portia don't live with men they don't love.

Portia said that she would put the ring on her finger in the future, when she is ready.

Trust her.

She lived with her first husband and she HATED him, genius.

Stop it.

Don't fuck this up.

"Where are you?" Portia says.

I look around. "I'm in the elevator with you."

She kisses me, looks up into my eyes, and says, "You ready to get lucky?"

"Always," I say. "We have good seats. About fifteen feet off the corner of the stage. I hear they throw fake blood on the people in the front row, so I decided to go with—"

"Everything is perfect," she says, and then kisses me again. "Exactly as I want it. You thought of everything. *Everything.*"

The room overlooks the river, and it's not bad, but a little average for what I paid, although I'm no expert on hotel rooms.

"You've probably stayed in better with your husband, right?" I say.

Why the hell did you just say that?

"He never made me this happy—*ever*," she says, and when I look into her eyes I know she's telling the truth, but it doesn't make me feel any better, knowing that I will never be able to give her what her husband did. I mean, first-grade teachers aren't ever going to be multimillionaires.

She's taking off my clothes now, and then I'm on the bed naked and she's running her mane of hair up and down my body, which tickles in all the right ways. Portia is way better at sex than I am, which makes me feel rather uncomfortable, because she had to learn all the sex stuff somewhere.

Don't think about that.

Don't fuck this up.

It's already fucked up, I think as the ring around her neck sweeps up and down my abdomen along with her hair and the nun's little silver Jesus Christ on the cross.

Just be here.

Just be happy.

You've made it this far.

My cell phone starts to ring.

I ignore it at first, but then I realize it must be my nephew. "I have to make sure it's not Tommy," I say. "I promised I'd pick up if he called."

She gives me a disappointed look, but nods.

"Tommy?" I say into the phone. He tells me he's okay, and I confirm that we are indeed at the hotel.

Portia is doing a very titillating striptease over by the window, the afternoon sun dancing up and down her naked skin.

Tommy lets me know that Johnny Rotten is there, and that his mom sent him to his room. "They're kissing again."

"Yuck," I say.

He asks if Portia is his aunt yet, and I say, "Still working on it," before I hang up.

When I return my attention to Portia, she says, "Nothing turns me on more than an uncle who breaks away from hot steamy sex to make sure his nephew is emotionally taken care of."

"I'm sorry, but—"

"I'm serious," she says, and then she takes a wild leap and lands on top of me.

"You pounce like a puma."

"Watched a lot of metal videos when I was a little girl," she says, and before long I'm inside her, and she's moving on top of me, and I feel hot, overwhelmed, in love, like I don't deserve this, like I'd do anything to keep it going—and I realize that I haven't loved anything or anyone like this since I was on junk, that Portia is my new fix, and not just the sex, which is amazing, but just spending time with her, seeing her smile, talking with her.

She comes, but keeps going for me, and it only takes another thirty seconds or so for me to finish, at which point she collapses on me, and we just lie there, still united.

"You're shaking," she says when she finally picks her head up.

I don't know what to say.

I'm embarrassed.

"It was such good sex," I offer.

She picks up the ring around her neck, kisses it, and says, "Trust me, Chuck Bass. Good things ahead. I just need to do it my way this time. Okay?"

"Okay," I say.

She kisses me on the lips. "Now I will shower and make myself look super hot for you . . . *and Vince Neil.*"

She winks, and then she's off me and in the bathroom.

When she comes out again, her hair's teased out a little and she's wearing heavy black eyeliner and raspberry red lipstick. She has on these tight jeans, four-inch heels, and a black tank top. "Not bad for a last-minute pack job and having no idea where the hell we were going, right?"

"I'm not letting Vince Neil anywhere near you," I say.

Because the casino comped us drinks at a restaurant called Tuscany, Portia insists we eat there, which makes me feel like a poor asshole. I tell her we can eat wherever she wants. "It's your night," I say. But she insists.

They seat us at a table for two in front of a fake bald mountain, water flowing over beige rocks—all indoors, of course.

We are in the mall portion of the casino—I can see a Tiffany's and a Coach store, and I hope to God Portia isn't interested in purchasing expensive items tonight, because I don't have the funds for that. I've budgeted enough for concert T-shirts, this dinner, and maybe coffee in the morning. But the name-brand shit her first husband bought her is looking worn and old lately, and I know how much she loves high-end fashion. I also know I will never be able to buy her that stuff on a regular basis.

I wonder if my financial situation kept her from putting on my ring.

Portia orders a pink grapefruit Cosmo, and I order a diet tonic water.

We clink glasses, and Portia says, "To our future."

"I'll drink to that."

We drink.

Portia says, "Remember the video for 'Looks That Kill,' where it's some postapocalyptic world and there are all of these women running around in loincloths and the boys of Mötley Crüe are herding them into a pen with torches? And then the woman leader comes to free all of the herded women in the pen, which she does, and she seduces the members of Mötley Crüe and even jumps over walls like a superhero?"

"How could I forget?"

"And then in the end the Mötley Crüe boys surround her with their fists in the air, and they all disappear into a flaming pentagram?"

"That's the best part!"

"I used to imagine I was that leader of women in the video, the one Mötley Crüe could not herd into a pen. A freer of women. Do you think that made me a feminist even before I knew what the word meant?"

"Couldn't tell you for certain," I say, and then laugh. "But I'll go with it if it makes you happy tonight."

"You think that's stupid, right?"

"It was just a music video. It didn't mean anything," I say, and then instantly wish I hadn't, because Portia loves to talk about stuff like this—get all deep and philosophical—and I want her to be happy tonight.

I'm relieved when she smiles and takes another gulp of her pink drink.

"As someone who lists Gloria Steinem as a hero, I probably shouldn't like Mötley Crüe—a band who will most likely have strippers onstage tonight," she says. "A band that's notorious for objectifying women. I tell myself I'm grandfathering Mötley Crüe in, because I listened to them before I knew any better."

"Like letting the racism of a beloved uncle slide?"

"Exactly! This music—Mötley Crüe—it's our childhood. It's what we have. It raised us, for good, bad, or indifferent."

I glance at the ring hanging around her neck and say, "It's that for me—but it's a bit more too. It kept raising me even after I became an adult."

I really wish I hadn't said that, because I don't want to talk about my past tonight.

"How so?" Portia asks, and then I know there's no turning back.

"I mean, as a former junkie."

She cocks her head to the side, sips her pink Cosmo, and says, "Mötley Crüe did do a lot of drugs."

"They say Nikki Sixx used to do five thousand dollars' worth of drugs a day. And that was in the eighties. Can you imagine?"

"You sound impressed," she says.

"Many years of my adult life, I didn't make five thousand dollars *a year*."

Why did I just say that?

"But what really impresses me is Nikki Sixx's sobriety," I say, and wonder if it sounds too soapbox, too former-drug-addict-turned-reformer. But for some reason I keep on going anyway, maybe because I really believe it. "When I was in rehab, one of the counselors—his name was Grover, which is an unusual name, and he was an unusual guy—he saw me draw a pentagram and the words *Mötley Crüe* in my notebook, with the little dots over the *o* and *u* and he asked me if I had ever seen the Nikki Sixx episode of *I Survived*. When I said I hadn't, he pulled out this VHS tape and we watched it together. It was all about how much drugs Nikki Sixx did, how he didn't even enjoy playing music anymore, didn't even care that he was a rock star, crashed cars, ended up alone on the holidays, paranoid in a closet, died twice and was brought back to life by an EMT Mötley Crüe fan who gave him adrenaline shots even though he was already pronounced dead. How he didn't even go to his grandmother's funeral, because he was so strung out. He was very close with his grandmother apparently. The episode ends with Nikki hitting rock bottom, but then getting clean and discovering that playing music sober could be a rush too. And then he started a charitable organization that helps teen drug addicts. They can learn how to make and produce music. I remember Nikki saying that music can give them a goal, something to focus on. When Grover showed me that episode, something clicked, and I decided if Nikki Sixx could beat addiction and make *Dr. Feelgood* sober, well, then maybe I could get sober and become an elementary school teacher."

Portia is staring at me intensely, and I can't tell whether it's love or regret or concern, so I go for a joke. "That line always gets big applause at Narcotics Anonymous meetings."

Now she's looking at me with those eyes that scare me, because they make me feel like she really loves me and maybe even admires me—and she's nodding supportively.

"Anyway, Nikki Sixx is my hero. Stupid as it sounds, saying that at forty-three years of age."

"I love you."

"I love you too."

"I admire you," she says. "You were brave. You fought to get here—right here, with me. And I won't forget it."

My phone rings, and I check it. "It's Tommy. Do you mind?"

"Go ahead," she says, but she seems to mind a little.

"Little man," I say. "You good?"

"Are you at the concert?"

"Not yet. We're eating dinner. Everything okay?"

"Johnny Rotten left."

"Good, right?"

"Mom's crying."

"Why?"

"Not sure."

"You okay?"

"I'm being brave," Tommy says.

"You're the bravest."

"I'm going to sleep soon. Just wanted to say good night."

"We'll see you tomorrow, buddy. And tomorrow is *soon*."

"You'll tell me all about the Mötley Crüe show? We'll listen to Portia's *Too Fast for Love* vinyl?"

"Swear on my life."

"And you'll answer the phone if I have a bad dream again?"

"You won't have any bad dreams. The Quiet Riot mask is protecting you, remember? That thing is super powerful!"

We say good-bye and hang up, and I tell Portia I'm sorry. "Sounds like my sister and Johnny Rotten had a fight. Tommy just needed—"

"You're a good uncle."

"I just answer the phone when he calls."

"Bullshit," she says, and then gives me a smile so beautiful, I'm forced to look away.

We dip bread in some sort of hummus-like mash, which is pretty good, and then we have the gnocchi, which I think is excellent, but Portia says is overcooked, and I wonder how she knows things like that. Who can tell the difference between properly cooked and overcooked pasta?

"Did you tell Tommy you were going to propose tonight?" she says.

"We hid the ring in his bed for a few weeks. He was my partner in crime."

"Whose idea was it to give me the *Too Fast for Love* vinyl?"

"All his."

"I'm going to tell Tommy you and I are getting married eventually," she says. "I'll make him understand. Don't worry."

"Okay."

"Because we are getting engaged and married eventually."

"Good."

After dinner, we walk arm in arm around the casino, digesting. We pass Judge Judy slot machines and a woman with a rhinestone belt buckle that spells JOURNEY, find a Thunder Moon and a Peeping Frog Moon on the carpet, and then we are in the mob of people assembled outside the concert.

"Everyone got old," Portia says as we look around at a crowd mostly made up of people who seem to be at least ten years older than we are. "When did that happen?"

There is a weird mix of grizzled bikers with neck tattoos and pointy beards, fake bikers cleanly shaved and in shiny new leather that has obviously never seen the open road, parents with their teenage kids who were taught about 1980s rock just like Tommy was, dweebs in acid-washed jeans and pastel polo shirts who look like they weigh 110 pounds soaking wet, women in leather bustiers and corsets and stiletto heels, and us.

Inside we purchase concert T-shirts and little *Theatre of Pain* key chains with the tragedy and comedy masks before listening to a local band as we wait for Mötley Crüe to take the stage.

Portia and I hold hands and take in the scene until Mötley Crüe make their entrance carrying scantily clad women on their shoulders and medieval banners that feature the letters MC in white and red, swinging a giant incense burner that looks like what a priest would carry. The crowd goes wild.

They open with "Saints of Los Angeles," and instantly we are teenagers again, banging our heads and flying the devil horns. By the time they're playing "Wild Side," I'm completely transported. There are strippers dancing and singing and doing acrobatics on chains hanging down from the ceiling and at certain points simulating lesbian sex, and the lights and swagger and noise, and Tommy Lee's drum set, which is connected to a giant O and becomes a sort of drumming roller coaster at times, spinning him upside down forty feet in the air as he bangs away during his lengthy drum solo mid-show. My role model Nikki Sixx is mostly on our side of the stage. I'm only maybe twenty feet from him, and as he plays his bass and spits water at the crowd and bangs his almost Muppet-like explosion of black hair, I wish I could thank him for doing that *I Survived* documentary and writing *The Heroin Diaries*. They play many of my favorite songs: "Shout at the Devil," "Home Sweet Home," "Live Wire," "Too Fast for Love," "Dr. Feelgood"—and Portia dances her little ass off and loses herself too, forgetting about the degradation of women and her feminist views of rock.

At one point Vince Neil says, "We're old motherfuckers up here," and the crowd roars because it's mostly made up of old motherfuckers too.

They finish with "Kickstart My Heart," during which Nikki Sixx spits fake blood all over the people in the front rows before he and Tommy Lee throw buckets of fake blood into the crowd and then call it a night.

When the lights go up, Portia turns toward me and says, "As a feminist, I know I should absolutely hate Mötley Crüe, but I can't deny it. They scratch the primal itch within us all."

"It's only rock and roll. Just a show," I say, loudly, because my ears are ringing now.

"I wish you could talk to Nikki Sixx," she says, yelling too, as we make our way to the exit. "Even though he spits blood on people, I bet he'd be cool to you. I bet he'd be proud of you for cleaning up. I wish I could get you backstage."

"Yeah, me too. Except you'd probably try to fuck Vince Neil."

"Jealous much? Your phone," she says.

"What?" I say. Everyone exiting the concert is talking very loudly, because no one can hear now.

"Your phone! It's ringing!"

I pull it from my pocket. It's not ringing anymore.

There are fourteen messages.

I jump out of line and make my way to the center of an empty row.

Portia follows and says, "What's wrong?"

I punch in my code and listen to the first few messages.

My mind starts spinning.

I feel as though I may vomit.

"I fucked up bad, Portia. I fucked up really bad."

"What's wrong? Tell me, Chuck. You're freaking me out."

I hold up my finger and listen to the rest of the messages.

I'm punching my thigh hard now, as I hear how scared my nephew is and mentally put together the pieces.

"Stop hitting yourself, Chuck. Stop that! Tell me what's wrong. *WHAT'S WRONG?*"

When I hear the message from Lisa at the Manor, saying that Tommy is safe with her, I look at Portia. "Danielle shot up in the apartment."

"Shot up?"

"Heroin. I'm not sure, but I think she might have OD'd. Tommy found her passed out with the needle in her arm. He's been calling me all night. I have to call him."

"Call him!"

I get Lisa.

She tells me that she's managed to get Tommy to fall asleep at her home, but that he was very upset.

Then she says, "It's bad, Chuck, really bad. I don't want to be the one to tell you."

"Just fucking say it!" I scream.

Lisa starts crying as she tries to get out all the words. "Tommy came into the bar, screaming and crying. We went to the apartment. Found Danielle on the floor. We called an ambulance, but it was too late. She's gone. I'm not sure that Tommy understands that yet, and I didn't know what you'd want me to tell him, so . . ."

I black out for a while, although I continue to move somehow, and when I come to, I'm in my truck, trying to get it to start, but the engine won't turn over, and then I'm punching the steering wheel, cursing incoherently, kicking the floor and screaming and crying, and Portia is telling me it's going to be okay.

"I let Tommy down," I keep saying. "I should have been there for him. I should have answered the phone when he called. My fucking father never was there for me, and now Tommy is going to think that—"

"Shhhh," she says, and then I'm sobbing into her chest like a baby for what feels like forever, moaning and completely losing my shit, before I'm overcome with it all and I pass out with my head in her lap.

When I wake up, my neck hurts, and Portia's looking down at me.

"Shit! We have to go home!" I say.

"It's okay. Tommy's with Lisa. We'll be home soon."

"How long was I out?" I say.

"Only a half hour or so," she says, and tries to smile.

Her eyes are red.

"What are we going to do?"

"We're going to check out of the hotel and rent a car. I'm going to drive. We'll pick up Tommy and bring him to our place, where he'll live from now on. We'll make sure Tommy is okay, and then we'll figure it out."

"Figure *what* out?" I say.

"Everything."

CHAPTER 29

The diary under Danielle's pillow tells us everything we need to know. Her boyfriend wasn't collecting for bookies. He was a full-time drug dealer more than willing to supply my sister, provided that she screwed him on a regular basis, of course. The worst part is this: she loved him, and yet she was afraid the feeling wasn't mutual. And I think she did drugs with him at first as a way to prove her love for him—sharing his interests, so to speak. But his product was a bit stronger than what she remembered from our days, and therefore the cravings were more intense. Everything happened quicker than she could handle. And her new boyfriend didn't like girls who couldn't handle their highs. That was the gist, anyway.

Johnny Rotten doesn't show at the memorial service—which is good, because my plan is to punch his face into a bloody pulp whenever I see him next—but Portia's mother miraculously does, and she even wears the dress Portia purchased for her, shedding the old stained pink sweat suit for a day. The Crab and all of my teacher friends attend, which touches me deeply. Danielle's hairy boss and a few other waitresses pay their respects, along with a bunch of people from the Manor. Wearing the black suit, black tie, white dress shirt, and black shoes and belt Portia picked out for me at Men's Wearhouse, I mumble a bunch of gibberish in front of the small crowd at the funeral home, mostly about growing up with Danielle and watching cartoons when we were little and then falling in love with metal in the 1980s, and how maybe I wished we were into classical music instead because classical music fans tend to avoid heroin and live longer, and what a good mom she was—how she loved Tommy so much—which is when I lose it and break down crying, maybe because I feel like it's all bullshit.

The worst part is that my getting emotional scares Tommy. He's sitting in the front row, dressed exactly like me because Portia also bought him a funeral suit and accessories, and I can tell that Portia doesn't know whether she should keep holding Tommy's little hand or come to me. Finally, she comes to me, which makes me feel weak, since my nephew who lost his mom is handling this better than me. She rubs my back and whispers, "You're okay," in my ear over and over.

"I should have put the pieces together. I should have saved her—"

There are maybe two dozen people seated in rows of chairs facing me, and I feel like it's my fault that my sister's funeral isn't better attended, like I'm the reason her life turned out so pathetic and ended much too early.

"I'm sorry. I'm so sorry," I say through tears.

"You're doing fine," Portia says.

I look over at the casket and see Danielle looking almost blue and waxy. The coroner found track marks up and down the inside of her thighs. She'd been using for weeks, the knowledge of which hasn't done much to ease my conscience. But it's not time for guilt. I need to make it through today. I have the rest of my life to deal with guilt.

A few people stand and tell stories about Danielle, none of them all that interesting. Diner patrons who always asked to be seated in her section, a few exaggerated tales about how much fun Danielle was to drink with at the Manor. Tommy talks about singing with her, and Portia tells a story about being in Mr. Vernon's class with Danielle, but most of it doesn't really register in my mind. I keep glancing over at Danielle and thinking that a decade or so ago it could have easily been me in that box. Why wasn't it? My fists clench as I think of Randall Street.

When there are no more stories left to tell, people make their way to their cars, and I ask the funeral director if Tommy and I can have a private moment.

They clear the room and close the doors.

Portia leaves too.

I do my best to keep it together as I say, "I want you to take a good look at your mom, Tommy, because when we close this lid, you won't ever see her again."

He looks at Danielle. "It doesn't really look like her."

"I know, but it is. And she loved you so much. She just did a dumb thing, and now Aunt Portia and I will take care of you."

"Aunt Portia wore the ring on her finger today," he says. "She wasn't wearing it before. Why?"

"I'm not sure. We'll have to ask her later."

"Will she be my mom now?"

He's looking up at me with this very concerned look, and it wrecks me.

"You'll always have your real mom with you in your heart," I say, at the same time thinking, What the hell am I telling the kid? What does that even mean? Having someone in your heart, like religious people say about Jesus. "She'll always be with you. And Portia and I will be with you too. I'm trying my best to make sure Portia becomes your official aunt, and I'm pretty sure that will happen, but I will never ever leave you, Tommy. Do you hear me? I'm with you for life."

"I know," he says, and then looks at his mom.

"It's okay to cry," I say.

"I did already, when you weren't looking."

"You can cry when I'm looking, Tommy. Didn't you see me crying earlier? It's okay. Real men let it out. So go ahead if you need to."

Tommy leans his little head against my thigh. "Can I kiss her good-bye just once?"

"Sure, but it's not going to feel like her, okay? Just so you know."

"Okay."

I hold him up so that he can reach, and he kisses Danielle on the cheek once. I hear him whisper, "Don't worry, I'll take care of Uncle Chuck."

After I put him down again, I say, "You don't have to take care of anybody but yourself. You hear me? And we're going to take care of you. You are the little kid. You get to be taken care of."

My voice is stern, but I want him to get the message.

He nods once, and then the tears come.

"I don't want my mommy to die," he says before he throws himself at me and then cries into my brand-new tie.

"I know. I know. I know," I keep saying over and over, because I don't know what else to say, and it's all I can do to contain the rage I feel whenever I think about Randall Street. "I don't want your mommy to die either. But we have each other still, and we are going to kick ass living together, you hear me? Absolutely kick ass."

He just keeps crying into my shirt, and so I rub his back until it's all out.

We put my sister in the ground without any religious fanfare, eat sandwiches at the Manor, and then Portia and I lower the futon in her office and get Tommy to sleep by lying on either side of him and telling him stories about when his mom was a kid, teasing her hair out like Axl Rose. The little guy manages to laugh a few times, which makes me proud, although he checks several more times to make sure his Quiet Riot mask is hanging above his makeshift new bed in Portia's apartment.

It's there.

We made certain.

After he's out, Portia and I watch the kid breathe for a long time, making absolutely sure he's sound asleep, before we leave him.

And then I'm finally alone in the kitchen with Portia, who has poured herself a glass of wine.

"You're wearing your engagement ring, I see."

"Let's talk about this later. We just buried your sister."

"I don't want you to pity me. I don't want you to wear that ring just so I'll feel better."

"I don't pity you. I love you. There was never any question about that. I just wasn't sure I was ready to get married again—officially married."

"Why?"

She looks into her wine for a moment. "Because our life together is going really well. I didn't want to tinker with it, you know? I wanted things to stay just the way they were for as long as possible. And maybe I want to accomplish something first—at least one thing, as a single woman."

Portia runs her index finger around the edge of her wineglass for a few seconds. "But now we have a real chance to make sure a good little kid has a shot at a good decent normal-*ish* childhood. We didn't ask for this situation, but here it is, and we have a choice."

"So you put the ring on for my six-year-old nephew, not me?"

"Don't be an asshole, Chuck." Portia smiles in a way that makes it impossible to take offense.

I stare at the kitchen ceiling. "You know, when I was up there today, speaking about Danielle, I thought about using again. For the first time in years, I wanted a fix. Even though junk killed her. I wanted to get high. I also wanted to kill Randall Street. I seriously want to kill him."

"So what's keeping you from getting high, throwing away all the work you've done?" Portia says, avoiding the second part of my confession.

"You. And Tommy. And the idea that I might be a good teacher. The Official Member of the Human Race card Mr. Vernon gave us. Choosing to be the person we want to be, right? But I can't do this alone. So I have to know right now, Portia, are you in or out?"

"I was always in, Chuck. Always."

"Then why'd you put the ring on today?"

"Because it's just a ring, okay? If it helps you and Tommy feel more secure, I'll wear it. But I'm in regardless. I was before I put it on. I'm wearing it for you too, in a show of solidarity. Maybe mostly for Tommy, because I know what it feels like to be alone as a kid—like you have to take care of yourself *and* the adults in your life. It's fucked, okay? I didn't want Tommy to feel doomed. And I wanted you to feel strong. Because you're never going to use again. We're going to make a good life for ourselves. We're going to make it together."

I look her in the eyes. "Portia, I knew she was using again. Some part of me knew."

She reaches across the table and squeezes my hand. "You didn't. Maybe you suspected."

"I should have saved her. She shot up for the first time with me. Did you know that? I introduced her to heroin."

"That was when you were addicted. You were sick. And you also reached out to her when you were healthy. Tried to help. She refused your help. And she left you with her problems, which you don't even see as problems because you are a good brother and an even better uncle. So don't do this to yourself."

I shake my head and stare at the table. "I don't know if I can raise him. I'm an ex-junkie with monstrous student loans. I don't have any answers."

She holds up her ring finger. "You're my fiancé. And what did I tell you in the truck? We're going to figure it out together."

"You sure picked a winner to fall in love with, huh?"

"You *are* a winner, Chuck Bass. I don't marry losers anymore. Been there, done that. This time around, it's only winners for me."

I marvel at this woman who can take control when needed.

"I just feel so guilty," I say, shaking my head. "How did I miss the signs?"

And then I'm crying again and Portia is holding me, kissing my neck and whispering reassuring words.

CHAPTER 30

A few awful weeks go by. I feel mad, powerless, like I might explode, although I mostly keep it together for Tommy and Portia—and I wait.

Then, late one Tuesday night after Portia and Tommy are asleep in bed, Jon Rivers the cop—in plain clothes—picks me up and takes me to the Manor. We get a booth by the jukebox. He orders a Bud bottle, and I have an ice water with lemon. Once Lisa serves our drinks, she returns to staring at her phone on the other side of the empty barroom, and Jon says, "He's clean. I'm sorry. No record. Nothing prior to suggest that he's dealing. No way we can pull a warrant to search his place. The diary's not enough."

"You found nothing else?"

Jon takes a sip of his beer. "He very well might be a small-time drug dealer, but it doesn't look like he's selling now. Maybe he's laying low. Maybe he only deals to friends and was smart enough to take a vacation after your sister's overdose. Off the record, I had a contact watch his grandmother's place for a week. He's there, but nothing's going on. Nothing illegal at all."

"He killed my sister," I say.

"From what the neighbors and Tommy said, Randall Street wasn't even in the apartment when Danielle OD'd. We have nothing on him, Chuck."

"You know he gave her the drugs."

"I *know* what your sister alluded to in her diary and how you feel about it. But we can't exactly bring her in for questioning. And—believe me—I sympathize. But I also can't bust into his grandmother's house and arrest him just because you want me to. That's not how the law works. I'd need a warrant. And for that we need more evidence."

"What's the point of having cops if they're never allowed to catch the fucking bad guys?" I say, and then immediately feel embarrassed, because I know Jon's already done more than he probably should.

He looks down at the table. "Listen, Chuck. I like you a lot, which is why I looked into this thing a little. You've done me a few solids in the past, which I haven't forgotten. But there's nothing I can do right now—as a police officer—to give you a sense of revenge or justice or whatever you're after. And I'm worried you might be thinking about taking matters into your own hands. The law says no. And as a friend, I officially say no too. I want to make that clear before I give you this next piece of information."

I study his face and can see that he absolutely wishes he could exact justice for me.

Jon lowers his voice. "The genius is right here in Oaklyn. His grandmother's house just so happens to be within walking distance of this very bar. The old lady isn't around. There's another elderly woman who lives across the street. She's apparently very nosy and shares your deep hatred of Randall Street. Likes to call into the station with her theories. We've been talking to her, and she says Randall hasn't gone out for days. She's been watching the house like a hawk. Day and night. Just waiting to call the police on him once she sees something suspicious. Apparently Randall's grandmother left for Florida just to escape him, and the old lady across the street misses her knitting buddy. Says all of her other friends have died, and she can't afford to winter in Florida."

"When a regular heroin user doesn't leave the house for days, it means one of two things: he's either getting clean or he has a supply stockpiled," I say.

"It's a shame that I can't just bust in there and find out for myself. If only there were some sort of need for the police to enter the house. If only someone else busted in there and caused some sort of disturbance that the old lady across the street might be able to officially report, but we can't wish for that and expect it to just happen. And without a warrant, we'd have to see the drugs right out in the open to search further, which is a distinct possibility if Randall's shooting up in there."

My knee is going up and down, quick as a sewing machine needle.

Jon looks around the bar. "The place is right off Kendall Boulevard. On Congress Avenue. A run-down sky-blue number. Only one painted that color on the street. I can't tell you the actual address for legal reasons. I wouldn't want you anywhere near that house, Chuck. If the law caught you there, it would be a very sticky situation. So don't you dare get caught anywhere near that property. You understand?"

"I do," I say. "You're being crystal clear."

"Again, my condolences," Jon says, and then downs the remainder of his beer in several quick, nervous gulps.

I nod. "Thank you, Jon."

"Don't do anything stupid," he says. "Maybe spend the rest of the night talking with Lisa. That sounds like a good idea. She'd do anything for you. Even though you're not in here as much as you used to be. Did you know we're sort of dating, Lisa and me? Keeping it quiet, but yeah. I like her a lot. I *trust* her too."

After Jon leaves, I sit in the booth alone, gripping my pint of ice water and thinking, until Lisa says, "Anything else, Chuck?"

"What?" I say, surprised to find her standing right next to me.

"Can I get you anything else?"

"Just a check."

"On the house."

"No, I'll pay."

"For water?"

"For the beer."

"We always give the cops free beer. You know that," Lisa says, chewing her gum nervously. "Jon says you and I should talk tonight for a few hours. Maybe you need to talk? So if anyone asks where you were, tomorrow, I'll just tell them you were right here with me. No one comes in the back bar after eleven on Tuesdays. No one. Which you already know. So as far as anyone else knows, we had the whole place to ourselves tonight. Maybe we even talked in private back in the kitchen."

I'm not quite sure what to say.

When the silence starts to get too awkward, Lisa says, "Danielle was my friend too. You can trust Jon. He wants the same thing you do. And you and me go back years, Chuck."

"Why are you and Jon doing this?"

"I was the one who took in Tommy that night, remember? The one who saw Danielle with a needle sticking out of her arm. So why do you think I'm doing this? Jon's your friend. He wants to do the right thing. So go, okay? Do what you have to do."

We lock eyes for a long time, and then Lisa says, "Be careful, Chuck. Will ya?"

I nod once, leave, and make my way down the train tracks parallel to Manor Avenue, headed toward Congress.

I'm not even really thinking about Danielle or Johnny Rotten or revenge—I'm just moving forward like a force of nature, maybe a storm cloud. I have no idea what I'll do when I find the man who supplied my sister with the drugs that killed her, but I keep moving forward nonetheless.

When I spot the sky-blue house, I notice that there's a light on across the street. I glance over and see an elderly woman knitting, framed by a bay window. So I walk by Jon's informer with my hands in my pockets and my head down. At the end of the block I look around and see no one, so I walk up the driveway of an unlit home and then—jumping fences and navigating backyards—I make my way back to the sky-blue home.

I spent years robbing homes for drug money, so I've had more than enough practice.

I'm a decent lock pick and can break a window making minimal sound, but I always try the door first. You'd be surprised how many times people forget to lock doors in suburban neighborhoods. And I suggest you always lock yours, because sometimes I just searched for the unlocked entryway—trying every back door in a neighborhood—and never once did I come home empty-handed.

There's a second-floor light on, but the blind is pulled. The rest of the house is dark.

When I try the screen door, it's locked, so I check the windows within reach, and they're all locked too. There's a rather large flowerpot on a little wooden bench, and when I lift it up, I find a key. It opens the screen door, but the actual back door is locked and requires a different key. It's an old wooden frame that doesn't feel very secure, and when I feel around, some of it is rotten. After pulling my sleeve down over my fingertips, I turn the knob, and push with my shoulder.

It gives a quarter inch before catching.

I can feel my heart beating harder now.

I silently count to three and then send my full weight crashing into the door, which opens with a crack—and then silence.

No footsteps, no yelling, no dogs barking, no lights switching on.

I wait a few minutes before I make my way up three little steps and into the kitchen. The blue moonlight streaming through the window reveals that the appliances and cabinets haven't been updated since the 1970s. Everything looks a grayish blue. There are used dishes and utensils on the counter, and on a small round table too. Some old cartons of half-eaten Chinese food are decomposing next to the sink. The trashcan is overflowing with the ripped-open packaging of microwavable food. Still no sounds.

As I enter the living room, I can see light leaking down from the stairs, which are carpeted and therefore quiet when climbed.

I reach the second floor with ease, although my shirt is beginning to feel heavy with sweat.

There's a half-opened door at the end of the hallway, so I move toward it stealthily, relying on the old instincts. It's like I've stopped taking steps and am being silently pulled across ice by a rope.

When I'm in front of the door, I listen for a good five minutes, but hear nothing.

The hinges creak when I push the door open, but it doesn't matter.

Randall Street is hunched over on the floor, the middle of his spine against the wall. His chin is resting on his chest and he's rubbing the top of his head in a circular pattern. His gear is in front of him.

Needle.

Spoon.

Lighter.

Cotton balls.

Small baggie of powder.

Rubber tube tourniquet limply tied around his arm.

A bag of pills—every color of the rainbow represented—suggests he's popping meds like candy.

A marijuana bong and a large baggie of weed.

A few empty beer cans.

Half a bottle of Jack Daniel's.

An ashtray full of cigarette butts and a half-empty carton of Camels.

The bedroom reeks of smoke and body odor.

Randall's so high—off a combo of chemicals that he couldn't remember, let alone re-create—he has no idea I'm even in the room.

When I was walking up the stairs, I was pretty certain I wanted to beat him to death, but he looks so pathetic below me now that I can't even muster up the ire to spit on him, let alone strike him repetitively.

I look at the walls and see posters of rock bands—the Sex Pistols, Guns N' Roses, Metallica, Slayer. It's not unlike many of the small rooms Danielle and I used to share when we were kids.

Randall's moaning now, and rubbing the top of his head more intensely.

Before I know what I'm doing, I take three swift steps, and like an NFL punter I kick Randall Street hard in the stomach. The impact makes this thumping sound, like dropping a bowling ball from a roof and hearing it land on a pillow laid out on the grass.

He lets out a long moan and then rolls onto his side in the fetal position, whispering, "Why? Why? Why?"

I snap back into reality.

This isn't me.

Not anymore, anyway.

I've done the work to change myself back into a human being.

I'm an elementary school teacher.

And I'm all Tommy has.

Plus, Portia would be so disappointed.

I no longer want to kick or punch the moaning Randall, so I search the room for his stash. The worst thing I can do to Randall Street is send him to jail, where men much worse than me will do the punishing. I quickly find two larger bags of heroin in Randall's sock drawer, which is a terrible hiding place. That alone lets me know just how far gone he is. Who knows, maybe he really misses my sister, and that's what the drug binge is about? The size of the bags more than suggests Randall is dealing. I leave one on the kitchen table and one on the coffee table in the living room as presents for Jon and his boys.

Once I've done that, I open the front door and flick the front lights on and off until I see the woman across the street pick up a phone. I leave the front door wide open.

On a whim, I go back upstairs to take one last look at Randall Street. His left cheek is on the carpet, and he's puked up a puddle of bile that now spreads from his mouth like a speech bubble in a newspaper cartoon. I'm just about to go when I see the small bag of H and needle on the floor.

It reaches out to me like the hand of a drowning friend.

Before I know what I'm doing, I've scooped up Randall's personal gear and then I've left his grandmother's house through the busted back door and I've jumped the fence and I'm running into the woods, knowing that the drug in my hand can make all of the guilt and anxiety and regret vanish instantly—I can be blissfully apathetic again—and suddenly I'm panting behind a huge tree and I've got the dirt and water in the spoon and the flame from the lighter is licking the silver underbelly and the smack is liquefying and then I'm sucking it up through the little cotton ball and into the needle as easily as I'm breathing air and every part of my body is begging me to stick the thin metal into my arm so I'm pulling up the sleeve of my coat and just before the needle enters my skin I start to hyperventilate and I'm smart enough to visualize my Official Member of the Human Race card—

. . . you become exactly whomever you choose to be.

—I pull out my cell phone and hit the one button and it rings and rings and rings and fucking rings and then I'm hearing Kirk Avery's voice message for the first time in my life because he's never before failed to pick up when I've called him and it all seems like a sign that I should shoot the hit into my veins and I'm thinking I just might when my phone buzzes and it's Portia and I hesitate but then pick up and she says, "Where the hell are you?" and so I tell her an abbreviated version of the truth, choking out the words, and she says she's on her way and I push the plunger of the needle so that the hit sprays into the night air and when there is none left I stab a tree and break off the point and I dump the rest of the junk into a mud puddle and then I'm burying the remaining evidence and covering the freshly packed earth with leaves and I'm saying, "Thank you, thank you, thank you, thank you," as I run as fast as I can back to the Manor with the sound of police sirens wailing behind me.

I'm mentally reciting the Official Member of the Human Race card like the words to a prayer when Portia pulls up.

. . . ugliness and beauty, heartache and joy—
the great highs and lows of existence . . .

Tommy's in the car, wearing his PJs under his winter coat.

"Why are you crying, Uncle Chuck?" he says from the backseat. "What's wrong?"

"Nothing at all," I say to him, and then to Portia, "I'm so sorry."

"I forgive you," Tommy says as Portia drives us home without saying anything at all.

I throw my clothes and coat into the laundry and immediately shower the sweat off me, making sure to get the dirt out from under my fingernails.

I look at myself in the bathroom mirror. My eyes look bad, guilty—like I know how fucked my behavior tonight was and believe I should be punished.

"Never again," I say to my reflection. "Never again."

Once she has Tommy back in bed, Portia makes tea and I tell her the extended version of everything that happened earlier in the evening, my voice shaking the whole time.

When I finish, I say, "Does my kicking Randall Street in the stomach make me a bad person? I'm supposed to be an elementary teacher at a Catholic school where we're all about nonviolence. I have a picture of Mother Teresa hanging in my classroom. What's happening to me?"

"You didn't shoot up when you had a chance, and I'm proud of you for that," Portia says, which makes me feel a little better, until she starts shaking her head and poking my chest hard with her index finger, tapping out the syllables of her words. "But you risked our future tonight, and I'm pissed as hell about that part. What if the cops find Randall dead? What about fingerprints? You could end up in jail! You think I want to bring Tommy to speak with his uncle through glass?"

The doorbell rings.

Portia and I look at each other. It's almost two in the morning.

It rings again.

"This isn't good," Portia says.

I walk down the steps and find Officer Jon Rivers standing in front of our apartment.

"Can I come in?" he says.

"Is that necessary?"

"Afraid so."

"Okay, then," I say, and then follow him up the stairs.

"To what do we owe this unexpected pleasure, Jon?" Portia says, acting for me. She's transformed her face and now looks remarkably composed. "Can I fix you some tea?"

"No need," Jon says. "I'll get straight to the point. What follows is confidential. Between us only. Understood?"

We both nod.

Jon continues. "Just wanted to let you know that we arrested Randall Street tonight and took him to the hospital. We received a call from an old woman who reported a break-in across the street from her. When we investigated, we found the front door wide open, so we entered. The back door had been kicked in as well. Randall was incoherent and high on junk and pills and alcohol and what-have-you in a bedroom upstairs, so I don't think he'll be able to answer any of our questions with credibility. He was pretty beat up. Looked like someone stole his gear, because we found no needles. Bags of heroin were in clear view, so we searched the house and discovered quite a bit more. Off the record, it's the most I've ever seen in one place. That's a lot of heroin that won't go into the arms of people like Danielle. The majority of it was behind the insulation in the attic—again off the record. The old lady across the street has been telling us that Randall was dealing for months, but we didn't have anything strong to go on until tonight. A few people on the force suspected that you, Chuck, might have gone there looking for revenge. But I told them we were at the Manor together this evening. They talked to Lisa, who confirmed that, and said you stayed to chat with her for a few hours before Portia picked you up a little after midnight. I assume you've been here ever since. If you can confirm that, Portia, I'll be on my way."

"That's what happened, Jon. Exactly," Portia says. "Cross my heart."

"Lisa said you had Tommy in the car with you," Jon says to Portia. "Can the boy confirm the same story?"

"He was half asleep," Portia says. "But yes."

"Okay then. Randall was so high, I doubt he'll remember anything. Given his connection to your sister's overdose, I thought you'd like to know immediately what was going on," Jon says and then squeezes my shoulder. "Maybe you'll rest a little easier tonight. That's the purpose of this visit. And to let you know the *official* story."

"Thanks, Jon," I say.

Once Jon is gone, Portia hugs me fiercely. "That's the last time you go rogue on me, right? I'm giving you one pass because your sister died. Just one and only one."

"I swear to God, Portia. *I swear to God*," I say as I hug her back with equal ferocity, both of us trembling.

The next morning Tommy asks if he was in a car the night before, and we tell him he must have been dreaming, which he believes without asking further questions.

Kirk Avery calls me back later that day. "I saw you tried to reach me last night. I was out on a friend's boat overnight fishing, and I forgot my phone charger. Ran out of juice. Of all the nights for you to call. Please tell me you weren't jonesing. I'd never forgive myself."

I think about the needle stuck in the tree—my shooting a perfectly good heroin hit into the night air—and I finally know for certain that I will never ever use again.

"I'm fine," I tell Kirk. "Catch anything?"

"Oh, thank god," he says, and then goes on to tell me about the "big one" that got away, like it always does.

And I wonder how many lies it takes to make the world go around.

CHAPTER 31

It's late May when Portia finally calls her husband to begin the divorce proceedings. Apparently he's now engaged to the young woman Portia caught him screwing a year or so before. He also says that he has sold his pornography business, conquered his sex addiction problem, and now wants to take his life in a radically different direction. He's had a lawyer draw up the divorce papers, and without Portia even asking, he offers her what I consider an obscene amount of money if she will only fly to Florida immediately so that he and his new "love" can begin to move on with "the next phase of their lives." And then he invites us—Portia, Tommy, and me—to Tampa Bay as his guests, all expenses paid. All Portia needs to do is sign the papers in person. Ken's even agreed to pay for any lawyer she names to review everything on her behalf.

I'm shocked.

"It doesn't seem right," Portia tells me in our kitchen while she is overwatering yet another spider plant. She's killed three already this year. "I keep feeling like I'm walking into a trap. This is not the man I know."

"If he wants to move on so much," I say, "why wouldn't he have tried to contact you before?"

"Oh, he has," she says.

"What?"

"Ken's been calling my cell once a day for *months* now, leaving these pathetic messages, practically begging for me to 'give him closure.' His lawyers have sent legal notices to my mother's home too."

"And you've been ignoring it all?"

"Yep. Fuck him. This will be on *my* terms."

"Why haven't you told me about this before?"

"You never asked," she says. "And I didn't want to make it weird for you."

It's true that I've avoided asking about her husband, maybe because I didn't want to push her, or maybe I hoped that she was taking care of the divorce quietly and would just surprise me one day with the news, giving it to me like a present.

When it's clear I'm not going to say anything else, Portia says, "I don't have much experience getting divorced, you know. I knew it would mean going back to Florida and seeing him again, and I didn't want to do that until I was ready, okay? This isn't an easy thing for me."

"Listen," I say, "who cares why he's being so generous? I'm thrilled. Let's go. The sooner you get divorced, the sooner we can get married."

"Should I take his money?"

"Isn't it your money too? You were married."

"I don't know that I want money made from misogynistic porn, especially since the girls were never fairly compensated."

I think about how she's been spending Ken's "misogynistic porn" money for the past year and wonder what the difference is now, but I don't say anything about that. Portia seems conflicted, and I just want her with me. Period.

"I'm behind you regardless of what you decide about the money," I say. The truth is, I have very mixed feelings about how much Ken Humes has already funded my life.

"I can't believe he's going to marry Khaleesi."

"Khaleesi?" I say.

"His new little whore. She's about twelve years old."

"Why do you care who he's with?" I say, before I can stop myself.

"You're okay with men in their forties dating twelve-year-olds?"

"She's not actually twelve."

"Oh, she's probably twenty by now."

"Okay, gross. But you're going to be free and clear of him soon, right? And then we can move on."

We take Tommy out of school, and I beg the Crab to let me use my three annual sick days. Because I have perfect attendance and the Crab wants me to marry Portia so that Rocksford Catholic Elementary's first-grade teacher is officially a family man, Mother Catherine reluctantly agrees, but bargains for me to do some upcoming curriculum work for free in exchange for the time off.

And then we're at the Philadelphia airport, which blows Tommy's mind, because he's never flown before. I've only traveled by air a handful of times in my life, but Portia is a veteran, negotiating everything with confidence and ease.

"Why don't we have to wait in the long lines like everyone else?" Tommy asks.

"Because we're flying first class, mister," she tells Tommy. "We fly in the front of the plane, where there is more room, and the flight attendants will be a lot nicer to us. Also, we get to board and exit the plane first. And there are snacks!"

"Why do we get those things?"

"Because we paid more money than everyone else."

"Why?" Tommy says.

"Because my first husband is treating, and also because we're worth it. You know, I never flew on a plane until I was in my mid-twenties. So you're already ahead of where I was when I was your age. You're living the high life."

Tommy takes in the security scan with wide eyes, and then he gleefully examines every part of the airport, but he loves looking at the planes the most.

He's not scared at all when we take off. He gazes out his window with a huge smile on his face as clouds pass by like no big deal.

I must admit, I could get used to first class.

The flight attendants call me Mr. Bass and treat me like I'm the president.

There's a car with tinted windows waiting for us in Tampa Bay, like we're movie stars, and it takes us directly to Ken Humes's mansion. That's exactly what it is too, a mansion. A huge white home with palm trees growing on the front lawn and white columns.

Columns.

"You used to live here?" Tommy asks.

"Unfortunately," Portia says.

"Why would you ever leave?" Tommy says, and I'm thinking the same thing. I've never even been inside a house this nice, and I will never ever own one, no matter how hard I work and how much I save. I could teach for two hundred years and still not be able to put a down payment on this sort of place, let alone afford the mortgage. Hell, I'd never be able to afford the electric bill.

When Ken and Julie answer the door, they are dressed in expensive-looking casual clothes—he's in boat shoes, khakis, and one of those Cuban-looking cigar maker's shirts, and she's wearing this sheer white dress and gold sandals. I can feel Portia bristling and worry that her claws might come out before we even enter.

"Welcome, friends," Ken says.

"Yes, welcome," Julie echoes.

The age difference between them is striking, although it's clear that Ken is the type of man everyone is attracted to. Money and looks. Must be nice.

I can see the muscles in Portia's body tensing.

"Hello, young man!" Ken says to Tommy.

"Yo," Tommy says, doing his best Rocky.

"Come inside," Julie says, and then we are sitting on a huge L-shaped white couch that is softer and more comfortable than anything I have ever slept in, let alone sat on.

"Can I offer anyone any juice, water, seltzer?" Julie says.

"How about some wine?" Portia says.

Julie and Ken look at each other, smile, and then Ken says, "We don't drink alcohol here."

"What?" Portia says. "The hell you don't. You have a fully stocked wine cellar collectively worth more than most men make in ten years."

I can't help thinking that I am most men.

"I'll have juice," Tommy says.

"What kind?" Julie says. "We have carrot, kiwi, pineapple, coconut-lime, and pomegranate."

Tommy makes wide eyes at me because he's never had any of those, and Portia says, "We'll all have the pineapple."

"Excellent!" Julie says and then heads for the kitchen.

"You seriously don't drink anymore?" Portia says to Ken.

"My drinking and smoking days are behind me," he says.

"You don't smoke cigars either?"

"Well, someone ruined my supply—destroyed my humidor too."

"I'm not sorry," Portia says. "What did you do with the wine collection?"

"Donated it. To the church. They had an auction."

"St. Mark's?" Portia says.

"There's a new priest there. Father Martin. He and I have become good friends. He's my spiritual adviser. He's been counseling me on that addiction problem I had." He raises his hand to his mouth so

Tommy won't see, mouths *Sex addiction* to me, and then says, "Best to be honest about it with other adults. Honesty is the path to freedom." To Portia he says, "I've been working on myself. I'm serious this time. Julie and I have been working together. When you pointed my own gun at me"—Ken glances over at Tommy here—"and how you left, well, it had a profound impact. It changed my life."

Julie returns with a silver tray and five highball glasses filled with pineapple juice. "Father Martin calls Ken King David. Says God's called him to a new life. He says I am Ken's Bathsheba—that our pairing came of sin, but that we will redeem ourselves. So we will serve in the fields of the Lord. Here, have some juice."

Tommy is staring hard at his sneakers.

I can tell Portia is baffled.

This is beyond weird for me.

So we all take a glass and sip.

"So you're a religious man now?" I ask, when the silence gets uncomfortable.

"In some ways, I always was, but that's exactly what this is all about," Ken says. "Atoning for our sins. We want to make sure your family is taken care of, finalize the divorce, marry ourselves, and then Julie and I are headed for Honduras, where we will do missionary work. We're going to build a school for kids who don't have one. Father Martin set the whole thing up. We're funding it, but we're actually going to help build it too."

"You're going to build a school? You—Ken Humes?" Portia says. "Have you even held a hammer in your hand before?"

"I know it sounds crazy, right?" Ken says, and there is no ill will in his voice. He really does seem to be a man at peace. "But Portia, the me you knew—that was the old me. I'm trying to be the new me now."

Julie takes Ken's hand in hers and holds it on her lap like a small puppy.

"God is all-powerful," Ken says. "And He has provided us with a mission—"

"Bullshit," Portia says. "You are a disgusting pig who exploited young women"—she points to Julie—"*continues* to exploit young women for your own gain so that—"

"I am not being exploited," Julie says. "Quite the contrary. You haven't been here for the past year. Ken has made radical changes in his life. The amount of charity he's already done would—"

"It's okay, Julie." Ken pats her hand. "Portia has a right to feel angry—she experienced the old Ken, who was all that she says he was. I'm sorry I was the old Ken when you were with me, Portia. I am truly sorry. But I am no longer that man."

"This is infuriating!" Portia says. "You were hideous to me. You cheated on me multiple times and insisted on making the basest, most sexist films, no matter how many times I talked about making films for women too. But there was no money in that, right? It was easier to exploit teenage girls who were looking for attention. Oh, how you belittled my ambitions—systematically made sure I always felt dumb and worthless. And now you 'find God' and think you can wash your soul clean with money—don't you see why that would infuriate everyone who intimately knew the 'old Ken'?"

He nods. "I do. But if you did not stand with me on the road to Damascus when God struck me down and forced me to see what I had not seen before, how could you—"

"You are not St. Fucking Paul, Ken!" Portia yells.

Tommy moves a little closer to me.

"No, I'm not," Ken says. "I am just a man who has a choice. And I am choosing to build a school for children who have no school. I am choosing to take care of you financially. And I am choosing to marry the woman who inspired my transformation."

Julie squeezes Ken's hand, and they gaze into each other's eyes lovingly.

"This is really bullshit," Portia says. "Such a fucking joke."

Julie glances over at Tommy and whispers, "The child."

"Oh, please. The last time I saw you, you were humping my husband in my own bed."

"Okay," I finally say. "Maybe Tommy and I will take a walk outside."

"I'm sorry," Ken says. "I thought we could all do this in a civil manner. Portia, I thought you'd be happy to know that I'm a changed man. I'm happy for you. I pray for you every day now."

Julie says, "I pray for you too. All three of you."

"This is getting way too creepy." Portia sets her pineapple juice down on the glass coffee table and walks out the front door.

"Well," I say. "I guess this means Tommy and I should probably get going too."

"Let me give Portia what is rightfully hers," Ken says to me. "She told me you're a first-grade teacher."

"When did she tell you that?" I say, hearing the jealousy in my voice.

"Last week, on the phone. She says it's a religious school, right?"

"Uncle Chuck's the best teacher there is," Tommy says.

"I bet he is," Ken says. "So surely Uncle Chuck understands the importance of making sure kids in Central America get an education. It will go easier down there with the priests and churches if Julie and I are married. We need Portia to grant me a divorce first. You and I both want to officially start new lives, right? Why drag this out?"

"Listen," I say, "I feel like it's not my place to get involved here. Whatever happened between the two of you—well, I'm grateful you screwed it up, because now Portia's with me."

"*Us*," Tommy says.

"As it was meant to be," Ken says. "Father Martin has told me many times—all for a reason." He stands and walks over to a small desk on the other side of the room and pulls out a large envelope. "If you are going to be Portia's husband, you'll want to look out for her best interests. Have someone look these papers over. You'll see that we have been more than fair. Any lawyer will tell you we've been generous to the point of foolishness. We just want to move on—atone and try to put some good in the world. But we need to put this unfortunate business behind us first."

"We could have made this ugly and uncomfortable for everyone," Julie says. "We have the means and the right lawyers to force Portia's hand."

"But we'd rather be Christian about this," Ken says. "Read over the papers. You'll be a very well compensated man if you can get her to let go of her pride and sign."

"If you have the means to get what you want, then why give Portia such a generous settlement?"

Ken smiles sadly at me. "Personal transformation takes patience and work. And a little help from the right woman. From what Portia said about you on the phone and from what I've gathered today, I can tell that the three of you are good for each other. But Portia can be a little, well, *stubborn*. I won't provide you with an owner's manual—and please don't tell her I used that term, or her feminism will have her foaming at the mouth. But it's time for all of us to move on."

I look into Ken's eyes and find no lies, which is tough, because I want to hate this guy.

I nod once, take the envelope, and then Tommy and I join Portia outside.

The car takes us to a gulf-front hotel in Clearwater. We eat dinner and walk the beach. We hang Tommy's Quiet Riot mask over one of the headboards, get him to sleep, and then talk on the balcony with a partial view of the water, as the waves roll in end-lessly through moonlight.

Portia's on her fourth glass of wine when she says, "Why did you take the papers from Ken?"

"He handed them to me," I say.

"Why didn't you leave when I did?"

"I tried, but he kept talking."

"You didn't have to be polite to him."

"What was it you said to me earlier—you didn't have much practice with divorce? Well, I don't have much practice helping the woman I love through one either."

She shakes her head. "It's not fair. His getting away so squeaky clean like this—buying his absolution from that priest."

"Would you rather he continue to be an asshole for the rest of his life?" I say. "Keep underpaying and exploiting young women? Because building a school for poor kids sure seems like what I'd vote for."

"It's just that—" She doesn't finish.

"What?"

She downs her wine, and then with a shaky voice she says, "Why did he change for her and not me? I would have loved to do all that charity work. How is it that she got him to—"

"Maybe you're supposed to do cool stuff with *me* instead. If you haven't noticed, I'm sitting right across from you. I'm here. I want to be with you. And I'm sorry I don't have a lot of money—"

"It was never about the money. Jesus."

"Then what?"

"I don't know. There was Mr. Vernon and then Ken. Both of them—I couldn't save them. I failed."

"Do you want me to go swimming in the gulf after a big break-fast tomorrow morning? I can cramp up and you can swim out and save me. We could call the local news crews and have them cover it on TV. I'd do that for you. No sweat."

She laughs.

Thank god she laughs!

"I'm being stupid, right?" she says.

"It's a lot to take in."

"Did you think she looked like his daughter?"

"First thing I thought when they opened the door."

"It's creepy, right?"

"Yep. But it's also none of our business. And we can be free and clear of them easily enough. Don't you think that it's all a nice twist of fate, Portia? I mean, if Ken was half as bad as you made him sound— and I absolutely believe he was all you said he was—his lawyers could have made things awful for you. Maybe the guy really just wants to do the right thing here and move on. And maybe that means we get to move on too. Get busy living the rest of our lives together."

Portia's silent for a long time. "I think I just need some time, Chuck, out here. I just want to think. Would I be a complete bitch if I asked you to leave me alone for a few hours?"

"Like go inside?"

"Yeah," she says in this quivery voice that suggests tears are coming.

So I go inside, brush my teeth, plop down onto the queen-size mattress, and listen to Tommy breathing in the next bed. I wonder if Portia is crying outside, and what that would mean. Does part of her still love Ken? It's got to be normal to mourn a failed marriage, especially since they were together for years. There would probably be something wrong with Portia if she weren't a little upset tonight, I tell myself, but it's hard to swallow.

Around three in the morning I hear the sliding door open and listen to Portia make her way through the dark to the bathroom.

She's in there a while, but she finally comes to bed and pulls my arm over her so that we are spooning.

"I love you," I whisper into her ear.

"Love you too," she says.

In the morning Tommy wakes me up, and we find Portia on the balcony reading over the divorce papers.

She signs later that day at Ken's lawyers' office in downtown Tampa Bay.

Tommy and I go along for moral support, and so does Julie, who—in another white sundress—looks even younger than she did when we all first met.

When everything is inked and legal, Julie squeezes Ken's arm, and he immediately asks if he can take us all out for a big meal, just to clear the air, so to speak.

Without missing a beat, Portia says, "No thanks, Ken. We're going to Disney World tonight."

"Seriously?" Tommy says.

"Seriously," Portia answers.

And the next thing I know, we're on a first-class flight to Orlando.

We spend our last day in the Magic Kingdom. Even though Tommy doesn't bring up the fact that his mother once promised him a trip here, I think about that a lot, but still mostly manage to relish the smile plastered on the little guy's face as he enjoys the various rides and shows and gets his picture taken with all of the characters.

Danielle would have loved this day, I keep thinking.

The week after I complete my first year of teaching first grade, with Tommy and Portia's mom acting as our only witnesses, Portia and I are married by a justice of the peace.

We tell Tommy he can pick the honeymoon destination, since he's going with us, and when he says he wants to go back to Disney

World so he can see the other parks and spend more than a day down there, we laugh and book it, because why the hell not.

Maybe you think a Disney vacation isn't as romantic as going to Hawaii or Paris or somewhere in Greece or Italy or Fiji or the Caribbean, but Portia and I never got to go to Disney World when we were kids, and so we do it up for a week in Orlando with Tommy, who doesn't have a single bad dream in the Magic Kingdom.

CHAPTER 32

It's a blistering hot July, and we've got our air conditioning on full blast as Tommy, Portia, and I eat corn on the cob and salted tomato slices at the kitchen table. We're talking about maybe driving south for a mini-vacation somewhere when Portia's phone buzzes.

"Who's that?" Tommy asks.

"It's an e-mail from a literary agent I queried," Portia says, and goes into her office.

A few seconds later she starts screaming like she just accidentally cut off a finger.

Tommy and I run to her. She hugs us both, and we all start jumping up and down.

The huge smile on her face is so beautiful.

"What the hell is going on?" I say.

She seems incapable of speech, so she points to her computer screen.

Tommy and I read the e-mail from some agent at an agency I've never heard of before, but then again, I haven't heard of *any* literary agencies. There's a lot of praise for Portia's novel—"an aching tale of loss and redemption" sticks out in my memory—and then the man says he'd like to represent Portia.

"So this means he's going to publish your book?" Tommy says.

"I think it means he wants to be her agent," I say.

Portia says, "Hell yes, it does!"

"It means he'll try to sell Portia's book to a publishing house."

"So people can read it?" Tommy says. "I want to read it."

To Portia, I say, "Congratulations. Seriously."

Portia puts her arms around Tommy and me, and we do another family hug, during which Portia breaks down crying, but it's a happy cry, which makes Tommy and me laugh.

"What the hell, Portia?" I say. "You okay?"

"I am," she says and then adds, "I just never thought I'd actually find representation in New York City. Me. *Portia Kane.*"

She's been submitting her manuscript for a few weeks now and hadn't heard anything before today. I don't know if this is a quick response or not, and I'm not really sure if Portia knows either. She's sort of doing this blindly, with no advice from anyone really, because she doesn't know any other published authors personally. She purchased a few how-to books off the Internet and just jumped in. Even though I believe in Portia, it's a little hard for me to accept it can happen this fast—that you just get an e-mail one day, and then you have a literary agent representing your book.

"Maybe you should call this guy?" I say, doing my best to be supportive. "It says he'd like to speak as soon as possible, right?"

"It's Saturday night, though."

"It does say *as soon as possible.*"

"So you think I should call right now? Do you think that would make me look too eager? Or lame for being home on a Saturday night?"

"He's e-mailing you on a Saturday night," I say.

"Yeah," Tommy says.

"Okay, I'll call him. But you have to leave the room."

I kiss Portia once on the lips and say, "I'm proud of you," before Tommy and I load the dishwasher.

Ten or so minutes later we hear Portia screaming in her room again.

"What did he say?" Tommy asks, once we're back in Portia's office.

"He loves it," Portia says, pushing the palms of her hands against her heart. "And he wants to start submitting on Monday, first thing in the morning."

"Submitting?" Tommy says.

"My book to *real* publishing houses in New York City," Portia says. "My book!"

Then she starts screaming again, pushes past us, throws Mötley Crüe's *Shout at the Devil* album on the turntable, and cues up "Looks That Kill."

We're all jumping on and off the couch, playing air guitars and drums, making guitar solo faces, and screaming the lyrics.

And it feels so good to be rocking out to Mötley Crüe in celebration of Portia's accomplishment. I watch Tommy spazzing with us, and it's the happiest I've seen him since his mother died. He didn't even look this happy at Disney World. And I can tell that he's feeding off Portia's good energy.

There are more calls from the agent on Monday morning after the manuscript has been pitched and sent to several houses, and then a few days after that, there is a small bidding war for Portia's novel, during which she has to talk to real editors on the phone and decide which one is right for her. "How do you choose?" she keeps asking me. "Besides going with the top bidder?"

The bidding gets up into the six-figure range, and I tell her that she should pick the editor she feels most comfortable with, because she will already be pulling in more than four times my yearly teaching salary with the sale.

It all seems too good to be true, but maybe it really is this simple. After all, what the hell do I know about the publishing world? Still, part of me is waiting for the catch, although I don't say that to

Portia. She's just so damn thrilled, and I don't want to do anything to ruin this moment for her.

She actually goes with the second highest offer because that editor seemed to "get the book more," which I'm not really sure *I* get, but we hire Lisa (Jon the cop's there too, because they're living together now) to babysit Tommy and go out to dinner in Philadelphia to celebrate regardless. Portia keeps saying, "I know Mr. Vernon will read this book. I just know it," which makes me nervous, because who knows if Mr. Vernon is still alive? And the last time we saw him, he made it pretty damn clear that he never wanted to interact with us again, let alone read a book written by a former student.

I wonder if Portia will be on TV talk shows and radio programs and if someone will make a movie out of her book. A part of me deep down worries she might lose interest in me once she becomes famous, but I try my best to kill that part and just be happy for my wife.

Over the next six months Portia takes trips to New York City, each one requiring her to buy a new designer outfit, heels, and a handbag, plus get her hair and nails done. While I love seeing her doing what she wants—not to mention that she looks amazingly hot when done up—I also worry about the fact that I can't provide her with any of these things, like her first husband did. I start to feel a little irrelevant.

Portia does lunches with her agent and editor and many people from her publishing house, which they pay for, and a few times they even pay for her to stay overnight in a hotel, which sort of blows this Catholic elementary school teacher's mind.

Each time, Portia returns home glowing and raving about how smart and classy her editor Nancy is, and how her agent gets her work and wants the next book as soon as she can write it. She once again starts spending all of her time alone in her office, and I begin to see what our life is going to look like over the next decade or so.

I eat most of my dinners alone with Tommy while Portia works, sometimes twelve hours a day, writing the new book, editing *Love May Fail*, working on her new website, endlessly chitchatting with other writers and readers on social media sites. And when we do spend time together, she asks me over and over again if I think Mr. Vernon will read her novel, to the point where I actually tell her she can't ask me that anymore.

But I have to admit that I have never seen anyone more full of joy and hope than Portia as she awaits the publication of her book. Her ecstasy rivals the memory of my first heroin hit, which worries me more than I let on. Such highs always come with even worse lows, in my experience. The ex-junkie in me waits for the yang to follow the yin, so to speak, as the dutiful husband in me tries his best to wear a smile and be supportive.

Mr. Yang sends his first calling card when Portia's book is slapped with a dreadful neon-green cover that I pretend to love, because her publisher doesn't offer to change it. Her agent says the bright color will "pop on the shelf," but Portia hates it and insists it's going to hurt her sales, although she does her best to feign enthusiasm in her e-mails to her editor and manages to maintain a positive attitude. But then the authors to whom Portia's publisher mails advance review copies, hoping to get supportive quotes for the cover, fail to respond. Even though Portia's agent tells her that it's hard for first-time authors to get what he calls "blurbs," it doesn't help—especially since Portia easily finds hundreds of first-time novels covered in the flattering words of more established authors.

Mr. Yang officially shows up about six weeks before the publication of Portia's novel in the form of something called a *Kirkus* review. Even though her agent calls her and says that *Kirkus* is notoriously snarky—that one negative review means nothing in the grand scheme of a publication—Portia cries when she reads it, which makes me want to find the anonymous author of the review and beat the snot out of him. It's not so much what the reviewer writes that pisses me off, but the high and mighty tone in which he trashes Portia's first book as "a painfully sentimental look at a more than slightly nauseating (and highly improbable) friendship between a wooden cliché of a teacher and the most annoying student you are likely to encounter on the printed page." The on-the-printed-page part really annoys me—where the fuck *else* would you encounter the main character of a novel? You'd think a reviewer of books would be able to write better. And I wonder why no one reviews the reviews. A reviewer who carelessly belittles the best effort of an artist—talk about cliché.

"It's bullshit," I tell Portia. "Your book is beautiful."

"I don't know if I can handle this," she says. "How public this is. I didn't realize how awful it is to be reviewed like this. I spent so much time on this book. It's the best thing that ever came out of me."

"And this reviewer is an asshole. Probably someone who wants to publish a book and can't. I'm sure there will be better reviews."

But there aren't.

In fact, the reviews get worse.

It seems like every week some publication reviews Portia's book with enough venom to kill twenty men.

Publishers Weekly calls *Love May Fail* "ridiculous," and then ends by writing, "Just cut the first two words from the title and you will have your review."

And then all of the advance-copy reader reviews begin popping up on the Internet via various websites and blogs, and those are even uglier. I keep telling Portia not to read them. She's losing weight, not sleeping, drinking too much, and seems to be suffering more pain than I thought a book publication was capable of inflicting.

She gets a few nice blog reviews, which I find by googling. I print those out, highlight the most positive parts—"This book gave me so much hope," and "I can't wait for a sequel!!!" and "A read that made me want to be a better person," and even "This novel saved my life"—and hang them up on the refrigerator, but she doesn't seem to care, even as the collection grows.

The *Philadelphia Inquirer* gives her a little hometown love the week before the official publication date, calling *Love May Fail* "a charming look at love and faith . . . not to be missed," but it feels a little after the fact, maybe even unconvincing, like praise from one's own mother.

On the day of her publication we go to three local bookstores so that we can see her book on the shelves.

Two don't have it in stock.

The third has a single copy on a back shelf, far away from the displays and the large stacks by the registers of the books that the store is pushing hardest.

It's easy to see that *Love May Fail* doesn't even have a chance.

We throw a small launch party for Portia at the Manor, and I make sure we have books there for her to sign. All of our friends are incredibly enthusiastic and supportive, but Portia just doesn't seem into it. The light in her eyes is pretty much gone.

Only a few weeks after *Love May Fail* hits bookstore shelves, Portia's editor calls, saying she is leaving publishing for personal reasons, but that her colleagues will make sure *Love May Fail* gets a fair shake. Portia's convinced that the poor early response after the six-figure advance is why her editor is leaving, even though her agent assures her that these things happen all the time in New York—both editors leaving houses and highly sought-after books failing to live up to the hype.

"So are we *failing*?" Portia asks.

"It's a strange game," her agent responds, which sends Portia even further south.

The publishing house stops communicating with her.

There are no TV or radio appearances.

Her agent's e-mails become few and far between.

And I want to ask Portia how a business like this can work. How can you pay so much money for something and then not promote it?

About a month or so after Portia's small launch party, once we have Tommy in bed, Portia pours herself a rather enormous glass of wine and sits down on the couch next to me.

"You can stop pretending," she says.

"What?" I say, looking up from reading her novel for the third time.

"That you enjoy it."

"But I do," I say, and it's not a lie. I still find it thrilling to hold a Portia Kane novel in my hand. Even a *neon-green* Portia Kane novel.

"I'm letting go of the whole writing thing," she says. "It was a mistake."

"You're a good writer, Portia. With a different publisher, better marketing—"

"Everyone hated it. And then they cut their losses. I've researched it. Other writers have had the same experience. And now they say it will be infinitely harder to get another publishing deal because my first book lost them so much money. Every publishing house in the world will have access to my sales numbers, which are and will remain shitty. Couple that with my reviews, and there's no point."

I don't know what else I can do to save my wife, so—even though I don't believe it's true—I say, "Well, at least you got a few thousand copies out there into the world. So that gives you a chance."

"No one in publishing cares about a few thousand copies," she says. "That's *nothing* to them."

"No," I say, trying to be the man I admire. "But it's a chance for Mr. Vernon to find your book and read it."

I see her face light up for a fraction of a second as she sips her wine, but then she halfheartedly says, "Maybe," and the light is gone again.

Time passes.

Mr. Vernon doesn't contact Portia.

She throws herself into the writing of her next book, but the joy and enthusiasm are gone.

On the first night of June, the Crystal Lake Diner—the place where Danielle waitressed—catches fire. No one is hurt, but just like that a South Jersey landmark is gutted. All of the booths and the stools and thousands of diner customers' good memories go up in flames. It's a sad twist of fate losing a public place that you've shared with a community for your entire life. And it's also one less link to Danielle—one less memento. The diner might as well have been in Portia's backyard, as she grew up right down the street. It's also like losing a time machine, because just walking into that place instantly transported many of us back to high school—late night fries after binge drinking in the woods.

"That's where I reconnected with Danielle," Portia says when she hears about the news. "And my reconnecting with Danielle led me to you and all that followed."

"Yeah, so?" I say.

"It just seems like an extremely bad omen, doesn't it?"

"Everyone got out safely, at least. That's good, right?"

"I don't know, Chuck. I just don't know anymore." She bursts into tears, which scares me. I mean, we're all sad about the fire, but Portia sobs and sobs in my arms for almost an hour.

Six months after the publication date, Portia receives a devastating e-mail from her agent. There will be no *Love May Fail* paperback release. The sales were so low that the publisher has decided to disassociate its name from Portia Kane.

Right around the one-year anniversary of her publication date, something inside of Portia finally breaks.

She stops writing and begins to spend her days taking long walks and sitting on park benches, mindlessly feeding squirrels and pigeons.

She repaints (multiple times) every room in our new close-to-my-work home in Pennsylvania.

Volunteers a lot at Tommy's new school.

Buys cookbooks and fattens me up with endless gourmet meals that would sell in the best restaurants in any major city in the world.

Bakes dozens of different pies for our neighbors.

She buys an old truck that looks remarkably like the one I had when we first met, and begins trash-picking furniture, refinishing the pieces in our basement, and selling them at flea markets. She barely makes a profit and doesn't seem to get any joy out of the process, downing Advil for sore wrists and elbows at an alarming rate.

Even our sex life becomes routine. She never initiates or refuses, but participates with an unspoken sense of obligation that borders on offensive and often leaves me feeling depressed. Whenever I ask if I'm doing something wrong, Portia says, "You are the best lover I will ever have," which seems like a way around talking straight about the problem. Still, I don't push her. I feel as though she's healing that broken heart of hers the best she can—and I, of all people, know that recovery takes time.

The worst part is that Tommy misses the old Portia. He doesn't exactly say anything about the change, but I can read his eyes and body language. The little man is sort of careful around her now, almost as if he has reverted to taking care of his mother figure, which breaks my heart. He's forever volunteering to help with chores around the house—like carrying in groceries or taking out the garbage or dusting or folding laundry or weeding the flower beds—and Portia usually says that it's easier to do the work herself, and while that frees up Tommy to play with his friends on the block, it also leaves him feeling confused and maybe even rejected, although I never ask him about his feelings about Portia. It's too painful for me to address my own, let alone deal with the effect my wife's depression is having on the boy we are raising.

Saying she doesn't have the emotional energy, Portia even stops making the drive back across the bridge to see her mother. More and more time passes in between trips east, and we only go when I pester her about visiting the old woman.

Time passes, and Mrs. Kane stares at the Buy from Home Network and Tommy grows and I teach and bartend and Portia finds things to keep herself occupied, at least superficially.

I plan little weekend family vacations and surprise dinners in the city, buy tickets to plays and musicals I think she will like, take her to a comedy club, allow Tommy to buy tickets to a few rock concerts we go to as a family. I even skip lunches to save my own money and buy designer clothes for Portia. She refuses to spend any of "Ken's money" on anything but the mortgage and essentials for Tommy, saying, "What do I need new outfits for?" While she always says thank you and smiles whenever she opens the wrapped boxes I give her, nothing I do ever makes her eyes light up the way they once did, and she never wears what I buy, unless I make a specific request.

Ken and Julie send postcards from Honduras, along with short reports on the missionary work they are doing. Portia rips the first few up with a rage that scares me enough to throw away the future notes without letting my wife read them first.

"Maybe you should try writing again," I sometimes dare to say when her crying wakes me up in the middle of the night, and she'll always respond, "I'm okay. Just go back to sleep."

The world is a hard place and can be hardest on the hopeful, but I just can't seem to let go of the woman I married—the one who believed wildly in possibility.

CHAPTER 33

On Tommy's ninth birthday, I lead my first-grade class to the after-school pickup with a bit of a lift in my step. In my front pocket are tickets to the monster truck rally that Tommy and his best friend Marcus have been wanting to attend. Marcus and I are going to surprise Tommy with a night of hugely obscene vehicles, five-foot-high tires driving over and crushing normal cars before bursting through flames and soaring off ramps over bikini girls as heavy metal music blasts from gigantic speakers hung above.

Basically a nine-year-old boy's dream.

Portia has agreed to go, mostly—I think—because it's Tommy's birthday, and he specifically requested that she be a part of things. She hasn't really been all that social lately, turning down invitations from friends and complaining about being tired far more than seems possible, especially because she's been going to bed early and sleeping twelve hours a night. Tommy has playfully nicknamed her "Sleeping Beauty."

Once my last student has made her way into her parent's car, I lock up my classroom and attempt to leave the building, but the Crab—who has somehow held on to the role of principal, even though she is approaching her two hundredth birthday—sticks her head out of the office. "Just the man I was looking for," she says. "I hope you're not attempting to leave early, Mr. Bass. The teacher's handbook states that you may not leave the building before three thirty without permission from administration, which as you very well know means me. And as I have given you no such permission, I *know* you weren't about to exit this building."

The Crab and I have become friends. Her evaluations of my lessons are always marked EXEMPLARY, and I haven't left for a higher-paying public school teaching position yet, which I believe both baffles and impresses Mother Catherine—we both know she'd write me a recommendation letter if I asked. The truth is, I like teaching here, and Mother Catherine is a fantastic principal who puts the needs of the kids first over the politics of parents who pay hard-earned cash to send their children to a Catholic school. I actually respect the Crab—a lot. And Portia has more than enough money left over from her first marriage for us to live comfortably.

"It's Tommy's birthday," I explain. "We're going to see a monster truck show."

"Well, I certainly wouldn't want to make you late for such a cerebral event as monster truck night, Mr. Bass, but I'm afraid I need to speak with you in my office before you leave. Something urgent has just come up. And since you are technically still on the clock, I suggest you follow me."

I swallow hard and scan my brain for any possible trouble that could potentially ambush me once the Crab closes her office door behind us. It doesn't take much for a teacher to be swept up into a shit storm. Some parent's boss makes them feel powerless during the day, so when they come home they call Mother Catherine and—with godlike confidence—critique my lesson plans. Or maybe somebody forgot about the peanut ban and stuck a threatening PB&J in a lunchbox, which would have the food allergy moms shooting nuclear warheads at everyone if only they had the capability, and since they don't, they call and scream until mushroom clouds come out of the phone. This is just par for the course when you are a teacher.

"Sit," the Crab tells me once we are in her office, and I do as I am told.

"Crazy parent call?" I guess.

"No," she says.

"So?"

"How's your marriage?" Mother Catherine says, confusing me.

I blink and then go for a joke. "How's yours?"

"If you wish to know the thoughts of my husband, I suggest you get down on your knees and ask Him yourself."

"I just might do that, Mother Catherine."

"Indulge me. Please. How *is* your marriage, Mr. Bass?"

"Why are you asking?"

"You are aware that Portia and I speak from time to time? That we have a . . . *a relationship.*"

"Yes," I say, and wonder where this is headed.

"I'd like to speak to you now as a friend and not your boss. May I have your permission?"

"Sure," I say, and begin to feel my palms getting sweaty.

"Portia tells me many things about you. I do believe the woman has mistaken me for a priest, because she has been confessing to me. Only I'm not bound by God to keep what she tells me a secret. Again—not a priest. We both know I would never tell anyone else her secrets, but husband and wife are one flesh, and therefore there should be no secrets between you and Portia."

"Secrets?" I say, imagining the worst.

"You are a good man, Chuck Bass. One of the best teachers we have here in this school—one of the best teachers I have ever seen in action—mostly because you care so much about the kids. That's what makes teachers great—empathy. Anyone can learn the subject matter. But caring, well you can't teach someone that. You either have it in you or you don't."

"What does this have to do with my marriage?"

"You are very good to Portia. And she knows it."

"I love her."

"And she loves you too, but she's stuck. You see it plainly, and she knows you see it, which makes it hard for her. Your Tommy sees it too, but pretends he doesn't just so she won't feel bad, which ends up making her feel even worse, because she doesn't know how to get unstuck and she very much wants to—for you and Tommy and herself too. She's had a crisis of faith, although she wouldn't put it that way."

I don't know what the Crab wants me to say. "I've been trying to—"

"You have been a good husband, better than Portia ever dreamed possible."

I just look at the Crab in her habit and wonder what this is all about.

"Portia and I have been praying together, did you know that?"

I shake my head.

"I have the sisters praying for Portia, and nun prayers are very powerful. I pray for Portia too. Every night. There are some people who are meant to tend the light, and that can be a difficult job over the long haul. Just look at what happened to my husband."

"Mother Catherine, I appreciate your prayers and the kind words. I really do. But why did you bring me into your office today?"

The Crab grins. "So direct, Mr. Bass."

I shrug playfully, because I did not mean to be offensive.

She's smiling too much, I think, just before she says, "Do you remember that when I first interviewed you, I said that Portia and I were linked?"

I don't remember that specifically, but it sounds like the type of mystical Catholic talk the Crab often uses, so I nod.

"Well, my dear friend Sister Maeve's prodigal son has come home."

It takes a second to sink in. "Mr. Vernon is alive? He's back in the Philadelphia area?"

"No, he's not in the Philadelphia area," she says. "But he *is* alive. We have been communicating. He finally responded to the letters his mother and I wrote him when she was dying and he was in the Vermont wilderness, feeling sorry for himself. Took him some time to get up the courage. But he finally got around to it."

"He's really alive?"

"Very much so."

"Does Portia know about this?" I say, thinking that Mr. Vernon's being alive—actual proof—is the one thing capable of putting the light back in her eyes. It seems like a miracle, because we'd completely given up.

"She hasn't a clue," the Crab says.

"Why didn't you tell her yourself already?"

"Because opportunities like this don't come along very often. Chances to resurrect people. Make them whole again. In my experience, it's best to do it with a little style and flair—panache even, don't you think? Heighten the experience. Make it memorable— epic. Be a little romantic about it."

"I'm not sure I understand, Mother. I'm sorry."

"Yes, you do, Mr. Bass. You absolutely do," Mother Catherine says, and then she slides an envelope across her desk.

"That's from him? Mr. Vernon?" I pick up the envelope—my heart is trying its best to punch through my rib cage. "Do I have to read it here in front of you?"

"You are free to go, Mr. Bass. Enjoy your monster truck rally. Happy birthday to Tommy. And have fun resurrecting our girl. She's got work to do yet."

The Crab and I look into each other's eyes for a moment, and then I say, "Thank you, Mother Catherine."

She nods with a quiet confidence, and the light in her eyes glows brighter than I have ever seen it shine before.

I jet out of the building and across the parking lot.

Inside my car, I rip open the envelope with trembling hands.

My eyes race back and forth, but I can't get the words into my head fast enough—and when I finish, I have to reread the letter immediately just to make sure I fully comprehend.

Once I'm sure I understand what Mr. Vernon is suggesting, in the privacy of my vehicle, I raise two sets of devil horns above my head, stick out my tongue, and scream like a proper metalhead for a good three minutes.

EPILOGUE:

Portia Kane

John Figler is a law-abiding high-school student. He says in his letter that he has read almost everything of mine and is now prepared to state the single idea that lies at the core of my life's work so far. The words are his: "Love may fail, but courtesy will prevail."

—Kurt Vonnegut Jr., *Jailbird*

CHAPTER 34

When my phone's navigational system tells me I'm close enough to see the spot, I search the triangle of grass at the heart of this little western Massachusetts town, which looks just as Chuck described. I immediately spot Mr. Vernon sitting on a park bench with a small yellow dog in his lap, basking in the midafternoon sun.

I park my truck at a distance and watch him for a time. He's wearing a blue turtleneck, which makes him look like a sea captain or an elderly Ernest Hemingway. He's also looking up at the clouds, petting his rather calm dog. Mr. Vernon's peaceful expression seems very much at home on his face. I fight the urge to smack it off. I also want to give my former teacher a fierce hug.

My mind flashes on the last time I saw him caning his way into the Oaklyn police station. I can't believe how much time has passed.

It's a strange mix of emotions—excitement, anger, relief, and even disbelief.

So much of the past is being dredged up.

And yet we've come full circle somehow.

Chuck was right—I need closure, which is why I'm here. I haven't been able to move on.

I'm stuck.

Desperate.

I find myself walking toward Mr. Vernon.

He recognizes me now, even though I have on sunglasses and a silk scarf tied around my neck, but he doesn't stand, maybe because of the dog on his lap.

He's scratching the dog's floppy ears and smiling, peaceful as the Buddha.

When I'm within earshot, in an overly dramatic voice, Mr. Vernon says, " 'The Teacher is here and is calling for you.' "

"What? Who said that?" The bitchiness in my voice embarrasses me, even though I have a right to be bitter.

"Martha says that to Mary. John 11:28. Am I not your Lazarus?" he says. "My mother was big on making me memorize biblical verses when I was little. I can damn near quote the whole New Testament."

"I think that teacher reference would make you Jesus, right? You *are* the teacher."

"I'm definitely not Jesus. No, *you'd* be Jesus in this metaphor. I am the metaphorical Lazarus, and you are—"

"Oh, fuck metaphors already. This isn't English class, for Christ's sake. And fuck you for leaving me like that at the Manor. That was a mean, horrible, cowardly thing to do. We've been worried for *years*!"

"In all fairness, yours was a pretty dirty trick played at a time when I was in crisis. You were deceitful," he says. "You didn't take into account the emotional shock that—"

"We were throwing you *a party*!"

"Well, I didn't *want* a party."

I smile proudly. "Well, you invited me here today. So I must have been right about something."

"True." He nods.

"And I still haven't forgiven you, for the record."

"Well, I forgave you. Officially," he says. "Quite some time ago."

"I remain pretty pissed off."

"And yet you came to see me." He's lost weight, and the skin hanging from his jaw sags red and loose, which maybe explains the slightly outdated turtleneck choice. Mr. Vernon's wrinkles have deepened, and yet he looks younger somehow, less stressed, maybe even at peace.

"What the hell is this about?" I say and then laugh in spite of myself. "Why have I driven all the way up here? Am I out of my mind? It's like we're yoked in some strange way. Like we're—I don't know. I'm too tired to be clever these days."

"Will you sit with me?" he says, and pats the empty bench next to him.

Sitting down next to Mr. Vernon feels wonderful, maybe because I'm truly exhausted after the six-hour drive—not to mention the toll that my failed life has taken on me—but I can't resist saying, "I knew you wouldn't kill yourself. You're better than that."

"I really don't think it's a question of being 'better,' but being *sick*. It's more of a mathematical equation maybe. When the bad tips the scales egregiously . . . I had a couple of close calls, if you really want to know. Spent some time at a facility. Nice place on a lake. It was good for me. I took some meds for a while. Talked to a few shrinks. Some good. Some crazier than me. Even wrote a letter to Edmond Atherton. Forgave him too. Spent a lot of time wrapped up in a wool blanket, sitting on an Adirondack chair watching loons—listening to them call to each other across the water. Have you ever heard a loon call? Beautifully haunting. Healing. They just keep calling and hope for the best. There's something to be learned from that."

The mania that was in his eyes the last time I saw him—it's vanished.

Mr. Vernon has found something.

"Who's this?" I point to the little somewhat-poodle-looking mutt that seems to be a permanent part of Mr. Vernon's lap, if the dog's comfort level is any indication.

Mr. Vernon smiles proud as any father. "This here is Mr. Yo-Yo Ma."

"You named your *yellow* dog Yo-Yo Ma? Seriously? Isn't that racist?" I say before I can stop myself.

"I certainly didn't intend it to be." He shrugs off my accusation, looking down at his pet the way mothers gaze at newborn babies. "No one will ever replace Albert Camus, but Yo-Yo Ma is my new buddy. Well, I've had him for almost a year now, so he's not exactly *new*. But our life together feels fresh—like we're still at the beginning. It's a *new* life for us—for me."

"What do you mean? *What* new life?"

He smiles at me. "I read your book."

My heart skips a few beats. "When?"

"At the right time," he says rather ominously.

"The critics crucified me."

"I don't read critics," he says. "I read novelists."

I wait for him to say more, but he doesn't.

Finally, in this embarrassingly small, needy little-girl voice, I ask, "Did you like it?"

He looks into my eyes for an awkwardly long time. Then, rather than answer, he says, "Come on, Yo-Yo Ma. Let's show Ms. Kane what we've been up to lately."

The little mutt jumps down onto the grass, and Mr. Vernon stands with his wooden cane in one hand and the leash in his other. "Your book inspired me to do some volunteer work. Every Tuesday afternoon now. And today just happens to be Tuesday. Come on. I'll show you."

I follow Mr. Vernon, the familiar rhythm of his cane making me flash on our time together in Vermont and New York City as he crosses the street and little Yo-Yo Ma's nails click on the concrete and asphalt. Then we walk for several blocks without saying a word. I need Mr. Vernon to help me believe again, and yet I fear he's going to let me down. The whole time my heart pounds at the thought of where he might be leading me, but my brain does its best to kill any hopes that arise, popping every beautiful shiny bubble that floats up from my subconscious, even though deep down I'm pretty sure Mr. Vernon is going to show me something wonderful.

"This is it," he says. "Where I volunteer."

It's a large tan brick building with some sort of World War II military cannon out front.

These words are etched in stone over the entrance:

Garvey Public High School

I start to feel lightheaded.

"Are you really teaching again?" I ask, wondering why he's not in his classroom, if so. It seems like the time when a typical school day ends, but too early for teachers to leave the building.

"No, I'm not technically teaching. Not employed, anyway. No paycheck. Like I said before, I'm *volunteering*."

"For what?"

Instead of answering, he says, "I want you to see something."

We don't go inside, which surprises me. I follow him to the side of the building, which is striped by three rows of rectangular windows.

Mr. Vernon turns around and faces me.

We lock eyes.

"The books we read in literature classes—just innocuous letters and symbols on paper, until we run the words through our brains and allow the fiction to manifest in the real world."

"How do we allow fiction to manifest?"

"Through our actions."

"What actions?" I laugh.

"Some students beat the hell out of you with a baseball bat, and some students save you by writing novels. And we've got to thank our saviors no matter how many times we feel attacked and broken, because we damn well need them. So that's what today is about. Thank you, Portia, for *Love May Fail*."

"I'm not sure I understand what's going on here. Why did we need to come to the side of the building?"

"Look up"—he points to the third-floor row of windows, which open en masse—"and meet the Garvey Public High School Fiction Writing Club."

Dozens of smiling young faces appear, arms emerge, and then paper airplanes are dive-bombing and gliding and loop-de-looping through the air above. The sky is full of the written thoughts of young people, and I'm instantly transported back almost three decades to when I threw a paper airplane out of a good ol' HTHS window, when I first was challenged to believe in possibility and a life that was something more than my mother would ever know.

I start to cry again.

Mr. Vernon puts his arm around me. "Remember—this is your fault. You did this. The relentless Portia Kane. *You*."

Arms keep popping out of the windows above, and paper airplanes continue to soar down toward us.

Before I have a chance to say anything, about two dozen high school kids pour out of the school and surround me. Each holds a neon-green copy of my book.

"You bastard. You're actually teaching *Love May Fail*?" I ask Mr. Vernon.

"But courtesy will prevail," he says proudly, finishing the opening rhyming quote from Vonnegut's *Jailbird*. "And they genuinely love it. Just look at their faces. You can't fake that level of enthusiasm, right, my future novelists?" His club members are beaming, nodding shyly, and smiling like they're actually meeting a *real* fiction writer for the first time. It's a weird dynamic, because I don't feel like a "real" novelist. But Mr. Vernon's huge, knowing grin somehow makes everything okay again, and I realize that this isn't about Mr. Vernon, or me, or even my novel. It's about something much larger. Cosmic forces are at work today. And maybe "real" is whatever you believe it is, in any given time or place.

I survey the young writers—they're smiling naively, completely unaware of all that is to follow in their adulthoods, excitedly taking part in this good moment. Several young women are looking at me like maybe they're exactly where I was when I was their age, desperately needing what Mr. Vernon offers, forging their own life philosophies in notebooks, or maybe on laptops and iPads or whatever fiction-minded kids use to dream these days.

And then, just like that, I'm back in my body again.

Everything is tingling.

I knew.

And now maybe I know again.

So when the kids ask with what seems like bona fide enthusiasm—even though I feel a little silly and self-conscious about it, not to mention the pathetically little practice I have—I sign their books.

Mr. Vernon stands proudly at the edge of the crowd, both hands on his cane. Yo-Yo Ma sits patiently by his master's feet, looking up with unabashed adoration.

Another thought hits me hard as a lawn dart to the eye: this moment is so terribly unimportant to the rest of the world, yet it means everything to me somehow—and it's enough.

So I sign and I sign and I sign.

The kids actually seem starstruck as they gape at my official author autograph and smile back appreciatively in a way that lets me know that a powerful teacher and a truly kind man prepped them for this good moment.

And at one point, I look up and see it.

The spark in Mr. Vernon's eye—it's back.

ACKNOWLEDGMENTS

My beautiful headbanging wife/first reader, Al, who is largely responsible for everything good in my life; super second reader, Liz Jensen, who has faithfully answered e-mails with brilliance and hilarity for years now; the amazing Doug Stewart, agent extraordinaire and best third reader in the entire world; Sister Kim Miller (aka Miller Time), who taught me many wonderful things about nuns; Mark Wiltsey, for helping me with all things Haddon Township and for being a true brother; editors Jennifer Barth and Jennifer Lambert, for pushing me (very hard) to tell the best story I possibly could; my film agent, Rich Green, who routinely makes magic happen out west; my mother, who long ago made sure I would always believe in the impossible; my father, who first brought me to Oaklyn, the town I love so much; my passionate little sister, Megan, and her husband Aaron; my loyal little brother, Micah, and his wife Kelly; Barb and Peague, for allowing us to work on this (and every) book in the Vermont house; my friend and dedicated web master, Tim Rayworth, and his wife, Beth, who conjures a delicious celebration pie whenever I get good career news; Ben Lipchak, for showing up and doing the work; Mr. Canada, aka Scott Caldwell, for being Mr. Canada; Evan Roskos, a true friend in writing, coffee talks, and mental health; Dr. Len Altamura, who always picks up the phone; Scott Humfeld, steady as the sun; Roland Merullo, who has often shared wisdom over early-morning diner eggs; Bill and

Acknowledgments

Mo Rhoda, friends for decades; all of the many people at Harper-Collins (and publishing houses around the world) who have worked tirelessly to promote this book; everyone at Sterling Lord Literistic and all of the foreign agents too; the many foreign editors who have made translations available; every single person who has ever purchased one of my novels, said or written something nice about my work, or attended one of my talks and stood in line afterward just to speak with me; the many devoted and big-hearted teachers who cared wildly and helped make me who I am today; and my former students, especially those of you who are following along.